Pūrākau

Pūrākau

MĀORI
MYTHS
RETOLD
BY
MĀORI
WRITERS

EDITED
BY WITI
IHIMAERA
AND WHITI
HEREAKA

VINTAGE

VINTAGE

UK | USA | Canada | Ireland | Australia
India | New Zealand | South Africa | China

Vintage is an imprint of the Penguin Random House group of companies,
whose addresses can be found at global.penguinrandomhouse.com.

Penguin
Random House
New Zealand

First published by Penguin Random House New Zealand, 2019

10 9 8 7 6 5 4 3 2 1

Design by Rachel Clark © Penguin Random House New Zealand
Cover art by James Ormsby
Prepress by Image Centre Group
Printed and bound in Australia by Griffin Press, an Accredited ISO AS/NZS 14001
Environmental Management Systems Printer

A catalogue record for this book is available from
the National Library of New Zealand.

ISBN 978-0-14-377296-5
eISBN 978-0-14-377297-2

The assistance of Creative New Zealand towards the production
of this book is gratefully acknowledged by the publisher

ARTS COUNCIL OF NEW ZEALAND TOI AOTEAROA

penguin.co.nz

MIX
Paper | Supporting
responsible forestry
FSC® C018684

CONTENTS

PART TWO: THE ANCESTORS

PART THREE: THE SEA TO THE LAND

PART FOUR: MYTHICAL BEINGS

PART FIVE: RAROHENGA

EPILOGUE: THE FUTURE

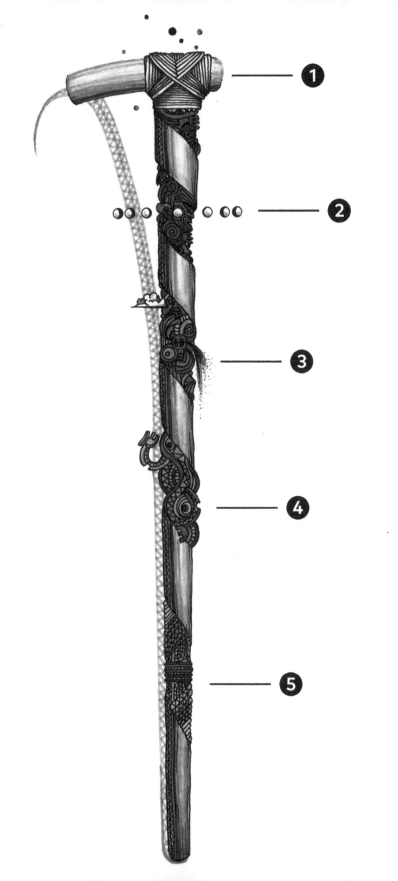

James Ormsby Decodes his Tokotoko Form

The drawing of a tokotoko, the walking–talking stick held by speakers on the marae, depicts the versions of the creation myth that tell of Tāne using his trees to help separate Ranginui and Papatūānuku. It was Tāne, too, who became the progenitor of humankind, so the tokotoko shaft also represents his ure. The tokotoko has small forms extending from it, with a thin shadow of aho, or fishing, lines behind.

There are five sections down the shaft, which relate directly to the book's parts: Creation; The Ancestors; The Sea to the Land; Mythical Beings; and Rarohenga.

(1) At the top, Matariki stars drift behind the handle/ure, spilling whakapapa marks. The lashing of the handle's binding symbolises the whakapapa or the layered stages of creation itself (Te Kore, Te Pō, Te Ao, etc). A crushed Māui attempts to separate the handle from the shaft, the first part of the creation. (2) Beneath this, a moon cycle orbits the ancestors. (3) The water cycle (encompassing cloud, waterfall and rainbow colours) floats from the third part of the tokotoko, referencing the Sea to the Land section. (4) Further down, taniwha arms escape from the tokotoko to depict the mythical beings. (5) The fifth part of the book, Rarohenga or the underworld, is represented with whakarei lines (customary whakairo or carving ornamentation).

Ngā mihi —
James F. Ormsby

Introduction

BY WITI IHIMAERA & WHITI HEREAKA

1.

Gods and monsters are at the very beginning of all cultures.

Horus and Set battled each other for the rule of Egypt. Zeus and his fellow gods arbitrated over the world from the heights of Mount Olympus. In the Norse pantheon, Odin presided over Valhalla, riding his winged eight-legged horse, Sleipnir, over the land. Ahura Mazda was a god of light in Persia fighting against Ahriman, the Spirit of Darkness, who controlled a three-headed demon known as Aži Dahāka.

In New Zealand, where Earth and Sky were the first parents, one of their sons — the mighty Tānemahuta — did nothing less than raise the sky so that life and light could flood the world between. This act might have freed the sons, but it also led to aeons-long battles between them.

Such tales come from long-ago times when people saw divinity in *everything*. They worshipped the gods, and from their veneration developed entire belief systems which flourished long before Christianity.

Mazdayasna (or Zoroastrianism) was one of the world's oldest extant religions. Hinduism was particularly polytheistic, with 33 million gods and goddesses. The Celts, who could count 1200 named deities, were, like Māori, animists. They believed that all aspects of the natural world were imbued with spirits and, therefore, gods were forces within nature. For instance, the sun was a god, the wind was a god, the ocean was a god and so on. Whenever thunder boomed, the gods were said to be walking overhead. If the crops failed, the gods must have been angry at some slight and therefore needed to be appeased.

Pity the poor human race. You negotiated your way through life very carefully.

One misstep and you could be zapped.

2.

Scientists consider that Māori came from the last of the migrations out of Africa, making the final *push* from Asia into Polynesia and then down to Aotearoa. Thus Māori share our gods and monsters with other Polynesian cultures. However, it is astounding that from a people considered to be the youngest of all human populations has come one of the most magnificent and richest inventories of origin narratives. From our ancestral homeland, Hawaiki (Ra'iātea, French Polynesia) around 700 AD, we carried our atua and taniwha with us and installed them in the new land.

Are the stories, myths and folklore imaginary? Not to Māori. The narratives that have come down — as Māori say, i ngā wā o mua, from the times in front of us — may be fabulous and fantastic but they are also real. They are so actual that today, although mostly Christianised now, Māori still ritually acknowledge sky and earth whenever in formal Māori settings:

Ko Ranginui kei runga — The Sky Father is above.
Ko Papatūānuku kei raro — The Earth Mother is below.

In so doing, Māori affirm the first parents of most indigenous civilisations and our kinship with all native peoples.

Not only do Māori do this, but we still pay homage to our gods (for instance, the first fish of any catch is ritually returned to Tangaroa, the sea god). We are also still able to establish our mythology on the landscape. In 2002, Transit New Zealand modified its roading plans for State Highway One when local Māori protested that the upgrade would infringe on the habitat of taniwha, swamp-living monsters.

Our funeral services may begin within a Christian setting but, most often, they end with the farewelling of our dead back to Hawaiki.

The Māori inventory of gods and monsters is still, therefore, relevant today.

Nor is there any separation of the 'fanciful' stories of our origin, i.e. mythology and folklore, from the believable or factual, the real from the imagined, rational from the irrational, or what can be believed in and what cannot. Māori do not make those distinctions. It's all history, fluid, holistic, inclusive — not necessarily linear — and it may be being told backwards, which is why, to orient ourselves, we always place our origin stories in front. The stories are actually the beginning of a whakapapa, a genealogy. And what they establish is the beginning of a distinctive world view.

First, there are the accounts of the origin and development of the universe. The stories provide a logical account of the coming of light, increasing by degrees and intensity until, lo, comes the dawning of the first day. Everything is happening all at once and over many aeons; Māori call this period of the making of the solar system 'the time when the world was shining'. And it is during these first days that the Sky Father and Earth Mother appear in the genealogy, tightly wrapped in each other.

Second are the accounts which relate the genealogy of the epic

Māori pantheon of gods. The primal children are all male and there are more than seventy. Among them are Tānemahuta, god of forests; Tangaroa, god of the oceans; Rongomaraeroa, god of agriculture; Tāwhirimātea, god of winds; and Haumiatiketike, god of the fern root and wilderness plantations. It is Tānemahuta, god of the forests, who devises the plan to separate the parents. This creates huge dissent between the brothers — those who side with him and those who don't. However, as earlier mentioned, Tānemahuta prevails, kicking with his feet at the sky until Ranginui is pushed forcibly upward and the strand of light which becomes the envelope for existence is created. There is a price, however: rolling wars between the atua during which Tūmatauenga takes upon himself the title of god of war and Rongomaraeroa assumes a second role as god of peace.

Doesn't sound as if much has changed, eh.

Everything is still happening simultaneously, events overlapping. In the events described, while they are fighting, the gods also begin to create overworlds and underworlds. Some people say there are as many as twenty heavens and the same number of worlds below, and each is the place of many kingdoms and inhabitants. Between them is Te Ao Tūroa and, here, the gods really outdo themselves. They create a place that is as bountiful as it is beautiful, a world of trees, fishes, ferns, foods, wind systems and so on. However, in the process, their fighting escalates as they bicker over borders and territories.

It is during this time that Tānemahuta becomes more than god of forests. His mother, Papatūānuku, provides him with the female element that will allow him to create the first woman, Hineahuone.

So the third of the major accounts of the whakapapa comes into play. This is the genealogy dealing with arrival of humankind and our relationships with the gods and the many worlds we have inherited.

The holistic nature of the world is extraordinary. The gods come and go overhead, underground, all around. Mountains move and fall in love with each other. Humankind can converse with trees, fishes and birds. And we share Te Ao Tūroa with supernatural beings like tipua (demons); maero (wilderness beings); ogresses and giants; flying men; taniwha (serpents, dragons and supernatural kidnappers); patupaiarehe (fairy folk); ponaturi (sea devils); and so on.

It's certainly a time when humankind needs heroes and heroines who can begin to negotiate with the gods for our tino rangatiratanga, sovereignty. Thus arise the splendid narratives concerning the exploits of Māui, the half-god, half-human hero who tamed the sun, fished up Aotearoa from the sea, and tried to obtain immortality for us. It is also the time of Tāwhaki, three generations later, who climbed the many heavens to secure the baskets of knowledge so that, although we were mortal, we could build one generation after another on the accomplishments of our kind. In this period comes Rata, who built a canoe, and he appears in the genealogy as one of our major waka builders. The great sea-going canoes enable the eventual departure from Hawaiki and arrival in Aotearoa.

In New Zealand, the whakapapa becomes replenished and enriched by tribal stories of the continuing relationship with all our worlds, but set in our own iwi landscapes. Fights with giant birds above mountains that Air New Zealand flies over. Encounters with taniwha that jealously guard their territories in rivers, swamps and entrances to our harbours. Here, also, we meet with the fairy folk, many of whom form the basis of some of our most enduring love stories.

What is interesting in the early genealogy is that, ultimately, humankind commits to a kaupapa. The planet created by the gods for us must be cared for. Not only that, but we have a duty as kaitiaki, conservators, to pass our legacy from one generation to another. To improve and add value in each generation, and to keep the whakapapa going forward into the future.

We're not doing a good job of it.

3.

The times of gods and monsters may be far behind the world now. The deities and demons are human today, existing among our own kind.

Nevertheless, the stories — as mythologies and folklore — have become huge repositories from which a terrific amount of imaginative work has sprung. Greek mythology is fortunate to have had Homer, Herodotus, Thucydides and others creating the basic library from the 12th century BC. In the case of the pre-Christian Norse, German and Viking worlds, the stories initially existed only as a few fragile source stems collected by the eighth-century monk, Bede.

In New Zealand, the Māori repository — oral — was kept by tohunga, priests and scholars, and primarily archived within whare wānanga — houses of learning. Different tribes and generations passed on their own versions of the stories so, for instance, some say that Tāne gathered the three baskets of knowledge but others that it was Tāwhaki. Some say Tiki was the first human to be created rather than Hineahuone. Not until the early 19th century, once Pākehā story collectors like Johannes C. Andersen, Elsdon Best and Reverend J. F. H. Wohlers spoke to local Māori keepers of the whakapapa like Te Rangikaheke or Te Whatahoro, did the diverse oral stories begin to be transcribed into English.

Subsequently, every generation has been marked by the work of sterling folklorists and story collectors who have painstakingly pieced together larger and more panoramic views. Often, as earlier alluded to, these exist in various versions and sometimes contradict each other, but they are all versions of what might be called our first origins. In New Zealand, a huge amount of recovery has occurred since the establishment of the Waitangi Tribunal in 1975. Here, most land claims were characterised by genealogies including those from our earliest inventories. Using mythology to prove the existence or not of certain historical figures, or to map out locations in the ancient world, has authenticated our earlier stories within legal process.

'This is where we start,' writes Whiti Hereaka in the prologue that begins *Pūrākau: Māori myths retold by Māori writers*.

'We are creatures of words,' she continues. 'We are creatures of imagination. We live on the edges of dreams and the margins of thought. We live in the whisper of the page.'

With these words Hereaka speaks for a new generation of creative writers among the Māori iwi, writers who have begun to explore their origin stories in a different, imaginative way. While the primary stories are considered sacrosanct, there has been a huge amount of interest in looking at contemporary society against a mythical template, either explicit or implicit. By doing so, certain truths reflecting society or that might have contemporary worth can be compared or contrasted — or affirmed.

The stories keep our gods and monsters as alive in our literature as they are in our landscape. Keri Hulme's 'Getting It' concerns the surprise arrival at a courtroom land dispute of claimants from legendary times, and is as pertinent to Waitangi Tribunal dealings today. Paula Morris's 'Real Life' creates a biography of the famed heavens-climbing hero Tāwhaki against the background of homelessness in Auckland, where the Sky Tower is the tip of a taiaha pointing into the sky. Kelly Ana Morey in 'Blind' imagines the ogress Rūruhi-Kerepō as an inmate of Kingseat mental asylum in a story that is also about elderly within the hospital system.

Witi Ihimaera's 'The Potato' takes that simple tuber as the subject for a story about feeding the world. And David Geary, in the virtuosic 'Māui Goes to Hollywood', considers Māui's death as occurring within a dreamlike setting — part-nightclub, part carnival — which could be the world in the Trump era.

Indeed, in *Pūrākau* Māoridom's best writers act as modern-day storytellers for the same purposes as their forebears. They mirror political events within fabular settings — and endeavour to be entertaining and instructional while they are at it. Take, for instance, Hemi Kelly's clever story 'Rata', or Tina Makereti's 'Shapeshifter', which invokes Pānia of the Reef. While the DNA of the origin story is honoured, Makereti shifts the telling to Pānia (the sculpture), thus offering us a glimpse of what Pānia sees today. The retelling sits in relation to the origin story through audience memory — but offering contemporary relevance.

Thus, like the oral tale spinners of old, the writers assembled in the collection are aware of storytelling as performance and, therefore, you can expect great drama and style in the indigenous fashion. 'Strike from the page,' Whiti Hereaka says, 'all that has been written before. Let the words and letters slip from your mind; pile them one upon another obliterating their meaning — their ink bleeds into the white spaces: they become pōngerengere, dark and suffocating.'

The first Māori poet to be published, Hone Tuwhare, led the way in the 1950s, and we represent his stunning poetics with 'We, Who Live in Darkness'. Similarly, Patricia Grace has been an exemplar of Māori writing since the 1960s, and 'Hine-ahu-one' is a perfect word portrait in miniature by one of our best literary stylists. Renée keeps on surprising with her trademark lilt and humour, as in 'Te Pura, Warrior Taniwha of Te Wairoa', and affirms just why she continues to be admired today. Ngāhuia Te Awekotuku shows in 'Kurungaituku' the qualities that have made her one of our leading academics: her story is marked by nuance and sly inflection.

Then there's Apirana Taylor who, in 'Hine Tai', aces a story that is deceptively simple but, as in all of Taylor's work, watch out for those subtexts.

These are quality stories in their own right, cleverly juxtaposing their Māori literary qualities of ihi, mana, wehi and aroha within the expected standards of the very best of postmodern literature. They counterpoint the mythical world with the most challenging of our contemporary realities, cumulatively underscoring this book with a powerful social commentary. Among them is Kelly Joseph's unforgettable and searing 'Hinepūkohurangi and Uenuku', Briar Grace-Smith's 'Born. Still.' and Whiti Hereaka's 'Papatūānuku' imagining the goddess as a mother bringing up her sons in a setting that reflects the reality of any mum trying to get by without a man in the house. These three narratives reverse the usual trope where often it's the story of the hero that gets the space and the woman's story gets sidelined.

The kanohi ki te kanohi reflections of reality are not surprising but we hadn't expected them to be so evident in a book on mythology. It is perhaps an indication of how integral the myths are to our lives that they can be both otherworldly while also being so easily grounded in the everyday. If you think the humans are the heroes here, however, you need only read Frazer Rangihuna's totally fabulous 'Īhe & Her' to get a complex reading that gives as much ambiguous mana to *her* as to him.

And then there's Nic Low's 'Te Ara Poutini' and David Geary's 'Rarohenga and the Reformation'. Both will resonate with sci-fi, fantasy and graphic novel aficionados, as well as addicts of pop culture from King Kong to Godzilla, from Fritz Lang's *Metropolis* to Ridley Scott's and Denis Villeneuve's *Blade Runner* and *Blade Runner 2045*. Low's dazzling narrative is a Māori origin story, Kāi Tahu to boot, that will remind some of the Marvel Cinematic

Universe — except that it's the *Māori* literary equivalent. And there's only one way to describe Geary's astonishing state-of-the-art story: it's a mutant work, a mindmeld. Both take Māori fiction 'somewhere else' and are worthy entrants to any sci-fi hall of fame. We might add Briar Grace-Smith's story, with its apocalyptic setting, to the list also.

4.

While faithful to their inheritance, the writers in *Pūrākau* have shaped the material in their own way and told the stories in their own distinctive manner. A few of the contemporary versions have been previously published and others have been written especially for this collection. Some of the origin stories may not be so well known, so the writers have provided notes on them that can be found in their biographies at the end of the book.

Finally, we ask you to imagine the book as a tokotoko, as conceived by James Ormsby in his superb cover design.

The tokotoko is the symbol of the storyteller. The tokotoko also evokes the pou that Tāne might have used to separate his parents. James has pictorialised the carved ceremonial walking stick with the myths spiralling down it.

Everything comes from the Creation, so that is at the top, in the handle: Te Pō (Kore), the separation, Hineahuone and Hinetītama stories leading to Tāne's staff. Here are grouped the thrilling narratives of the world spawned by Tāne and opened up with his brothers (mountains, forests, seas, rivers and so on). Next come the stories of the ancestors of Hawaiki: Māui, Tāwhaki and other heroes prior to the great sailings of legendary canoes southward to Aotearoa. Here follow the stories of New Zealand where a people

— our forebears — lived not just with gods and monsters but also in a landscape, seascape and skyscape of incredible diversity and potency.

Finally, at the bottom of the tokotoko are stories of Rarohenga, a place famed for arts and culture.

We hand the tokotoko to you to grasp in your strong hands. To gain strength and inspiration from. To wield as a staff, a wayfinder, a symbol of who we are.

Carry it on into the future to show the next generation who they can be.

Prologue

BY WHITI HEREAKA

This is where we start. Let it be blank. Blank is different from nothing. Nothing suggests, well, nothing. No. Thing. But blank is possibility — it may be filled, it may change, or it may remain. Blank.

Listen closely to the blank, the black, the dark. Let it invade you, colonise you, assimilate to it. This world is dark and all that there is, is darkness: a black void blankness. It is everything. It is Te Kore.

Te Kore, endless Te Kore, the void that stretches forever because there are no boundaries, no time. There is just Te Kore.

Te Kore, endless Te Kore. The void that has no substance. We cannot perceive it. We do not exist; there is just Te Kore.

Te Kore, endless Te Kore. The beginning and the end. All the things that have been and will be, but cannot manifest in . . .

Te Kore, endless Te Kore . . .

. . . everything, every possible thing, is enfolded together so very tightly that enormous heat is generated. It is the heat of creation, the blank feeling its potential.

And in the infinite void of Te Kore there is a hum, a hum of recognition: a prediction of change. We have started something. It is a beginning and in less than a second everything expands into . . .

Te Pō.

The darkness at last a presence, there is no longer an empty void. There is the night that stretches on.

Te Pō.

And in the darkness, the hum grows stronger. It is the hum of many voices, of infinite voices. It is all that has been, that will be, finding its form. Finding its will to be. Particles combine and divide, the ripples of their coupling and divorce spread out and become great waves. Everything has changed.

Te Pō.

The darkness envelops. It invades. It is you and us and we are darkness.

Te Pō.

The darkness is complete, oppressive. It defines and shapes our form. It pushes down, and we push back.

Te Pō.

The darkness is our comfort, yet we continue to repulse it. The darkness that had defined our forms has been replaced with space.

Te Pō.

The darkness is now an absence of light. We have perceived this. Our eyes have opened.

Te Pō.

And in the darkness, we listen for the hum. It is both within us and without us.

Te Pō.

The darkness is a womb, it has nurtured us but we cannot stay within its confines forever.

Te Pō.

And in the darkness, we realise that we are not alone. We are many who dwell in the darkness of . . .

Te Pō.

The darkness, O the darkness that has nurtured us, that has oppressed us and defined us. The darkness that is us, must inevitably arc into light.

Ki te whaiao, ki te ao mārama.

All that was held in Te Kore, all that has expanded into Te Pō, is but a pinprick of light. It is the seed of potential. It is minute, this particle of light. It is tempting to say insignificant; but because it holds our attention it *is* significant — we've imbued it with importance.

Watch as it continues to grow: the heat and light increase at a rate impossible for us to fathom. To our slow senses it is as if we are witnessing a great explosion. One moment we can hardly see the light, the next we are surrounded by it.

Thus, this tiny speck has become the centre.

Let us meet here at the centre. The centre of all that is known, all that will be. We will create a world here from a few words, we will make a place where we will be comfortable.

Let us first build a whare where we can share our stories. A whare tapere: a house of storytelling and games. A pātaka kōrero: a storehouse of language. Dig foundations in the light, holes for posts: four. Our whare will be a simple rectangular shape; symmetry soothes and pleases. From afar, our whare shines in the blank: it is a tiny speck in the great abyss of Te Pō. It carries us all. It is so small in the vastness, so vulnerable. How is it not crushed by the black? Be comforted by the thought that eventually night arcs into day.

We must continue. Walls. Plain for now, but by the end of our telling they will be carved by words and deeds — life, if you'd call it that, frozen in the moment. Past, present, future simultaneous. As it is, as it should be.

Below is the blank, the black so vast and unlimited that your head spins with vertigo. A floor, then, is a necessity. Let us throw a mat on the floor. It's finely woven from flax fibre. The warp and the weft are tight, so that none of the blank shows through the minute holes, the pinpricks, the specks. Not a particle of blank shows through. The floor supports and yields. It is comfortable sitting here; perhaps even lying here, letting our words lull you to sleep.

Above are ridgepole and rafters: the backbone and ribs of the whare that envelops us. Do you imagine yourself the heart? Keeping the rhythm of the place, letting the whare live? The kōwhaiwhai patterns have yet to be painted on the rafters and ridge — they too are blank; waiting for their story to begin.

What more do you need to be comfortable? A roof overhead, thatched as they were in old times; a window to let in some air; a door so that you can leave this place when it is time. Across the window we will place a sliding panel, so that we might shut out the world if we choose to. We will borrow it from a whare carved by expert hands long ago, or, perhaps, from this point of time, that whare has yet to be built. Perhaps it is our whare that will inspire the carver: his dreams are of our pare, lintel and our door. It does not matter that he died long before you were born. Our whare exists out of time.

The whare, now whole, must be blessed so that we may dwell together. We take water into our mouths, let it drip from tongue to hand and cast the drops into the corners. The water both cleanses and nourishes the seeds of potential here — we stand at the beginning and the end of a journey. We open a path so that our words might be fruitful, so that we may hear them and be satiated. We welcome you to this place that we have created, we welcome those whose lives we will invoke here, or at least, the parts of their lives that we have glimpsed.

Let this place be filled with the things that we will need for the telling — the siren song of beautiful patupaiarehe; the fine cloaks and weapons that Hatupatu stole are propped up against a wall; rows of tiny milk teeth, sown like seeds in a flower bed; the glint of Poutini's dark, green scales as he escapes with his love.

A miromiro sings — *Tihi-oly-oly-oly* — a lament for a lost lover.

Let this place be filled with love and betrayal, with death and life, with human and non-human, with upheaval and change.

These are the things we need for the telling. These are the things of story.

The whare is now brimming with story. Listen now, even the posts are whispering secrets — they know stories too. Stories that perhaps you don't want to hear.

Events slide in and out of view. The endless loop that these scenes play upon twist ever so slightly so that they mirror themselves.

Beginning.

Middle.

End.

Middle.

Beginning.

Te Kore.

Te Pō.

Te whaiao.

Te Pō.

Te Kore.

We pick a place on the continuum. This is where we start. It is at once a beginning, a middle and an end.

Stories, stories, stories — our lives are coloured and shaped by them: when we gather and share gossip, or sit silently alone with a book — the words come alive in our minds.

There must be pleasure in both the hearing and the telling of the story. It is a selfish storyteller who hoards the pleasure for themselves, who inflicts boredom upon their audience just so their voice is heard. It is, after all, a privilege to be heard — and one not many are allowed. There are always those who will speak for others, who take control of the narrative.

The stories live through us and us through them. A skilled story-teller will shape the narrative to beguile you, ensnare and bind your attention: because a story is born and lives in the space between the storyteller and their audience. The storyteller cannot hold their story too tightly to themselves. To live, it must have room to grow. Remember how the gods separated the sky father Ranginui from his wife Papatūānuku — the earth mother. Rangi and Papa held each other in such a tight embrace that their children could not thrive. It is only when Tānemahuta forced them apart that life could flourish. Is it not the same for a story?

It lives in the telling.

We live in the telling.

But that is telling.

We are creatures of words. We are creatures of imagination. We live on the edges of dreams and the margins of thought. We live in the whisper of the page.

Does it follow that a story must die as it ends, as you close the pages of the book — or does it live on within you, nestled deep in the folds of your mind?

A story, then, is a dangerous thing for the reader; to allow yourself to open your mind and your heart to creatures who need *you* to survive, who need *you* to live. Ah, but you will face whatever danger there might be, your craving for us is *that* strong. Our relationship is symbiotic — but is it mutual, or parasitic?

Look at the book in your hands: the leaves opened, the spine cracked. The words on the pages are like a pulsing heart — you can see life here. You can feel it in your hands. Through these pages, through these words, we live. We want to be heard. We want to exist again, at least in your mind. We need to tell you our stories so that you'll let us in and we can breathe again.

Unread, these pages are a burrow buried beneath the ash and debris of a violent eruption — here we will wait for the return of the beings that create us. We are bound and unbound. In this form we can exist in many places, in many minds at once — but these words cannot adequately convey the actual experience of our lives. These shapes and groups that you think of as *words* are just ghosts, the faint outline of a life, an approximation.

Still, it is enough for you to glimpse the world of the other. Through stories you are immortal; a god capable of living one hundred lifetimes or more. Through stories, you can achieve the impossible and travel through time. Past, present, future — all able to be lived and felt by you. The lives you can live within a story are endless. The lives you can consume are countless.

How will you remember us? Those whose deeds are remembered and celebrated, and those whose deeds serve as a warning. The betrayed lover, the foolish man, the neglected kaitiaki. The liar. The thief. The murderer. The giant. The monster. The ogress.

The story. The teller. The audience.

Perhaps our names are familiar to you, perhaps you think you know our stories. Because our names are our story, they are us. They become part of the words that have been spoken about us, written about us, they bind us like the aka vine — their whispers encircle and define us. We have all found ourselves clothed in a character that wasn't familiar — in skin that was pulled and stretched to fit another idea of us. It is a partial truth. Not ours, but theirs.

Perhaps a story can only be told in slivers; no one can perceive the whole, the truth. Because is it ever truly possible for anyone to understand the life of another completely? We will tell you our stories anyway. It is enough for you to have a taste, to run your tongue along the edge of the blade. It is enough for us to get a foothold.

Strike from the page all that has been written before. Let the words and letters slip from your mind; pile them upon one another obliterating their meaning — their ink bleeds into the white spaces: they become pōngerengere, dark and suffocating.

Listen closely to the blank, the black, the dark. Let it invade you, colonise you; assimilate it. This world is dark and all that there is, is darkness: a black void blankness.

Let it be blank. This is where we start.

PART ONE

creation

CHAPTER 1
THE BEGINNING

———

Te Pō

———

Te Pō

BY PATRICIA GRACE

I am aged in aeons, being Te Pō, the Night, that came from Te Kore, the Nothing.

First there was Te Kore that could neither be felt nor sensed. This was the void, the silence, where there was no movement and none to move, no sound and none to hear, no shape and none to see.

It was out of this nothingness that Increase and Consciousness, and I, Te Pō, were born.

I am aged in Aeons, and I am Night of many nights, Night of many darknesses — Night of great darkness, long darkness, utter darkness, birth and death darkness; of darkness unseen, darkness touchable and untouchable, and of every kind of darkness that can be.

In my womb lay Papatūānuku who was conceived in Darkness, born into Darkness — and who matured in Darkness, and in Darkness became mated with the Sky.

Then Papatūānuku too conceived, and bore many children among the many long ages of Te Pō.

CHAPTER 2
RANGINUI AND PAPATŪĀNUKU

———

We, Who Live in Darkness

———

Papatūānuku

———

We, Who Live in Darkness

BY HONE TUWHARE

It had been a long long time of it
wriggling and squirming in the swamp of night.
And what was time, anyway? Black intensities
of black on black on black feeding on itself?
Something immense? Immeasureless?

No more.
There just had to be a beginning somehow.
For on reaching the top of a slow rise suddenly
eyes I never knew I possessed were stung by it
forcing me to hide my face in the earth.

It was light, my brothers. Light.
A most beautiful sight infiltered past
the armpit hairs of the father. Why, I could
even see to count all the fingers of my hands
held out to it; see the stain — the clutch of
good earth on them.

But then he moved.
And darkness came down even more oppressively
it seemed and I drew back tense; angry.

Brothers, let us kill him — push him off.

Papatūānuku

BY WHITI HEREAKA

In the end it was their son Tāne that separated them. She knows
it's repugnant to admit that, even to herself. Those who say that it
is not fair to blame the children have not met stubborn, tenacious,
persistent Tāne. He was always a wilful child.

All of their sons, at one point or another, had come between them;
but it was Tāne who had pushed and pushed until they could no
longer embrace each other. And Rangi had left.

Her boys are strong willed. Tangaroa, changeable Tangaroa —
calm one moment, a tantrum the next. Tāwhirimātea, strident in
his beliefs, always trying to stir something up. Tū is smart, cunning
even, and is always looking for a fight. Haumia is tough and wild,
she's given up trying to tame him; and Rongo, the quiet one, the
peace broker, steadfast, stoic and stubborn.

Perhaps the relationship would have survived if she and Rangi
had waited, had spent more time together as a couple alone. Been
rational and cool headed: planned their family, prepared themselves.
It makes her laugh. How could she have prepared herself for her
children? You know what they say about best-laid plans. As if you
can plan for love, plan for life.

Still, perhaps if she and Rangi had been strict with them. Brought
them up to be . . . different. Six perfect little gentlemen, who
wouldn't dream of raising their voices or arguing with each other,

or — *heavens!* — their parents. It is a fleeting fantasy. Those docile, obedient children are blank faced in her mind, the thought of their cloying voices chanting *Mummy! Mummy!* makes her shiver.

Ah, my sons. I wouldn't have you any other way.

She can't blame Tāne. Not entirely. There must have been signs before. Sometimes she thinks of herself clinging to Rangi, her grip so tight that her fingernails dug into his skin. Maybe her intense need for him pushed him away. She can't remember the last time they actually talked — really talked. And they haven't been alone together since they had kids. Apart from their children, she doesn't know what they have in common. Rangi was always the one with his head in the clouds. She was always the grounded one.

Why didn't they fight harder to stay together? They should have held on until their fingernails were ripped from their beds. Maybe Tāne's pushing was the excuse they'd both been looking for.

It's strange to think about it, but perhaps they started separating the moment they came together. All their past decisions led here.

She has a terrible crick in her neck — had it for years, but it's flared up again from the stress, probably, or maybe from the relief. She moves her head left to right and then back again, trying to release the muscle. She reaches for the knot just underneath her shoulder blade, trying to dig in with her fingers, but it is just out of reach. There's pain in doing nothing and pain in trying to free it. She's not sure which is worse. Her forehead tightens, another headache is on the way. She'll lie down until it goes away.

Her bed is vast and empty.

They were so cramped before, living on top of one another really. It was no place for growing boys. She heard them grumbling amongst themselves. Perhaps they thought that she couldn't hear them — their bickering and their plans.

We need more room!

I can't breathe here.

We should kill them!

There was a hush after Tū had said it. Of course she didn't believe he meant it — *although, there's a darkness to him, something in the way he stares like he's always plotting his next move* — of course he didn't mean it. Of course he didn't, what would Tū know of death?

It's irrational and paranoid to think that her children were plotting against her. Sure, sometimes it felt like they ganged up on her, but that's what children do, isn't it? They test the limits and push boundaries, that's how they grow.

She closes her eyes as if she is trying to shut the thought out. Why would her own children want to hurt her so badly? Hurt themselves? Because, despite their bravado, she knows that they miss Rangi too.

Her pillow is wet. She wipes her face with the back of her hand as she sits up. She never was a pretty crier — her eyes puff up immediately and hūpē runs freely from her nose.

She shivers and pulls a shawl around her. She feels cold all the time now, more if she's been crying. Maybe the need for warmth is a comfort thing, mental rather than physical. Tāne gave her the shawl. He can be so thoughtful and generous that it makes her feel guilty about dwelling on his flaws.

Funny, she never thought that green was her colour but this suits her so well. Maybe she doesn't know anything about herself at all. She looks at herself in the mirror. Really looks — her own face is like that of a stranger, she has trouble recognising herself. She knew Rangi's face so well, his eyes flecked with light, his nose, his lips . . . almost every pore and whisker, she knew it so intimately. She studies herself — her smile, her frown. Looking at herself makes her think of what she is missing, his lips on hers, their shared breath. Does she have real sympathy for the woman in the glass? That woman is a stranger to her.

It is too quiet. With the shawl wrapped tightly around her, she goes in search of her boys. Surely their chatter will chase these useless thoughts away. *Where are they?* The homestead is empty.

The boys have scattered — did they hear her crying and flee? No, she can't imagine that they'd be so callous. They're exploring, the novelty of having so much room is still new to them. They've made this place their own; each staking out their territory, busy with their interests. Rongo will be nearby in the garden, digging neat furrows into the ground. Tāne and Haumia will be in the bush — Tāne has probably claimed the tallest tree and Haumia will be hanging out in the scrub land. Tangaroa will be at the beach. Tū could be with any of them, it depends on his mood or if he's annoyed his brothers — which he often has.

She wanders around the homestead, checking each empty room until she's back in her own. Even if the old place was cramped, at least she wasn't alone. Who has she to talk to here? Her sad reflection in the mirror? She looks at herself again, tired and sad. Has she always looked this way? She reaches out and touches her reflected cheek: so cold and hard.

She had thought that her family was all that she wanted, all that she needed. She's devoted herself to them and now what? What is there left for her now?

She was happy before. They were happy before, weren't they?

She feels numb. She doesn't know who she is. She has always been defined in relation to Rangi — their love, their embrace, their children. She can't remember life without him. Did a time ever exist when she was just herself?

She flops on the bed, stretches out like a starfish and stares at the blank ceiling. That's what her life is now. Nothing, wall to wall. She can't remember what life was like without Rangi, in her mind he was always there — before love, partnership and children. If she tries to think of a time when she was on her own there's a deep void in her memory. He was her light in the dark.

There is nothing without him. She is nothing without him.

And yet, here she is. She still exists, even if their relationship doesn't.

The ceiling is so blank. She stares up at it, relaxing her eyes so everything is sort of blurry. There are no edges anymore. There is not an absence of a thing, but the potential for anything.

No, not yet. I am not ready to stop wallowing.

Ah, but there is a flutter within her. It is excitement and hope and . . .

'No!'

Her own voice surprises her. She didn't mean to speak.

The smell of rain is in the air. It reminds her of Rangi. It is the smell of their love, their lust. Petrichor, the musk of the earth and sky combined.

Rangi was her first love, her one and only love, but now she wonders if it was real. Had they simply settled for one another? Had they been too scared to live without one another, too scared of the unknown?

Since the separation, she can finally see Rangi as another being. When they were together it was easy to think of themselves as one organism, or to be frank, one orgasm. Sex had always been passionate, they had always been hungry for one another.

She can still feel his fingers digging into her hips, the prickle of nerves running right down her spine from his breath on her neck.

She reaches out her leg and kicks her door closed; it would be just her luck if one of the boys wandered in now.

Eyes closed, she conjures him. Imagines that they are his rough fingers brushing her nipples, his hands squeezing her breasts. Even though she had been with him for so long, even though they had made love hundreds of times she's finding it hard to keep him in her mind. She pushes a finger into the cleft of her vulva, seeking out her clit, her sticky pubic hair tangles around her fingers and a clenching warmth spreads from her clit to deep within her.

And then her mind wanders to all of the jobs she has to do and the moment is gone. She grinds the heel of her palm into her pubic bone — trying to convince herself that it is his weight upon her, determined not to give up . . .

She groans and sighs, but it is not from pleasure. How long has it been? She's showing, so five or so months. Another sigh. It's been far too long.

They were never shy with one another. Their love was intense and oppressive. Is that why their boys wanted them to be apart? The disgust one has for the sex life of one's parents?

She was happy with Rangi. She felt whole. She was satisfied.

Now she is apart from him, she has the clarity to ask whether being filled is the same as being fulfilled.

She looks at her hand. The dent in her ring finger is still there. The skin is pale and smooth, like a scar. She supposes that it is.

Is it time to finally learn who she is?

She is a mother.

So she does what good mothers do — *isn't this what good mothers do?* She forgets her own feelings, forgets *herself*, and concentrates on her children. She focuses on how they are coping rather than how she still yearns for him.

Her boys are too young to understand, they have no experience of love that is all consuming. She loves their father still.

It would be so much easier if she hated him — at least then she'd have anger to distract her from the hole he's left. If she hated him then she wouldn't miss him right?

It is so lonely here. She has no one to talk to about her grief. She can't burden her children with it. Not that her boys have ever considered her feelings; she is their mother, a being who lives only for them.

Is that all she is, all that she's ever been, a mother? Now that she has the room to breathe, the room to think, will she find something more? She rubs her temples, guilt pinches between her eyebrows. What kind of mother wishes for something other than her children? She wishes she knew another mother so she could ask — though she never would, no one can know she doubts herself.

The love she has — *had* — for Rangi is dwarfed by the love she has for her children, and yet . . .

Sometimes she feels like her throat is constricted by resentment — she tries to suppress the part of her that hates those boys of hers. The boys that ruined her love. Her boys, her boys. The story will always focus on her boys.

No one can understand her loneliness.

As if in response, the baby in her womb turns, sending tremors throughout her body. She has named her youngest son Rūaumoko. He will be a son: she always bears boys. Poor Rūaumoko. He will never know his father. Not like his brothers have.

Her only comfort is the thought that it was good for her boys; the separation. Each of their reactions at the beginning had been so different. Tū had brooded, at times it seemed as if he was jealous of Tāne; as if *he* wanted to be the one who had separated his parents. Rongo had become withdrawn and when she picked up Haumia he held her so tightly like he wanted to be buried in her. Even Tangaroa clung to her. He was always there: at her arm, her knee, her hip. Of course she's glad he's found his independence now — that they all have — but when she was focused on them she didn't have to think of her own pain. Now it seems like there is nothing else to think about.

Freed from his father's shadow, Tāne has flourished. He has made a life for himself. She can see that soon he will be ready to pursue a love of his own.

It is good for them. It is good for us. She repeats the words over and over until it is the truth.

Most of their boys had stayed with her. Only Tāwhirimātea has gone with his father. The look on his face as he followed Rangi. She had not known her son to be so angry before. He was angry at her she supposed. He blamed her for the break-up.

Everyone is on edge when Tāwhirimātea visits. He takes pleasure in destroying his brothers' precious things. When did he become so cruel, so angry? She shields Rongo and Haumia from Tāwhirimātea. The older siblings need to work it out amongst themselves.

Tāwhirimātea goes after Tāne first, shaking the tree Tāne has climbed — trying to shake him out. Tāwhirimātea tries to get at his brother, ripping the lower branches of the tree. Tāne ignores him, which only fuels Tāwhirimātea's rage. Should she intervene? Tāne laughs and she's relieved — *just brothers being brothers.*

Tāwhirimātea manipulates Tangaroa to fight against Tāne with him. They hurl water at Tāne, but he doesn't budge. Tāwhirimātea leaves to get more ammunition and Tangaroa looks at the tree in front of him and then up to his brother in the branches above him. Without Tāwhirimātea's encouragement, Tangaroa's anger quickly subsides and he wanders off down to the beach again.

It is Tū who fights back against Tāwhirimātea. While Tāwhirimātea is spurred by his anger, Tū fights because he enjoys the violence. Tū yearns for the bruises and the blood. The fight is vicious and physical — Tū punching Tāwhirimātea over and over again. She yells at Tū to stop and is grateful that he listens, she's not sure if she could have stopped him physically. Tū crows at his victory, proud that he has beaten his brother.

However, Tū hasn't finished fighting yet. It is like he just can't stop his rage now that he's unleashed it. Angry that none of his brothers stood with him against Tāwhirimātea, Tū finds any excuse to argue and fight.

She is disgusted by her sons — where did the love go? How has she let such cruelty take seed? She cannot bear to see Tāwhirimātea's rage and humiliation. She cannot bear to see Tū's arrogance.

Rangi calls her, pleads for them to be together again. He pours his grief over her and suddenly she feels the weight of him again, pressing down upon her. She didn't realise that she had been drowning under him. That alone she could breathe. She can't muster any sympathy — why should she be burdened with his pain?

She still loves him, will always love him, but she needs to put herself first. She's not strong enough yet to save them all.

Her arms are heavy. It's like she's spent all this time reaching out for him, trying to cling to what was. For now she must put the things that remind her of Rangi away. She packs the shirt that still smells like him into Tāwhirimātea's bag — he can take it back to his father.

She turns the photos of them together around. One day she'll be able to look at them again. Hopefully, one day soon.

When he comes to pick up Tāwhirimātea, she turns away before closing the door. She doesn't have to see him leave again.

She sits at the window looking out over her land. Her boys are out exploring again, it's nice to have a moment to herself. Time to think. It's getting dark, soon they'll come home and tell her about the things they made and discovered. One day, she'll tell them about her discoveries too. As the light fades she can see herself reflected in the glass. She reaches out to touch her cheek — the glass is still a little warm under her fingertips.

'There you are, Papa.'

Yes. It was good for them. It was good for us. We needed room to grow.

CHAPTER 3
MANKIND AND MORTALITY

Skin and Bones

Hine-ahu-one

Hine-tītama — Ask the Posts of the House

Skin and Bones

BY TINA MAKERETI

He was lonely. It's what you'd expect really. A man in his situation. He was surrounded by the good earth, his plantation, his stock, a nice river in the valley for fishing. He thought he should be happy. Fulfilled. But something was missing.

It was spring. He went about the place tilling and planting and from time to time felt an urge. He'd look down and see his own weighty erection and think *What am I supposed to do with this?*

He worked hard. There's a massive amount of work to do when you first start out on a place. He needed to get everything working in rhythm with everything else. He wanted to be self-sufficient. So he added in fruit trees and feed crops, and found he enjoyed the birdlife that came to fossick in his orchards.

Despite this, at night the urge all but overcame him. He would thrash about in his bed, the mass of the pulsing thing between his legs making it impossible to lie comfortably. Nothing would relieve it. His own desperate fumblings had little effect. He tried dousing it in cold water, strapping it down with bandages. He prayed for relief.

Even though there was no one else around, he felt betrayed by his own neediness. When he stopped for a breather and a drink he no longer surveyed his land proudly as he wiped the sweat from his brow. He frowned. The birdsong no longer reached his ears.

He saw that the shed needed painting, the weeds needed pulling and the trees needed fertilising. He saw that it was not good.

———

There came a day so hot the earth beneath his fingers was warm to touch. He had watered it in preparation for his seedlings, and now he sat and ate his lunch beside it, running his left hand through the dirt as if it were sand on a beach. He was hard again, as he was almost constantly these days. It occurred to him that it would be pleasant to unsheathe his penis in the warm sunlit air. He looked far around himself. Of course, there was no one there. He hadn't seen any of his brothers since they had that fight last winter, during which Tāwhiri destroyed several of his crops and crashed into his house, causing the roof to collapse. *Tāne, you gotta get him back for that,* Tū had goaded, *I'll back you up!* But he'd rejected Tū's advice, so Tū turned on him as well. The only one he was on speaking terms with at the moment was Rongo, but he lived miles away.

His meal finished, he thought *why the heck not?* and pulled off his pants. His left hand was still dirty, but rather than cleaning it he let it be, finding himself even more aroused by the odour of the earth. He stroked himself, but this still felt like his own hand, so he fell to his knees and began moulding the soil into a pleasing shape so that he could lie against it. At the last moment, he made a hollow deep into the mound he had formed, and, no longer thinking rationally at all, he inserted himself there.

Well. For a man as inexperienced as Tāne, this was a revelation. It was warm and soft but unyielding enough to cause a pleasing friction as he rubbed himself in and out, astonished by the pleasure of it. He released his seed quickly and lay spent against the earth like a babe on the breast of his mother. Oh, the relief! For the first time in days he felt calm deep down to his belly, and his loins did not scream fiery need at him.

For many days after that he experimented with his mound, forming it in different ways each time to see how it best fitted him. He gained much pleasure from coupling with his little plot of sacred soil, but he found it best to do so in the afternoon, once the sun had warmed the earth for the day.

Days turned to weeks and weeks to months, and Tāne became frustrated again. The autumn chill brought with it frost and rains that, for his crops' sake, should have pleased him. But his mound turned to watery mud, and he rarely got a chance to lie there. His desire would come to him at night, and he wished for something that could relieve the ache that had moved from between his legs up into his chest.

This ache had all of him now. On the rare occasions he could enjoy the physical delight of his earthy adventures, he would return to his bed spent but still yearning. For all the cold winter he carried a pressure within, a need for more than simple bodily indulgence.

He couldn't figure out what he was missing.

———

By the following spring, as the sun's warmth released sweet blossom buds from hibernation and the insects and birds began emerging from their winter nests, Tāne was desolate. He came to the soil desperately, but without passion. His orchards suffered. He neglected his stock. His house was left unswept. He no longer gained any joy from hunting, gathering and cooking his meals. Instead he ate whatever food he found while he worked — fruit, seeds, the occasional huhu grub.

One day after a sun-shower Tāne dozed under a tree in his orchard, where it was relatively dry. His eyes were half closed, his mind drifting. He thought about all the adventure he'd had in his life, all that he had created on his land. But he did so without the pride he was accustomed to experiencing over such thoughts. *What is happening to me?* he thought.

Slowly he became aware of the fantails in the foliage chattering excitedly, the cicada buzzing steadily faster, the tui's call becoming more melodic and enchanting than he remembered. With his eyes fully closed now, the world around him was a riot of fervent sound, each creature vying for the attention of its peers. *I am alone*, Tāne thought, *that is the problem*. But who did he yearn for? He opened his eyes to the flutter of numerous wings, feathered or dry-leaf crisp, clasping talons and searching feelers, buzzing and twittering declarations of love — the ardent couplings of all creatures in the canopy. *Oh*, he thought, *oh*. And he laughed — for how could it have taken him so long to realise this?

He called his mother, asking her what he should do about finding a partner. She did not know of any available young women. Indeed, no women were known in the area at all. She felt for her son. Even though she and her husband were separated now, she remembered their time together as the happiest time of her life. *You may have to be creative*, she told him, *let your imagination guide you. Do you know of the place called Kurawaka?*

Tāne felt the world tilt for a moment, a path clearing before him. The place his mother had named was the same place he had been visiting all this time.

He made his way to the spot he held in such affection, all the way beseeching the heavens and the earth to help him in his quest. There, he fell to his knees and scooped the soil into his arms, bringing it to his face and inhaling deeply. *Yes*, he thought, *oh god yes please let this be it*. Then slowly, affectionately, he began to work. At first, it was easy: he wanted the creation to be like him, his mirror, his equal. He formed the arms and the legs, the neck, the head, the shape of the torso. Here, he took liberty, remembering the various forms he had tried the summer before, adding shape in ways that he had found most pleasing. There were things he did not know or understand, so he let instinct guide him — adding folds, a dimple or two. He was enchanted by the figure that emerged under his fingertips.

All that was left was the face of his beloved. This was difficult. He formed something resembling what he knew of his own features: a nose, two eyes, lips. Touching his face, he realised the features he had moulded were softer than his own. He hoped this new person would accept the roughness of his face and body. Laid out before him now, the figure was smooth and rounded, like the hills in the far distance. He was at once excited and anxious. He knew of the old magic, how the life force could be shared, how creatures could be brought into being, but he had never tried to make someone like himself before. Who would she be? Would she even want him? Would the magic work?

His mother had told him to be creative. A leap of faith was required. He opened his mouth, not yet sure of the words, closed his eyes, and attempted to find the sound. If he could just find the right note, the words would come . . . he was sure of it. His voice sounded awkward at first, so unsure. But he was right. After a moment of hesitation his throat began to hum with vibration, and the chant coursed through him like a powerful shifting tide.

This was it. If it didn't work he would be crushed. He wanted to prolong the moment of anticipation, the moment of not knowing. And then it was time. He leaned over and looked at her dear face, gathered up all the power of the desire inside him, and blew a warm constant stream of air into her nostrils. He took all of the air in his lungs and blew it into her, sending with it all his intentions.

There was a pause.

And then she sneezed. *Tihei mauri ora*, he whispered. He helped her sit up, break away from the earth beneath her. A layer of soil fell away from her skin, and he could see her in her true form, glistening and alive and the deep red-brown colour of the earth that had formed her. Silent laughter filled him even as tears formed in his eyes. He clasped her to him, pressing his nose against hers so that they could breathe together for a while.

She was smiling as she lifted her face to look into his eyes. He felt heat rise to his face. He didn't know where to look. She was here. Alive.

'I'm Hine,' she said, 'I'm so glad you figured it out. I've been waiting for ages.'

He was stunned.

'Aw, look at you,' she said, 'you're all skin and bones. Let's make a feast. Time for a celebration, don't you think?'

Hine-ahu-one

BY PATRICIA GRACE

I sneezed and therefore I lived.

Tāne the procreator set the parents apart so that there could be light and growth; so that people could be generated on earth.

After the separation of Rangi and Papa, Tāne wished to justify his deed by joining the male and heavenly element of himself to the female earthly element that I am, in order to generate mortal beings.

He searched everywhere for me, the uha of mankind, but I was hidden from him. He found instead the uha of plant life, and, by joining the male element of himself to this female element, gave growth to the plant life on earth. He found the uha of the various creatures of earth and gave growth to animal life.

It was Papatūānuku, the earth mother, who kept me hidden, keeping secret the hiding place of the uha of mankind. Then, when all was ready on earth for mortal being, she told Tāne to form woman from clay at Kurawaka.

So Tāne went to Kurawaka, the pubic area of Papatūānuku, and formed a new shape for me from her clay, being assisted in this by the Great Being and the many godly beings of the high heavens, who gifted or shaped the different parts of me.

Tāne blew on me, my eyes opened and I drew breath. I sneezed and was alive. But Tāne's searching was not yet over. He sought a way in which to combine our two elements — and so produce mortal life.

He searched my body, acting in its orifices. These first contacts produced earwax, tears, mucus, saliva, sweat and excreta. But in acting within my clitoral opening our male and female elements came together and Hine-tītama was conceived.

Within my human shape, I, Hine-ahu-one, held first human life.

Hine-tītama — Ask the Posts of the House

BY WITI IHIMAERA

1.

I am flying backwards in business class from Bangkok. It's a strange
feeling, but I'm getting accustomed to it. Passengers are in rows
of six in a herringbone pattern, alternating one passenger facing
forwards and one backwards. I am reminded of boyhood days when
my cousins and I slept top and toe in the same crowded community
arrangement, sometimes four per bed — except that my fellow
passengers aren't as attractive or congenial.

I've been on business in the UK, with a brief stopover in Thailand.
I've never liked Bangkok — too hot and fetid. Not even the
fevered joys of Patpong have ever convinced me to stay. Too many
disgusting foreigners seeking sex with underage Thai girls and boys.

Why is it that business class always attracts such arrogant people?
When I boarded the onward flight to New Zealand via Sydney a
stupid pasty-faced overweight Englishman of the kind I thought
was extinct in the tropics told me I was sitting in his seat. He didn't
even apologise when I read his ticket back to him and pointed out
that he was over by the door — suitably next to the toilet. Then a
woman, somewhat overdressed with fake diamonds, insisted that
I move my carry-on luggage from the compartment above where

she was sitting so that she could park her faux leather overnight bag and toiletries in 'her' space: I asked to see her ticket for the compartment.

I should be accustomed to such ignorant behaviour. Brown faces like mine are no longer a rarity in business class, but it appears that some passengers persist in believing that the sun has not set on the Empire. Some still seem incensed that I am not travelling in steerage where they consider I belong.

Yes, I am in a mood. It has nothing to do with my business negotiations in England — I am board chairman of a New Zealand publishing company — which in fact have gone very well. No, it's the business concerning Talia that is bothering me. Over the last three weeks I have been able to put it 'on hold'. However, now that I am heading home across the Pacific, I am also having to confront the inevitability of sorting it out.

I should introduce myself: I am Isaac Tairāwhiti Jnr. Although my father, Isaac Senior, died twelve years ago, people still call me Junior to distinguish me from him.

Come to think of it, flying backwards is an appropriate physical position to be in as I think about the whole messy business involving my granddaughter. After all, Māori people always say we walk backwards into the future, meaning that we put the past before us. That's supposed to be positive but, in this case, the past is a burden that I wouldn't mind being divested of. Yet, how can I do that? Since I became a successful businessman — some thirty years ago now — the burden was thrust upon me. My extended whānau elevated me to their head — not that that was entirely consensual — but, listen, for a constantly cash-strapped family, it was either take me or go into bankruptcy.

It's actually been a surprising elevation, given my early childhood as the runt of the clan; weak, a cissy with a club foot who couldn't dive for pāua or do a haka without toppling over. Still, over the years they've got used to it and so have I, and whatever residual grievances they may harbour against me, they have forgiven because of my capacity to help them whenever they are in need. Their financial problems are easily sorted out: Uncle Solomon seeking injections of cash whenever the mortgage on papakāinga land needs paying; Cousin Bella, asking for another loan because she's spent her money at the Auckland casino; Nephew Rāwiri, inevitably in debt to some Black Power gang who are threatening to kill him for not paying for his drugs; Whaea Hera, needing a home for her hopeless brood in South Auckland. I'm also usually happy to donate to a mokopuna's wedding or university education, or to buy jerseys for the local rugby team.

All these family requests are easily solved by my signature to a cheque. But it's the problems to do with blood, history, whakapapa, old squabbles and feuds — skeletons rattling in the whānau cupboard — that won't go away.

Talia is the daughter of my only child, Makareti. She's the sweetest girl imaginable. Now nineteen and in her second year at the University of Auckland, she is doing very well.

Makareti and Glen, her husband, also have three very boisterous boys — Glen Junior, eleven; Rāwiri, nine; and Simon, eight. I call them, affectionately, Huey, Dewey and Louie, after characters in an ancient Walt Disney cartoon I watched as a boy. Every second weekend they get delivered to me by Makareti so I can take them out to Rainbow's End. The boys run me ragged, of course, wanting to go on every ride including the roller coaster — I use my club foot as an excuse not to squeeze on with them — but Dewey (alias Rāwiri) is on to me: on our last visit we went on the bumper car circuit and I was the best and most ferocious driver on the course. Surveying the wreckage he said, with an exaggerated sigh, 'Poor Pāpā, winning like that — and him with his club foot and all, too!' I fed him lots of candyfloss and popcorn and he got his comeuppance when he threw up. 'Pāpā, you don't play fair,' he wailed.

'The first rule of survival,' I answered. The sooner he realised, the better.

I love the boys but of all Makareti's children, the one closest to my heart is Talia. It's not just a matter of the prettiness which she has had ever since she was a baby. Throughout all these years I have watched with excitement the development of her enquiring mind and intelligence. When she finishes university, I'm hoping to bring her into the business. Meanwhile, whereas I take the boys to Rainbow's End, Talia has a monthly dinner with me at a restaurant.

Our fine-dining date is part of the agreement we made when I decided to pay her fees rather than her taking out a student loan. I'm supposed to play the stern grandfather checking on my investment and she is able to play the penitent granddaughter for only getting As instead of A+s in her essays. But really, the dinner is just an excuse to show Talia off to my friends and to watch as she turns the heads of the young men who wish they were having dinner with her rather than the old goat she ends up with.

If this sounds like I am besotted with my granddaughter, I will not deny it. Apart from which I have a special bond to Talia and to Makareti through Makareti's mother, Georgina. When I was cradling Georgina's head in my lap, almost forty years ago, watching her coughing up blood, she said to me, 'Promise me, Isaac, that you will look after Makareti? Promise.'

'I promise,' I answered, watching her life ebbing away — and raging inside that this was happening, despairing at the unfairness of it all.

'Nor do I want anybody to know what happened to us,' Georgina said, digging her fingers into me fiercely. 'Nobody is to know the secret. Promise me.'

I have kept both promises all these years. But a month ago, Whaea Hera, my aging aunt in South Auckland, in some ugly fit of temper, let the secret out.

2.

A dismal morning, and the plane has landed at Sydney airport.

Last night I could hardly cope with my anger at what Hera had done so, immediately after a midnight dinner, I took a sleeping pill. But I couldn't sleep at all.

'Pāpā Isaac,' Talia had wailed over the telephone to me when I was in the UK, 'please tell me it's not true. Please, Pāpā, please!'

All the blood drained from my face and I immediately telephoned my daughter Makareti. 'Yes, Dad,' she sobbed, 'that whole horrible story. Talia knows it now. I denied it of course, but Talia didn't believe me.'

'Who told her?' I asked. I could barely stand. A huge hole had opened from the past and something terrifying and ugly had been thrown through it to land stinking and rotten at my feet.

'Whaea Hera — but why should she do that? We never did anything to her, Dad.'

My heart went out to my daughter. She was really the bravest one among us. I rang Hera immediately. 'What did you tell Talia?' I was so angry that my forehead was popping with veins and my eyeballs were ready to explode.

'It was her own fault,' Hera answered. 'Putting on airs, pretending that she's better than the rest of us. It was time she was taken down a peg or two. She was getting whakahīhī. Somebody had to teach her a lesson.'

'You count yourself lucky, Hera, that I'm out of the country,' I said to her. 'But when I get back, I'm coming for you.' I could scarcely control myself. If I had been in the same room as my aunt I would have broken every bone in her worthless body.

I look out the window of the plane. My club foot is throbbing badly; I shall blame Aunt Hera. It's because of my foot that the Australian customs authorities provided a wheelchair for me at the air bridge. The other passengers had to wait as I got in it. Mr Pasty-Faced Overweight Englishman voiced his irritation. Perhaps Australia is his final destination, in which case they thoroughly deserve each other. Of course Diamond Lil also remonstrated at what she considered to be my privileged treatment. I rolled up my left trouser leg and took the sock off to reveal my 'cloven horse's hoof' — the sight of it would put anybody off their breakfast. I was about to show her my right foot, where the condition is not so severe, but, gasping for air, she quickly passed me by, clutching her paste diamonds to her pneumatic chest.

I fully meant to make her day, but her reaction took me back to childhood. When I was born my unsuspecting parents were absolutely shocked by my deformity, especially my father, who was a highly regarded sportsman in Māori tennis, rugby and wrestling. As for my mother, Rewa, she took the blame on herself, but loved me unconditionally. She wasn't prepared to accept that I would always be like *this,* and I began a correction therapy known as the Ponseti method. At six weeks I had an Achilles tenotomy, an incision in the tendon, on both my feet. At three months, a special type of splint called a Denis Browne bar, otherwise known as a foot abduction brace, was attached to my feet. I wore it nearly full time for three months and then at night and during naps for the next three years. My mother liked to tell me that I was a brave baby and hardly ever cried when the splint had to be periodically realigned. Perhaps my stoicism dates from boyhood.

Mum's persistence enabled me to eventually walk, albeit with specially built shoes and a cane. I don't blame my father, Isaac Senior, for not bonding with me. The sight of his first male child stumping along on his ankles, calling 'Daddy, daddy, daddy' must have seemed grossly unfair. I would never be the sportsman son to kick a football around with and he would never be able to stand on the spectator line watching me as I scored a try.

As for my cousin Georgina, she was my heart's companion. She was the eldest child of my father's eldest brother, Aaron, and his gentle wife Auntie Agnes. She should have been a boy though, not a girl — you know, eldest son of an eldest son — and so had been as unwelcome to her father as I had been to mine. No wonder we became each other's special friend. When we were infants Georgina protected me from all the roistering, loud, bullying children, both male and female, in the community. At five years of age she took to coming around to my house on her tricycle, leveraging me into the tray on the back, and taking me for long rides to the marae. If anybody ridiculed me, she gave them a bloodied nose. By the time she was eight, she piggybacked me from schoolroom to playground.

I still have a startling memory of a game of baseball at school. Much to my chagrin, Georgina picked me to play on her side — usually I would have been propped under a tree along with Big Wallace or Four Eyes Sally. But no, Georgina insisted that I play and that was that. By then I had a cane to help me walk and when the umpire said 'Batter up!' I hobbled up to the plate, balanced, swung once, swung twice, and then in a fit of exasperation swung really high and hard — and my bat connected with the ball. 'Quick!' Georgina yelled. I jumped onto her back and she was away, running like crazy to first base — and we made it! From there, we stole a run to second base and although she carried me to third base, Georgina was tiring. 'You've got to help me run home,' she panted. 'I can't carry you any more so we'll just have to do it three-legged. If I strap your bad leg to my leg with my belt, and you lean on me, I can run for the both of us.'

My heart was thumping like mad. 'What if I fall down? In front of everybody?'

'You won't fall down,' Georgina said grumpily. She draped my arms around her neck and said, 'Hold on tight.' We were lucky that Hiria Jones was the batter. When she hit the ball it soared over the fence into Mr Haddock's backyard. 'Come on, Isaac!' Georgina cried.

I will remember every bone-wrenching, juddering, excruciatingly painful step we took until the day I die. I can still hear my cousins and classmates yelling out to Georgina, 'Drop him! Run by yourself! Quick!' From the corner of my eye I saw Kepa Karaka retrieve the ball and throw it back towards the diamond. But most of all I remember Georgina's face, intent, focused, dragging me along with her. 'Dive, cuz, dive!' she yelled.

I fell forward, falling home, falling with Georgina in a tangle onto the home plate.

'Safe!'

Georgina was laughing and laughing. 'You did it, Isaac, you did it!'

Not I did it or we did it.

You did it.

Ah, memories of small victories are sweet when you are a handicapped child. Remembering that baseball game has obviously put a beatific grin on my face, if the responsive smiles from passengers following me back from the first class lounge onto the plane are anything to go by. Not so Madame Cubic Zirconia; I wish I had Dewey's trick cushion, the one that emits a fart when compressed, to put on her seat as she settles down. Instead, as the plane rises across the morning sea, I try to think higher thoughts and turn my loving memories to Georgina again.

By the time we were teenagers we were still very close. My mother approved of the relationship even when it looked suspiciously like love. 'Between cousins is all right,' she said. As Georgina entered puberty though, she traded in her tomboyishness for beauty and, therefore, testosterone-driven boys started to crowd me out, driving me insane with jealousy. At that point we were catching the school bus to high school in the nearby city, however, so the pursuit of a higher learning began to mitigate my raging hormones.

Did I enjoy high school? Did I *what*! I compensated for my physical deficiencies by providing evidence of my intelligence. I grabbed at every scholastic and cultural experience available, getting excellent grades in all academic subjects. I entered speech contests, joined the stamp club and successfully auditioned for the annual Gilbert and Sullivan dramatic production — I was a pegleg sailor in *The Pirates of Penzance*. By such means did I distinguish myself with the academic triumphs that are the last bastion of the nerdy student in The Also Ran Competition of Life.

Still, Georgina and I could never really let go of each other; or, at least, I could never let go of her. While there were always other boys, I was the one with whom she shared a romance, chaste yes, but heart driven. What she loved most was when I would read to her the dreadful romance novels she loved like R.D. Blackmore's *Lorna Doone*, usually in the suitably wild river setting just behind the marae. On another occasion, after I had read to her *Of Human Bondage* by W. Somerset Maugham, she arranged that we should play truant from high school and go and see the film with Laurence Harvey and Kim Novak. The main character played by Harvey, you will recall, has a club foot, and has a doomed relationship with the Novak character who, eventually, leaves him. Well, a club foot can never be romanticised and, give me a break, maybe Harvey could get away with it being incredibly handsome, but I could not. Even so, Georgina burst out, 'I wouldn't desert you, cousin, not ever!' And I, with a lump in my throat and welling up with unaccustomed sentimentality, vowed I would love her forever.

Yet, Georgina could be such an idiot. On one occasion she asked me, 'Did you know that Lord Byron had a club foot?' as if that would make me feel better. Why, oh why, did she then have to spoil it by adding that Joseph Goebbels also had a club foot and wore a metal leg brace for most of his life? Georgina had found his name on a list of people with club feet and had thought he was a German film star.

Remembering, I lift an imaginary champagne flute to my lips. 'This one's for you, my gorgeous, funny, exasperating cousin. If I was to admit to loving anybody, it would be you. I loved you, I idolised you, I was loyal to you.'

Yes, indeed I was. Then Auntie Agnes, Georgina's mother, died of emphysema — and I could do nothing to save Georgina.

3.

It's usually a thrill to arrive in New Zealand again, but my excitement has been undercut by this gloomy business involving Talia, my granddaughter. And as I disembark, I realise that I actually loathe flying.

At least I have the comfort of parting ways with Mrs Faux Diamonds. As I go through customs I watch her walking ahead. Aha, she has been stopped by a customs agent. I wonder how much she will have to pay for trying to enter the country with the half-eaten banana and biscuit I managed to secrete into one of her carry-on bags?

Victorious, I know young Dewey would only roll his eyes as I sail past her and out into the public waiting area. There, I see Sefulu, the young driver for my company. You can't miss him. He's a big brute of a boy who used to be a sumo wrestler in Japan.

'Hello Mr Tairāwhiti,' Sefulu salutes. 'The car's just outside.'

We speed along the motorway into the city. I call up Talia and, although I am usually irritated when her singsong answerphone clicks on, I am relieved not to have to talk to her personally.

'Talia? This is your grandfather speaking. You must already have gone into university, but I just wanted to let you know that I am back from overseas. I know you are hurting over what Whaea Hera has told you. Why don't you come over to the Herne Bay house tonight. And afterwards we can go to dinner?'

Then I call Makareti. As soon as she hears my voice, she bursts into tears. 'Oh, Dad, I'm so glad you're home. Talia has been absolutely terrified, screaming, crying, trying to get the truth out of me. I can't keep stonewalling her.'

'But you've kept denying the story, haven't you?' I ask.

'Yes.'

I close my eyes with relief. Then, 'I'll go over to see Whaea Hera as soon as I've dropped my bags at the house. Once I know what she's done, that will make it easier for me to know what to do when Talia comes to see me tonight.'

I disconnect the call. I see Sefulu looking anxiously at me. 'So we have a job later, Mr Tairāwhiti?' he asks.

'Yes,' I tell him. 'In Manurewa.' That's where Hera lives with her gang of boys. 'It could involve some rough stuff. I hope you've been working out today.'

Now, I should introduce you to my great, passionate, flawed clan. As I've already mentioned, Uncle Aaron, Georgina's father, was the oldest, and head of the extended whānau. My father, Isaac Senior, was the second in the family. Following them came my uncles

Joseph, David, Abraham and Solomon — though their names were disguised as Hōhepa, Rāwiri, Aperahama and Horomona. Rounding out the whānau were Leah, Rebecca and Hera (Sarah). If you're wondering about their biblical referentiality, blame the early Christian missionaries; they totally blitzed Māoridom with their bibles and baptisms.

Although I speak of them grudgingly, when I was growing up my father and his brothers were all larger than life and super-human. Having saintly names could not sublimate their sexual personalities — they were smiling, physically imposing beings who strode through life with careless charm and abandon. As young men they had all been notoriously phallus-driven, creating the template by which my own weedy masculinity could only be measured in the negative.

Uncle Aaron's amatory exploits were legendary. He was indulged in his escapades by his brothers and doting sisters: Hera forever proclaimed that women were always throwing themselves at him — it was their fault, not his. When he married Auntie Agnes, the whole family breathed a sigh of relief. Yet when she was carrying Georgina in her womb, and Uncle Aaron had his first extramarital affair, the family, despite professing the Christian values of fidelity, forgave him. Apparently he was too much of a man for one woman — and it was more convenient to accept that this was his natural condition.

Indeed my father and uncles were more like the god brothers of Māori mythology. That was their default position. Around Uncle Aaron, a particular arrogant mythology developed. He was Tānemahuta, god of forests, but he wished to create a race that was in his image: humankind. To do this he needed to create a woman. Accordingly he asked the Earth Mother, Papatūānuku, to help him. 'Haere atu koe ki a Kurawaka,' she told him. 'Go to Kurawaka, my sexual cleft, and from the red clay you find there, make a woman to mate with.'

The woman Tānemahuta created was named Hineahuone, Woman made of clay. He took her in his arms, pressed his nose to hers in the first hongi, shared his godly breath with her, and she passed from inanimate to animate being.

She opened her eyes and sneezed, 'Tihei mauri ora!'

Hineahuone's role in the narrative was to become the mother of a beautiful daughter, Hine-tītama, Girl of the Dawn. After she gave birth, having served her function, Hineahuone disappeared from the story; I've often wondered what happened to her.

Meantime humanity became Tānemahuta's marvellous playthings. Just like the god, Uncle Aaron was granted immunity for anything he did with them too.

It's all related, this business of Talia, her mother Makareti and my dear cousin Georgina — and it all began with Georgina.

At the time that her mother, Auntie Agnes, was hospitalised, I was fifteen and dux of my high school. On the recommendation of my headmaster, Mr Burns, I was awarded a fellowship to a prestigious Christchurch boarding college with an excellent upper school. When Mr Burns mentioned it to my father, he surprised me with his pride; Mum's tears were heartfelt.

The one desolating aspect was that I would have to say goodbye to Georgina. I arranged to meet her at the wild river in the hills behind the marae. She sensed my reluctance to leave her.

'There's nothing here for you, Isaac,' she said. 'You have to make your way through life with your brains.'

Life was changing for Georgina too, and not for the better. 'I have to leave school,' she said. 'With Mum in hospital, Auntie Hera says I have to look after Dad and the boys.' Georgina was referring to her two younger brothers Ramon and William. 'Auntie says it's a waste for a girl to be educated anyway.'

On my last day in the village, before departing for Christchurch,

I went to say goodbye to Georgina — and to Aunt Agnes who had, in the interim, been released from hospital as they could do nothing further for her. Uncle Aaron met me at the door. 'Don't stay too long with your aunt, boy, you'll tire her out. And Georgina has her work to do, so make your goodbyes quick.'

I paid my respects to Aunt Agnes and held her hand for a moment. She was hooked to a machine that gave her regular bursts of oxygen. It was awful hearing her gasp for air. In between one inhalation and the next she motioned me closer. I thought that it was so she could give me a kiss of farewell. Instead she whispered in my ear.

'Your uncle is looking at her.'

Forgive me, but at the time I didn't understand the import of what she was saying. The remark slipped past me. After all — and I'm not making excuses — I was already committed to catching a train to Christchurch. At Lyttelton Harbour, I was met by my housemaster, Mr Fox, and driven to the school where I was enrolled in accountancy, mathematics, English and history. When Mr Fox enquired what sports I might like to take up, I surprised him by asking about the pugilistic art of boxing. On his part, noting the way I was nervously flicking my cane, he joked that I should take fencing instruction. I decided to take both.

By the time I settled into boarding school and my lessons, my whānau, the valley and Georgina were receding from my consciousness. I was surprised and pleased that my fellow students were of a Southern gentlemanly calibre and did not draw attention to my club foot. Indeed I was treated as an equal and, in academic competition, I soon proved to some of the Cantabrians' finest sons that I was a force to be reckoned with. In boxing, while my balance was an impediment, my reach compensated. I also soon valued my fencing instruction when, during a school visit into the city, some callow youths set upon one of my classmates; my cane became my épée and I drove them off.

Then, a month after I had arrived in Christchurch, Mum wrote to me that Aunt Agnes had died. Mr Fox gave me permission to telephone from the school office. 'Should I come home for the tangi?' I asked.

'Agnes has already been buried,' Mum answered.

'What's Georgina's phone number? I'd like to call her and ask if she's okay.'

'Your uncle doesn't have a telephone in the house anymore,' Mum said. 'I'll let her know you asked after her. Things are going to change now for Georgina. She will have to be the mother of the family. She is in God's hands.'

Again, I suppose I should have read the signs but I didn't. Forgive me but I was frankly enjoying my schooling — making fond friendships with future professors, judges and captains of industry that have proved their worth by being sustained throughout my adulthood. I didn't even notice when my mother stopped giving me news of Georgina in her occasional letters.

At the end of the year I sat the examination for university entrance and, having done that, prepared to go home. I said goodbye to a friend I had become particularly fond of — Anthony Walcott, whose parents had a large high-country estate inland of Timaru — and caught the train to Picton. That evening I crossed over the Cook Strait by ferry and, in Wellington, embarked on the long, tiring train trip to Gisborne.

The train arrived in the early evening and my parents were waiting on the platform. Mum cried sentimental tears; in the past they would have stained my shoulders, but now they left wet patches just below the breast pocket of my school blazer. 'Goodness,' she laughed, 'haven't you grown, son!' She prodded my body to discern my musculature and pointed out to Dad the signs I bore of surprising adolescent strength. But all he was concerned about was my elocution.

'Is that how they talk down in Christchurch?' he asked. 'Like an Englishman? Now that you're home, we'll fix that.'

After dinner, I couldn't wait any longer. I had to see Georgina.

'Isn't it late?' Mum asked, exchanging meaningful glances with Dad.

'No,' I answered. 'I wrote to Georgina telling her I was arriving today. She'll be expecting me and, if she isn't, then I'll be a surprise for her.' While in Christchurch I had found a poster of the Hollywood film, *Lorna Doone,* just the right present for her romantic sensibilities.

The twilight was falling and the hills were darkening with shadows. I imagined Georgina's face when she opened the door to me. Would she jump into my arms and smother me with hugs and kisses? But when I knocked on the door, it was Uncle Aaron who answered. He took one puzzled look at me, realised who I was, and laughed out loud.

'Hello, boy!' he said. Then he turned and shouted down the hallway, 'Georgina, it's your old boyfriend.' He let me in. 'Come in, come in. We've just finished dinner.'

When Aunt Agnes had been alive the house had always been full of noise. Ramon and William were often running around the room, chasing each other. Georgina was always busy helping her mother with the housework. Not any longer. The boys were sitting at the table, waiting and watching their father. When he appeared with me they asked him, 'May we be excused now, Dad?'

All this time, Georgina had been sitting, her face downcast, at the table in the place where her mother had once presided. I walked up to her and went to kiss her cheek.

'No, don't . . .' she said. She gave a frightened look at her father.

Uncle Aaron laughed again. 'What's wrong with you, Georgina?

You've been looking forward to seeing your boyfriend. Give him a kiss.'

Have you ever seen a person with dead eyes? And Georgina's lips were so cold, so cold. Quickly, she got up from her chair, collected some of the dishes and carried them to the kitchen.

Uncle Aaron began to laugh and laugh.

It was then that I knew what was happening.

'Your uncle is looking at her,' Aunt Agnes had whispered.

When I returned home, I couldn't help it — I threw up into the toilet bowl. My parents were waiting in the sitting room for me and the first words I spoke to them were, 'Please tell me it's not true. Please . . .'

'We tried to stop it,' Mum began. 'When rumours started that Aaron was being intimate with Georgina, and even though Aaron was the oldest, I told your father to go over to his brother's house and tell him that what he was doing should end.'

I was so angry, I lashed out at Dad. 'Why did you have to wait for Mum to tell you?!'

'Don't you use that tone of voice with me!' my father answered. 'You might be growing into your maturity now, but you know nothing. We all tried to make our brother see sense, all of us, all the brothers and sisters.'

'But you failed,' I moaned. 'Georgina's still there.'

My father sighed, 'You tell him, dear,' he said to Mum. 'Our son has never listened to me.'

'She wouldn't leave him,' Mum answered.

'Wouldn't or couldn't?' My voice was rising. 'Georgina's too afraid to leave. Uncle Aaron must be threatening her in some way.'

But Dad was insistent. 'That they've been together all this time, we've all got used to it. It's too late to do anything, and that's the end of it, Isaac. Let it go. There's nothing any of us can do now.'

'Oh no?' I answered. 'We'll see about that.'

Over the following week I went to my other uncles and aunties. What did my uncles say? 'Who are you, boy? Respect your elders. This is none of your business. This is our business.'

And my aunties? They had surrounded Uncle Aaron and Georgina with a wall so that the secret could remain behind it.

Aunt Leah explained it to me this way: 'Just before your Auntie Agnes died, it was she who called Georgina in on her deathbed. It was she, her own mother, who told Georgina that she should go and lie with her father and give him comfort.'

I couldn't believe my ears. 'Auntie Agnes would never have done such a thing.' Aunt Leah was always making up stories and then making herself believe them. And her two younger sisters were as gaga as she was.

'To lose a wife is a terrible thing,' Aunt Rebecca added. 'But when that wife paves the way for a man to gain another partner, it is a blessing.'

However, it was Whaea Hera who took the cake. When I went to visit her she preened herself in her self-righteousness and turned to Genesis, chapter 19, verse 30 in her bible. 'You will recall, nephew,' she began, 'that the prophet, Lot, had just lost his wife. Against the Lord's instructions, she had looked back at the twin cities of Sodom and Gomorrah and had been turned into a pillar of salt. Poor Lot, his two daughters saw that he was disconsolate at the loss — and that he also needed an heir — and so they went unto him.'

Hera closed her bible and looked heavenward.

'In likewise, your cousin Georgina is doing her duty just as Lot's daughters did. Her union is sanctified by their example.'

I couldn't stand it. I wanted to poke her sanctimonious balloon and burst it. 'Bullshit, Auntie. Bull*shit*!'

She looked at me affronted. 'Don't you dare use bad language to me, Isaac Tairāwhiti. Whakahīhī. Too big for your boots. Know your place, boy.'

'All you women, you should know better, you should be looking after your own. By not acting against your brother, you too are guilty, are complicit in what he is doing.'

I held my hands up in despair. 'And I count myself guilty too.'

Throughout the rest of the summer I tried to talk to Georgina: on the road as she was passing by; at church on Sundays; or down on the marae whenever there was a tribal gathering. But word of my opposition had got around. Uncle Aaron was supported. I found myself being cold-shouldered.

In desperation, one morning, I waited until Uncle Aaron had left the house and Georgina was alone with her two brothers. I didn't even bother to knock.

Ramon looked at me, scared. 'You're not supposed to be here,' he said. 'You better get out now.'

'I'm not leaving without Georgina,' I answered. I went down the hallway to her room. It was empty. I found her, instead, in the marital bedroom.

'Hello, Isaac,' she smiled. 'Just like you, isn't it, to be like young John Ridd in *Lorna Doone* and try to rescue me.'

She was lying on the bed, resting. I sat beside her. She put her head on my shoulder.

'Come with me,' I said.

'Where shall we go?' she asked. 'There's nowhere to run. Anyway it's too late. I belong to my father. I've always belonged to him.'

'What bizarre logic takes you to that idea?' I asked her. Oh, I recognise the symptoms now: the victim begins to relate to the perpetrator. But no matter what I tried to tell my cousin — 'Get out of the house, come away now, with me' — it was no use.

She shook her head, bewildered. Stressed out, she started to scream at me. 'I don't even understand half of what you're saying,

Isaac! All your big words, they're not real! Where I am, *this* is real! Here! Here! Here!' And then she began to rock back and forth. 'And there's something else. I'm having a baby.'

Her words terrorised me. 'A baby?!'

'I'll be a good mother,' she said.

We were interrupted by a noise at the door. I heard Uncle Aaron hitting Ramon and William and their cries of pain. Then Uncle Aaron spoke to someone else: 'They must be in the bedroom.' Then he came into the room with my father.

'I've come to take you home, son,' Dad said. 'Nobody should ever come between a man and his wife.'

'His wife?' I asked incredulously. 'Georgina is not Uncle Aaron's wife. She's his daughter!'

Uncle Aaron's face stilled. I could tell he was angry — but Dad was there. Aaron turned to Isaac Senior and laughed softly. 'Don't worry, brother, real men don't hit cripples.'

I got up from the bed. I think Uncle Aaron was surprised at how fast I could move. What's more, until that time, I don't think he had realised how much I had grown. I was eye to eye with him now, and he didn't tower over me. 'Real men might not hit cripples,' I said. 'They also don't commit incest. As for cripples, we have no problem hitting sexual abusers.'

I let him have it. A good old slap, a backhander, rather than a punch to the guts.

There's something about slapping a man, particularly when it's done by another man, that is more shocking than using fisticuffs. It sends a different kind of message: 'You are contemptible and, indeed, you are beneath contempt.' No wonder that, in the old days, slapping a man across the face with a glove was prelude to a duel with swords.

Of course Uncle Aaron slammed me. I went down and he put a foot to my throat. As quick as I could I reached for my cane, aimed it at his crotch and pushed. With a cry of surprise he fell backwards.

'Congratulations,' I said to him. 'Real men do hit cripples after all.'

Then I was up and attacking him. Parrying with my cane, flicking at his chest, mentally quartering him for the coup de grâce.

Oh, I should have done it. Stabbed Uncle Aaron at his heart. Pushed on the cane with all my strength, and killed him. I'd get off lightly for his murder. After all, I was only seventeen. I didn't know what I was doing, judge. Sorry jury, after all, look at me, I'm a cripple.

Dad said, 'Don't.'

The weeks flew past. I received notification from my friend Anthony Walcott, who telephoned from Timaru, that we had both been successful in obtaining University Entrance. 'Which university are you going to?' he asked, presuming that I would go on to further academic studies. I turned the question back on him and when he said that he was thinking of Canterbury I told him I would join him there.

Matters had been strained between me and my father so I was not surprised that he would support my higher education. At the railway station taking me south he said to me, 'The family and I have had a talk. Don't come back, son, not for a while anyhow.'

'Oh, I see, the family that sleeps together stays together, eh Dad?'

When I arrived in Christchurch I couldn't rest. I telephoned the police and made an anonymous report on Uncle Aaron. Police in those days were not as committed about tackling cases of domestic violence, rape or child molestation. They turned a blind eye.

I was flatting with Anthony and a couple of other boys, and in the middle of the night I was called to the phone. When I answered it, Uncle Aaron's voice came down the line, 'I know it was you, boy.'

I began my life as a university student. The following winter,

Auntie Hera passed through Christchurch and dropped off a parcel from my mother: in it was a polo-necked jersey she had knitted to keep me warm.

'By the way,' Hera said, 'your Uncle Aaron and his wife have had a baby girl.' Then she added, 'It's better if we all accept the situation. No use causing any more trouble, boy.'

The cousin I loved called Georgina was being erased and in her place was a person who looked like her and talked like her but who was now 'Uncle Aaron's wife'.

And so Makareti came howling into the world.

That night after Auntie Hera left, I had a dream. I was back in the playground of my primary school and the umpire said, 'Batter up!' I hobbled to the plate, balanced on my cane, swung once, swung twice, and then in a fit of exasperation swung really high and hard — and my bat connected with the ball.

'Quick!' Georgina yelled. But instead of me jumping on her back it was she who jumped onto mine. 'You've got to carry me, cuz,' she said. My throat was dry. How could I do it? I began to stomp my way towards first base, but the closer I got the further away it was.

'Quickly, Isaac,' Georgina pleaded as she began to slide off my shoulders. Please, cuz!' Georgina screamed again. Oh, I tried, I tried so hard, but I stumbled and fell and, when I looked back, Georgina was lying on the ground.

When I awoke, my sheets were drenched with sweat. I pulled them around me and gave a deep groan.

'I'm so sorry, Georgina,' I sobbed.

4.

Sefulu has delivered me home to Herne Bay. He takes my suitcases to the bedroom and starts to unpack them.

'After this, I'll wait at the car for you,' he says.

'I won't be long,' I tell him. 'I'll just have a quick shower, and South Auckland here we come.'

While I am dressing, the telephone rings; my dear granddaughter Talia, returning my call. As soon as she hears my voice, 'Isaac Tairāwhiti speaking,' she bursts into tears.

The sound breaks my heart. 'Don't cry, darling,' I console her.

'Whaea Hera was so awful,' Talia cries. 'She told me many horrible things about . . . about . . .'

'You mustn't believe what Hera told you,' I answer. 'I will tell you the truth when you arrive tonight and we have our little talk. Yes, at seven o'clock. And then, are you free for dinner? Good.'

I ring Cibo and make a reservation. 'Your best table, by the window, as private as possible,' I say. Then I ring Aunt Hera and, when she answers the telephone in that smarmy voice of hers, I hang up.

Good, she is at home.

I put on a sports jacket, take up my cane and go out to Sefulu. 'Take me to Manurewa,' I tell him.

Three years after I began university at Canterbury I graduated with a bachelor's degree in commerce. I had made some semblance of peace with my extended whānau — and I couldn't keep on being angry with Dad — so, from time to time, I returned home for the occasional, very brief, visit.

On one of those visits I bumped into Georgina at church. It was a sunny day and I was overjoyed to see my heart's companion. She was vivacious, with lustrous eyes and skin, and nothing about her gave any sense that she was a victim.

'Isaac? Isaac!' Georgina called. She ran towards me and almost bowled me to the ground as we hugged. 'You must meet Makareti,' she said. 'Makareti? Haramai. Come and meet your uncle.'

A shy three-year-old child toddled over to me and, trustingly, put her arms up so I could hold her.

'Hello, Makareti,' I said as I breathed her in. I wasn't accustomed to children but tried my best to make a crook in my arm so that she could stay there while I spoke to her mother.

Georgina and I chatted on the church steps, and she was bright and happy. Across the way I saw Uncle Aaron, but not Ramon or William. 'They left home a few years ago,' Georgina said. 'They were arguing with Dad about me and so he threw them out.' She had blossomed into a young woman saddled with an increasingly aging husband. Not only that, but growing maturity had given her a stronger sense of independence; she was aware and knowing.

For instance, she thought I was examining Makareti. Instead of being offended she smiled, 'No, she bears no mark of sin upon her. And when she was born I had her baptised immediately. The sin is her father's and mine, not hers.'

I was astonished that Georgina had come to this understanding with such clarity.

And then Uncle Aaron joined us. 'The old boyfriend is back home again,' he laughed. He put out his hand but I did not shake it. He made a gesture that he didn't care about my reaction and motioned to Georgina that it was time they left. Makareti skipped ahead in the sunlight.

Uncle Aaron glanced at the little girl — and the same sunlight unmasked him.

Uncontrollably I began to shiver. My memory went back to Auntie Agnes when she had whispered in my ear: 'Your uncle is looking at her.'

I walked swiftly after Georgina and grabbed her arm. She laughed, surprised.

'Be careful,' I said. My mouth was dry with terror.

It wasn't over.

Shortly after that visit, my parents Isaac Senior and Rewa came down to Canterbury. I took them out to dinner with a few friends, including Anthony and a young girl, Felicity, whom I was dating. After dinner, my mother said, 'I like your girlfriend.'

That's when I told her and Dad that I had been offered a scholarship to York University in Toronto, Canada. 'I think I'll take it,' I said.

By that time I was a young man with my own life ahead of me — and there was nothing I could do about my cousin Georgina and her situation. I thought, maybe, I might be wrong about seeing Uncle Aaron look at Makareti.

Something happens to the mind and memory, and I had anaesthetised myself from thinking about those parts of my life that couldn't be fixed. Why? Of course it was guilt. About not being able to help Georgina. Sure, every now and then I had fantastic ideas about returning to her house and, this time, picking her up in my arms and getting her out of there. But that only happens in sentimental films. As Georgina had hinted some time before, real life is not like that.

'You must come home before you go to Canada,' Mum pleaded. 'Dad and I would like to give you a twenty-first birthday and the key to adulthood.'

Naturally I couldn't refuse. I invited Felicity, Anthony, my old housemaster Mr Fox and a number of other university friends to the birthday. We decided to make an extended four-day weekend visit of the occasion.

Mum and Dad were delighted to see us all. I hadn't realised how gracious a hostess my mother could be until I saw her in action with my friends. 'Please call me Auntie Rewa,' she told them. When I remarked to her how terrific I thought she was, she said, 'I've never had the chance to show you how much I loved you, son. So I'm doing it all at once while I have the chance because, when you go overseas, who knows when I will see you again.'

As for Isaac Senior, he enjoyed having young people in the house and taking them on excursions around the countryside, showing them the marae and the various historic sites of the tribe. 'Isaac Junior has never shown much interest in his Māori side,' Dad told them. As for my extended whānau, it was interesting to see their reaction to my friends, especially to Felicity and Anthony — Felicity's father was a member of parliament, and somebody down at the marae clicked on Anthony's surname, Walcott, and realised his father had been a famous All Black.

The only blot on the long weekend was the absence of Georgina in any of the family and friends get-togethers. 'Things are not going too well between Uncle Aaron and Georgina,' Mum explained. 'They are having a lot of arguments. Your uncle has been violent to Georgina. Just be careful, son, and don't make things worse. Georgina stays in the house; she's so devoted to her daughter and won't let her out of her sight. And sometimes Uncle Aaron won't let any of the family in. When Dad went over there to tell him about your birthday party, Aaron came to the door with a rifle and told him to clear off. "Tell that crippled son of yours I don't want him to set foot on my property, either. I heard what he told Georgina, warning her against me." Something's happening in that house, son.'

Uncle Aaron could not stop Georgina getting a message to me though. She telephoned from a neighbour's house just before all the guests were due to go down to the marae for the birthday feast.

'I'm sorry I won't be able to come to your birthday. I would love to, but if I do I have to come alone, and I can't leave Makareti with . . . him. I rang you to wish you all the best.'

I could hear Makareti crying down the phone.

'You were right to warn me,' Georgina said.

The evening was lovely and warm, with just enough of a breeze to take the heat off the day. The whānau had pitched in, helping to elevate the party to one of those family occasions that would long be remembered as one of the best ever. The marae was strung with lightbulbs and the dining hall was festooned with balloons and streamers. When Mum and Dad and my friends walked through the door I was surprised to see my uncles and aunties arrayed in their evening finery preparing to give us a rousing welcome.

'Karangatia rā! Karangatia rā! Pōwhiritia rā, ngā iwi o te motu!'

Anthony turned to me, 'Wow,' he said, 'what a wonderful family.'

I am sorry to say that my cynicism had the best of me. 'Yes,' I nodded. 'We put on a good show.' It was just that they caught me unawares with their obvious tribute to me, singing and dancing as if their reputation depended on it. Was I wrong about them? In all the years I was growing up in their bosom, was I the one who was dysfunctional and not them? Had I made the effort to know them, really get to know them?

I looked at my parents. Although my father had never said he loved me, Isaac Senior was standing up tall and as proud as a soldier. My mother has always been sentimental. There she was, gripping onto Dad's arm, looking at him as if to say, 'See? See how the whānau honours our son?'

The celebration proceeded. We sat down to a huge birthday feast. Tray after tray of food came out of the kitchen and Auntie Hera wobbled regularly to my side in newly purchased high-heels to ask, 'Is the kai all right, nephew?' The mutton, chicken and fish were brought in from the earth oven and, unaccustomed as I was to Māori gesture, I managed a fair enough thumbs-up sign to Uncle Horomona. During the dinner the usual speeches were presented: the ones from Uncle Hōhepa and Rāwiri were filled with heroic memories of myself that I couldn't remember — perhaps they had mistaken me for somebody else. Anthony told stories of riotous evenings when we had gone on the town, proving I was just as bad a bloke as everybody else in the dining room. Mr Fox rescued my reputation by praising Mum and Dad for having a son of whom great things were expected.

The highlight came when Dad presented me with a huge silver key with glittering ribbons tied to it. 'Son, you are now an adult,' he said. 'Open the doorway to adulthood and go through.'

All the while, in my mind I was pleading for him, 'Say it, say it, Dad, despite my disability say that you love me.' He never did.

I made a suitable reply. I realised that occasions like birthdays were really opportunities to say not only 'We want to honour you' but also 'We want to tell you how sorry we are for any misdeeds between us. It's time to move on.' Birthdays were times of forgiveness as well as unity. I thanked Mum and Dad and the family for the occasion. I apologised for my long absences from everyone but assured them that I always knew where I belonged. I forgot all the skeletons in the family cupboard and, instead, dwelt on the good memories.

My uncles and aunts sighed with relief at my diplomacy. For one night, at least, I could eat crow and be a good and obedient son of the whānau.

It was just before dawn, a few hours after Mum and Dad, Felicity, Anthony, Mr Fox and I had managed to make our tipsy way home, that I was suddenly woken up by a sharp, loud sound. I was puzzled by it, listened for it again, and tried to get back to sleep. But the telephone rang and I saw the light switch on in the hallway as Dad answered it. He came to my bedroom.

'Something's happening over at Aaron's and Georgina's,' he said. 'We better get over there.'

My heart filled with dread. Dad was already backing the car out of the garage. I dressed quickly and joined him. We sped along the road and turned in at Uncle Aaron's driveway. As we were approaching the house, Auntie Hera appeared in the headlights — she was the one who had telephoned. She was in her dressing gown and she waved us down.

'It's Georgina,' she said to Dad. 'I think she's shot our brother. She's got his rifle and won't let anyone in the house.'

A few other people from the village had gathered with torch lights. Among them was Uncle Horomona; he was talking to Georgina through the front door.

'Go away,' she called. 'Don't anybody try to come in.'

I was out of the car in a flash. 'Georgina? It's me.'

'Isaac?' The door opened a little, and the muzzle of the rifle poked through.

'Let's rush her,' Uncle Horomona said.

'No,' I answered with as much force as I could muster — and Uncle Horomona stepped back. 'Georgina will talk to me. Don't anybody make a move until I come back out. Is that understood?'

I walked up to the door. Georgina opened it further, smiled, and said, 'Isaac, I knew you would come.' Makareti was beside her, hugging her mother around the knees. 'Will you take Makareti out? And then return to me?' She kissed Makareti. 'Stop crying now, darling. Go with Uncle Isaac.'

I took Makareti and gave her to Auntie Hera. 'Oh, thank God that the baby is unharmed,' she said.

When I went back to the house, Georgina let me in, locked the door behind us, and took me to the main bedroom. She looked as if she hadn't slept for weeks; she had dark circles under her eyes and her face was filled with fatigue. Uncle Aaron was lying in the bed, still alive, his chest bloodied from a bullet wound. He was breathing hoarsely, his eyes wide with fear.

'Get help,' he whispered. 'Get help for me. I don't want to die.'

Georgina patted his hand. 'There, there, Dad.' Then she looked up at me. 'Will you stay with me, Isaac?' she asked. 'Dad's been interfering with Makareti, and he has to pay.' Her eyes were burning with purpose. 'I'm so tired, cousin, and I want to sleep. But I have to wait until he has gone from this life. Will you wait with me?'

'Of course, cousin,' I answered.

So, we waited. Uncle Aaron tried to get out of bed; Georgina restrained him. He pleaded with her, sobbing for forgiveness, but she only nodded her head and settled him down again.

Outside I heard more cars arriving, car doors slamming, and raised voices. 'What's going on? What's happening?' People were banging loudly on the door. They would soon break it down.

Then Uncle Aaron stilled. I took his pulse. I nodded to Georgina, 'He's gone.'

She closed her eyes and, with strange tenderness, kissed both his cheeks. She gave a deep sigh and, before I could stop her, slammed the rifle butt between her feet, bent her chest over the barrel, reached down for the trigger and pressed it. The sound was shockingly loud in the room. The smell of cordite was acrid. I heard the front door cracking open. Dad and Uncle Horomona burst into the room.

I caught Georgina as she fell. 'No, Georgina!'

'Promise me you will look after Makareti,' she said.

'I promise.'

There was blood everywhere, and gouts of blood were coming out of Georgina's mouth every time she exhaled. 'Nobody is to know the secret. Promise me.'

She gave a huge gasp and her eyes started to flicker. 'Oh cousin, if I go to hell will you come to get me?'

The sun burst across the hills.

5.

And now Sefulu and I turn off the motorway into South Auckland.

It's the Māori and Pasifika part of the city. Sometimes Makareti loves to bring me and the boys here to the Ōtara Market before letting us loose at Rainbow's End. 'Time you had a walk on the wild side,' she likes to tease me. 'Get you out of Hernia Bay or Ponsnobby or Gay Lynn and among real live mean-as people.'

Makareti forgets that I have visited quite a few dangerous neighbourhoods in my time: black shantytowns in Johannesburg, Hispanic hotspots in Los Angeles, slums in Rio de Janeiro — and to prove that I'm not colourblind, I've also been in the middle of white supremacists' riots in Hamburg.

South Auckland's reputation is unfair, though. There *are* good people here.

However, there are also people like Whaea Hera and her boys.

'It's the grey house, isn't it, Mr Tairāwhiti?' Sefulu asks. He has turned into a cul-de-sac and is pointing at the third house in the crescent. I own the house: when Auntie Hera decided to leave the village and come to Auckland to stay with her daughter and that hopeless gang of crims her daughter supports — her tattooed freak of a husband, Bojangles, and her two sons Ace and Rooter — they had no place to stay. I bought them the house as part of my — let's call it — lay-by arrangement to keep Hera in line on family matters. Well, she has just welshed on the deal.

Sefulu pulls in at the kerb. For a moment I sit there, having another of my headaches, wondering about my aunt's viciousness. What did she say to Talia?

'Time for the showdown,' I say to Sefulu. I take a deep breath, open the door of the car and step out. I see the front curtains open and Hera's face looking out the window. I hear her yell to Ace and Rooter. Quickly I give Sefulu his instructions: 'I want you to go to the front door. Hera will have her two boys blocking the way. But if I know her, she'll try to get out the back. You keep the boys occupied while I deal to her.'

Sefulu and I walk quickly to the front door. 'What the fuck do you want?' Rooter asks. Sefulu diverts their attention while I walk as fast as I can to the backyard. I am just in time. The door opens and Hera steps out, a lumbering antiquity, making for the garage, fumbling with the keys to her car.

'Going somewhere?' I ask her. I put out my cane and, with a yelp, she trips over it and falls on her driveway. I take my cane and give her a good hard belt on her big arse, oh, it feels so good to hear her cry out.

'I want to know every venomous word you spat at my granddaughter, you disgusting old bitch.'

'Talia's never been your granddaughter,' Hera answers with surprising spirit.

'Wrong answer,' I say to her, and I give her another whack, this time across her kidneys.

Aunt Hera groans but this time she is not so defiant. She's looking around for her two boys, where the fuck are they? Then, 'I told Talia everything.'

'Everything?' Another stroke of my cane across her face keeps her in submission. 'Did you tell her about Uncle Aaron?'

'No.'

'And the night Georgina killed him?'

'She's heard the rumours,' Hera spits back. 'She's a big girl, she can put two and two together all by herself. She doesn't need me or anybody else to join the dots.'

I lean against the house and watch as Hera gets up. I leave her there and walk back to the car. Seeing me, Sefulu stops belting into Ace and Rooter. Hera is not finished yet though. She has one last lot of venom to spit out, 'That girl was always too whakahīhī,' she yells. 'Always showing off how educated she is. She needed to be brought down a peg or two. Somebody had to tell her that she has tainted blood. She's not as good as the rest of us and she never will be. She's lucky that the sin doesn't show in her . . .'

'The sin is yours, Hera, for not stopping Uncle Aaron from committing incest.'

'She better watch out — it will come out in her own kids if she has any. Or in their kids. Sooner or later . . .'

Sefulu has to restrain me from going back and killing her.

'I'm giving you to the end of the week to get the fuck out of my house, Hera. You, your daughter, her husband, your grandsons, go find another rock to crawl under.'

The mess — there was a lot of it following the night and day Georgina killed Uncle Aaron.

Of course, she was vilified in the press. After all, hadn't she shown her guilt by killing herself?

There was a police inquiry of course; I delayed my trip to Canada to give evidence at the inquest. In Makareti's interests, the incest was hushed up.

The judge awarded custody of Makareti to my parents — Dad being the second son after Aaron. My mother soon came to delight in the task. After the whole affair had quietened down I took Makareti to visit Georgina's grave. While we were sitting there, digging the earth so that Makareti could plant her daisies and daffodils, I kept thinking about what to do about my promises to Georgina concerning Makareti's parentage and keeping everything secret.

The answer was simple. I spoke to Mum and Dad and they agreed. I then spoke to my extended whānau and, although there were some voices in dissent, particularly those of Auntie Leah and Auntie Hera, the consensus ruled.

I became Makareti's father. In the family whakapapa, Makareti's line shows that I am her dad and Georgina is her mother, and that my parents are her grandparents. I've managed to erase Uncle Aaron in the same way he had tried to erase my cousin Georgina when he took her 'to wife'.

I never married. While I am attracted to women and have the occasional affair, I am really not the kind of man that women marry.

Later.

It is ten minutes to seven and I am back in my house, expecting Talia. I think of her grandmother, my cousin Georgina. There's a room two inches behind the eyes where all my memories are kept. For as long as I live, Georgina will always inhabit that room, safe from the world, safe from pain.

Showered and shaved, I am dressed in a blazer and dark trousers. I've spoken to Makareti again and reassured her that my meeting with Talia will go well. Makareti has asked if I want to take Huey, Dewey and Louie to Rainbow's End this weekend. I remember a previous weekend when a man came up to me and Makareti and complimented us on the family. Huey was puzzled. 'We're just a normal family like everybody else, aren't we Mum? Aren't we, Pāpā?'

Oh, there did come a time when Makareti was in her teens that somebody whispered to her, just like Auntie Hera has whispered to Talia — perhaps it was Hera that time also — that her family history was a lie. I can remember Makareti coming crying and wailing to me, just as Talia will be doing soon.

When it happened, I recalled the story of Hine-tītama, Girl of the Dawn, whose mother had been made of clay. She grew up a very beautiful young woman and Tāne, her father, desired her. He made her his wife and in the fullness of time, she bore children.

But Hine-tītama wanted to know her lineage, or whakapapa, so that she could tell her children — they represented the first tribes of humankind. She knew who her mother was but she didn't know who her father was. When she asked Tāne, he was evasive. In the end she turned to the birds of the forest for the answer and they told her, 'Ask the posts of the house.'

The Māori meeting house is a world of its own. It has a head which you see when you approach from the outside and, when you enter, you are within the body of the house. You are literally within the stomach of the tribal ancestor who begat the tribe and with whom the tribe is associated. There are a number of carved posts which support the structure of the meeting house; the main ones are the poutokomanawa, the heart post, and the poutāhuhu, the ridge post. In the old days, the pou, which also included the wall posts, were said to be living, sacred, able to talk.

When Hine-tītama entered the whare she put her question to the posts of the house: 'Who is my father?' The first post answered, 'Tāne the husband is also Tāne the father.' Hine-tītama would not believe the response so she asked the second post. Again the reply came back, 'Tāne is both the father and the husband.' Still she wouldn't believe the answer. She therefore asked every post of the house, and when they all responded, 'Tāne, Tāne, Tāne,' she realised the truth.

Hine-tītama was the first of all women of the world to take the blame upon herself; not the man but the woman. She was overwhelmed with shame. She was not worthy to stay in the overworld, the world of light. But she also had her children to consider. How could she save them from guilt? She resolved that she had to leave and go to the underworld, Te Pō, the world below. There, within the womb of Papa, the Earth Mother, she could find sanctuary and, possibly, prepare her children for their redemption.

By means of a powerful karakia, Hine-tītama therefore weakened Tāne so that he would not follow her. Once he was incapacitated, she hastened to Rarohenga. At the entrance to the underworld she was confronted by the guard, Kūwatawata, who told her, 'Turn back, turn back before it is too late. If you enter here you will never be able to return.'

Still, Hine-tītama knew she had to go onward.

When Tāne arose from sleep and realised what she had done, he managed to reach her just before she turned to enter the underworld. Weeping, he said, 'Please don't go.'

Her words to him? They were of love and of sacrifice. 'Haere atu, Tāne. Hāpaia ngā tamariki i te Ao. Go back, husband and father. Go back to the light and raise our children. Then, when they grow old and die, let me lovingly gather them in.'

Hine-tītama achieved her transcendence. She became Hinenuitepō, which some have translated as 'The Goddess of Death'. I say to you, look to the literal translation of her name: just as the full name of Tāne is Tānenuiārangi, Great Father of the Overworld, let us acknowledge Hinenuitepō's nurturing role as Great Mother of the Underworld. Hers is the redemptive role and it is through her that we achieve forgiveness.

Seven o'clock. I'm getting nervous.

I have opened the sliding doors and am looking across the front terrace. I want to be able to see Talia when she arrives. I plan to smile at her reassuringly and welcome her into my arms.

I am having a gin and tonic, but my hands are trembling and the ice is clinking like icebergs ready to sink the *Titanic*. I am not usually as anxious as this. Is that my Talia now? Stopping her car and getting out of it?

If it is, I better wipe my eyes, otherwise she'll see that her stupid old grandfather has been crying — and that would not do my reputation as a stern old goat any good.

Shall I tell her the truth? Oh, when her mother Makareti had asked me, those many years ago, despite what Georgina had asked me — to keep the secret — I had come to believe that secrets were wrong. Makareti? Well, she was made of steel — she still is — and I thought she could bear the news that Uncle Aaron had been her father.

She had laid a hand gently on my arm and asked, 'When does it stop, Dad?'

And now, this evening, I ponder my brave Makareti's question.

Must Talia take on the burden, too, of something that wasn't her fault? Must the sins of the father continue to be visited on the heads of the children?

I stand to greet Talia. My club foot is aching badly. Talia looks up at me, her eyes glowing. 'Pāpā? Pāpā . . .'

Oh, how I love this child so. Makareti's daughter. Georgina's granddaughter.

Truth or lie? What would *you* say if your circumstances were mine?

In the gathering night I tell her what I think she should hear.

the ancestors

CHAPTER 4
MĀUI

———

Headnote to a Māui Tale

———

Born. Still.

———

Māui Goes to Hollywood

———

Me aro koe ki te hā o Hineahuone!

———

Headnote to a Māui Tale

BY KERI HULME

There are many stories told:
how, surprising his mother by a month or more
she deemed him unready for life and laid him on seaweed,
covered with meconium and that strange slick of foetal fat
and lastly, as a comfort to small disorderly souls,
his parent's long and treasured hair —
parent?
Ah, thereby a tale: tikitiki a Taranga in the North
but tikitiki a Te Raka in the South and he,
in at least one telling, was father to the youngest,
the man who could fly, who borrowed fire every morning for the
    world
from his incendiary grandfather, Mahuika,
who in turn, flitting from time to time and space to space
spent a long life brooding in abyssal deeps
as mother to islands
— but I hear you snap That was his grandmother! Mahuika!
    Grandmother!

Well, it is a weird family tree: I mean it was definitely his auntie
who rescued him from the sea and nurtured him on sunlight and
    water until

he came full term
(which, for a trickster, is a longer or a shorter time)
but, was she really The Wind? Or just one among many?

And there is speculation, much later on, about the number
of sisters Irawaru had
but none over the fact he turned Irawaru into the first dog
— not the kindest thing to do to your brother-in-law
even if you can't stand the lazy sod —
but then, no-one ever accused him of kindness —
heroic prowess, ungodly ingenuity, devastating wit? O *yes*
but there is that small difficulty with the not-fully-formed-human
being, well, not fully human . . .

Anyway, it *was* Tuna the father of the eels
(and sometimes half the bush as well)
whom he slew for taking indecent liberties with one
or both, or more
of the aforesaid wives,
and there is no doubt his end:
crushed between the thighs of Hinenuitepō.

(I have not gone into the hasty sun;
the mystic jawbone of that grandmother,
or the fishing up of (yawn) o so many islands —
I do admit to a friendship with fantails)

— seriously, there he was slithering and wriggling bellydown
stopping the outlet of Death and She
watching beady-eyed already — talk about Tuna's revenge
heh!

Was it just
his mana She killed?
Or the man (or whatever)
himself?

It all depends
on what story
you hear.

Born. Still.

The Birth and Return of
Māui-Tikitiki-a-Taranga
(as observed by his sister, Hina)

BY BRIAR GRACE-SMITH

Hina's hair trailed down her back like a wave of fizzing, hissing sea foam. Her eyes were shiny, as if someone had smoothed cling wrap over two buttons of the greyest sky and pushed them deep into the lunar whiteness of her skin. She was the only girl in a home full of brothers. Like so many male prime ministers and presidents, these four boys, named Māui-mua, Māui-taha, Māui-pae and Māui-roto spent their time trying to prove to each other that they were the best at anything and everything that they happened to be doing — be it boxing, scoring goals, pissing or nose-picking. The brothers were like an extension of the same person: except for small differences they all looked similar and once one started an action, they all copied it, only the next in line would do it more loudly, violently and with much more swag. From sunset to sunset poor Hina was smothered in a boy-tsunami of legs, arms, body odour and noise.

It was only in her mother's presence that there was peace.

The children's mother Taranga was a lighthouse in a raging testosteronic sea. Straight backed and sure footed, she glided through the turbulent boys, negotiating the trouble spots, picking up clothes and toys with her feet, tossing them into the air and catching them in her long-fingered hands. Her voice was a laser-strike of honey that broke through the two-metre-thick wall of thumping, banging and shouting, forcing the brothers to all shut up and listen.

'Brush your teeth, you fullas, and get to bed, I'll be checking on you in fifteen minutes,' she would say, and, anxious to please, all four brothers would jump to their feet at once, sprint to the bathroom and begin the squirt, scrub, spit and rinse of tooth brushing.

Taranga secretly embraced the boys' need to be the same. It made things so much easier than raising a group of kids who wanted to be different. The boys all liked to wear the same clothes, so shopping was easy and, at mealtimes, they stood in a line with plates in hand, happy to be dished up whatever servings and amounts of pretend meat and veges the one next to them was eating. The family lived in a time when the world had been destroyed by war and there was nothing alive anymore to eat or drink, excepting of course, people, and one result of living in a world that had no life was that no more life could be made.

'I am so lucky to have had youse and I must remember to treasure every moment,' Taranga would often say to her children, and indeed when she was with them she gave them all of her attention. The only time she drifted off was when she would sit on the couch and let Hina plait her blue-black hair. As her hair was brushed, oiled, parted and plaited, the light in her bright eyes would go out, and Hina knew that Taranga was thinking about their father, a man that none of the children had ever known. Their father, Makea-tu-tara was the leader of the rebellion and he lived in the underworld but no one knew where that was.

Anyway, on one particular morning, Hina awoke to her brothers barking and rolling around on the floor like puppies, the toilet seat up and the walls plastered with their artificial Weetbix, and she knew straight away that Taranga wasn't home. This was surprising because her mother never left the apartment building without telling Hina, her most sensible child, first. 'I'm going to the warehouse to trade for more fake food,' she would say or 'I'm going to visit Mahuika and have a glass of her bootleg because I am losing the plot.'

Mahuika was Hina's grandmother. Her eyes and freckles were the colour of flames. She wore bright kaftans and was forever flashing her long, well-manicured and glittery nails. Mahuika lived in a penthouse in another apartment building, on the better side of town. Mahuika was the only person in the city who knew how to make fire out of nothing, and her services were in high demand, especially during times when there was no power, which was most days. Any source of brightness was treasured. The sun outside had long since been smothered by ash and pollution. No one was sure if it even existed anymore. The world outside was eternally grey.

Knowing that something must be wrong for her mum to disappear unspoken, Hina unbolted the apartment door and walked in her tippy-toed way along the hallway. She stepped into the lift and pushed the button. As she waited for it to move she listened to the southerly — which had long ago become trapped in the lift shaft — scream and whip its dragon-like tail. She breathed in the sting of urine that snaked its way into her senses from the dark, sticky corners of the lift and as the light around her began to dance she closed her eyes so she didn't see the ancient faces that appeared mid-flicker. So, by the time the lift closed its rusty jaws, Hina was flying so deeply inside the cosmos of her six-year-old thoughts, it took her a moment to realise that she wasn't the only non-ghost in the space.

There on the floor, a pile of long limbs and hair, was Taranga. Hina could see that in her arms she held something. A baby. An umbilicus, twisted and striped like a candy cane, trailed from the baby's puku up inside the place between her mother's legs.

The baby's face was as smooth as a pebble, his nose had no holes for breathing air and his eyes were welded shut, and because he hadn't been ready to trade the water of Taranga's womb for the land, his feet and hands were webbed.

Hina gasped and bent down to touch him and felt that he was cold. Without taking her eyes from her baby, Taranga said, 'His name is Māui-Tikitiki-a-Taranga, and he is the last child ever to be born into this world, Hina. We must do what we can for him. Push on my puku girl.'

Hina pressed down on the bulge of her mother's belly. Taranga exhaled deeply and out gushed the placenta. Three times the size of the baby, it was purply and translucent, like a jellyfish, with what looked like a tangle of blue and purple electrical wiring showing just beneath its surface. Unlike the baby, it pulsed and throbbed with life.

'Now cut off my hair and weave your brother a basket so he can be warm,' Taranga instructed her daughter.

Hina extracted the pocket-knife she kept hitched to her belt and ran her finger along the blade lightly. A gift left to her by her underworld father and crafted from underworld steel, it was always sharp. Hina watched it draw a thin line of blood. Then, taking a handful of her mother's slippery, shiny hair, Hina began to cut.

Wearing orange radiation suits and masks, Hina, Taranga and the baby, who had been placed against his mother's breast, zig-zagged, ducked and dodged their way through the city. They had to be careful of snipers who crouched in waiting on the rooftops ready to shoot anyone who passed. If they were killed, their bodies would be sold and consumed by royalty or sold to the scientists for testing, but human cells died quickly outside of the body and the days of cloning were long gone. The human race was all but dead.

Taranga and Hina climbed the two thousand stairs that led to the top of the giant wall that kept the monster sea from escaping into the city. The sea raged below, its surface littered with plastic, polystyrene and tin. Hina had grown up listening to her mother's stories about swimming in that sea. 'It was my favourite place,' she told her. 'There was a beach with sand to lie on and dig up. The water didn't sting you and there were fish with scales and wiggling eyes,' she said, trying hard to remember. 'My dad would put out a net and catch enough to feed us, and all of our cousins, aunts and uncles. Now, just like the land, the sea is dead.'

Taranga held her baby, wrapped in hair, one last time. She took off her radiation visor, kissed him and she cried.

Finally she raised him skywards and called out to the gods to guide and protect him: 'E ngā atua, manaakitia tā mātou pēpē.'

Then with a scream she cast the baby into the foaming waves. For a moment it looked as if he might fly.

Hina had never forgotten that morning. Sometimes, she would close her eyes and imagine her little brother floating through the ocean, swaddled in hair, tied with his umbilicus to his placenta charging forward, lighting up the deep dark ocean and showing Māui number 5 the way to a new home.

———

Ten years later, Hina was lying on her bed listening as the noise of her brothers snoring, tossing, turning and sleep-talking began to thicken. Suddenly, she heard five loud and sharp knocks at the door. She heard her mother's feet slide over the linoleum floor in a hurry to open it. Who could it be? She heard her mother gasp and begin to wail, and she smelt the sharp smell of the sea. Peeking around the corner of her door, she saw a skinny boy with hair like seaweed and big dark eyes. His hands and his feet were webbed. Pulling out of his mother's grasp, he looked at her and smiled cheekily. She knew that Māui number 5 had returned and that he was not like her other brothers. He would be her friend and they'd have many adventures together.

One day, Hina would plait the sacred rope that Māui 5 would use to snare the sun, pulling it like a fish from the darkness and flooding the world with light.

He would charm their grandmother Mahuika so much that she would give him every single one of her magical glittery nails. Each nail would hold a flame, and he would bring fire back into the world.

He would follow their mother to the underworld, and meet their father Makea-tu-tara.

Using the jawbone of his other grandmother, Murirangawhenua, he would fish up a new, clean land, full of life, with forests and rivers and trees. That land would become their home. More babies would be born.

His brothers would always be jealous of him, and so he would become Hina's closest friend. Still, despite that love, one day he would hurt his sister so deeply that she would take her own life.

Māui Goes to Hollywood

BY DAVID GEARY

No man is a motu.
— Hone Donne

MOTU IHOP

Elvis, Marilyn and Māui were hanging at the IHOP across from the Chinese Theatre.

'I think it's bad taste,' said Elvis, glaring out the window at the Paul Walker impersonator.

'It's just too soon,' said Marilyn.

'Well,' said Māui, 'he was the star of *The Fast and the Furious*, so being quick off the mark is kind of . . .'

Elvis cut him off.

'He tries to get suckers to pay him 200 bucks to drive them in a crappy convertible to the tree Walker crashed and burned beside, but it's not even the same tree.'

'It's sick,' spat Marilyn.

'Oh come on,' teased Māui, 'aren't you both cashing in on the tragic deaths of . . .'

'Elvis's death wasn't tragic,' laughed Marilyn. 'He died on the can, one deep-fried triple-cheese burger too many, 350 pounds of self-loathing.'

'That was so tragic,' said Elvis.

'No, not. If he was alive today, he'd be on *My 600-lb Life* — celebrity edition. Marilyn's death was tragic. Murdered by Kennedy's goons because he was worried she'd blow the lid on their affair, and then they made it look like an O.D.'

'I suppose you think 9/11 was an inside job, too?'

'It was.'

'And we never walked on the moon?'

'The shadows are all wrong. Stanley Kubrick made a deal with NASA, and . . .'

'And Elvis is alive and well?'

'Well, his spirit lives on, honey, just look at you.'

Elvis gave his cheesy grin and Marilyn batted her false eyelashes at him. She pouted and he kissed her cheek, careful not to smudge her lipstick. They were an item.

'You're just lucky, Māui, that you never died,' said Marilyn slurping up the dregs of her trim-milk smoothie.

'Actually, he did die,' said Māui.

'Not in the movie,' said Elvis. 'That Lin-Manuel Miranda is a genius.'

'Did I tell you I almost got into *Hamilton*?' said Marilyn.

'Yes,' Elvis and Māui replied in unison, 'many times.'

'So there might be a *Moana* sequel?' asked Elvis. 'And he'll die?'

'Um, nah — not with how he died,' smirked Māui.

'What? How did he snuff it?' asked Marilyn.

'He can't die,' said Elvis. 'He's like The Rock.'

'He'll live forever with perfect pecs,' cooed Marilyn.

'He's not like The Rock,' said Māui, cutting up another apple-potato pancake.

'Then how did he die?' asked Marilyn, stabbing a fork into a piece of Māui's pancake.

'It's a bit rude — like eating other people's food without asking,' said Māui.

'Rude! I love rude,' said Marilyn, a struggling stand-up comedian from Nebraska.

'Okay, well, he . . . he tried to crawl up through the Goddess of Death while she was sleeping and grab her heart and climb out her mouth, and become immortal. But she woke up mid . . . um . . . wriggle, and she crushed him. So now we all have to die.'

'Hold on. What?' said Elvis.

'What did he try to crawl up through?' asked Marilyn.

'Her . . . you know . . . lady bits,' blushed Māui.

'You mean her pussy?' snickered Elvis, a yoga teacher from Austin.

'Oh for fuck's sake, can we just call a vajajay a vajajay,' said Marilyn. 'Did Oprah fight for nothing?'

'Did the vagina have teeth?' asked Elvis, dead serious.

'Um . . . maybe. Sharp obsidian pointed ones in some stories, yeah,' said Māui.

'Vagina dentata!' Elvis and Marilyn belted out together and high-fived. The IHOP — International House of Pancakes — stopped mid-munch. Māui hunkered down and sipped his lukewarm coffee.

'Sigmund Freud . . .' began Elvis.

'As in Kentucky Freud's Chicken — it's mother-fuckin' good!' quipped Marilyn.

'You know,' said Māui, all stern and eyebrows, 'this is a family restaurant.'

'Sorry, but it's clearly just another fear-of-the-female male myth,' said Marilyn. 'Same as how all the old fairytales about evil stepmothers were originally cautionary tales about men preying on girls and women.'

'Is that right?' said Māui, stumped. 'Let's get back to preying on tourists.' Māui gestured to the waitress with his mighty roll-on-tattooed arm.

'We got this,' beamed Marilyn, throwing down a twenty.

'You've been going through a dry spell,' agreed Elvis, and threw down a ten.

'Actually, that's kind of why we asked you over here,' said Marilyn.

Māui got the tingles. 'Oh, I just thought you were being matey.'

'Your Māui schtick is,' said Marilyn, 'getting old-hat. *Moana* came out years ago now.'

'And it never won the Oscar for animation,' said Elvis.

'And your tatts are getting . . . tatty,' said Marilyn.

'And Māui never wore shades in the movie,' said Elvis.

'That . . . movie . . . isn't . . .' stuttered Māui. 'I have trouble with the sun.'

'Plus, you don't have a permit,' said Marilyn, lowering Māui's shades with her pinkie, and fixing his bloodshot brown eyes with her steely blue ones. 'If the city catches you there's a big fine. A couple of grand.'

'And you're illegal, right,' said Elvis, 'so 45's got you in his crosshairs.'

Marilyn stood up and smoothed her famous white dress down.

'Best of luck, big boy.'

She blew him a kiss and sashayed out. Elvis took out his comb, dragged it through his hair while checking himself in the reflection on the serviette box.

'I'm sorry, man. Marilyn is kind of the boss down here. And she's in with the cops, so what she said about illegals — that's her firing a warning shot.'

'You said that.'

'Hey, maybe you want to do a farewell Māori haka dance thing. She can't object to that. And you could get a decent stash to send you on your way.'

Elvis offered his sweaty hand. Māui batted it aside. Dark clouds rolled in. The migraine-train. His fingers flexed and made fists. Māui was going to smash something, or someone. Elvis left the building.

MOTU KING-HITS

Māui had been cut before. The Warriors cut him. The Manly Sea Eagles cut him. He always smashed something, or someone. Māui felt the roimata coming, pushed his shades back up the bridge of his nose, up over the rough ridge that went East then West. Too many hit-ups, smash-ups, facials. His last chance came when the North Queensland Cowboys threw him a lifeline. A one-year deal. Do or die.

Once upon a time he'd been a young flyer, played in the centres and carved it up. But as he'd got older he got pulled in closer to the pack. Now all the Cowboys wanted him to do was hit the gym, bulk up and take the 'don't-ask vitamins'. They just wanted a big hunk of meat to do the hard yards, and a hit-man to slow the opposition's flyers down. Āe, Māui had developed a bit of a rep for that. Ever since some bright spark from the Sunshine Coast lit everyone up, and got a big head about it — so big he could barely fit it through the posts. Māui got the bros together, set a trap, left a gap, and then slammed the gate shut with a gang-tackle that cut the kid in half. Broke his jaw in three places. Oh, he came back, but was never the same. Gun-shy after that. You can find it on an NRL King-Hits DVD.

Back at the IHOP, Māui tried to clear the clouds away by

thinking about all the king-hits he'd laid on others in the past. Maybe that would help him through wanting to smash something, or someone, right now.

Māui squinted through his shades. Across the street, Elvis was talking to a cop, and Marilyn was making friends with Paul Walker. She'd be riding in his convertible before the sun set over Hollywood.

MOTU POKIES PALACE

Townsville, Australia. North Queensland Cowboys NRL Club. Sparrow's fart. The burble of pokies and gurgle of dough down the drain.

Māui roundhouse-punched his beloved fishing pokie, the screen glitched and reset. He slouched over to the ATM, jammed in his card, punched in some numbers, waited, then hammered it with his fist.

CREDIT LIMIT REACHED

Māui punched the ATM again, right in its stupid face. He got tingles. Someone was watching — the cleaner. He'd seen her before. She'd busted him doing coke in the toilets with his old Eftpos card. It didn't work in Aussie but reminded him of the old country so he couldn't throw it away. Coke was okay. It went through your system faster than dope. You could do a line on Saturday night and pass a test Monday morning. It was a purely recreational drug.

'You got eye trouble?'

'No.'

'Then what are you looking at?'

'Just wondering if you're going to break that machine?'

'What do you care?'

'Well, I'll have to clean it up, if . . .'

Māui punched it again. The screen cracked.

'You know there are cameras in here Māui, right?'

'How do you know my name?' Māui was in disguise. He was wearing a studded leather jacket with the collar up and the long blonde wig he'd swiped from the boys Vice-Versa team-building night, when the players all wore dresses and the cheerleaders all wore suits, and everyone got munted, and then it was all on, and he woke up on a yacht. He told himself he looked like some weird heavy-metal biker that no one wanted to mess with.

'Who else knows it's me?' asked Māui.

'Everyone,' said the cleaner.

'Everyone?'

'Everyone.'

'Why don't they say anything?'

'They're afraid of you.'

'Oh. Oh. So they should be. What's your name?'

'Tilly.'

'Tilly, that's a bit silly . . . Tilly.'

'It's short for Matilda.'

'Want to go waltzing? Are you afraid of me?'

'How about I call you a taxi?' said Tilly.

'Sure. Call me a taxi. I'm a taxi,' cracked up Māui, his trickster powers clearly fading. Once the joker in every pack, he was now reduced to bad dad jokes.

'You need to go home.'

'How about I come home with you?'

'Nah, my place is a shithole,' said Tilly.

'But you're a cleaner.'

'Yeah, I clean all day and night here, I ain't cleaning when I get home.'

MOTU CROSS

They went back to Māui's place. He lived in a basement. His place was a shithole, but she wanted his body.

'Where's your phone?' asked Māui as she lifted his shirt and admired his abs and pecs.

'What do you care?'

'I don't want you taking any photos and putting them on social media. The club is very clear about that.'

'Oh, fuck you, I'm going home,' and she grabbed her croc-skin bag.

'No. Stay. Stay. I'm sorry. I'm sorry, it's just everyone wants a piece of us, wants to bring us down. It ain't like the old days when you could get away with all sorts of shit. You know, what no one realises is how boring it is being a pro-athlete. That's why I was doing that coke that time. I'm so bored. And you know Andre Agassi, one of the greatest tennis players of all time, he said he hated tennis, said he did speed to do the vacuuming to keep himself sane. You, you just see the highlight reels, the king-hits, the sensational tries, not the relentless grind. Not the pain, and painkillers. How everyone loves you when you're a winner, and trashes you when you don't get the Ws. And after games we need to wind down, and the pokies, they . . .'

'You're there every night.'

'Are you spying on me?'

'You talk too much. Are we fucking or what? 'Cause I got a shift at ten.'

'Yeah, we're . . . but can't we just talk a little bit. What mob are you?'

'Oh no, I don't want to be your girlfriend.'

Tilly became Māui's girlfriend. Well, his booty call. Well, they got into a routine. Māui played pokies in his strange disguise 'til she finished her shift and then they went home together. They didn't talk too much. Then, they progressed to playing some pool together at the club to help him relax the night before home games, and he introduced her to some of the boys. It was all good 'til the night she hit him with the jigger. They were playing pool, and she was whipping his arse, as per usual. He had been a little distracted by the replay of another game though, where some legend destined for the NRL Hall of Fame had brought his kids onto the field after the end of his final game. They interviewed him with one cute kid on his shoulders. Māui was triggered. Tilly sunk the black with all Māui's balls still on the table.

'Down-trou! Down-trou!'

Māui counted all the balls, nodded, and dropped his trou, let it all hang out. A punter went to take a photo, but Māui sneered and they ran away real quick.

'Okay, big boy,' said Tilly, 'time to zip up.'

'Nah, nah, I want to say something.' Māui got down on one knee, his pants still around his ankles. 'I want kids,' he blurted.

'Don't look at me,' said Tilly, cracking up. 'You're a total loose unit.'

'Nah! I'd be a good father!'

'You? Nah. You'd be another dead-beat dad.'

'Don't say that.'

'If I got up the duff to you, I'd get rid of it.'

Another trigger. Māui zipped up and clocked her. Tilly fell down beside the pool table. She came up swinging the jigger and smacked Māui across the temple with the butt end. He came for her but she threw the jigger like a spear and the cross branded him right on the forehead. Māui bellowed. Some of the boys stepped in, held him back, then Māui just grinned. The hard man. Tilly grabbed her croc-bag and walked out. Māui threw the boys off, made as if to follow her, but then reeled around and racked up to play himself. He grabbed the triangle but then he couldn't work out which way it went around, or where the black 8 ball went, and he rubbed his temple, his forehead, and blacked out. Māui's head bounced twice then settled on the green felt.

MOTU FRIDGE

The day after Māui got out of hospital, Doc — the Cowboys' doctor — knocked gently on Māui's basement door.

'Māui? Māui, you home?'

Doc heard some heavy shuffling from inside and the lock turning. It opened a crack and from the darkness inside, Māui whispered, 'Who is it?'

'Doc.'

'Doc who?'

'Doc — Doc, from the team.'

'What do you want?'

'Just came to check how you're doing, mate. I see you're keeping the lights off like the specialist said. And you weren't answering your phone.'

'Had to turn it off. Loud noises are like bright lights.'

Doc came in and closed the door quick behind him. Pitch black. He clawed his way around the furniture and they sat on the leather sofas in the dark together.

'So how you feeling?'

'Peachy. Can't move faster than a snail without wanting to spew.

Like if I don't balance my head just right it might fall off.'

'Oh, well, takes time right,' said Doc holding up a bag. 'The boys all chipped in for some of your fave food, drinks, tunes and some DVDs. They even got you that *Moana* movie with The Rock in it. It's good. I seen it with the kids.'

'I can't watch no fucking DVDs. Can't look at screens. The light stabs my eyes.'

'Yeah, but just for when you're feeling a bit better. Look is your girlfriend, she taking care of you?'

'Doubt it. All her stuff is gone. Must have cleared all out while I was at the game.'

'One of the boys said you clocked her at the club.'

'Nah, I just . . . pushed her.'

'And that she clocked you?'

'Nah, she's . . .'

'Māui, the club watched the CCTV footage. They saw it all. That was one hell of a jigger-chuck. She could be an Olympic javelin thrower with the right sort of coaching.'

'What do you want?'

'I want to say that you shouldn't have been playing the next day if she KO'd you the night before. The guys who took you home fessed up, said you were totally out to it when they dropped you off here.'

'I was just . . . sleeping. Tired, that's all.'

'Look, you need to ring your agent. They've been trying to get in touch too.'

'Are you cutting me? Is that why you're here?'

'Māui, mate, your bell has been rung one too many times. The specialist reckons one more concussion and it could be lights out for good. You'll get a payout. But maybe you should think about going home?'

'Home to what?'

'Um . . . coaching? I'm sure you're a legend in your hometown.'

'Yeah, I got a star on the footpath in Feilding.'

'Really?'

'Nah. Back there they just know me as Maurice.'

'Maurice?'

'Yeah, when I finally got out, I changed my name.'

'So you're not really Māui?'

'Nah. He was just some Māori super-hero my Nan told me stories about. As a kid I just wanted to be smart and strong like him.'

'So what name is on your contract with us? I mean did you change your name legally?'

'You know I've come back before.'

'Mate, have you seen the hit the Raiders put on you?'

'No.'

'It was massive. Your signature topknot — it just totally unravels as your noggin snaps back. The munthead who coathangered you is up before the judiciary and he'll get six weeks at least.'

'Will it make it to the next King-Hits DVD?'

'Bound to. Probably be on the cover. But the clincher was these other two clowns turn up and spear-tackle you into the turf. They'll get three weeks if not more. You just lay there twitching 'til they could get the cart out. It was ugly. Not a good look for the NRL. Not with all this talk about head-bins and concussions. Mate, you ain't coming back.'

'Don't say that.'

'You know quite a few of our guys retire and get into security. We could set you up . . .'

'Shut up. You hear that?'

'Eh?'

'That voice, that moaning?'

'Ah . . . no.'

'Sitting here in the dark I've been hearing things, this voice mainly, but I can't work out what it's saying. Kind of a chant . . . you hear that?'

'Um, nah. But your fridge has got a bit of a drone.'

'I think it's my Nan. She's another reason I can't go back to friendly Feilding. I stole something from her. See, she didn't trust banks. Kept her cash in a Griffins biscuit tin under the bed. And she didn't trust doctors, or hospitals, 'cause that's where you go to die. She liked the old medicine, but most of the ones who knew all that stuff were gone. And she had these ingrown toenails and she'd get me to try and clip them and dig out the toe jam, but Jesus they stank. And she was on the turps to kill the pain, and pouring it on her feet, too. I . . . I just couldn't take it any more so I stole her biscuit tin and ran away to Auckland to have a trial with the Warriors. I didn't think about her for a long time, tried not to anyway, but then one day I saw this old kuia in a wheelchair on the sideline of a game, and I got the guilts so rung up my cousin back home. He said they found her with gangrene and they had to cut off her feet. And her teeth had gone rotten, 'cause she didn't trust dentists neither, so she'd lost some of her jaw. Which would be the worst, 'cause she could talk up a storm. She'd tell stories of the old people, trying to get me interested, but I was just a leaguey meathead. Yeah, my poor old Nan, she had the real gift of the gab. But now, according to my cousin, she was sitting in a wheelchair with her stumps begging outside the Warewhare. And no one dared mention my name to her. It was so bad that if I was playing on TV then the whole whānau, and anyone who knew me, was yelling for the opposition to smash me. So I guess they got what they wanted, eh. Like if you get a rep as a hit-man, then you got a target on you 'cause every other wannabe hit-man/enforcer wants to make their mark on you, right? . . . You hear that? She's chanting something at me now. But I'm koretake — useless. Used to know all that te reo when I was living with her as a kid, but I lost it. Now I just got a few words that come back, but my powers have faded. Now she's probably dead and come to haunt me, call me over to the other side, 'cause I'll be dead soon, too.'

'. . . Yeah, mate. That's not good talk, bro,' said Doc. 'In fact, I've come to . . . um . . . I've got some pamphlets for you. Some reading.'

'I can't turn on the light to read.'

'Well, they're about . . .'

'Suicide?'

'Yeah. Are you having any of those, those sorts of thoughts?'

'Um . . . nah. Does that make you feel better?'

'Um . . . it's not about how I feel.'

'Isn't it? Don't you want to just be able to say you did due diligence on sad-sack Māui and then fucked off?'

'Mate. Mate, it's not like that.'

'Yes, it is! You got better things to do than deal with some messed-up headcase. You got some young flyers to get up to speed, so fuck off and tell them I'm doing good. That I can't watch their fucking DVD. And you know what? It is okay really. It's just me and my thoughts all floating around me — like little islands I paddle in and out of in my waka. I don't even have to go to any more boring fucking practices, and do stupid gutbusters, and listen to pep talks, and pretend I like everyone, and . . .'

'So, let me summarise. You can't go back to Feilding, but you need to get out of this basement . . . eventually.'

'Because the club is paying the rent?'

'Yeah. So where do you think you will go?'

'Disneyland. I've never been to Disneyland.'

'Are you sure . . .?'

'Yeah. It's the happiest place on Earth.'

Doc took the groceries to the fridge. When he opened it the drone noise changed to a higher pitch, and he thought he did indeed hear a voice coming from inside the icebox. He couldn't make out any words, but it sounded like some old lady in pain, that they were calling for help and no one was coming. Doc threw the groceries inside and slammed the door shut. The usual drone noise returned.

'Um . . . you might want to look at that fridge.'

'Did you hear her in there?' said Māui.

'I heard something.'

'Oh, good, then I'm not going pōrangi.'

'I'll come back to check on you at the end of the week.'

'Yeah, whatevs.'

'And turn your phone on.'

Māui didn't turn his phone on, but he did try to watch the *Moana* video with his shades on in the dark. It was still too much, so he just listened to it. The first time he was all over Māui. But the second he was all about the girl, and how she'd never know how far she could go. Then he was feeling a bit better and watched all the DVD extras, and finally he watched the movie again and this time all he could think about was how great the ancestors were, and how they weren't just Polynesian fishermen blown off course. Nah, we know where we are, and we know where we're going.

MOTU DISNEYLAND

Māui went to Disneyland. Just watching the rides made him dizzy all over again. The happy families everywhere made him sad. He walked out into the heat and some Mexican-looking dude was selling knock-offs out the back of a van.

'Hola! What's your name, amigo?'

'Maurice . . . Māui.'

'Māui! Māui! It's a sign, amigo! You were meant to meet me! And, man, have I got a deal for you! They had all these complaints about Disney marketing a Māui Halloween costume, complete with tattoos. PC people saying it was like wearing a brown man's skin, and minstrels all over, so they had to pull them all. But I got one — one only — and I can sell it to you for fifty bucks.'

'I'll give you five.'

'Come on, this is you, Māui! This is your skin! Twenty?'

'Ten. Final offer.'

'Sold.'

So Māui got the costume. He didn't think it would fit — but it stretched and wasn't too bad. He knew all the words to all the songs, so he went down to the Chinese Theatre and starting singing: 'You're welcome . . .'

MOTU ONE MORE CUP OF COFFEE BEFORE I GO . . . TO THE VALLEY BELOW?

'You want a top-up, love?'

'Huh?' Māui woke up with a start, a pool of drool on the table, the motu in his head still floating around.

'Listen, love, you can't sleep here. Manager won't like it. Have some more coffee.'

The waitress poured Māui another cup. He adjusted his sunnies.

She was strangely familiar, strange and familiar. There was something about her jawbone. He got tingles. Māui had come across fa'afafine at some of the PI celebrations he'd been at with the Warriors. They scared him, so he'd never actually talked to one but he could see how someone could be fooled.

'Where are you from?' asked Māui.

'Santa Monica. I like the beach. And there's just the right amount of freaks.'

'But before that?'

'Oh, Compton. My dad was black and my mum was American Samoan. I'm a spicy combo, like The Rock. We're distantly related somehow.'

'To The Rock? To Dwayne Johnson?'

'Yeah. You must know him considering you're playing Māui across the street, right?'

'Oh, yeah, I was. But Marilyn just cut me.'

'Bitch. Never tips. So you got an agent?'

'Um . . . not for acting stuff . . . yet. But I'm working on it. Going to break in like how Arnie and The Rock did. I'm . . . I was a big shot in rugby league in Aussie for a while. I'm Māori.'

'I know, I can tell. Can you do the haka?'

'Yeah, of course.'

'It's just, we're doing a fundraising show for the Pacific Islands hit by Hurricane Ivanka, and a haka would be a great thing to have on the bill.'

'Can't you do one?'

'I could, but I've got my own act. Anyhow, here's a flyer. I've got to clear tables.' She sashayed away.

'Hold on, what's your name?'

The waitress leaned in so Māui could read her name tag. She was gorgeous, smelt of frangipani perfume. Everything looked . . . real.

'Sina,' she said.

'Sinner?'

'Sina.'

She glanced down. Māui dropped a serviette over his hard-on. 'Thanks, um, for the coffee. Am I supposed to tip?'

'Yeah. But not if you come to the show.'

Māui threw a ten on the table and hurried out.

MOTU THE UNDERGROUND

Māui wandered around for a few hours, torn about whether to go or not, but then there, right in front of him, was the venue, The Underground. He could hear the Pacific Island drums coming from inside. He went down the stairs. There were a lot of fa'afafine, all dressed up to the nines and fabulous.

Māui couldn't see Sina anywhere. The lights were bright. There were bound to be strobes. He thought about leaving but then the show was starting and he slunk up the back in the shadows with his shades on.

The drums got louder and the crowd went wild. The MC strode out in foot-high heels, tight black dress and wrapped in fairy lights. It was Sina. Other girls joined her and they lip-synched to Beyoncé's 'Run the World (Girls)'. The crowd went nuts, and then out came the other acts: slap dances, fire-dancers, a choir, fa'afafine doing slam-dance knee drops that Māui just couldn't watch. His arthritic knees sung back in pain. He was triggered. The music was too loud, the lights were too bright. A mirror ball started. His head spun. Dark clouds rolled in. He closed his eyes, the spew rose up his gullet. He had to go. Māui gagged, stumbled towards the EXIT sign, but then he heard his name.

'. . . Māui!'

He froze. Everyone was chanting his name, 'Māui! Māui! Māui!' The spotlight fell on him.

'Please welcome to the stage,' said Sina, 'the big man, the demigod, the great hunk of love that is Māui!'

Māui tried to leave, but then Sina was there in front of him, whispering in his ear, 'Where are your tatts?'

'Um . . . my back pocket.'

'Then let's get them on. Arms up.'

Māui did as he was told and lifted his arms up. Sina stripped off his 'I ❤ LA' T-shirt as the crowd whistled and threw money. She reached into his back pocket and took out the roll-on Māui tatts from *Moana*. She rolled them slowly down over his arms and torso. It was hot, hot, hot.

The song, 'You're Welcome', blasted out over the PA as Sina led Māui down to the stage. Muscle memory kicked in. His body started twitching, doing the moves automatically that he'd rehearsed over and over in the basement in Townsville.

The crowd stood up, clapped, threw money. He was nailing it. Māui finished and they yelled, 'More! More! More!'

Māui broke into a hoary Hori version of Te Rauparaha's 'Ka Mate' haka, knowing full well his Nan was cursing him for honouring the bastard who'd butchered 400 of their tīpuna on a hill above Whanganui. Still, just like T.R., he found himself stepping up out of the darkness and into the sunshine.

'Ladies and gentlemen, a big round of applause for Māui!' said Sina. The mobile phone cameras flashed — he was a star born again. 'Now who would like to see us do a little act together?'

They stomped their feet and cheered. Māui looked at Sina, sweating bullets.

'Does everyone know how Māui died?' asked Sina.

There were howls of laughter. Māui got the tingles. 'I'll play Hine-nui-te-pō, and let's see if Māui can come up through my thighs,' said Sina.

The crowd became hysterical. They were clapping, cheering and throwing more money.

Māui wasn't so sure about this, but there Sina stood in her foot-high heels, legs akimbo, as she reprised Beyoncé. Māui paused.

The crowd chanted his name, 'Māui! Māui! Māui!'

He had no choice. He got down on his knees, wincing as the arthritis spikes stabbed in, and crawled towards Sina/Hine, through under her legs, but then she dropped down onto his back, and slapped his butt to ride him around like a horse. The cameras flashed. Māui bucked and Sina fell off his back onto her butt.

She and Māui got up ready to rumble. He made fists. She made fists back at him. He didn't know whether to bash her or pash her. She puckered up. He kissed her. Slow and deep. The crowd went wild. Sina broke off, took Māui's hand and they bowed.

Another fa'afafine approached with a bucket as Māui fumbled his sunnies back on. Sina read out the piece of paper in the bucket.

'Quiet! We've raised $4322! And I'm sure we could raise more. Who wants Māui's signature?'

Māui signed signatures for another hour with 'You're Welcome!'

Sina changed and joined him wearing another black dress and jacket, greenstone earrings and a bone hook pendant.

'So where are you staying?'

'Backpackers,' said Māui.

'Come home with me . . . I have a spare bed.'

MOTU SANTA MONICA

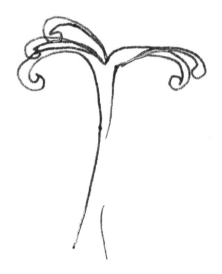

They drove in the taxi through the City of Angels. Māui laid his heavy head on the window sill, looked up at the palm trees and motu floating by. Sina took him into her balcony apartment. Māui took out his phone.

'Don't,' said Sina.

'But there'll be photos of me, of us, all over the internet. My fans will . . . I have to explain. I'm . . .'

'You're whatever you want to be.'

'I'm a joke.'

'No, you're a good sport. You helped us raise five grand for a great cause.'

'Who are you?'

'Me . . . I'm Sina, a healer. I have healing hands. Now, take off your clothes, beefcake, and let me lay my hands on you.'

Māui did as he was told, lay face down on the bed.

Sina touched his temples, crown, busted nose, compounded neck vertebrae, separated shoulder, torn rotator cuffs, intercostal trauma and sternum crack, arthritic hip, medial ligaments, serrated patella, torn hammies, ruptured Achilles, and then she sucked his gnarled toes 'til he blubbed like a baby.

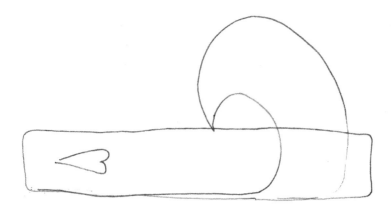

MOTU TAPU

Māui was back in his dark basement. He went to find the door
and it was wide open. No, there was no door. He felt a cool breeze,
the warm smell of colitas rising up through the air and he climbed
up the steps. Just like Te Rauparaha coming out of his kūmara
pit, Māui felt a haka coming on, but this time he resisted. He was
learning.

The street outside was dark, a stray dog howled somewhere . . . or
was it a coyote? Then Sina was there, and Māui was wearing electric
blue speedos, and rollerblades and headphones, and he didn't care.
His footie boots were in his hand and he threw them up over the
wires. He snapped a picture and posted it to Instagram.

Guess who just retired?

Māui and Sina rollerbladed down the parade at Santa Monica
hand in hand. There were sideshows, and they were all for Māui,
all about Māui. You could go fishing with his brothers and pull up
a giant fish that turned into an island and win a giant panda. You
could trick an old lady into giving you fire. You could turn your
brother-in-law into a dog . . . Or was it a coyote?

'Come on, we're going to miss the big ride,' said Sina.

'What ride?'

Sina took Māui's hand and they bladed down the pier to the heart-shaped boats. They took off their blades and pedalled out onto the water towards a large pontoon in the shape of an arch. As they got closer, Māui lifted his sunnies to read the sign.

'The Tunnel of Love?'

'The Tunnel of Love. That's where we're going. You know Hine-nui-te-pō wasn't just the Goddess of Death, she was also the Goddess of Night, she was a healer. She takes us back to where we once belonged. So, there's no need to be scared because you're with me now.'

They pedalled under the lights, into the darkness. Māui closed his eyes and Elvis sang to him, 'Are You Lonesome Tonight?' and Marilyn cooed 'Happy Birthday to You' and then way off in the distance he heard chanting. Calling. Calling his name.

'Oh my god,' said Māui, turning to Sina, 'I've spent my whole life trying to be hard, the hard man, the star of the show. I'm so fucking exhausted.'

'I know,' soothed Sina.

'But now I want to be soft.'

'I know.'

'I want to be soft with someone.'

'I know, so just let go.'

'Be soft for someone.'

'I know. Believe me, I know.'

Māui and Sina sailed on into the darkness and the chanting, the chanting grew louder.

Me aro koe ki te hā o Hineahuone!

BY JACQUELINE CARTER

If Hinetītama
can become Hinenuitepō

crushing

the next man who tried to interfere with her
between her thighs

then I too can deal to any man
that would enter me without my permission.

If our tūpuna wāhine
can have the courage and the vision

to leave their homelands
in search of new homes

then I too can leave any place
that does not nourish and support me.

If that great ancestress Wairaka
can summon the strength of any man

and drag that great ancestral waka
from the sea with her own bare hands

then I shall not allow myself
let alone anyone else
to think of me as less
than his or her equal.

This is what we mean
when we speak of mana wāhine
it is the strength that is within us
by virtue of our descent from Hineahuone

which is why
when you meet a woman
you really
ought to hongi

to pay heed
to the strength
that is woman.

CHAPTER 5
TĀWHAKI
AND RATA

———

Tāwhaki: Real Life

———

Rata

———

Tāwhaki: Real Life

BY PAULA MORRIS

Because T had no money for the bus, he set off on foot for his grandmother's house. The walk to Ōtara took him around three hours, and it rained most of the way. The squalls were so heavy at times that T's feet sloshed in his work boots, and his sodden jeans stuck to his legs.

Nana's house was easy to spot from a distance. On the bare-bones veranda sat two red velveteen armchairs. Most days his grandmother kept vigil in one of the chairs, and today was no exception. She wore something long, dark and shapeless. Her slippers looked like mismatched carpet.

Sprawled on the other chair was one of his nieces, Tash — fifteen, and lumpy in sweatpants and a hoodie, as though she was about to do some exercise. Tash never did any exercise.

Neither his grandmother or his niece noticed him standing on the footpath. His grandmother was blind and Tash was transfixed by her phone.

'Hi, Nana,' he said in a loud voice. 'It's me, T. I've come to visit you.'

'Oh yes,' she said. 'Thought you'd be around sooner or later.'

'Why aren't you at work?' Tash said, glancing up from her phone.

'Why aren't you at school?' he asked her. The site where he'd been labouring had closed. The developer was bankrupt and the builders couldn't get in to pick up their tools. He hadn't been paid for two weeks.

'I'm sick,' Tash replied. 'And I have to look after Nana Miri.'

'I don't need anyone looking after me,' said his grandmother. 'And I don't need to be stuck looking after anyone else, neither.'

'I don't need anyone looking after *me*,' Tash said, face twisting into a sulk.

'Good,' said Nana Miri. 'Everyone looks after themselves here. So bugger off, the lot of you.'

The conversation wasn't going well. 'The thing is,' T said, 'I do need somewhere to stay for a few days. Doesn't have to be in the house. I could sleep in the shed.'

'Shed's as wet as you.' Tash smirked at him. 'The roof's got a hole in it and someone smashed in the window.'

'Your dad smashed in the window!' shrieked Nana Miri, pointing in T's general direction — but he thought she meant to point at Tash. Tash's father was Jase, one of the worst of T's brothers, volatile and vengeful, and always out of his head on something chemical. T's own father, Nana's oldest son, was long dead.

'I could fix the window, Nana,' he said in a soft voice. 'I can fix anything you need.'

Nana was shaking her head.

'My house is full,' she said. 'Full with the bones of dead men. Skeletons to the rafters. Skulls jamming up the cupboards.'

'Yuck,' said Tash.

'The thing is,' T said again, trying to sound calm and capable, and not at all like any of his brothers, 'I don't have anywhere else to go. I just need to get back on my feet.'

'What about your girlfriend?' Now, Tash was interested. 'Did she dump you?'

T said nothing. They'd been evicted from the house in Glen Innes. The land had been sold. Developers were building townhouses —

two and three storeys, with tiny balconies and patios, and nowhere to hang the washing. Maria had whisked away the baby, little Arahuta, to her mother's place in Avondale, and T had never been welcome there. Too many of his brothers and sisters had been on Home D. Too many of his uncles and cousins were in gangs, or in prison. They were the worst kind of family, Maria's mother said. The apple never fell far from the tree, she said — even though T was clean and always had been.

'You boys are all useless,' Nana announced. She leaned back in her chair and smiled in a sinister way, as though she really did have a house crammed with bones. 'Where are you when I need to go to the podiatrist?'

'I have to go with her,' said Tash. 'It's disgusting.'

'You sit in the waiting room!' Nana snapped.

'I have to put the nail polish on you after,' Tash said. 'The fungal stuff.'

'Just a couple of nights,' said T. Rain was falling again. His feet were swollen and spongy. But Nana shook her head.

'No room,' she said.

'Hey, you could sleep in the shed and she wouldn't know,' said Tash. 'Just keep quiet in there.'

'*You* keep quiet!' shouted Nana. 'I'm blind, not deaf. I hear everything you fellas say, and a lot more besides. You know nothing. Nothing about anything.'

'I'm trying to learn things on the internet,' Tash said, waving the phone that Nana couldn't see. 'I'm learning about geology and rocks and glaciers! But you keep interrupting me.'

T's phone was dead and he had no money to pay the bill.

'I'd take you to the podiatrist, Nana,' he said. 'But I don't have a car anymore.'

'Duh! We catch a taxi,' said Tash. 'The podiatrist is a lady. She's from Afghanistan.'

'They know how to treat old people with respect,' muttered Nana.

'Yeah, like, the Taliban blow them up with bombs over there! That's why she moved to New Zealand.'

Nana ignored this. She appeared to be staring straight at T, as though she could sense his forlorn presence on the footpath, or hear the rain prickling his jacket.

'Go live in the bush.' Nana waved a magisterial hand at him. 'Go live in the trees with the birds. It'll be good for you. Come back next week and take me to the podiatrist. Maybe then I'll let you fix the shed.'

'You should be a negotiator for the UN, Nana,' Tash told her, and then both fell silent. Cars swished past. Light was already seeping from the day. T said goodbye and walked back up the road. He walked and walked, squelching his way along the Great South Road until he reached the flash car dealerships, then the shops in Newmarket, and then the long uphill grind of Khyber Pass. Wasn't that a place in Afghanistan?

He kept walking, passed by flotillas of buses and cars shrill with lights, until he reached the old cemetery, the one tumbling down Grafton Gully, broken bottles like deadly flowers among the leaning gravestones. Perhaps that's what his grandmother meant by the bush, but T didn't think so. On he walked, wending his way past the university, the students hooded and sluggish in the rain, its buildings a maze he'd never dared to enter. When he reached Albert Park, and the lumpy tentacles of its biggest tree, T stopped. He couldn't walk another step. This was where he'd stay, among the birds, until his luck changed.

———

Three nights in, the winter cold and dank, T was learning how to sleep rough. There were public toilets in the park. In the bins around the university he could find the remnants of half-eaten lunches. The trees were better than a doorway where the drunks could spew on him or kick him in, where he might wake up with his shoes missing, face damp with someone else's piss. In the park, T could hear the morning, and smell it, before he opened his eyes. The birds started talking; branches quivered in the wind. The park smelled heavy, of mud and moss and worms writhing in the wet grass.

He learned about the 7 a.m. shuffle down Queen Street when the night shelters emptied, about the druggies and the runaways and the old fellas who talked to themselves. He learned about the trek up to the City Mission to slump in the queue outside, everyone draped in stinking blankets, waiting for something hot to eat, and how to lean away from the people with rattling, liquid coughs, how never to meet anyone's eyes. He learned how to fish flattened cardboard out of the skip behind the Central Library. At the Mission he asked for a bin bag and for a blue fleece, ragged around the hem but clean, because that was another thing he learned — to have no pride, to have no shame.

In this weather, staying dry at night was a problem. The park's bandstand was barricaded with scaffolding, and the back porch of the Language School was already taken. That space had been claimed by Taniwha — the name that T had given to the guy with the dreads and the wheely cart — and Taniwha didn't look like one for sharing.

Inside one of the largest trees in the park T found a hollow, and after he'd cleared out the rubbish — cans, fast-food bags, and paper cups dribbled with coffee — it wasn't too bad. He tucked in a damp square of cardboard and then the bin liner, to shield his jeans from dirt and rat droppings. The hollow was just big enough for him to sit with his head lowered and his knees knocking his chin. He hunched there, peering out like a ruru.

The rain still found a way in. T's face and hair misted, and the rats kept waking him up, scratching around and squeaking. Twice on the fourth night someone tried to chuck stuff in — a beer bottle and an empty cigarette packet.

This might be the lowest point of his life, he thought — sleeping in a rubbish bin. At least Maria and the baby were in a real house, safe and warm. He missed them so much he felt gnawed at inside, a pain worse than hunger. Every day at the library he waited his turn for one of the public computers and sent Maria an email, checking in, telling lies about staying at his grandmother's and looking for work. Maria never replied.

On the fourth night in the park something took hold of him, a restlessness like a tug, pulling him out of his hollow. A real ruru, T knew, wouldn't sleep so close to the ground, waiting to get eaten. He clambered out, leaving everything behind, and stumbling on ridged roots that in the dark felt like low stone walls. When he tried to get a foothold on the trunk, his boots slithered and his hands stung, bitten by shards of bark. The tree was alive — of course, he knew that. He'd hauled enough wood in his time, hammered nails into hundreds of boards. But tonight the tree was a creature, a brute that wanted to throw him off. T reached for a branch, stubbing his fingers, and hauled himself up. His feet skidded and the branch creaked with the wind and his weight, but T steadied himself. Thunder rumbled and for an instant the sky was shot through with darting light, just enough to reveal the next branch. He reached for it, his hands ready this time for the scales of its skin.

The higher he climbed, the more the tree rocked and shuddered. Branches thinned but beyond them T could see no stars: they were smudged out by clouds as grey and roiling as Rotorua mud. The Sky Tower, lit red, looked out of focus in the haze, immune to the lightning sparks. Thunder grumbled again, close enough to shake the tree. T reached for the highest branch: it bent towards him like a bow. There was no reason for him to climb the tree like this, his skin slick with cold rain, wind cutting through his jacket, lightning jabbing at him and the thunder so discontent, so complaining, that it might be the voice of his grandmother. He just couldn't stay huddled in the tree's bowels anymore, trying to make himself disappear.

T held his face up to the rain, dizzied by the swirling tumble of clouds. Up here he was exposed, draped across several branches like a too-heavy Christmas decoration. The sky was a mystery to him, even on a clear night. How could the ancestors have read its language so fluently? How could they have found answers to anything, or paths to anywhere?

Above him dark clouds split and billowed, and when lightning flashed again, T thought he could make something out. It was the face of his grandmother, her eyes wide open, jaw contorting when the cloud shape shifted into another face, one he didn't recognise. Another face and another face and another; some calm and puffy-cheeked, like the moon, others agape and angry, glowering at him from the sky, their faces as angular as scraped skulls. One might be his father, but T wasn't sure — it was so long since his father died, a knife to the guts in a pub near Khyber Pass. Thunder crashed from the face's mouth and T shook with the force of it, with the anger and fear his father's death had breathed into all of them. T and all his brothers, their inheritance nothing but blood on the footpath and the rage of it, the rage.

'You bastard!' he shouted at the clouds, but they were already forming themselves into a new face and then into another, lightning crackling behind their eyes. The Sky Tower was the tip of a taiaha, pointing into the sky. He didn't know any of these faces but they must know him. At night, when he was a kid, T used to sit out on the front step of their house, away from the racket and stench of his brothers. He'd stare up at the sky, trying to make sense of the stars, but he'd never known the names of anything. He couldn't crack the code. Now, the thunder was speaking to him in a way the stars never could. Maybe, back then, he'd crept around too much, stayed too close to the ground.

Something harder than rain hit him on the arm and then the leg. It couldn't be hail — not in this drizzle. Another sharp ping on his shoulder and T reached out his hand to grab whatever it was, half-expecting a small rock of ice. But it was just a stone. And another stone, bouncing off his head. T managed to catch that one as well, though he almost skidded off his branch, and scraped his knuckles trying to right himself.

Someone was pelting him with stones.

'Bugger off!' he shouted, not looking down.

'You're gonna kill yourself, mate!' The voice was a man's. Nobody he knew. 'Lightning'll hit you up there!' Most of the rough sleepers looked out for each other — that was another thing T had learned.

The cloud faces were gone. Now, they were just a grey smear on the sky. The thunder's rumble was softer, more distant, moving out to sea.

T pocketed the two stones so he'd have his hands free for the descent. He'd take those back to his grandmother's to give to Tash, if she was still hanging around. They might be useful for her school project — geology? geography? — because they were actual stones, not just pictures on the internet. These she could turn over in her hand and feel how smooth and rounded they were in real life. He'd tell her that there was more to the world than the internet could possibly contain. She needed to put her phone down. Maybe climb a tree, or climb inside one.

He would take his grandmother to the podiatrist. He would fix her shed roof and window with his grandfather's tools, and make her a walking stick. He would walk all the way out west on the Great North Road, to Avondale to see Maria and little Arahuta. If no one would give him a place to sleep, he'd keep walking towards the great hills and gullies of Waikumete Cemetery. Trees stretched along the ridge there, and when he climbed them, T would see the full sweep of the Waitakere Ranges and all the way back to the city, the Sky Tower a distant beacon. He wouldn't bleed to death after a fight like his father. He wouldn't fester and rot like his brothers, smashing doors and windows and people, poisoning themselves and everyone they touched.

Up in the tree tops, this city was his. The stars and the clouds and the thunder were his. T had climbed his way to heaven, one branch at a time, and there was nothing he couldn't do or see or understand, nothing he couldn't become if he put his mind to it, nothing that could stop him once he got back on his feet.

Rata

BY HĒMI KELLY

'Nanny Moko, my stomach's sore.'

'What have you been eating? Have you been in that lolly jar again?' Nanny Moko asked Tāwhai. 'Go to the toilet.'

'But I don't need to go toilet. Have you got any Nurofen?' he asked.

'Any what?!' she snapped. 'Look! There's a pantry full of rongoā in that bush out there.'

Nanny Moko didn't believe in Pākehā medicine, as she referred to it. Her grandfather, who raised her, taught her about rongoā, the medicine of the bush. That's what she was known for. There were always people coming and going from the house. They would come from all over the place seeking her care.

'Me haere tāua ki te ngahere. Some koromiko will do the trick. Nurofen, by jingos!' Nanny Moko walked towards the back door shaking her head in disapproval. She pulled on her coat and gumboots, and stepped outside. 'Kia tere, e moko!'

Tāwhai managed to slip into his gumboots and catch up to her. He was rubbing his puku in the hope that she might feel sorry for him and slow down — just a little bit. Tāwhai wasn't putting it on: he did have an upset stomach but if it persisted, which he quietly hoped it did, he might get a sick day or two.

'Kaua e takaroa!'

Nanny Moko wasn't falling for it and she steamed ahead. The

whānau had celebrated her 75th birthday earlier in the year. Despite her age, she was quick, like her tongue, and if there was one thing Nanny Moko couldn't stand it was dawdling.

Tāwhai was the oldest of the grandchildren. He was sent to live with Nanny Moko during the winter months of the year. It was his responsibility, his mother would tell him, to keep her company. Koro had passed away two years earlier.

Rural Te Kōpua was poles apart from the hustle and bustle of central Wellington. The nearest town, Te Awamutu, was about 15 kilometres away. That didn't bother Tāwhai; he enjoyed living with Nanny Moko and spending time 'back home', as everyone referred to it. He was in his second year of high school so he was familiar with the teachers and he had made mates at the local college from his previous stay.

There weren't many people living at Te Kōpua now: most had moved into town. Nanny Moko's home wasn't far from the marae. It was nestled in between the Waipā River and Kakepuku, a burly maunga whose upper half was covered in native bush where Nanny Moko collected her rongoā. The lower half of the maunga, once dotted with old kāinga, was all farmland now.

'Just about there,' Nanny Moko told Tāwhai, who was still rubbing his puku. Tāwhai had accompanied her to the bush many times. He would hold her kete, listening and watching as they went. He wasn't that enthusiastic about their outings as they almost always took place in the early morning when all he could think about was the underside of his duvet.

'Anei te kawakawa. Don't get the pretty leaves, you want the ones that have been eaten by the ngārara. If it's good for them, it's good for us.

'We just need the koromiko then we'll return home. I want to be home before the sun sets.'

Tāwhai didn't know why. It was a peaceful evening and he could do with a nice stroll home after almost sprinting all the way here to keep up with Nanny Moko.

'Why don't we want to be here after dark, Nan?' he asked.

'Well, for one, we won't be able to see where we're going because you forgot the torch,' she chuckled. 'And you might find yourself in unwanted company.'

'Who?' asked Tāwhai. 'There's no one out here.'

'This is the home of Te Tini-o-Hakuturi and the Patupaiarehe. They like to roam the bush at night. They're the true kaitiaki here, we're just visitors.'

Tāwhai was curious. 'Who's Te Tini-o-Hakuturi? Are they like the Patupaiarehe?'

'Not quite. The Hakuturi are all the children of Tāne who live in the forest, all the insects and all the birds. The Patupaiarehe are small, fair-skinned creatures like you.' Nanny Moko gave Tāwhai a grin. His father's Irish genes had trumped his mother's. His mother was Nanny Moko's eldest daughter. 'They might even mistake you for one of them and marry you off to one of their misty maidens.' Nanny Moko laughed.

When they approached the bush edge on Kakepuku, Tāwhai noticed the mist had started to settle on the upper slopes of the mauna. Nanny Moko had told him that the Patupaiarehe used the mist as a vehicle to travel to and from the adjacent mauna, Pirongia.

'You know, there was a girl here when I was growing up, a cousin of mine, we called her Patupaiarehe. Her hair was a reddish colour and her skin much fairer than ours, yet her mother was as dark as night. We didn't know her father but the old people would say that her mother had an affair with one of the Patupaiarehe folk.'

'Maybe she had an affair with a Pākehā,' Tāwhai said. Nan let out a loud laugh.

'Maybe,' she replied. 'Heoi anō.'

That was something Nan always said when she wanted to change the subject.

'You know the right time to collect rongoā is in the morning before sunrise, nē?' She shot Tāwhai one of her typical sideways glances. 'We're only here at this hour because it's an emergency. Now, when you leave in the morning, you say your karakia, keeping in mind exactly what plants you need. You go without eating or drinking. "Me haere maroke koe," the old people would say. They wouldn't even talk to anyone. You need to maintain a clear mind. The old people who lived here knew when Koro was going to get rongoā. If people acknowledged him as we passed in the morning he would remain silent and carry on.'

'Isn't that rude?' Tāwhai asked.

'That was tikanga. People knew at that point exactly what he was doing and they respected that. Things have changed now.'

Tāwhai and Nanny Moko arrived at the foot of the bush; it was half-light so Nanny Moko started inspecting the nearest koromiko she could find. 'Make sure you take the rau from the eastern side, Moko,' she said moving towards the back of a nearby bush. 'Never take from the shady side, because it doesn't have the same healing properties as this side. Then you karakia again.'

Nanny Moko had never explained all of this before. She just did it and Tāwhai followed without question. He knew what she was doing but didn't always understand why.

'Why do we karakia?' he asked, following her to the eastern side of the koromiko.

Nanny Moko stopped what she was doing and looked at him. 'Imagine you needed something extremely important that only one person could give you. If that person freely gave you what you needed, what is the least you could do?'

Tāwhai paused. 'Ah — say thank you?' He was sure the answer couldn't be that simple.

'Āe. Karakia is our way of saying thank you.' Nanny Moko continued inspecting the koromiko. 'We acknowledge Tāne and his tamariki and our connection to them through our whakapapa. We came much later than all of them, so they're senior to us in the scheme of things and, as we take, we give back. You don't want to make the same mistake Rata did.'

'Ko wai a Rata?' Tāwhai asked.

'Rata — your tupuna. Ha! Anei!' Nanny Moko had found the particular rau she was after. 'Here we go. You see the small shoots in the middle at the tip of the branch? This is what you need. Kōrero mai.'

She began to recite a karakia.

'Nāu, e Tāne, i toko ai te rangi ki runga,

I puta ai te ao mārama.

Ka kīia ai koe ko Tāne-te-waiora,

Homai rā te waiora

E kimihia nei, e rapua nei,

Kia ora ai ō uri.

Hui ē, tāiki ē!'

She snapped off two shoots from the tip of one branch and Tāwhai copied her, taking one from another branch.

'Ka nui tēnā. That's enough. We only take what we need. Now, let's get home.'

On the walk home, the sun was waning behind the foothills of Pirongia. Tāwhai turned back towards Kakepuku and watched the mist envelop their majestic maunga. Who was Rata, he wondered, and what was his mistake?

'Fill up the woodbin when we get back, please.' Nanny Moko said.

It was Tāwhai's job to light the fire and keep it going. At Nanny Moko's, fire meant hot water, hot food and dry clothes. She would often remind him that if it weren't for Māui and his trickster ways there wouldn't be any fire. She had a knack for storytelling and pointing out the relevance of the pakiwaitara she told.

'Nan, will you tell me about Rata?' Tāwhai asked.

'Okay, but let's get inside first.'

By the time Tāwhai had filled the woodbin and hung up their coats, Nanny Moko was sitting at the fireplace, separating the rau she had collected earlier that day into two piles.

'Haere mai. Kainga ēnei. They will settle your puku.'

Tāwhai took the shoots of koromiko from her hand and chewed them before swallowing. They weren't as bad as he'd thought.

'Your tupuna, Rata, was born many years ago. He was the grandson of the great Tāwhaki. According to some iwi it was Tāne who ascended the heavens to fetch the baskets of knowledge; however our old people spoke of Tāwhaki. He had to work around his blind kuia, Whaititiri, before he could return with the baskets intact. Tāwhaki had a son named Wahieroa and Wahieroa had Rata. When Rata was only a baby his father was killed by Matuku-tangotango on an expedition to a far-away place named Pariroa.'

Nanny Moko passed Tāwhai one of the piles of rongoā to hold.

'Now, all of these events took place in Hawaiki long before our tūpuna made their home here,' she said. 'When Rata grew older he asked his mother about his father. His mother explained that his father had been killed by Matuku when Rata was just an infant. Rata would often question his mother about the location of Matuku's home but she was hesitant to tell him; she knew his intentions and was fearful that if Rata went after Matuku he too may never return to her.

'"What good is it to you?" she would say. "In order to get there you need a waka, which you don't have."

'Rata would retort, "I will build my own waka and sail to this place to avenge my father's death."

'That was the tikanga in those times: just as Tāwhaki had avenged his father's death, Rata was determined to do the same. Rata's mother would ask him, "How will you build a waka?" She knew that Rata would eventually find out where Matuku's village was, and, after some time, she gave in to Rata's unwavering persistence.

"'Sail towards the rising sun," she instructed him, "there you will find Pariroa, the home of Matuku." After saying this, she handed Rata an old toki, "You will need this to fashion your waka."'

'Weren't there any spare waka in the pā?' Tāwhai asked. Nanny Moko smiled, as though she was impressed by his wit.

'Well, Rata's mother was aware of the scale of the task at hand and wanted to test her son's determination. In order to go, he would need to build his own waka, and to do that he needed a toki; however, the toki she gave him was blunt. After handing Rata the toki, she instructed him to visit his elderly kuia, Hine-tua-hōanga, who lived in solitude on the outer edges of the pā. When Rata approached Hine-tua-hōanga's home, he saw her sitting hunched over in front of her small shack. She peered at him and said, "Rata, what brings you here?" Rata was nervous; he had heard many tales about Hine-tua-hōanga and her aged sandstone body. "My mother told me that you would help me sharpen my toki," he replied.

'Then Rata told her about his mission to avenge his father's death. He also told her that he needed to sharpen the toki in order to fashion his waka. At that, Hine-tua-hōanga agreed and slowly turned away from Rata, revealing her coarse sandstone back. She ordered him to rub the blade of his toki against her and as he did she recited her karakia, "Kia koi, kia koi, kia koi."

'Rata thanked his kuia and returned home with his sharpened toki in hand. The next morning he made his way into the bush in search of a suitable tree for his waka. Quite often when we retell these pakiwaitara, Moko, we tell them as if the main character ventured alone, but that makes no sense. How on earth would Rata haul the huge tree from the forest all by himself?'

Tāwhai nodded in agreement.

'One man who accompanied him,' Nanny Moko continued, 'was Kāraerae, a tohunga at canoe-making. As soon as the party reached the area of the bush where the giant trees of Tāne stood, Rata spotted one that stood higher than the rest. Its upper branches pierced the forest canopy stretching towards the sun and its trunk was completely round — ideal for a sea-voyaging waka. Rata and his crew set to work hacking at the mighty tree.'

'Did Rata karakia first like we do?' Tāwhai asked.

Nanny Moko smiled but didn't answer the question. 'Finally at dusk the tree toppled to the ground, creating a resounding thud that could be heard from their village. Rata instructed his crew to head home for the night to rest. The next morning they returned to the area where they had left the tree but, lo and behold, there it was standing erect as if untouched! Kāraerae and the others were overcome with fear.

'"Nā wai tēnei mahi? Who is responsible for this?" they asked themselves in shock. Rata, on the other hand, was consumed with frustration as his mission to avenge his father's death had been delayed. Rata instructed the crew to set to work again and he himself began to hack away at the hefty trunk with his toki. At nightfall the tree crashed to the ground a second time. When they returned the next morning they were amazed to see the tree standing once more in its original upright position. After the third day, when the same thing happened, Rata was frustrated. He told his mother about his trouble with the mystical tree. She instructed him to visit his kaumātua, the wise tohunga Whakaihorangi.

'At Whakaihorangi's house, Rata complained that beings of the forest were pestering him and making him the butt of some joke. A stern Whakaihorangi told him to watch his words: Te Tini-o-Hakuturi were his ancestors and the kaitiaki of the forest. Whakaihorangi asked Rata to describe exactly what he and his men did every day, and it didn't take long for him to spot the mistake.

'"Aha!" he exclaimed. "You didn't recite the correct karakia – or in fact any karakia. Instead you carelessly chopped down your ancestor, a child of Tāne, for your own gain without offering anything in return."

'"How can I right this?" Rata asked.

'"Return to the tree and fell it once more. After felling the tree, cover the stump with the paretao fern and return here to meet me with some of the fern."'

'He aha te paretao?' Tāwhai couldn't help interrupting.

'Anā.' Nanny Moko pointed to one of the leaves that Tāwhai was holding.

'What are the two piles for, Nan?' Tāwhai asked her.

'This pile will be boiled and the rongoā taken internally as tea. Koinā ngā mea hei inu. And the pile you have is for making poultice and bandages, or will be used in a bath like the paretao. Koinā ngā mea hei ūkui.' Nanny Moko placed both piles to the side and continued.

'Rata did exactly as the old tohunga instructed. After he felled the tree he returned to find Whakaihorangi waiting for him. Whakaihorangi took the paretao and began reciting the ancient karakia connected with the felling of a giant tree for a whare or a waka.

'The next morning Rata and his party set out into the bush for the fourth time. To their relief, they found the tree they'd felled lying on the ground. The karakia of Whakaihorangi must have appeased Te Tini-o-Hakuturi. Rata and his crew were elated, and they set to work at once preparing the body of the waka. That evening Rata returned to his mother and told her of his success. She told him that his mission was incomplete and that he would need to call upon his kaumātua, Whakaihorangi, once more to perform the final blessings over the waka. This would ensure safe passage over the sea.

'The next day the village gathered at the beach. As Whakaihorangi chanted the ancient karakia, Rata's waka was dragged to the water's edge and given the name Aniuwaru. And soon, Rata and his tauā set out towards the rising sun, bound for Pariroa, the land of Matuku-tangotango.

'Aī! Look at the time, Moko! We better get to bed. You have school tomorrow.'

'Did Rata kill Matuku and return to his mother?' Tāwhai asked.

'We'll have to save that part of the story for tomorrow,' Nanny Moko replied, and Tāwhai got ready for bed. Before Nanny Moko turned out the light in his room, she sat down next to him.

'You see, Moko, we learn from our mistakes and, although Rata made a mistake, with the help of his elders, he corrected it. There was also a process he followed. He could have gone into the forest and cut down any old tree to build his waka. Instead, he carefully selected the right tree, and it was the karakia of Whakaihorangi that appeased Tāne and Te Tini-o-Hakuturi. That is what made the waka seaworthy.

'It's the same with our rongoā. Anybody can go and pick a leaf and eat it but it's the process we follow that makes it right. It's the time we go, the area we visit and the careful selection. The most important thing, though, is our acknowledgement of Tāne through karakia, as it's the karakia that gives the rongoā its healing properties that make us better.' Nanny Moko kissed Tāwhai on the head. She mumbled some indistinct words under her breath and placed her hand over his puku.

The next morning Tāwhai woke up early to the song of the tūī. His tummy ache had gone, which, unfortunately, meant he had to go to school. He wasn't upset though; he was grateful, grateful for his Nanny Moko and her karakia.

CHAPTER 6
MOON
AND MIST

———

Moon Story

———

Hinepūkohurangi and Uenuku

———

Moon Story

BY PATRICIA GRACE

On the night that Rona bad-mouthed Moon she did it because she wasn't in her right mind. Even before she tripped and fell she was feeling stressed. So much had happened that day and at the end of it she'd been left with far too many responsibilities.

Early that morning, in an enemy attack, one of their men had been killed. They'd been taken by surprise, and though at first they tried to defend themselves they found themselves greatly outnumbered. Some of their houses had been broken down and most of their stored food had been stolen from the pātaka. All they could do was take their children into the forest and hide until it was over.

Once the raiding party had gone on its way the men followed at a distance to make sure it was leaving the territory. They knew that one day there would have to be a reprisal but that would have to wait until they had built up strength by making suitable liaisons. Perhaps revenge would take place the following season or the one after, or maybe it would not take place until another generation had passed.

After the men had gone, the women and children set about fixing the houses, consoling the widow and finding enough food for everyone to eat. They also had to tend to one of the grandmothers now lying in the death shelter which had been erected for her.

While others had the task of seeing to the needs of the widowed and the dying, much of the responsibility for providing food and replenishing stocks was left to Rona and any children who were old enough to help.

It was late at night before she realised that the water containers were empty. There was no water for children who might wake in the night and no water for the dying grandmother who had not taken solid food for some days. Most people had fallen asleep by then or were keeping watch round the shelter.

So although her baby, sleeping on the mat by his grandmother, was now stirring and would soon wake and begin crying to be fed she thought she'd better go to the spring to fill the calabashes.

There was a cold wind blowing. Rona put a cloak over her shoulders and took up the containers, tying two at her waist and stringing the rest together to carry, then began running as quickly as she could along the track through the trees. The way was bleached by moonlight. The pumice path, the undergrowth, the fringes and fronds, the trees, the swathes of hanging kiekie were all decoloured except for a tinge of blue like mother's milk.

Rona was not halfway to the water hole, flying along, leaping the rocks and tangles along the way, when a big hairy cloud, dog-shaped, ran right across the moon's face, causing the pathway and the whole night to blacken. Running in darkness she did not see the looping tree root across her track. Rona tripped and fell, letting go of the calabashes which shattered against the stones and trees.

It was a heavy fall in which Rona banged her head hard enough to be knocked out for some minutes. There was a broken bone in her foot, she had bitten off the tip of her tongue and there was blood coming from a long gash in her shoulder.

Rona put full blame for her fall on the moon.

Perhaps in her stupor it didn't occur to her that it could have been more the fault of the passing cloud that the light was blocked out, or of the wind that had whistled the hairy dog across the moon's visage. Once she had gained consciousness it was all she could do to grasp the trunk of a small tree and pull herself up to sit with her back against it as the scraggy dog ran off and there was light once more. But because of her concussed state, the stresses of the day and the anxiety about her baby, maybe she could be excused for sounding off at the moon the way she did. Maybe there were extenuating circumstances.

Although really, no matter how you see it, it was an enormity to look the moon in the eye the way she did then, and call it a big bowl of boil-up in which the moon's own head simmered and steamed along with a mess of fern root, kūmara, vegetables, fruits and a variety of berry-filled birds.

No excuse for it.

There was no greater insult in the universe than to be compared to cooked food — for it to be insinuated that your mana was to be taken over by one who would eat you, and to imply that you were to be chewed, swallowed, digested and excreted.

There was no more low-down state of being than that of cooked food, and therefore no greater profanity than what emanated from Rona that night.

'Pokokōhua. Stupid Moon,' she yelled. 'Look what you've done. The calabashes are broken and I can't fetch water. My ankle is broken too, so I won't be able to make it to the spring anyway. I'll have to crawl home now but my head is in such a spin I hardly know which direction to take. I could get lost in the trees. Children will be crying for water. The dying grandmother will be parched. My baby will be awake and will have to be fed by one of the other mothers even though my own breasts are so full that they're stinging. Boiled head. Useless hua.'

It would have been a vile enough invective even levelled at one's peers, but now here was this earthling foul-mouthing a most ancient and venerable ancestor who had been around even before the time of the separation of Earth and Sky. Rona, even in her dazed state, would not have dreamed of disrespecting Earth in the same way, yet Moon is a close relative of Earth, indeed the very closest. Earth and Moon probably started out as conjoined twins. In fact they must still be conjoined twins in some mysterious way as there is definitely a push-me pull-you relationship between them. There's some dance in which the two are forever coordinated and where one could not exist without the other.

It was not only the words that Rona uttered that were so evil; during their delivery she displayed a pair of white, angry eyes and a set of bloodied teeth as well.

But in a way it was fortunate it was Moon she picked on otherwise it could have turned out much worse than it did for Rona.

If Rona had decided that it was the passing of the dog-shaped cloud that was the reason for the blackout, or that it was the fault of the whistling wind, and then if she'd aimed invective at Dog-cloud or Wind instead of Moon, it could have been the end of her.

Both Cloud and Wind are children of Tāwhirimātea who is the Great Coordinator of elements — wind, rain, storms, tornadoes, snowflakes, whirlwinds, thunder, sleet, hail — the whole orchestra. He too is a most ancient and venerable ancestor, though is of a later generation than Earth and Moon. He is subject to Moon's pull and has to mind his p's and k's when it comes to her.

In the days before the separation of his Earth and Sky parents, TM was only a whistle of stagnant breath squeaking about between their crushing bodies. However, he went from strength to strength after their separation and the coming of light. No one messes with TM. He can uproot whole forests, flatten houses, buildings, towns, cities and whip sea waves up to a fury. He's a scrapper from way back and you disrespect him or his offspring at your peril. Everyone knows that.

Anyway, no one with any sense vilifies those on whom their own existence depends.

If TM, being neither as austere nor as composed and measured as Moon, had been the one on the end of Rona's vitriol he probably would have struck her down right there. Her relatives could soon have been handing her corpse up into the trees so that the birds could clean her bones. Lesser beings, such as chiefs, kings, bishops, lords and commanders, have dished out far more severe punishments than what Moon decided on for Rona.

Never in all her centuries had Moon been maligned in such a manner. She'd never been maligned in any way at all. On the contrary, she had grown accustomed to adulation and exultation by prophets and poets throughout the ages. Even when stars galloped by on fiery sky horses and called, 'Howdy, Paleface' in seductive voices she didn't take umbrage. She took it as a kind of homage to candescent beauty. In fact she was pleased to have someone come by and call out to her. It was a solitary path she was on. Moon led a lonely existence.

It is often the case that conjoined twins are not equally endowed at birth, one being more favoured by circumstances than the other, and Earth had come out better off than Moon in many respects. Unlike Earth, Moon had no adornments to distract her, no offspring to amuse her, no light of her own, and she bathed only in reflected glory. But she had her own mana and didn't mind.

Even so, Moon knew that she now had to be firm, that she would need to come down strongly and make an example of Rona so that a lesson could be learned for all time.

'You'll have to come here and say that,' said Moon, and Rona felt herself being lifted from the ground. When she realised what was happening she grabbed hold of the tree she had been sitting against, hoping that it would anchor her. But the moon's pull was too great. The tree was uprooted and both woman and tree were taken on a journey skyward.

Early in the morning people came out of their sleeping houses wondering what had happened to Rona. Some had been waiting all night for water. They went off along the track to look for her, soon arriving at the place where she'd fallen. They found the broken calabashes and saw the disturbed soil where the tree had been uprooted. They saw blood on the ground and thought at first that Rona had been killed and taken away by their enemy.

It was a child, calling and pointing, who drew their attention to Rona who was being drawn upwards clutching a tree, her cloak and her long hair spreading behind her, the two calabashes still tied at her waist. They watched throughout that whole day as she journeyed, and by the time night came could see her caught up there in the centre of the moon.

At first they thought she had been swallowed and was being slowly digested by the moon. They were sorry about such a fate. But after several months, as they watched the moon diminish, hide itself for a time, then gradually reappear and grow again, they could see Rona hadn't been swallowed at all and hoped that Moon would one day return her to them.

Rona soon came to understand that Moon would never release her and that she would never see her children or her people again, so she decided she would have to make the best of the situation. Her new home was roomy and comfortable and she became aware that anxiety and stress were unknown in this new place. She found she could relax there. She realised too that war, though invented by the atua at the time of the separation of the Great Parents, had since been taken on exclusively by earth beings, her own kin, as part of their identity. War was now executed only in earthly panoramas. She was pleased to be above all that.

It was a long time before Rona's family accepted that she would never come back to them. They believed at first that she had become

Moon's servant. Some said they could see her sweeping Moon's floor or lighting her lamps and candles. Others said she was gathering Moon's firewood or shaking out bedclothes or shining the rings of the moon.

But after some generations the people decided that their ancestress, Rona, was not Moon's servant at all. They observed her seated at Moon's window. They saw her dancing in many rooms. They saw that her hair had been coiled up into a chiefly topknot and decorated with tall combs. They understood that Rona and Moon had become close companions, had become as one, as together they collated the seasons and rolled and unrolled the tides.

Hinepūkohurangi and Uenuku

BY KELLY JOSEPH

When she thought back, she sometimes wondered why she got involved with him in the first place. Of course she had been with other humans before; she was just as curious as the next celestial. Many of her kind enjoyed dipping into the realm of flesh and skin ever since their arrival by waka millennia ago. Hinepūkohurangi's flings were usually hot and fleeting; bodies cushioned on moss beside waterfalls or grinding against slippery rock faces. She'd disappear before the sun rose, leaving them spent beside the water wondering if it was a dream or reality. She would never see them again and that's the way she liked it.

The humans she took for lovers were always strong, matā kai kutu in their prime. Men or women, it didn't matter; she was attracted to their mana. Uenuku was different. He was shorter than her, with no broad shoulders inside his hoody. He also had no hips to speak of; when she first met him, his jeans sagged around a non-existent arse. She actually thought he was a child when she saw him beside that large camera. What was it about him? Maybe it was his eyes that drew her in, green with yellow towards the irises, like sunlit pools inside a cavern. Maybe it was those curious delicate hands of his, constantly moving, like an agitated pīwakawaka. Or maybe it was because she felt like she had met him before. From the very beginning he felt known to her.

That first night she watched him for a long while as he tinkered with his camera. Hinepūkohurangi remained hidden to him within the mist that plumed sphere-like from a fountain. His camera was large and old, like the ones they used a hundred years ago. It sat on a wooden tripod, with bellows the colour of blood, and a thick lens edged in brass that glinted under the full moon.

Occasionally Uenuku's upper body would disappear under a draped jacket and he'd look like a headless spectre. Hinepūkohurangi smiled at this. She liked how he worked with confident purpose. He cocked the shutter on the lens, went back under the jacket and fiddled with the bellows, adjusting the screws on the rail. Then he came out, grabbed a light-meter from his backpack and pointed it at the sky and around the fountain area. Returning to his camera, he fiddled with the lens some more. Then he slid a black box with sheet film inside, she guessed, into an opening near the back. He pulled out the dark slide protecting the film from light. He released the shutter using a cable release attached to the lens. Then he retrieved a large torch. Suddenly, he began whirling the torch around. He was a dervish of light. The beam revealed weed-filled concrete planters, tipped rubbish bins, tagging, shattered plastic orb-lighting, cigarette butts, glass shards, and benches splintered by drunks. All the grimy details of the abandoned plaza were exposed.

At last he pointed towards the fountain. The lights around it had been kicked out long ago. In his flare, Hinepūkohurangi, mesmerised by those eyes, those hands and his dance of light, let herself be completely seen.

He dropped his torch.

It rolled before coming to rest near her feet. He picked it up with a shaking hand and let the light sweep up her body from feet to knees, thighs to belly, nipples and clavicle, all barely concealed by her hair and diaphanous mists. Finally the beam came to her face. She blinked but did not look away.

'Holy fuck,' he whispered in awe.

'Manners man-child,' she said, smiling again.

'Shit! Sorry, sorry. Shit! I just got a hell of a fright. And you're so . . . Who . . . or what are you?'

'Ko Hinepūkohurangi ahau. Some call me the Mist Maiden. Nō Rangiora ahau, from Rangimamao. Ko Atua te iwi. I am the creator of fog, haze, and the low clouds that cling to mountainsides. And maker of mists of course.'

'Are you for real? I must be tripping . . .'

'Kāore, I'm real,' she said, taking his small shaking hand and bringing it to the side of her face. When he took it away he stared at it, astonished. His fingertips tingled and his palm was moist.

He cleared his throat and raised himself up to appear slightly braver and not intimidated by her. 'What are you doing here?'

'This used to be the place of my favourite waterfall. It once had so much wairua. It was my refuge. Then the people arrived. They felt the sacredness of the area too, placed a mauri behind the falls and a village was built nearby. Later when the others arrived, a town rose up. The mauri was stolen and put in a museum. Then they flattened everything, channelled the stream into a pipe and covered it with concrete pavers. I'm still grieving. Every now and then I come here to pay respects to all the life that was taken away.'

She drifted off. She could almost hear the water rushing over the rocks, see the manu flitting around in pursuit of bugs, smell the rich, damp earth with all the life it contained. She shook her head, back again once more with her feet firmly upon concrete.

'And you man-child, ko wai tō ingoa? And what brings you here?'

'My name is Uenuku. I'm taking photos for an upcoming show. It's my first solo show. You know, an exhibition — um — you probably don't have the foggiest what I'm talking about.' He looked at her sideways and she burst into laughter. His neck turned red, spreading to his cheeks.

'Nice pun, e hoa. I actually know all about your current society, your modern culture. I'm not ignorant or archaic just because I'm Atua.'

'Fair enough. I guess I've got a lot to learn . . . about you . . .' He smiled now, his eyes looking directly at her. Really looking.

It was Hinepūkohurangi who blushed then. She quickly changed the subject.

'Why the old camera? Why not digital?'

'Digital would be too easy. The big camera slows me down. It's hard. The process is laborious and it doesn't always work out. I like that, the uncertainty. It makes me see more. I take more in. And the details it captures are incredible. Digital can't touch the resolution and crispness of large format.' He looked at his hands, then up at her nervously. 'Let me show you something,' he said.

He led her to the camera. First he put the metal sheet back in and then he pulled the whole film holder out. He cocked the lens shutter and opened up the aperture to let the light in. Then he lifted the jacket for her to go under. She didn't hesitate. She never believed the old people's stories that cameras were taipō, goblins, with the power to suck out your mauri. They were just dark boxes with holes in them to let in light. Nothing to fear there.

Under the jacket the musky, oily smell of Uenuku was strong. She couldn't help but breathe more deeply. She was shielded from the reflections of the yellow streetlights, and on a large rectangle of glass the plaza was projected upside down and backwards. The way the plaza was illuminated onto the ground glass somehow made it different, otherworldly, almost magical. Almost.

'Auē!' she said. 'Neat!'

Encouraged, words suddenly flowed from him. 'I guess I'm here because I want to show people the things that are overlooked. Show the sublime in the ordinary. Get people to really see what is here.' He pulled the jacket off her gently.

She straightened to her full height. 'But there's nothing good here to see, e hoa. Not really,' she said.

'The ugly can be beautiful. All this detritus, they're markers of time, remnants of the human interaction with urban space, forgotten fringes, an archive of lost spirits . . .'

'Sounds like a bunch of pretentious kōrero tūtae to me. This place is tainted. Ruined. Doesn't matter how nicely you frame it or spin it with silken art-speak. You never felt what was here before, so you can't even begin to understand!' She closed her eyes, anger rising, 'You don't know what was lost.' The mists around her turned from white to a roiling steel grey. 'How could you know?' she said. 'A sleepwalking mortal. An entitled millennial one at that. What you're doing here is trivial. Indulgent.'

She saw something in his look then and she knew she had gone too far. Something crossed his face like a high cloud above the earth. It cast a shadow of hurt or anger or something . . . she couldn't read exactly what, but the expression was fierce and intense. Powerful. It turned her on.

She leaned in and kissed him. It was a long, warm, wet kiss. The feeling of familiarity returned, and when their bodies drew closer she felt utterly whole.

He tasted like Coke and tobacco. There was something inside him she could feel too. A sticky blackness. A sadness inside his chest that he hid from others. Also inside him, deeper, she could feel enormous potential; that potential came at her mind's eye as swirling colours. She kissed him harder.

Despite his earlier nervousness, his lips weren't shy at all. They left hers and travelled across to her ear. They lingered on her lobe before grazing her skin gently all the way down the side of her neck. She was electrified, her veins shivered. This was the first time a human had done that to her. Her mists turned to pink candyfloss around her — a shepherd's delight.

Uenuku leaned back, and grinned at her, 'That's a neat trick. You're like one of those ultrasonic diffusers.' He touched his lips, 'And you even made my lips tingle.' He laughed.

Hinepūkohurangi could tell he had already forgotten what she had said before, because now he was drinking her all in. His gaze wandered downwards. She let the mists around her dissolve so that he could see her more clearly, becoming naked. He stared at her for a long time before pulling her to him. Even if he was small in stature, his hard cock pushing against his jeans, pushing against her, felt large enough. It had been many years since she had been with a human, and those yearnings were awakening within her too.

A chirrup in the high branches above them startled her out of the moment and she looked up. In the branches were the black silhouettes of starlings, an inverse constellation against a deep blue sky.

Blue sky, not black. Her chest tightened. She pushed Uenuku back.

'What's up?' he asked.

She looked to the west and there the moon was setting over the hills. She looked to the east and saw how pale the sky was over the city skyline.

'I don't have long. If I linger until the sun rises I could get trapped here, separated from my celestial whānau.'

Other starlings were now joining the first in song. Then, from across the plaza, they heard a husky voice, summoning.

'Haere mai tuakana, i mua tonu i te whitinga o te rā!'

'Who's that?' Uenuku asked.

'Hinewai, my younger sister. Creator of the gentle rain that falls during foggy weather.'

'Sis, kia tere! Time to go.' Hinewai's voice was closer this time and more urgent. Then she appeared nearby, a vague shape at first, part woman, part drizzle. When she became more solid her disapproval was obvious. Hinepūkohurangi ignored her sister's rolling eyes and said to her, 'Āe. Haere atu!'

Hinewai rose towards the sky, beckoning her big sister to follow, worry on her brow.

'Stay for a bit longer . . . please?!' Uenuku said, grabbing for the Mist Maiden's arm. His hand passed straight through her.

Floating upwards she didn't mean to look back. She had never had the urge to do that before, she always left without attachment. This time she did. Below, Uenuku looked so small, so insignificant. Those green-yellow eyes shone from his upturned face, blazing with desire and regret. She tried to wave goodbye but she couldn't. Instead she touched her lips where his had been moments before. The starlings were deafening as the first rays of sun hit the plaza. Hinepūkohurangi was gone.

Uenuku schlepped back to his cottage in the valley. He passed puffy-eyed people, some munching on toast or drinking takeaway coffee, heading to work or university along the lichen-covered pavement. His camera was balanced over one shoulder, the bellows collapsed, the square body still attached to the tripod legs that he had also contracted. The flattened structure was easier to handle but it was still hefty. The tripod pressed into his skin so deeply it rubbed against bone. His lower back was killing him from the weight, but he liked this because pain gave him something to focus on.

The alternative was a playback of the night's events in vivid Technicolor. She was gone and he couldn't figure out if she had been a hallucination. She could easily have been a vision; he hadn't slept properly for weeks now because of the show. Also he kept forgetting to take his meds. If she was just a vision though, why was he left feeling so completely empty? His gut ached with that emptiness — and his lips still buzzed too.

The sickly-sweet scent of jasmine rose from a hedge — he was home. He paused at the ornate cast-iron gate and suddenly he saw with fresh eyes what a dump this place was. The timber siding was rotten and soft as Weetbix. The veranda was so crooked it threatened to collapse on anyone entering the front door. Inside the house was rough too. The leaky roof had left stains like topographical contour lines along the edges of the Victorian wallpaper. Smells inherited from the previous owner — cat piss and the aroma of countless mutton roast dinners — infused the musty carpet. Once, he even found a mushroom growing under his bed. The scrim walls breathed on windy days, billowing damp air like a bellows. That dank air entered his chest, leaving a rattling cough that had turned into pneumonia this past winter.

Uenuku knew this was only temporary, and it was practical. The rent was cheap so he could spend the rest of his meagre pay on photo supplies. Also the landlord didn't give a shit what he did to the place. It was due to be knocked down in six months anyway to make way for a new bypass. So until now, it hardly bothered him, the decay of the cottage. Still, this time, when he opened the squeaky gate and walked down the brick path, the place felt so lonely he almost cried. Almost.

Instead he got to work. There was another way to prove whether Hinepūkohurangi was real.

He went through the back door into the lean-to kitchen. Here he had set up a darkroom. The windows were painted over. On the bench were three large trays, already filled with fresh chemicals and covered in sheets of plastic. He took out the film holder from his backpack and grabbed a film-developing canister off a shelf. Inside the empty walk-in pantry it was light-proof once the door was shut. After pulling the door closed behind him he opened the film holder. He felt the notch in the film and placed the emulsion side inwards as he curled it into the canister, before popping on the lid. In the kitchen again, he rinsed the film with a wetting agent and water. He expertly measured the chemicals he needed and placed them into the canister one by one. After pouring and agitating then tipping each one out, he rinsed the film. Then he released the negative sheet from the canister, holding his breath in anticipation. Raising it up to the light, he could see there was an image there. Carefully, he squeegeed the water off. He got a loupe and held the negative up to the light.

There she was.

Her image was reverse, so that her black hair, her pupils and dark irises were transparent — he could see the room behind those parts. But it was definitely her face, supremely beautiful even in negative.

He breathed out, relieved. Here was evidence that he hadn't had an episode — a 'funny turn' as his mother liked to describe them. On the walk back from the plaza the familiar black heaviness had begun to spread out from his chest, seeping out to join the new emptiness in his gut that she left behind. But these feelings both lifted when he saw her face again. Now, something new warmed his chest. Now, he could let himself hope, just a little. Somehow, he might see her again.

He let the negative dry for a while longer before he stuck it into the enlarger.

Switching on the safe light, he pulled a sheet of paper from a box under the sink. He didn't need to do a test strip. He could tell from the density of the negative the approximate exposure he would need to make. He cranked the timer to five seconds, punched the button and the light momentarily shone through the negative onto the paper. When the enlarger clicked off he took the paper to the developing bath and dropped it in. He lifted the edge of the tray so that he could gently rock the print as the chemicals revealed the latent image.

He never got tired of the moment when the image appeared. It was alchemy.

Sitting there, amongst the garbage of the plaza, within the sphere of the fountain, she had been caught by the beam moments after they met.

He needed to see her more clearly.

Returning to the enlarger, he raised the head where the negative was held. Her face and body grew bigger, more central, while the rest of the image went beyond where the paper's edge would be. This time he took a moment to focus the image properly, using a grain finder. Once it was sharp, he took another sheet from the box, exposed it, then dropped it in the developer.

He rocked the tray as she slowly appeared. Deep brown eyes, long jet-black hair down to her waist, luminous skin, and a mouth that curled up in the corners when she smiled. He waited until the blacks were fully developed then moved the print to the stop bath, then to the fix and finally to the water bath.

The image floated under the water. His eyes were drawn to her mouth. She had smiled a lot. Laughed at him a lot. But for some reason he didn't mind her teasing. She was lofty, condescending and fierce one minute, then sensual, open and gentle the next. Changeable as mist. What she said about his photography being indulgent, that stung. He hadn't forgotten that. But what replayed in his mind was the kiss and the way she revealed herself to him. Let herself be vulnerable. And her intense beauty of course. It was beyond anything he had ever seen.

He turned on the overhead light. While the image was still in the water he traced his finger over her face. The resolution was so high she was almost holographic. It was still a poor substitution for her, a simulacrum, but it was all he had. The print was smooth under his fingers. He traced her outline until his fingers got wrinkly as walnuts.

A memory suddenly surfaced then, of himself as a little kid sitting in a cold bath looking down at his wrinkly fingers turning white. His mother was scrubbing at him with a rough flannel, yelling in his ear, trying to wipe clean the ink he had used to draw all over his body. His skin was getting sore from the rubbing. He had found a book on tā moko that day at the school library when he was hiding from the big boys who gave him wedgies and Chinese burns. He thought the warriors in the book looked cool. After school he went to his hiding spot under a kawakawa behind his house. There he had copied the designs from the book with a black ballpoint pen along his arms to his chest, down his legs and then, lastly, he worked on his face. Fuck knows why. He knew he would get in trouble, but he did it anyway. After the bath, his skin was so raw it bled. The ink, along with any illusions he could ever look like a warrior, were washed down the drain.

Back in the here and now, Uenuku finally took the print of Hinepūkohurangi from the water and squeegeed it. As he was pegging it up on the plastic line that criss-crossed the ceiling, there was a soft knock at the door. He wasn't expecting anyone.

'Fuck off. I'm busy,' he yelled. He was exhausted too. He didn't feel like talking to anyone. Plus he wanted to spend more time studying her photograph.

The door handle turned and Hinepūkohurangi appeared in the doorway. Sheepish. It was night behind her. How did that happen? He shook his head. Who cared? She was here. Not a figment in his mind, not a latent form imprinted on a sensitive silver emulsion, or a monochrome image on wet paper. Real. The light above her illuminated her cheekbones. Her curly-lipped smile. His heart palpitated 'til he felt like he might lose strength, buckle and fall face-first into his chemicals, but he managed to straighten himself enough to meet her in the middle of the room. They smiled at each other, giddy.

'He roa te wā,' she said with that same wry smile. She pointed to the print he had just made. 'Nice. Hope your model signed a release form for that.'

'Ha ha. Who suddenly made you the photography police?'

He took her hand gently, led her through the narrow hallway, past the lounge and into the front room where the bed was. They sat on it, side by side. He couldn't stop shaking. He excused himself, walked back to the lounge where his ciggies were. He lit one and took a few puffs to calm his nerves, then stubbed it out in the ashtray. When he came back she was already lying down with her mists dissolved. She was stunning — it hurt to look at her. She beckoned him over. He sat beside her and reached out, tracing her face with his fingers, then her whole body, slowly. Her skin was silk, unreal.

They fucked. The first time was rough and feral, desperate, like the world was about to end or like they would never see each other again. Later that night, the second and third times, they took their time, were more tender and attentive towards each other.

Afterwards, resting in each other's arms, they talked quietly.

'Why did you get into art?' Hinepūkohurangi asked.

'It was something I was good at. From since I was little. It was also an escape.'

'From what?'

Uenuku was silent. How could he even begin to tell her about his parents?

'Are you hungry? I haven't eaten all day,' he said. She shook her head so he went off to the lounge where he had the fridge. He pulled out a few snacks and brought them back to the bedroom.

'An escape from what?' repeated Hinepūkohurangi. Uenuku rolled his eyes. His ploy hadn't worked. He sat on the edge of the bed eating a banana.

'My parents are a bit . . . strange. I was an only child and they always treated me like an adult from a young age. I was more like a roommate than their child. Mostly they seemed annoyed about having to care for this small person in their house — and I was smaller than most, a weakling. On good days they just ignored me, but on bad days my mum would get into these rages if I did anything wrong, anything childlike. Sometimes I'd find her looking at me with such contempt. I have no idea why they decided to breed.'

He threw the banana peel in the corner and lay down next to her.

'They had these expectations. That I would be exactly like them, a little clone or something. When I told them I was doing a degree in fine arts I couldn't believe how happy they were — I was so relieved. My dad even slapped me on the back and shook my hand. "Finance is going to take you places, son," he said. When I clarified it was fine arts, not finance I'll never forget their confusion, their disappointment. Dad asked me bluntly, "What the hell's that good for?" And Mum, she was more subtle, but just as cutting. She said, "As long as you're happy Ue . . . maybe you can switch to something more practical later on eh."

'But fuck them, I'm going to show them. Prove myself through art.'

'Why? Why do you need to buy in to that? Just do it for the love of it. Do it for yourself.'

'I will. But I also want them to see me as something more than a burden.'

'You want them to be proud?'

'I guess. But more than that, I want them to respect me.'

Hinepūkohurangi said gently, 'I don't want to sound mean, but why are you so hung up? They were a bit weird and strict. Lots of parents are like that. Waiho atu. It's not worth it.'

'That's not even the worst of it. There are other things I'll never forgive them for.' She held his hand and he found courage through her touch. 'When I was a teenager I started to see things. It was voices at first. And then I began to see them, spirits. They were everywhere I went and they wanted to talk to me.'

'You're matekite. That's a gift.'

'My parents didn't think so. When I told them, they freaked out, found a psychologist to say I was schizo and then had me committed to the nearest psych ward. I was put on antipsychotics, got electroshock treatment. I was there for a year.

'The worst thing about it was that feeling of complete lack of power. I didn't have a choice. I was a puppet. I was an embarrassment, a problem that my parents wanted to hide.' He rolled over, turned his back on her.

'You have suffered for someone so young,' she said.

'Anyway, last night when you said that I was entitled, you were wrong. I don't expect anything to be handed to me on a plate. I'm going to work my guts out to succeed and I'm going to do whatever it takes. I'll show them that I'm a force.'

'Hoea tō waka,' she said quietly. 'But be careful.'

'Anyway, I'm tired. Let's go to sleep.' Her arms wrapped around him from behind. He felt protected, understood.

'Kairoro,' her breath was warm at his ear. 'Do you still see kēhua?'

'No,' he said, his voice carrying a sadness he couldn't hide. 'But sometimes I still feel things. Like at the plaza. There was something powerful there once . . .' He felt her arms holding him even tighter then, as he fell asleep.

From his dreams he could hear the birds begin to sing and Hinewai calling from outside the cottage. When Uenuku rolled over Hinepūkohurangi was already gone. The spot where she had been was still warm. The ache from the separation was there, but it was manageable.

Getting up for a shower he found a note on top of his jeans.

He read it in his head, with her voice.

'Don't tell anyone about me. I'll have to leave this realm and never come back. Seriously. OK? Promise me. Hei tēnei pō. xx.'

Of course she didn't have anything to worry about. He was great at keeping secrets.

For many weeks they followed the same routine. Hinepūkohurangi would come after dusk and they would make love. Then they would talk, eat, watch TV, fuck some more — in bed, on the couch and sometimes, her favourite, in the steamy shower. He took her into the darkroom while he developed photos for the upcoming show. He showed her how to make photograms using objects they found around the house. She was a quick learner. They did such mundane things that sometimes he forgot that she wasn't just a regular girlfriend.

One night Uenuku suggested they go out. They could meet up with some of his workmates, the other assistants from the City Gallery. They were beginning to tease him about how he didn't have a girlfriend. If they only knew about the goddess he shared his bed with maybe they'd stop being such dicks.

'Kāo. It's too risky. You can tell them about me later.'

'When?' he asked.

'Later.'

He tickled her feet. 'Maybe you can wear a disguise . . . maybe some sunglasses and a moustache,' he said.

'Ha ha. Don't think so,' she said. 'Moustaches make me sneeze.' She wrinkled her nose.

'Seriously. Why not now? I want to show you off.'

'It's just the way it is. The way of my people. Maybe once we have a pēpē,' she said, giving him a sideways glance.

'A baby? It's a bit early to be talking about kids isn't it? I'm not sure I even want one yet.'

'You will.'

'You don't know that.'

'You'll be better at parenting than your own mātua, if that's what you're worried about.'

'I'm not. Maybe there's just too many kids in the world already,' he said.

'There will be room for ours.'

He smiled a little. He quite liked the way that sounded. Ours. Our kid. Or kids.

'Too right. I'll be a fucking awesome dad,' he said, mostly to himself.

Hinepūkohurangi grinned at him, 'Āe. The best.'

That night they pumped the stereo and danced through the house, ate takeaways and fucked in the shower.

The exhibition was two weeks away. He was finding it hard to focus, to decide what to show. He rang to schedule a meeting with the director of the gallery, Katie, to discuss which work he needed to print, mat and frame.

'It's a bit late in the piece isn't it?' she said over the phone.

'I've been a bit busy.'

'With what? Or should I ask, with whom?'

He met her in the gallery after hours. She was in her mid-fifties and wore skin-tight black jeans, a tit-hugging black T-shirt, black leather boots, rectangular thick-rimmed glasses — also black. Mutton dressed as lamb, he thought. Black lamb. The only colourful thing she wore was a gigantic plastic red tiki. Her dyed-jet hair was tightly pulled back into a sleek ponytail. Her face was severe but attractive. Several raised moles were dotted about her face and for some reason he always seemed drawn to the one on the side of her nose when they spoke.

She was whip smart — a straight shooter who cut through the shit. He found her intimidating but mostly annoying. He only tolerated her because she was the owner of one of the most influential galleries in the country. He spread out the twenty contact prints he had made with something close to dread. The images of urban nightscapes had taken months to plan and shoot. She flicked through them quickly, occasionally pursing her lips. Finally she looked up at him over the rim of her glasses.

'Uenuku, honestly, you can do better than this. Something is distracting you.' She shot him a look with her piercing blue eyes. His attention went to the mole.

'We've talked about this before. You've got the talent to be Aotearoa's new indigenous art star. The next Michael Parekōwhai.'

She flicked a print she was holding onto the table for effect. 'But this series is just pedestrian. Art-student quality. It's a fail. I'm sorry, but it's true.'

You're not sorry, he thought. He looked out the window at the people in the street below. Happy people. Carefree. People enjoying the last of the sun's rays without worries about fucking upcoming shows.

'You need to quickly come up with something else. Something deeper. More shocking. Shake me out of my stupor. Surprise me. Open my eyes.'

He couldn't even speak. His anger and disappointment choked him. Instead he silently gathered up the contact prints and put them back into their folder. His hands were shaking again. There was so much riding on this show. He'd fucked up big time. He should have listened to Hinepūkohurangi.

The folder slipped out of his hands as he tried to stuff it into his backpack, and the contact sheets scattered onto the floor. The one print he hadn't shown her, the one from the first night he met Hinepūkohurangi, landed on top of the pile and Katie picked it up before he could.

'Now this is interesting. Who is she?'

'She's nobody.' He reached for the print but she jerked it out of his reach.

'She's my girlfriend,' he said feebly.

'There's something about her . . . I can't put my finger on it. She doesn't seem real.'

She's more real than you, you fake bitch. He wanted to say it so badly his tongue almost itched with the words.

'Where's she from?'

'Up north, the far far north. The islands . . . Yeah, she's um . . . PI.'

'No she's not.'

He stood there, stunned.

'Excuse me?' he said. What the fuck. Who does this woman think she is? He reached over and snatched the print and stuffed it roughly into his pack. Smashing it back in.

'She's Atua.'

Uenuku stopped midway through zipping the bag.

'I can tell,' she continued, 'because I've met one before myself, many years ago. A male one. I'll tell you about it over a beer sometime. Best — sex — ever.'

Uenuku wanted to puke.

'But listen, Ue. May I call you Ue? This is a gift. This is exactly what we need.'

'We?'

'You, I mean. Listen, do you see her frequently?'

'What business is it of yours?'

She exploded then and he actually flinched as she yelled, 'It's my fucking business because THIS is my fucking business, you twerp!!!' She gestured around the office, towards the gallery. 'I've got a shit-load riding on your little debutant show and I need you to come through with the goods!'

The better half of Uenuku wanted to spit in her face and run away, but something else was fighting that. A mixture of survival instinct and pride. His precious ego. He sat down on a swivel chair, defeated. He spoke quietly.

'She comes to me every night and she leaves before dawn. She can't stay in our world in the daytime,' he said. It almost felt good to be talking about her.

Katie listened. She was looking out the window, tapping her chin with a finger. He could almost hear the cogs turning. The synapses firing. He imagined a tiny devil dancing on her shoulder, whispering in her ear.

Finally she said, 'This is great material. People love the "other". Brown folk are hot right now. And you've got yourself a hot brown goddess. She's like a supermodel. She's a supermodel with super-powers. The viewers will eat that shit up.' She thought some more and then shot him a triumphant and hungry look, like she was about to eat his first-born child.

'Right, I've got it. We invite a select few attendees, VIPs, trustees and members of the gallery — exclusive types — to come to your house to view her. In your bed preferably. It could be a statement about everyday life meeting the sublime, the ordinary colliding with the gods, reality intersecting with spirit. We'll guarantee a life-changing experience. All you have to do is make sure that your lover doesn't leave. Fill in the chinks around the windows and doors. Paint the windows . . . whatever it takes. I'll leave that up to you. The main thing is to make sure she doesn't leave before the audience arrives.'

'That's nuts. I can't do that. I love her. I'm not just going to exploit her like that.'

'Yes, yes. Very earnest. Honourable. Fuck all that romantic crap! The stakes are too high. You can't afford to bring emotion into this. This is what you've wanted all along right? Fame. Attention. Respect. You'll get all that if you do this.'

He shook his head. This woman was mentally unstable.

Uenuku didn't commit to anything.

She touched his arm lightly as he made his way out, braying in an overly friendly voice, 'I'll call you soon to sort out the details. It's going to be so good, Ue. Really good. Remember — brown is the new black.' Then she got right into his bubble with her coffee breath, clinging on his arm. 'Your life is about to change my friend.'

He left. The darkness in his chest was spreading through his veins like Indian ink on a paper towel. At the bus stop he spewed in the gutter.

After Hinepūkohurangi left the next morning he texted Katie to tell her he didn't want to go through with the plan. She rang him straight away on his cell phone. She didn't mention the text.

'Good news. I had Kaden my PA ring around to all our people immediately after I saw you yesterday. Tix were priced at $1000 each and will come with a signed, limited-edition print — the one I saw yesterday with your lady muse. All 100 sold easily. Well done. Our guests will arrive at your house just after 8 a.m. on Saturday.'

'I don't want to do it,' Uenuku said.

'Well, you don't have much choice now . . . You'll make us look fucking stupid. My reputation is on the line. You do this and you'll be the next choice for the Venice Biennale for sure.'

Uenuku's grip on the phone was making his hand ache.

'Oh, and I went ahead and gave two free tickets to your parents. I knew you'd like them to be there. I told them that it will be the most talked-about art show in years to come. They said they'd be there to support you.'

Uenuku hung up on her then. Well played, you clever cunt. There would be no backing down now.

The night before the show, or happening, or whatever it had become, Uenuku was quiet. They were sitting together on the sofa, she had her long legs draped over his.

'Ki a koe rā hoki. Have I done something wrong?'

'No, no. It's just me. I'm just feeling hōhā. I'll get over it.'

'OK, because if I said or did something you'd tell me right?'

'Yeah, I would. Don't worry. I'm fine.'

They made love then, right there, but for the first time since they met, his cock kept getting soft.

'Something is definitely up,' she said, 'and it's not your ure.'

'Har fucking har,' he said. He rubbed at his limp dick absently.

'Sorry, that was poor taste,' she said.

'I'm just tired and stressed. My show opens tomorrow, remember.'

'He iti te hau marangai, e tū te pāhokahoka. Don't worry. You will knock their stupid white tennis socks off,' she said.

She tried stroking his cock, but he gently pushed her hand away.

He attempted a weak smile. 'Let's just get some sleep.'

As soon as he heard her breathing even out, he crept to where he had hidden all the supplies he needed. He used duct tape to cover the windows with blackout fabric he'd bought from the curtain shop. Then he used rags to fill in holes around the window and under the door. For good measure he changed the digital alarm clock by the bed, turning it back a few hours.

He settled on the bed beside her and watched her sleep until his own eyes closed. He woke when the first tūī in the kōwhai outside began to chant. Hinepūkohurangi began to stir too. She sleepily rubbed her eyes and stretched.

'Strange. I thought I heard the tūī sing.'

'It must be confused. It's still early.' He tapped the alarm clock. 'Look, it's only 3 a.m.'

Then Hinewai's voice could be heard outside. Hinepūkohurangi sat bolt upright.

'Hinewai, she's calling me.' She began to rise from the bed.

Uenuku panicked. 'Lie down! Now! For fuck's sake woman. Stop being so fucking paranoid.' He grabbed her arm and pulled her down onto the bed.

For some strange reason she didn't get up. Perhaps it was the shock of his treatment. She lay there, staring at the ceiling instead.

Hinewai's call became more persistent. The tone became more and more distraught, until it became a karanga of grief. Eventually her deep, resonant voice rose and disappeared.

Uenuku relaxed a little then. He held Hinepūkohurangi gently and stroked her face.

'You're only dreaming, silly. That wasn't your sister you heard. Just go to sleep, eh.'

Her eyes began to flicker and she nodded. Her lids closed. She squeezed his hand in hers — trusting.

When she woke again, Uenuku was already dressed, watching her in the dark. This time the birds outside in the trees were singing loudly — all of them. There were murmurs of a large crowd of people gathering too. Uenuku didn't stop her getting up this time. She came towards him and, at first, he thought she was going to hit him. He cringed, waiting for the slap. Instead, she reached inside the front pocket of his hoody where he kept his cell phone. She flipped it open. 8:14 a.m.

'Kāo, kāo, kāo!' she cried. She went to the window and pulled back the curtain. Saw the fabric stuck to the windows. 'No, please, no!' she whispered.

She walked to the door leading to the veranda. She stopped, turned and looked at him. Really looked.

He had seen that look before. On his mother's face twenty years ago. But there were other feelings there in her eyes too. Sadness. Betrayal. So much hurt.

'Kei te aroha au ki a koe, you stupid little man. He aha ai???' She didn't wait to hear his answer.

Turning the doorknob, she flung the door open. The light streamed into the room, illuminating her naked body. She stepped out into it, her head held high.

The viewers had arrived at the gallery at 7 a.m. Katie had Kaden set up champagne with strawberries, cheese and croissants and ham off the bone cut into delicate slices. They were given their limited-edition print and a map to Uenuku's house. There was a buzz in the room. A vibe that this was going to be a special day. Katie made a small speech telling everyone to expect to see aesthetic beyond their comprehension. Their world would shift. Open up.

There was a shuttle on offer, but still many people walked. A few drove. They gathered quietly in groups around the cottage. Anticipation made many of them rock back and forth on their feet, shifting weight. Katie melted into the background and watched the audience from the back.

At 8:15 the door opened and a woman stepped out. Not a woman, a goddess. There were gasps. Some held up their cell phones, clicking furiously. One person fainted.

The goddess was truly exceptional. Her proportions were perfect, golden. With the sun shining on her she glowed. She raised her arms and gathered something around her out of the air — droplets of water. They began to collect and swirl around her, covering her nakedness. Then she began to rise, a brown Botticelli. She rested a moment on the roof of the cottage, crouching near the painted finial. A cool fog began to descend into the valley.

She called down to them. Her voice rang across the courtyard. The birds in the kōwhai were silent. 'What is the truth? What is manipulated? What you crave is the aesthetic, the light flickering on Plato's cave. Projections. You are blind, ego-driven and false! These shadows won't last.' Then she directed her gaze at Uenuku, who stood there with tears streaking down his face. Her mists turned to a smouldering grey, a smog. 'True and infinite love was right in front of you and you squandered it. You didn't play by the rules and these are the consequences. We could have been a beautiful whānau. You blew it Uenuku. E kore a muri e hokia.'

Katie looked over at Uenuku, his face collapsing as he heard the word family and saw the way Hinepūkohurangi held her belly protectively. He moaned, comprehension washing over him — she was carrying their unborn child. Too late, too late. His face showed that he would never see the baby or her again. Uenuku quite lost his shit then.

He supplicated to begin with, 'Come down! I'm sorry. Please! Come back!'

Then he tried scaling the veranda. Grabbed for the sagging roof. It crumpled. The whole thing fell around him in a heap, leaving him covered in timber and rotting debris. His parents self-consciously stepped forward to help him. Uenuku spat at them, his eyes wild, rolling around in his head, unfocused. His parents backed away, scared.

It was quite uncomfortable watching all this, fascinating. Katie almost felt guilty for instigating it. Almost. Not quite.

Suddenly, Hinepūkohurangi broke out in karanga and the hair on Katie's head and neck prickled. The air shimmered around them as the words rose and fell. Hinepūkohurangi sang in her ancient Atua language and the words were like warm oil entering their ears, trickling down inside to their chests. The vibrational frequency of her voice began opening up the realm to her homeland above.

And then, when she was done, without a glance back, she rose into the sky towards her waiting family. Evaporated.

Those who heard Hinepūkohurangi that day were blessed. Her song was a fast track to ascension. Their hearts split open and the film over their eyes was wiped clear. They became awakened. Katie reached up to the clearing sky and smiled. She beamed at those around her. They smiled back, joyful tears overflowing.

Everywhere, everywhere, love and light.

Uenuku was impervious to the song. He made to leave. His parents tried to reason with him, begged him to stay. With their new insight, they could finally understand how badly they had hurt him. His mother even laid down on the ground at his feet to show how much she truly loved him. He walked right over her and out the gate. He never saw them again.

He searched for Hinepūkohurangi. He scaled the mist-cloaked ranges of the Ureweras, trudged through the brumous spray of West Coast beaches, sat for days near waterfalls in the remote Catlins, breathed in the toxic steam of White Island. And he returned again and again to the plaza where they met.

His back bent and his hair turned white, and yet still he looked. With age, he began to look more deeply. He meditated for days, his body almost turning to stone, to dust.

His longing became a tunnel, a gate, back and forth through time, through light. Time was no barrier to his yearning. He was a time traveller, fuelled by hope and desire.

He kept on looking.

One day, he reached so far back with his mind, Ranginui saw this feeble soul and took pity on him. He knew how it felt to be torn away from the one who owns your heart.

He transformed Uenuku into his fullest potentiality — pulled from him the colours that were always inside him; the latent spectrum. Water droplets dispersed and reflected. A bridge appeared. Spanning time and space.

Finally he would be near her again. They could be together. Into the infinite.

CHAPTER 7
KUPE

———

Kuramārōtini

———

Waka 86

———

Kuramārōtini

BY BRIAR WOOD

So the story goes
that trickster Kupe
cheated his friend
into diving overboard
to free the lines
then paddled rapidly away.

Some hoa.
Best to know that
legendary navigators take huge risks
and do not make the safest companions.

Ākuanei —
she asked herself —
what do I want —
home in Hawaiki
or the travelling years?

What does he want —
the waka my father gifted?
Matahourua and me?

Or maybe unhappiness
with the man she'd married
drove her to the coast.
It's possible —
she was curious and Hoturapa wasn't
the kind of man who liked a journey
so she chose Kupe.

Yet even an inveterate traveller
might become weary in a waka
on the open sea,
looking out for landfall.

Travelling direct to her destination —
as the future loomed towards her
she named that radiant land
on the horizon
Aotearoa.

Waka 86

BY ROBERT SULLIVAN

I am Kupe. I have the credit for finding
this new land, the parts of which

I named with parts of me, including
my son — I have left my son here,

the gods were appeased.
My soul will never forget this.

I have been quoted many times,
e hoki a Kupe? Did Kupe return?

The saying is meant to politely
refuse a request. But I do

return to this land. Thoughts
I placed here keep returning

to my ears. I am sorry
for correcting the saying,

but I have been returning
for a very long time now.

the sea to the land

CHAPTER 8
FROM THE SEA

———

A Story from the Sea

———

Shapeshifter

———

A Story from the Sea

BY WITI IHIMAERA

WHAKAPAPA OF A TOHORĀ

In the wrenching of power into their own hands, the six main architects of the Māori world soon found themselves at odds with their own ambitions of what to do with it.

Tānemahuta, Tangaroa, Rongomātāne and Haumiatiketike had finally separated their parents, Ranginui the sky above from Papatūānuku the earth below.

But Tāwhirimātea had loved his father and followed him up to the sky. From there he sent winds and hurricanes upon Tānemahuta's many forest kingdoms, and storms across the sea so violent that Tangaroa took refuge in the deepest depths below. The children of Rongomātāne and Haumiatiketike found themselves uprooted in Tāwhirimātea's cyclones.

As for Tūmatauenga, the sixth brother, he had proposed murdering the parents. There was no love lost therefore for his brothers, so he waged war on all of them.

Within this vicious maelstrom, even the brothers who had supported the separation fell out with each other. For instance, Tangaroa in his haste to escape Tāwhirimātea's cyclonic temper had left his children, the fish and ngārara to fend for themselves; the fish sought sanctuary in the sea but the lizards decided they would be safer within Tānemahuta's forests. Tangaroa therefore turned on Tānemahuta, sending the fish to fight against the reptiles in a long and bitter war. Similarly, the sea birds were eventually to wage war against the forest birds for sovereignty over land and sea; an uneasy truce established the boundaries between them — manu moana the sea birds and manu whenua the birds of the land.

Nobody knows how long the battles lasted to determine who would dominate and who wouldn't but, eventually, the six gods — aided by other god brothers numbering some seventy or so — began to lay the foundations for Te Ao Tūroa, the world of incandescent light between.

Ika-roa set about giving birth to the stars of the Milky Way. Uenuku began to fill the world with rainbows. Haumiatiketike went about the business of ensuring the flourishing of the fern root.

The gods also began to contract with one another. For instance, Tangaroa appointed the triad of Kiwa, Rona and Kaukau to assist his sovereign rule: Kiwa to be guardian of the southern ocean, Rona to help control the tides and Kaukau to aid the welfare of the sea's denizens. To the triad, two other gods, Takaaho and Te Pū-whakahara, brought a special suit: their offspring had been given lakes to live in, but they preferred to roam the freedom of the sea. The suit was accepted, and this was how sharks and whales were granted habitation of the ocean.

From the very beginning the whale was grateful for this release and this was why the whale family, the Wehenga kauiki, became known as the helpers of men lost at sea. Why? Because humankind and whales — as well as forests — had the same godparent in Tānemahuta.

Whenever asked, therefore, the whale would attend the call, as long as the mariner possessed the necessary authority and knew the way of talking to whales.

A PRINCE OF HAWAIKI

One of the people who called the whale was a young man named Paikea.

His name was Kahutia Te Rangi, and his story is but one of a number that come from a sea of stories — so many narratives of gods, monsters and men that arise from the great ocean of our ancestors.

He was the first-born son of Uenuku, one of the chiefs of Hawaiki. His brother, Ruatapu, was jealous of him and wanted to kill him. He planned to do this by taking Kahutia Te Rangi and the sons from other royal houses of Hawaiki out in a sea-going waka, and scuttling it.

However, as the waka foundered and Ruatapu swam among the princes clubbing them, a whale lifted Kahutia Te Rangi up and carried him to safety, swimming for many days and nights. It did not head back to Hawaiki though. Instead, it carried Kahutia Te Rangi southward on its migratory journey around the great Southern Ocean, heading for the rich krill feeding grounds at the bottom of the world.

Sometimes the seas and skies were calm. At other times there were fierce storms, mountainous waves, heavy rain and dark skies split by thunder and jagged lightning. Kahutia Te Rangi continued his karakia, however, and, early one morning, as the star Poutūterangi (Altair) appeared over a far distant mountain arising from the sea (Mount Hikurangi, 1756 metres high, the first place on the earth's surface to greet the sun every morning), he realised that the whale had brought him to a land only rumoured about in Hawaiki. This was the fabled, bounteous country of great beauty and richness called Aotearoa.

This is only one of the many versions of the whale rider story.

In another version Kahutia Te Rangi is described as not only a royal son of Hawaiki but also a man who, by mystical powers, could transform himself into a taniwha, a tipua, a whale even — operating fluidly between his human form and his ocean form.

And, why should we not believe this? After all, Hawaiki was a paradisiacal land, a Polynesian Eden, half real, half unreal, where man walked with the gods and communed with beasts, birds, forests and all animate and inanimate things.

In this version, the murderous Ruatapu pursued Kahutia Te Rangi to Aotearoa. It must have been a thrilling sea chase. Ruatapu summoned up a series of five tidal waves and sent them ahead of him, but Kahutia Te Rangi managed to get ashore and change back into his human form before they were able to swamp him. The waves then recoiled, returning to their source, where they overwhelmed he who had sent them — and so Ruatapu went to his watery grave. The local people say that if you come to Whangarā in September you can still see these tidal waves breaking on the shore.

There are many other variants to the story. Some say that Kahutia Te Rangi and Paikea were two different people; and the narrative concerning Paikea and his brother, Ruatapu, is still disputed. Others say the reason Kahutia Te Rangi was able to call on a whale to rescue him, or even to change into a whale, was because his genealogy connected him to beasts of the sea — to the porpoise and Portuguese man-of-war and, in particular, to large whales, including pike-nosed whales.

Another variation tells that Kahutia Te Rangi had to leave a wife and a son, Rongomai Tuaho, in Hawaiki when he eluded Ruatapu. Many years later, pining for his father, Rongomai Tuaho sent a magic bailer to Aotearoa to ascertain if his father was still alive. Another strand of the whale rider story is that the island you see close by the beach at Whangarā — Te Ana a Paikea — is the whale itself, transformed into a rock. You can reach the island at low tide, but at high tide in winter a stormy channel separates it from the mainland.

TE KAIEKE TOHORĀ

Third there was a story that began at Whangarā.

In the old days, in the days that have gone before us, the land and sea were without life, without vivacity. The tuatara, the ancient lizard with its third eye, was sentinel here, unblinking in the hot sun, watching and waiting to the east. The moa browsed in giant wingless herds across the southern island. Within the warm stomach of the rainforests, kiwi, weka and the other birds foraged for huhu and similar succulent insects. The forests were loud with the clatter of tree bark, the chatter of cicada and the murmur of fish-laden streams.

Sometimes the forests grew suddenly quiet and in wet bush could be heard the delicate sound of fairy laughter like sparkling glissandi.

The sea, too, teemed with fish but they also seemed to be waiting. They swam in brilliant shoals, like rains of glittering dust, throughout the greenstone depths — hāpuku, mangā, kahawai, tāmure, moki and warehou — herded by shark or mangō ururoa.

At other times, from far off, a white shape would be seen flying through the sea, but it would only be the serene flight of the tarawhai, the stingray with the spike on its tail. Waiting. Waiting for the seeding. Waiting for the gifting. Waiting for the blessing to come. Suddenly, the fish began to see the dark bellies of the canoes from the east. The first of the Ancients were coming, journeying from their island kingdom beyond the horizon.

Then, after a period, canoes were seen to be returning to the east, making long cracks on the surface sheen. The land and the sea sighed with gladness:

We have been found.
The news is being taken back to the place of the Ancients.
Our blessing will come soon.

In that waiting time, earth and sea began to feel the sharp pangs of need, for an end to the yearning. The forests sent sweet perfumes upon the eastern winds and garlands of pōhutukawa upon the eastern tides. The sea flashed continuously with flying fish, leaping high to look beyond the horizon and to be the first to announce the coming. In the shallows, the chameleon seahorses pranced at attention. The only reluctant ones were the fairy people who retreated with their silver laughter to caves in glistening waterfalls.

The sun rose and set, rose and set. Then one day, at its noon apex, the first sighting was made. Something spouting on the horizon. Then a dark shape rising from the greenstone depths of the ocean, a leviathan breaching through the surface and hurling itself skyward before falling seaward again. Underwater the muted thunder boomed like a great door opening far away, and both sea and land trembled from the impact of that downward plunging.

Suddenly the sea was filled with awesome singing, a song with eternity in it, a song to the land:

You have called and I have come,
bearing the gift of the gods.

The dark shape rising, and rising again. A whale, gigantic. A sea monster. Just as it burst through the sea, a flying fish leaping high in its ecstasy saw water and air streaming like thunderous foam from that noble beast and knew, ah yes, that the time had come.

The sacred sign was there, on the monster, a swirling moko pattern imprinted on the forehead.

Then, the flying fish saw that astride the head, as it broke skyward, was a man. He was wondrous to look upon. The water streamed away from him and he opened his mouth to gasp in the cold air. His eyes were shining with splendour. His body dazzled with diamond spray. Upon that beast he looked like a small tattooed figurine, dark brown, glistening and erect. He seemed, with all his strength, to be pulling the whale into the sky.

At that moment, when the boy breaks through the skin of sea, when he looks up through the sea and anticipates the whale leaping through it and into the sky, mythology blends with prose, fantasy with reality, past with present. And pūrākau begin to occupy a place between the real and the unreal, the natural and the supernatural.

Joins then with now.

Us with the whale rider.

Shapeshifter

BY TINA MAKERETI

Sometimes I think men just take what they want. See that fella over there? The one with the eyes like icy water and a puku that sticks out from his middle like he's swallowed a boulder? He just came up here before and kissed my tit. Got his wife to take a picture. Ha ha, look at me, I'm kissing Pānia's boob. Like that hasn't been done before. Jeez, you'd think they'd have a bit more class. I must've been felt up by half the country.

I've got nice boobs, the way they did me. Of course I'd still prefer the soft, fleshy kind at the end of the day. Wouldn't stand up to all that touching though. Good thing they did me in bronze. I've got nice legs too. I'm particularly proud of those.

Fifty-four this year and hardly any wear and tear on the old body. Which sounds like a good thing, but isn't so great for me in the long run. There are a lot of stories around about what I am and who I am, and how I got here. Some say I am really the reef out there; that I provide all the fish for the people, for my descendants. Some say I used to be a selkie, a seal-person who needed both sea and land to live. Some say that my family forced me back into the ocean, but others know it was my husband Karitoki's trickery that sent me back there. There is a little bit of true in all those stories. People find it hard to hold in their heads: that it can be this way *and* that way. That at one time I took on the skin and swiftness of the seal underwater, that I married an earthly man, that I became the reef. My spirit is as malleable as the shifting sand on the ocean floor.

The people loved me, for generations, so much so that they cast me in bronze, not knowing. Not knowing that it would attract me — this molten form of my body they made from their imaginations. The rising heat and lick of it — an element I'd never tasted before — a metallic swell that begged for my presence. Oh yes, I went there, all the way to the workshop in Italy, swept up in their excitement. I played in the bronze liquid, giggled as the bubbles popped and sizzled, delighted in it as it cooled. Then came a new feeling, a cold smoothness, not unpleasant, elegant. My new form was beautiful. I was taken back to Napier, and much admired. Though when I grew bored with this new game, I decided to return home as I had always done.

Have you ever had one of those bad dreams where you know it isn't real, and you know that all you have to do is open your eyes or move your finger to wake up, so you use your mind to try and make this happen, but you can't? Sometimes you imagine yourself awake, only to realise it's a dream within a dream. You keep sleeping, struggling against the confines of your mind, struggling to wake your inert body. This is how it has been for me, ever since the metal cooled and I realised I wanted to go home. I hear the people who come to see me say, 'Oh, they have really captured her spirit.' Nobody knows, this is exactly what happened.

What's a girl to do? I've always been one to make the best of a bad situation. Since I couldn't wipe the smile off my face, I thought I might as well go along with things, enjoy the fame. On the days I yearned to move my limbs and feel the waves against my skin, I thought of Karitoki, and couldn't help wondering if this wasn't some sort of utu for the way we parted.

The thing with Karitoki was he always wanted more. It wasn't enough that I gave myself to him at night. I loved every part of that man. Steamed up the place, we did. But I never saw the rest of his people. And he wanted everyone to meet the hot chick he'd scored. He didn't want me to go back to the ocean before sunrise.

'Look,' I said, 'these are the rules — I can be yours at night only. If I don't return to the sea, I'll die.'

Did he listen? Course not. He went to the tohunga to beg for tricks to keep me earth-bound. When I woke to him sneaking food past my lips I couldn't believe it.

'You would risk my life for this?' I said to him. 'To show me off to your mates?' And I stormed off, never to return, so that he was forever the loser with an imaginary girlfriend.

Look now. He is gone and I am forever on display — Karitoki's woman.

———

Apart from the odd fondle, the people treat me well. I have my regular visitors. There's one old fella who's been coming here for years. He likes to sit by my side and look out at the sea, and he talks to me. Once a year he comes early in the morning, when the moon is just setting, and those times he wears a uniform with medals on the front. He told me one day that I remind him of his first wife, another time that he thought it strange we had both been to Italy, the last place you'd expect to see two Māoris like us.

'I was there before you, my dear,' he said, 'but you would not have liked the Italy I saw. It was an ugly place.' Then he laughed a dry laugh that was more sadness than joy. 'I understand why people say it is beautiful. The land and ocean are almost as stunning as our own. I could not see any of that while I was there, of course. At first I was so homesick I could only see all the things that were not home. And I hated those things. After that, when we were at the front, well, that is a slow nightmare from which you cannot wake.'

Sometimes when he started talking like that he would touch my hand or hold my knee. Not in a rude way, more as reassurance. His hands were lined and bumpy like a map showing where rivers and mountains lie.

'I was nineteen,' he said, 'quite filled out for my age. But my mate Joseph, he still looked like a boy. Wide shoulders, but skinny. He needed a few more years to grow into his frame. We called him Twigs.' He has a walking stick, my soldier. Likes to tap it on the ground to punctuate his words, or wave it around when he gets really agitated. It is carved, a fierce tekoteko on top, notches and spirals that tell his story all the way down. He bangs it now. 'Twigs never left Italy.'

This man I understand. He holds himself proud, especially in that uniform. Most of all, I like that he talks to me as if he sees me: not my bronze shell, but my trapped watery spirit. He makes sure to look in the same direction that I am forced to gaze, and always comments on what he sees there.

'Ah! The clouds are magnificent today,' he will say, 'one never gets tired of this sky.'

Fortunately, this is true.

It's on one of these mornings he comes to me and says, 'I won't be able to come here anymore, love. The whānau want me home and I'm too old to fight them. The time has come, eh?'

The wind here can be wicked. It whips up around us, causing his hat to come loose. He reaches for it, and almost falls in his effort to grab the thing before it flies away. Readjusting it on his head, he takes out his handkerchief to wipe his eyes. They are bleary, moisture escaping from the corners. I cannot tell if this is because of the wind or something else. He walks around me, using his hands to guide himself around my form. If only I was an old woman, I could link my arm through his and go with him . . .

'Look at that,' he says, 'look at the black clouds in that red sky.

Was a sky like that we woke to the last morning I saw Twigs alive. You know it's not going to be a good day when you wake with that heavy feeling in your gut. That heavy feeling that chases you through your sleep, chases away your appetite. And then if that's the sky you wake to, well, you start to have very strange thoughts.' He leans his back against me, his backside propped on my foundation. Then he extends his arms forward, one hand on top of the other on top of the walking stick.

'Sorry to be a morbid sod, old girl.' Look who he's calling old. 'It's a terrible thing, when a boy like that dies. Just before the life goes out of them, just before they turn into that thing that is just a body with no spirit in it, they look like babies. I saw that with Twigs. I was with him right at the end. His eyes got big and then they closed and I watched the struggle in his face, and just at the moment he let go I thought — I bet he looked like this when he was a baby in his mother's arms. I didn't know I was right until my own babies were born and I couldn't look at them without seeing my mate.'

He has stopped wiping the tears now; he lets them run. 'Sometimes I couldn't be around my children because of that. I went to the pub instead. Let the missus take care of them. She looked like you, you know, did I ever tell you? I couldn't tell her, couldn't explain. What could I have said? It wasn't because I didn't care. It scared me silly, seeing Twigs in my own kids. Made me want to rip up the place, have a go at anyone who came near. I wanted to go back and kill again when that happened.

'So I just stayed away.'

He is quiet for some time after this. It is a good silence between us. He gives my knee a friendly rub. 'I will miss you. E noho rā.'

Then he walks away. Slow, deliberate steps. Halfway to the street he turns to me, salutes.

By the time the sun has warmed my bronze skin I have been photographed twice by tourists and petted several times by affectionate locals. It is a day like any other, clouds rolling in and scattering along the coast, the ocean green, then blue, then grey and choppy. A taste of salt and seaweed blows in from the water, stinging my nostrils and settling on my lips. I daydream I am floating in a kelp bed again, warmed by the alchemy of sun and water. At dusk I think of my old soldier and feel emptier than I ever have before. As darkness folds itself over the day, I see myself clearly — a metal husk, no companion for men of flesh and pulsing blood.

But there are worse things in this world. Me and Karitoki trying to one-up each other over aeons of time? What does it matter? We had our war, but people come here and all they see is the love. A beautiful Māori love story, they say. They don't know the rest of it. I have to admit — there was a whole lotta lovin'. And that evens the score a bit. Let him laugh, my husband. I'm not going anywhere for a few more aeons yet, anyway. These buggers will be swept away on some tide a thousand years from now, or maybe it'll be an earthquake or a star dropping out of the sky that'll return me to the sea.

———

'Ay Riki, there she is, there's your girly, Pānia.'

'Ooooh, Riki, is she your new girlfriend?'

'Hotter than your last girlfriend, eh bro?'

There's some high-pitched giggling at this.

'Yeah, shut up you lot. My koro said I have to look after her. S'not my idea.'

'What d'ya have to do to look after a statue?'

More giggles.

'I dunno. He said talk to her. Keep her company.'

'People are gonna think you're nuts, man.'

'Yeah, well youse can do it too.'

'Nah, why'd we wanna do that?'

'Cos I said so, that's why. Anyway, we can sing instead of talking. We can do our practice here.'

They approach me slowly, giggling, shuffling, not looking each other in the eye. Someone farts loudly and the whole group crumples laughing. Then, the boy, Riki, tells them to shut up again, begins to count off: 'tahi, rua . . .' And they sing. The song lifts me, an ancient lullaby, the notes calling me out of my shell to dance. Even though I cannot move, I lose myself for a moment — when the sea breeze hits me I am air, I am salt, and, at last, I am water.

They try to sing other songs. When they mess up the words they just hum instead. The humming is good. I don't know the songs, but they have harmony. Then, for a joke, they put my name into a song about doing it all night long. They're cheeky little thugs, but if I could make a sound, I'd be laughing. After three songs they start trailing off, lighting up smokes and opening cans. The boy, Riki, is the last to leave. He begins trailing after his mates, but turns, swiftly lifts his chin and looks straight at me.

'Laters,' he says.

Yes. I will be here. *Laters.*

CHAPTER 9
POUNAMU

———

I Have a Stone

———

Te Ara Poutini

———

I Have a Stone

BY KERI HULME

'I have a stone that once swam
ancient seas' — it lies
big eyed, gills agasp
thin as varnish on the shale
only lacquer left from life.

                              I am a fish
                              familiar of these seas
                              of deadly air and
                              I know the knife of age and

I know stone —

On this finger another ancient swimmer
flash flicker flares greenlightningblue:
you smile at my rocks
but I murmur opals; you
say ancestors and I breathe,
Bones —

Te Ara Poutini

BY NIC LOW

The monorail carried the tour group above the Arahura River, moving fast. Āhua sat with her nose hongi'ed to the glass. Her pale blue-green eyes didn't blink. Even a week into the tour, she still couldn't quite believe what she was seeing.

The carriage doors opened. 'Kia ora koutou,' a familiar voice announced.

Āhua and the other tourists turned from the windows. Tumuaki was standing in the aisle, dressed once more in his Ngāi Tahu tour guide's kiwi-feather cloak.

'Welcome to the last day of Te Ara Poutini, whānau,' he said. 'Feel free to tune out if you've heard this before, but for those who've just joined us for this final leg, gather round.'

About a third of the guests rose from their seats and clustered round Tumuaki. Āhua stayed put; she'd heard the story hundreds of times growing up.

'Our story begins in a sheltered bay on Tūhua Island in the Bay of Plenty.

'One day the guardian taniwha of pounamu, Poutini, was hiding there from his nemesis Whatipu, the guardian taniwha of grindstone. From his corner of the bay, Poutini spied a beautiful woman walking along the beach. He watched her strip naked and slip into the ocean to bathe. Poutini fell in love — or maybe it was lust.

Her name was Waitaiki, and he wanted her for himself.'

Tumuaki caught Āhua's eye and gave a small smile. She smirked.

'Poutini swam silently across the bay, and with a faint ripple, he snatched Waitaiki up and sped across the ocean with her to Tahanga on the Coromandel Peninsula. When they arrived she was freezing. Poutini lit a fire on the beach to keep her warm.

'Now, Waitaiki's husband was the powerful chief Tama-āhua. He found Waitaiki's discarded kākahu by the water, and knew something terrible had happened. He gathered his men and hurled his magic tekateka spear into the air. It hung quivering, pointing to Tahanga. They loaded their canoes and paddled to the mainland at full speed.

'When they arrived, they found the cold ashes of Poutini's fire. The taniwha had taken Waitaiki south to Whangamatā, where a new fire burned. And so a great chase began, all the way down through the North Island, and then the South Island. Poutini was finally cornered here in the Arahura at the stream we now call Waitaiki.

'Realising he could never defeat Tama-āhua in battle, Poutini hatched a desperate plan to keep his beloved close. He transformed Waitaiki into pounamu, then laid her in the river. She became the mother, and the motherlode, of greenstone. Poutini slipped out to the coast, Te Tai Poutini, where he guards her still.

'When Waitaiki's husband Tama-āhua arrived he grieved over his wife's cold and lifeless form. Before heading home, he named two mountains. The first, which you'll see out the right hand windows in about a minute, is Tūhua, named after their island home. The second is Tama-āhua, named for himself so he could watch over Waitaiki. The great chief then returned to Tūhua, where he remarried, and his descendants . . .'*

---

* Adapted from Tipene O'Regan, *He kōrero pūrākau mo ngā taunahanahatanga a ngā tūpuna: Place names of the ancestors*. Wellington: New Zealand Geographic Board, 1990, pp. 83–84.

'. . . *dreamed of revenge*,' Āhua thought.

The twenty-eight-year-old martial arts expert returned her gaze to the window, looking down at the enormous taniwha scrambling up the riverbed below. Poutini's scales glowed dark green against the wet stone. As he leapt from pool to pool his claws struck sparks off the boulders and dislodged small trees. His movements were part lizard, part fish, and wholly real. A naked woman with obsidian-dark hair clung to his back.

Āhua had been on the luxury tour for a week now, following Poutini and Waitaiki on their mythical journey south. She'd grown tired of her fellow tourists — mostly Ngāi Tahu from the east coast metropolises — but since the first day at Tūhua Resort, when Poutini's nostrils and gleaming eyes had surfaced from the bay, the taniwha hadn't gotten any less magical.

'Realistic, isn't he?'

Āhua looked up from the window again. Tumuaki was watching her with quick brown eyes.

'Realistic?' she said with a broad grin. 'I was just thinking he looks magical. Grab a seat.'

Tumuaki settled into the leather recliner opposite. For a moment they studied each other. He was young, perhaps twenty-two, with an athlete's slim muscular build. She let her gaze drift to the faint smile on his inked lips, remembering their taste from last night.

They both turned to the window, suddenly shy. Āhua watched Waitaiki's naked figure crouched low on Poutini's back, rolling her hips to match the creature's gait.

'I still can't believe it's all robotics,' she murmured.

'Even better than the real thing,' Tumuaki said. 'The finale this afternoon will blow your mind.'

'Already blown,' she said, and he had the decency to blush.

'You done any other Ngāi Tahu tourism trips?' he asked.

'I'd love to go whale watching.'

'They sighted a real whale last week.'

She grinned at him. 'Bullshit.'

He grinned back. 'Maybe they're robots, maybe they're not. But you could try our *Luminaries* tour while you're here on the coast. We've rebuilt Hokitika as a perfect replica of the book.'

'I'd rather go do *The Bone People* in Okarito. I've always loved Keri Hulme.'

'Me too. Maybe we could . . .'

Āhua's phone chimed.

It's time, her kaitiaki spoke in her ear.

'Excuse me,' she said. 'I'll be right back.'

Āhua walked down the aisle, feeling Tumuaki's eyes on her back. She passed through the boutique car with its softly lit cabinets of carved pounamu, then paused at the huge window outside the day spa.

The monorail had slowed to give them a good look at Poutini climbing the waterfall into the narrow, steep-sided second gorge. He moved swiftly, claws gripping the enormous jumbled stone blocks. The blue river surged off his back in billowing sprays. At the top he stood with the river pouring between his legs and turned to look back down the valley, watching for Waitaiki's husband Tama-āhua.

The door at the end of the corridor hissed open. A man in his late forties in travelling clothes — thatched cape, gaiters, pāraerae sandals — came and stood casually next to her at the window looking out. He was short, heavily built and compact, his movements as economical as her own. Deep hand-tapped tā moko of Ngāi Tahu design and rank framed his handsome face. He wore a tour pin on the lapel of his cape, but he hadn't been on the tour until today.

'Ko wai koe?' she murmured.

'Tama. Ko koe?'

'Āhua. We okay here?'

The man looked around the empty corridor and nodded. 'Brought you a souvenir.' He palmed her a beautiful long kōauau of forged steel.

She slipped it into her kete. 'Kia ora. Get ashore okay?'

'Timed it perfectly between patrols.'

Āhua heard hesitation in his voice. 'But?' she asked.

He grimaced, 'A fisherman spotted us at the river mouth.'

Āhua pictured the black Zodiac riding undetected through the booming coastal surf, then skimming up the wide flat waters of the Arahura River in the dark. A lantern gleaming on the bank. A figure standing abruptly, peering into the night.

'What happened?' she asked.

Kia tūpato,' her kaitiaki whispered in her ear.

The doors at the end of the corridor slid open. Two tour guides passed.

'Oh you know, we had a few beers . . .' Tama said.

'Kia ora,' the guides murmured. One lingered over Tama as if trying to place him. She was reading his moko rather than his expression. Like the moko kauae on Āhua's chin, the designs looked old, but they'd been lasered on by a corrupt southern tohunga just a month ago. They seemed to be working: the guide smiled.

Tama nodded and smiled back. '. . . and we had a good catch up,' he continued. 'You know, how his whānau are doing . . .'

The guides entered the day spa. The door hissed closed.

'. . . and then I shot him in the face,' Tama said quietly but provocatively.

His eyes were cold. They'd been training together for six years. And she finally realised that what she'd taken as professional distance was actually dislike. He didn't trust Āhua at all.

'You?' he said. 'No issues coming in the front door?'

'None,' she lied.

In the week spent tracing Poutini and Waitaiki's animatronic adventure through the North Island, the tour group had stayed in five-star whare in the bush, watched sunrises over Taupō, and collected carved taonga at each of the ancient quarries along the route. On New Year's Day 2038, they finally landed in Ngāi Tahu territory in Māwhera.

It had been sixteen years since the New New Zealand Wars, but border security between the sovereign tribal territories was still tight. At customs Āhua summoned all of her training to keep her heart rate steady. She stepped up to the desk for her iris scan. Her entire whakapapa lit up the screen in a glowing grid. Her mother's lines, the ones she knew, were from her home in Tūhua, but the system automatically highlighted the branching tree of her father's Ngāi Tahu ancestry. This was why she'd been chosen to infiltrate the tour. She tried not to hold her breath.

The official leaned in to hongi. 'Nau mai, haere mai e tōku whanauka. This your first time, eh?'

'Yeah, here to find my southern roots!' she said, doing her best impression of a born-again.

'Excellent,' the official said. 'And your roots are . . .'

The screen shifted. The names of Āhua's ancestors spread across a satellite map of Te Waipounamu, showing where they had lived and died.

'. . . in Arahura!' the official said. 'Great choice with the Poutini tour. Follow the green line to Wharenui 3. Your flight's pōwhiri starts in ten.'

The small carved gate opened. She stepped onto Ngāi Tahu soil. She was in.

A series of five-storey-high glass spheres dominated the arrivals concourse. Each was filled with towering sunlit kahikatea and rimu, with one of the southerner's signature black meeting houses nestled inside. Waiting out front of number 3, Āhua breathed in the moist, earthy, strangely familiar scent of the West Coast bush. She kept her head down to avoid the roving patrols of armed guards.

Once called on, she watched, fascinated, as the digital faces of the ancestral pou inside the whare came to life. She'd heard that Ngāi Tahu had developed the technology to simulate their ancestors. Throughout the speeches the carved pillars listened intently, nodding along, even kicking off the waiata at one point when an old man droned on too long. Above them the roof glittered like the night sky in a constellation of whakapapa showing the links between every person present. Āhua had a lot of cousins in the room. It was a nice touch, but as she and the other guests passed down the long line of locals to hongi each in turn, she felt uneasy. She wasn't really here to find her southern roots.

'Kia ora.'

Āhua found herself face-to-face with one of the Ngāi Tahu tour guides who would take them south. He had warm, quick brown eyes, and wore tā moko well, though he was young to have achieved such rank. As they clasped hands and pressed noses she could feel each of them lingering, inhaling deeply of the other's scent. Dressed flax, a hint of taramea perfume, the sweet musk of his skin. She heard muffled laughter from either side; they were holding up the line. She pulled back, grinning. He flashed her a grin of his own as they moved away.

At the feast afterwards, as he approached through the tables, she observed an alertness and confidence of movement which seemed out of place in a tour guide. She finished her mouthful of takahē and wiped her lips.

'Hey. I'm Tumuaki,' he said as he sat down. 'So your ancestors are from the Poutini coast like mine?'

'Hey. I'm Āhua. Some ancestors were, but I don't know much.'

'How much?'

'My dad was Ngāi Tahu, but I never knew him, and beyond that, nothing. I asked Mum about it when I was about ten, and you know what she did?'

Tumuaki raised an eyebrow, making his moko come alive. 'What?'

'Sat me down and told me how an evil Ngāi Tahu taniwha kidnapped my ancestor Waitaiki, and has kept her imprisoned up the Arahura ever since!'

'And you're here to see her for yourself. Are you really descended from Waitaiki?'

'No, but I am descended from Tama-āhua,' she said.

'Wow! So—'

'Anyway, it's my southern whakapapa I'm here to learn.'

After kai, in the coach on the way to the tour group's hotel, they pulled out their phones and traded whakapapa. Tumuaki spun the story of one Poutini Ngāi Tahu ancestor into the next, and Āhua felt herself carried along by his enthusiasm.

'So we're definitely cousins,' Tumuaki concluded.

'Mmm, close but not too close,' Āhua said. 'I have to ask: what do you do outside of guiding?'

'Like you can't guess! I see it in you, too.'

'What's your weapon?'

'Mere pounamu.'

'Close combat, eh?' she said, thinking of her own love of the greenstone blade. 'I teach taiaha. We should train together some time.'

'I'd like that.'

She smiled and flashed out a hand so fast he had no chance to react. Rather than strike him, she pressed her fingers to his cheek. He didn't flinch. His eyes gleamed.

I'm supposed to act like I'm on holiday, she thought. Fuck it. 'So what are you doing later on?' she said.

The day's last light filtered through the primeval forest outside the hotel, illuminating Tumuaki's muscular torso with dappled gold. He propped himself up on one elbow, and brushed a strand of hair from Āhua's sweating face, then traced the pattern of the Ngāi Tahu moko kauae across her chin. Āhua felt a strange frisson at the intimacy of his touch and the dishonesty of her tattoo.

'You know, Papakura was one of your ancestors,' Tumuaki said.

'Who's he?' she asked.

'She — one of our great warriors. That'll be where you get your combat skills from. She led war parties up and down this coast, and fought at . . .'

Āhua nodded, but couldn't take it all in. She lay back and stared at the ceiling, thinking, Why wasn't I told about this?

'Hey, would you like Papakura while you're here?' Tumuaki asked.

'Huh?' she asked.

'As a kaitiaki, I mean.'

Most people had a celebrity avatar as their kaitiaki, or personal guardian, on their phone. It gave them a thrill to get news and omens from a grizzled kuia like Maisey Rika. Tumuaki was offering something else here.

'You mean the ancestor?' Āhua asked.

'Well, a simulation.'

It'd be a breach of security protocol, but a kaitiaki was just a voice and a face. What's more, she was curious. 'Sure, why not?'

'I should tell you she's still in beta. They're all a bit . . . dark.'

'Dark?' Āhua sat up in bed.

'We fed the tribe's entire archive into a learning AI, and used it to create simulations of fifty tīpuna. The idea was to literally bring the archive to life so we could understand history just by chatting with our ancestors. But a lot of the source data was colonial.

The simulations turned out a bit — savage. Take her advice with a pinch of salt, okay?'

'Okay, sure. Let's do it.'

Tumuaki groped for his phone on the bedside table, then passed Āhua hers. She accepted his request, and blinked in surprise. She'd been expecting some wrinkled old crone; not this young woman with wild dark hair and clear skin and a serious mouth, her lips and chin inked deep green. Āhua realised with a start that the woman's moko was identical to the one she'd had lasered on. Papakura's eyes danced with recognition and mischievous life.

I'm your twenty-third great-grandmother, the voice in her ear said. *Welcome home.*

Long after Tumuaki had fallen asleep at her side, Āhua stayed up talking to the simulation. Each question about her father's people and their lives on this coast led to ten more. She watched digital re-enactments of the meeting at Rūnanga when Ngāi Tahu debated permanently settling the Poutini coast. She watched Tūterakiwhānoa force open the Māwhera Gorge with his enormous thighs. She watched her twenty-third great-grandmother wield a taiaha in battle, dancing as if she was the altar flame that burned at Māwhera, centuries ago.

Back in the upper Arahura, Āhua pushed Tumuaki and their meeting from her mind. Tama was watching her closely, his black eyes unblinking and cold.

'No issues coming in,' she reiterated as the monorail gently de-celerated, then finally came to a halt. 'We're here.'

They'd reached the creek known as Waitaiki, which was the source of pounamu, and ground zero for the myth and the tour. She and Tama bent their heads together and whispered a quick fierce karakia, then parted without a glance, strangers once more.

Āhua stepped down onto the platform. She turned in a slow circle, awed at the sacred place she'd heard so much about. The air was damp and cool. The mountains stood silently above. Great rivers of mist poured over the broken tops of the McArthur range into the valley below. Waitaiki Creek tumbled down to the Arahura in a foaming roar. Āhua could feel the wairua of the place. A quiet shiver of anticipation ran down her spine.

For generations her tribe had dreamed of retrieving their ancestor Waitaiki. The time had come.

She strolled down to the edge of the creek where the other guests were taking their places at tables discreetly positioned among mountain flax and hebe. Their faces were open, lit up with the unfamiliar beauty. Waiters brought cocktails. Āhua noted the positions of armed guards. She held up her phone as if taking a photo.

'Kaitiaki,' she murmured, 'why are they here? Protecting the guests?'

Protecting the stone. This is still the real source of pounamu.

'Okay. Run divination app. What are the omens?'

Her phone chimed a moment later. It was part old lore — analysis of clouds, GPS mapping of birds, the positions of stars — and part simulation using all available data.

By nightfall you will drink your enemy's blood, her kaitiaki said. *But your enemy is yourself.*

Āhua glanced sharply at her phone. She'd never had a response like that. 'What do you . . .'

'That's Arahura stone,' Tumuaki said.

He was standing at her elbow, just inside her personal space. He reached out to touch the inaka hei matau hanging at her throat. 'Bringing it home, eh?'

'No, this is Tūhua stone,' she said, putting her phone away.

Tumuaki raised an eyebrow. '*Tūhua* stone?'

Āhua kept her voice playful. 'Waitaiki's the mother of greenstone, and she's from Tūhua. So it's really ours.'

'Hah! You—'

The reedy blast of a pūkaea cut short Tumuaki's reply. Moments later a second trumpet joined, the note surging out then falling away in a plaintive echo of the human voice. The ground began to tremble. Cocktail glasses shook with a high-pitched ringing, then with a shuddering groan the taniwha burst from the river, clawed his way up the bank, then came to stand before them, poised and dripping, sniffing the air. His eyes flashed with the rainbow iridescence of pāua shell.

Waitaiki climbed from his back and slipped down onto the river bank, naked and shivering. The taniwha hauled driftwood into a heap and kindled it into flame with a quick karakia. Āhua watched with fascination and horror as Waitaiki and the creature folded themselves together beside the blaze, her arms draped across his neck, his tail encircling her body; concentric circles of life. The ancient deity and the young woman whispered to each other in low voices.

It was an ingenious piece of theatre, Āhua thought. What if Waitaiki wasn't kidnapped? What if she eloped?

Every now and then Poutini lifted his head and looked down the valley. On the horizon, something gleamed. The creature let out a rattling hiss. Āhua knew how the myth went: Waitaiki's husband had tracked them here, and was approaching fast.

'Here we go,' murmured Tumuaki. 'Wait 'til you see Tama-āhua's war party.'

'I can't wait,' she murmured back.

Poutini unfolded himself and stood with muscular grace, padding away from Waitaiki to stand in the riverbed just metres from the guests, his attention focused on the horizon like a hunting dog.

From this close, Āhua could see the twin rows of serrated shark's teeth gleaming in his jaw, the impossibly detailed matte-black tattooing on his hide, the ripple of muscles and tendons beneath. She knew they were the pistons and hydraulics of the tribe's best engineers, but the wairua felt strong.

Then with shocking clarity, Poutini began to karakia. The penetrating, otherworldly rhythm of the atua's war chant seemed to come from everywhere at once. He whipped his tail and stamped the ground, his eyes bulged and he seemed to grow in size. Sudden mist burst up from the creek, swirling at random then solidifying into Poutini's own form, again and again, until a rank of ten spectral taniwha stood ready to fight at his side. The gleam on the horizon grew brighter against the thundery grey day.

Poutini's chant reached a crescendo, then abruptly changed. The creature bowed his enormous head, took a deep inbreath, and then his war cry became a lament. Though he was of the atua, he knew he would never defeat Waitaiki's husband in battle.

The wraiths of mist disintegrated in brief showers of rain. Poutini keened with an unearthly sadness that rang from the stones. He turned and folded himself once more around Waitaiki. His tail encircled the woman, holding her close.

His embrace grew tight, and his lament sank to a rumbling dirge, and he began to squeeze, and squeeze harder, bearing down on his lover with the great remorseless pressure of the mountains themselves. If he couldn't have her, no one could. The piercing bone cry of a kōauau toroa joined in. Hairs stood up on the back of Āhua's neck, and she felt tears forming in her eyes.

Waitaiki started to struggle, and then kicked and screamed as her skin began to change. Poutini's tail coiled around her again and her breathing slowed and her struggles grew feeble. Poutini's spiritual essence crept through her veins. She and the taniwha both wept. Her feet stilled, now looking as if carved. Soon she would turn entirely to stone, and shatter, and the tourists would all get a piece to take home. Āhua couldn't watch.

She took several steps backwards, away from Tumuaki, and turned to look at the transfixed crowd. Even the guards were staring, though they saw it every day. Āhua scanned the many upturned faces.

There.

Tama had positioned himself on a small rise next to the booth that controlled the production. He was watching her intently, waiting for the signal. She flexed her fingers. The light in the sky grew brighter. She took the long silver kōauau from her kete and nodded.

Now.

As Āhua shook the kōauau, it telescoped out into a steel taiaha with a faint click, and as Tama brought up the barrel of his AR15, the light in the sky grew blinding, accompanied by the harsh scream of engines. As one, the crowd screamed as four jet-black helicopters tore overhead and a volley of rockets slammed into the monorail at their back, incinerating the sinuous white carriages in a series of brilliant flashes.

Tama began to fire in tight bursts into the clusters of guards. Āhua moved with a feeling of release, lashing the blade of her weapon into the chest of the nearest guard, cleaving his breast-bone with a metallic snap. She sliced another across the temple as she spun, then felled a third with a bloody thrust to the throat. They were dead before the first wave of molten glass from the explosions hit the ground.

Then she was sprinting through the smoke, head down, tearing into the next corpus of guards in a silver blur. Someone screamed at the guests to take cover. She heard the suppressed thump of Tama's semi-automatic, felt the huff of displaced air as rounds tore past.

Blood and fire filled her nostrils. Centuries of anticipation swarmed in her veins.

Overhead, the huge twin-rotored helicopters swung wide and circled back around. As Āhua moved through the chaotic crowd towards another body of guards, she glimpsed the great whipping steel cables beneath each helicopter, and the familiar shape of her own iwi insignia on their sides.

Tama disappeared into the production booth. Two shots. An instant later the animatronic Waitaiki ceased her struggles. Poutini lay down on the river bank, with just his chest rising, eyes blinking, gone into some holding pattern. The epic soundtrack of taonga pūoro cut out, leaving the crackle of flames, the vicious rattling thump of heavy-calibre fire from the helicopters, and thrilled screams from the crowd.

In the thick of the melee, something flashed into Āhua's vision. Without conscious thought she twitched the head of her taiaha up and felt a jarring impact. Another blow came in low and fast, and she found herself back-pedalling furiously, fending off lightning-fast strikes about her head.

Tumuaki. With a mere pounamu shimmering in his right hand.

She spun on the ball of her right foot, sweeping the head of her taiaha towards his belly, then at the last instant flashed the broad blade down into his head.

He danced sideways and parried with a glancing blow, then struck hard with a back-handed grip. Āhua rolled away and turned, coming back to standing, taiaha quivering in her hands. Did she really want to hurt him? She pukana'd, a high-pitched *yip*, and sprang forward. Tumuaki was expecting the attack, raised his mere to parry, but he hadn't expected her strength. She smashed the weapon from his hand, stepped forward and flicked the tongue of her taiaha around to rest against his carotid artery. The feathered collar of her weapon danced in time with their breathing. They were eye to eye, slick with sweat.

'What are you doing?' he whispered.

'Taking Waitaiki home,' she whispered back.

The air around them erupted in a whirlwind of downdraft as the choppers came in to land. Warriors in black fatigues jumped clear and forced the remaining guards into the dirt. Tumuaki was herded in with the rest of the tourists and guides.

The blades slowed, the din lessened. The cockpit of one opened and Āhua's great-uncle Tūhākari stepped down, wrapped in a long kahukurī, flanked by his own personal guards. He strode towards Āhua through billowing black smoke, pressed his nose to hers, then pulled her into a brief embrace.

'Well done,' he shouted in her ear. 'We'll get that filth off your face. You've earned your real moko kauae today.'

She had to fight a strange urge to pull away.

From another helicopter the engineering team deployed. Women in scuba gear slipped into the river, trailing steel cables and slings. They'd drilled the manoeuvre dozens of times, knowing they only had minutes before Ngāi Tahu scrambled a reactionary force.

Then the engines powered up, the rotors whipping faster and faster until they disappeared. The air buckled and shimmered from the heat of the exhausts. Tūhākari stood with his head bowed at the water's edge, chanting low and fast. The cables came taut. Slowly the choppers began to rise.

With a grinding, ripping rumble accompanied by a high and drawn-out scream, something began to rise from the waters. The helicopters' engines howled under the load and the aircraft rose higher and higher until the tremendous form of a woman breached the surface and came to hover above the boiling creek.

The real Waitaiki was as large as a whale. She lay on her side with her legs drawn to her chest as if sleeping. Her face was peaceful. Her hair swooped away in the direction of the current, chipped and scarred where a millennia of storms had torn fragments off and sent them tumbling into the sea. The pale green-grey inaka of her skin gleamed.

Āhua fingered the pounamu around her neck with a blood-flecked hand. Her taonga had come from this river, which meant it was part of Waitaiki herself. She thought of her tribe's plans to return her to the bay at Tūhua.

Her phone chimed.

There's no mana in running like a dog with a weka, her kaitiaki said in her ear. *Kill and eat every person here so your victory is complete. Or cut your ties.*

Āhua stared at Papakura's face on her phone. She couldn't understand what was happening. Her avatar simply delivered messages from her own system.

'You're meant to be my kaitiaki,' she stuttered.

I'm your twenty-third great-grandmother. Cut the tie. She belongs here. So do you.

'You're a simulation.'

I'm a child of Te Rorohikotākata, the Kāi Tahu AI. If she leaves there will be two generations of war. Your children's children will be consumed by fire.

'I don't have children.'

But you will.

Āhua looked up from her phone. Tumuaki was staring at her across the smoke.

Āhua walked to the water's edge and gazed up at the greenstone goddess. The scream of engines made it hard to think, but she'd made up her mind. She sheathed her taiaha behind her back, jumped to catch the nearest cable where it ran underneath Waitaiki, then hauled herself up until she was standing on top of the great stone figure. The downdraft blew her hair in wild tangles.

In her ear, Āhua heard Papakura begin to chant, something so ancient she barely understood the words. The karakia had been passed down from tohunga to student for generations until the chain of transmission broke with the missionaries, but the words had been transcribed into the archive by a Pākehā in 1834. The tribal AI had finally retrieved the chant from the archive after centuries lying dormant, and turned it back into speech. The syllables resounded with undiminished power.

Āhua unsheathed her taiaha, and cut the silver umbilical in two.

The helicopter bucked skywards like an ejector seat with the sudden release of tension. The cable whipped high into the air, catching in the light before snarling up into the rotors. The helicopter did a lazy backflip, then plunged towards the valley floor. Āhua leapt to the ground and rolled clear as the mother of pounamu crashed back into the river, pulling two other helicopters in and down. As their rotors touched, the guests wailed. Smoking fragments of blade strafed the tussock with a vicious hiss. Both helicopters plummeted into the river, and the third broke across the rocks with a roar. Suffocating heat flared over Āhua's face. The pilot of the last chopper hit the release on his cable and climbed free.

Āhua looked for Tumuaki and found him struggling in the grip of a soldier. In a few strides she was there. She pulled the mere from her own war belt and threw it back-handed. It caught the soldier behind the ear, dropping him to his knees, then she whipped it back into her hand by its cord and offered the weapon to Tumuaki, handle first. He cracked the soldier across the head.

'Why?' he asked.

'I changed my mind. Waitaiki's home is here,' she said, glancing up at the remaining helicopter. 'We need cover.'

'The production booth,' Tumuaki replied. 'There's an entire facility underneath.'

They moved fast through a tableau of grappling soldiers and

guards, lit by a dozen burning fires. As they reached the production booth, instinct made Āhua look up. A gust of wind cleared the smoke. Stalking towards them through the flames, gaze fixed, gun levelled, was Tama.

The bullet tore across the top of her thigh as she rolled behind the booth. Blood welled from the cut. Tumuaki was at her side, pressed into the dirt. Shots ricocheted overhead.

To her left, a guard lay sprawled. A rifle hung from his hands.

'There,' she said. 'Grab it when I say. Go!'

She hauled herself up and lunged to the right. Bullets whined. Tumuaki crawled to the guard's side and swung the rifle around, leaning it on the dead man's chest. His shot snapped into a boulder, spraying Tama with shards of rock. He dropped, clutching his face.

'Muskets made all the difference, eh?' Tumuaki yelled.

'I'd rather have a real taniwha!' she yelled back.

'We do!'

Overhead, the roar of the helicopter grew, and Āhua heard the sickening thump of heavy-calibre fire. The chopper dropped down into her line of view, skimming the tussock, and swung side-on to expose the open door where the gunner sat. Directly behind the helicopter she saw Poutini's huge motionless form, stretched out like a small hill.

Tumuaki vanished into the production booth.

As the gunner brought his weapon round, she saw a quiver go through the enormous serpent. The air flooded with the epic swell of taonga pūoro, backed by pounding of drums. Poutini's head rose and turned and his lips parted on gleaming teeth. He opened his mouth and roared. The gunner's finger closed on the trigger. Āhua watched, awestruck, as with a single fluid movement the guardian deity lunged forward and raked one enormous claw across the back of the helicopter, shearing off its tail.

As the gunner fired, the chopper began to spin wildly. Bullets raked the surrounding cliffs. The craft swirled sideways, caught a skid and tipped, disintegrating in a brilliant koru of fire.

Black scorch-marks covered Poutini's flanks. He lashed his tail into a crowd of soldiers. Tama scrambled to his feet and ran. The taniwha pounced, landing on him with an earth-shaking thump.

At the water's edge, Āhua's uncle Tūhākari began to chant. A wall of black cloud boiled up the valley towards them like a flash-flood. Poutini snarled and lashed out at the tohunga, but the chant held him back. Tūhākari's personal guard raked the taniwha's scales with automatic fire.

The storm broke. As Poutini fell back, clawing at the wind, Āhua reached Tūhākari's personal guard. She cut them down with swift strokes. Tūhākari turned and his chant faltered. Poutini snapped his head and torso between his jaws, shook him twice, and tossed him aside.

His body smashed through the cocktail bar, bounced and rolled. The soundtrack died away.

For a long moment, nothing moved beyond the lick of flames.

Āhua looked around. Pockets of guests cowered here and there. Away to her left, the animatronic Waitaiki went through her death throes in a pre-programmed loop. She shook, quivered, then shattered into a hundred gleaming jewels. Poutini stood watching with his enormous head on one side.

Then he turned to the real Waitaiki where she lay on her side, half out of the creek, eyes staring at the sky. The great serpent slid into the water and wrapped his limbs around her in a tight embrace. The pair sank beneath the waters with a gentle murmur.

Āhua reached for Tumuaki's hand. They took a bow. The guests began to holler and cheer.

'Great tour,' one of the guests muttered. 'But the ending was a bit much.'

CHAPTER 10
FROM THE EARTH

———

Moving Mountains

———

The Kūmara God Smiles Fatly

———

The Potato

———

Moving Mountains

BY CLAYTON TE KOHE

I can't remember the first time I heard The Thequetonics; their music has pervaded my life. It seeped into me as I slept in the back of the old Kingswood: the last remnant of my father's life before us kids came along. Later, they became the soundtrack of my childhood on the long car trips every summer to the beach, my legs sticking to the hot vinyl of my parents' van.

As a teenager, their music would punctuate the mix tapes I played in my beat-up Toyota Starlet — the songs that my mates and I sang so loudly that our voices threatened to peel off the already flaking orange paint-job.

I've nursed more than one broken heart while listening to 'A Different Door' playing on repeat. When I was younger, I'd binge-drink the cheap spirits that were sold in plastic bottles and belt out the lyrics:

I see you've chosen
A different door
I can't stop you
I won't stop you . . .

The song let me dwell in my sadness, but offered a little bit of hope. There was always a different door to choose.

Nowadays I drink top-shelf, but the song has the same effect — things are never entirely broken — except for The Thequetonics themselves.

The story of their infamous break up often eclipses their music. Almost everyone knows about the brawl that started on stage at Kings in Ōhākune.

'It was like they erupted,' a fan said at the time. 'All that rage — it was awesome, man.'

I've heard that all four members of the band walked out of Kings that night and have never talked to each other again — since 1983! It's hard to believe, since they all live relatively close to one another.

'It was like they erupted,' a fan said at the time. 'All that rage — it was awesome, man.'

I want to know what happened at Kings. Why had these four guys — close friends from what I understand — why had they fallen out so spectacularly, so publicly?

The Thequetonics were founded in the garage of charismatic frontman, Tom Southern. Southern and guitarist Ray Halliday were the heart of the band: the songs they wrote often sounded like their two guitars were in constant competition — their riffs developing like an epic battle. Supporting Southern and Halliday were bassist Pete Reed and Tau 'Eddy' Edwards on drums.

Their music was heavily influenced by the punk of the late 70s — a genre not readily associated with Māori musicians — although 'A Different Door' hints at a change of direction musically. 'A Different Door' sits comfortably next to 'Be Mine Tonight' and 'Blue Lady': a potent trio of songs that almost guaranteed you'd pull back in the day.

Hardcore fans nicknamed the band *The 'Tonics*. These days it's not uncommon to hear them called *The 'Te' Tonics* — reclaimed by young Māori fans, they're born again.

The 'Tonics have been called, somewhat unfairly, a one-hit wonder. Casual listeners may only remember 'A Different Door'. It was the band's only commercially successful single and was released after their split. The band had a loyal following though, before they imploded that cold July night in 1983.

It's that gig that has fuelled their ongoing appeal. If you believe the stories, half of the country was crammed into Kings in Ōhākune. A 'who's who' of New Zealand music claim to have been there that night. Claims that are often flimsy at best. A bootleg of the show made the band infamous. Legend has it that The 'Tonics made the recording themselves — perhaps in a moment of prescience. The bootleg tape captures the special magic their live performances were famous for.

Part of The 'Tonics' appeal was the fractious relationship between Southern and Halliday. Fans I've talked to describe the unbearable feeling of tension whenever they played, like at any moment something would kick off. That night, the aggressive competition between the two became manifest, coming to blows between them on stage, before an all-out brawl in the venue itself.

I acquired a copy of the bootleg in my twenties; a flatmate left it behind with a couple of old shirts and a pair of odd socks when he blew out of town. He was a useless flatmate, but he did have good taste in music. The tape was so precious that I only listened to it a few times; I was paranoid about stretching the tape, or, worst-case scenario, my Walkman destroying it.

I kept the tape even as cassette players disappeared from stereo systems. A few years back I got it converted to a digital file, paid extra so I could have both the original and a cleaned-up version. With the hiss of the cassette filtered out, the virtuosity of Halliday's riffs are astounding, the voice of Southern is both raw and melodic. But somehow the music loses a little bit of magic in the translation.

The 'Tonics were always a band that had grit, who needed a little bit of grime in their sound. Cleaned up they're no longer authentic.

I contacted Pete Reed and Tau 'Eddy' Edwards for an interview. I wanted to get them in the same room together — I thought that a reunion would be a bit of a scoop. Pete flat out refused, and threatened to cancel the interview. Eddy just sighed, 'I've been trying to get in touch with everyone, man. Thirty years of trying. I see Queenie every now and then in town, but she doesn't even give me the time of day.'

Queenie is the — if you'll pardon the expression — elephant in the room. The subreddits on The 'Tonics are rife with rumours about Queenie's part in The 'Tonics split. Usually, she's called a 'Yoko' before the discussion degenerates into the expected misogyny. I don't want to believe that The 'Tonics broke up over something so banal, so trite as a love triangle.

So I agreed to meet each of them separately. And after spending time with these two men — separated by 100 kilometres and 35 years — I'm not sure if there will ever be a truce between them.

Pete Reed has called Kawerau home on and off since the 80s. In the late 80s he lived for a stint in Melbourne, trying to crack the Australian scene; but he didn't last long across the ditch.

The hotel bar in Kawerau is much like the town itself: a remnant of a time gone by, holding on to its glory days of a few decades ago. A pub like this probably exists in every small town in New Zealand, aging clientele sharing the same old stories over a jug of mass-produced beer. It's the kind of place where I search for the least offensive, mediocre beer to order; but at least it's cheap and plentiful. It will probably be renovated soon — robbing it of any charm it now possesses. In the city, a place like this would be patronised by those who love kitschy nostalgia — the kids the Boomers call 'Hipsters' —

but here in Kawerau they play Fleetwood Mac unironically — even unapologetically.

in Kawerau they play Fleetwood Mac unironically — even unapologetically.

They know Pete well here. He is a man who is at once at home in these surroundings and totally incongruous to them. The locals wear shorts and jerseys that peacock their allegiance to their chosen sporting gangs: local, national and international. Pete's dressed in black — jeans, T-shirt and leather jacket — with his long, greying hair tied in a ponytail. Pete stands out. He attracts attention. It's intentional — that's the kind of guy Pete is.

'Hey, mate. Clayton, yeah?' Pete says as he shakes my hand. At first I'm taken aback by his voice, that whisky-stripped drawl so familiar to me. His backing vocals once lent an almost off-key power to Southern's voice.

I buy Pete a beer — not much of a payment to bare your soul, I know — and we settle down to talk about The 'Tonics.

It's only a couple of hours' drive south to Taupō, where I'm meeting Tau 'Eddy' Edwards on his lifestyle block off the Napier–Taupō road.

Unlike Pete, who seems to weigh every word, Eddy lacks any sort of guile.

'Oh man, look at you!' he says as he greets me. 'I bet Pete *hated* you. No offence, man.'

I ask Eddy why he thinks that. 'Your hair, your clothes, your shoes. Even your glasses, man. You look . . . what's the word? Slick. Yeah, slick. He hates . . . ah . . . artifice. Yeah, try-hard eh? No offence.'

Eddy is a plain-speaker, genuine. I believe him when he says he doesn't mean to offend. Still, it's hard not to feel it. I mustn't have my poker face on, because Eddy says, 'Don't take it personally though. Pete hates everyone, even me.'

In small doses I can't imagine hating Eddy, but being stuck in a van with him on tour? There's something in his golden-retriever eagerness that could make a man consider murder.

Eddy is a solid guy, he has the kind of body you would tag as #dadbod and your grandma would call 'barrel chested'. The kind of body that you can only get from actual manual labour. He's wearing a polo shirt and jeans — it looks like he's made an effort. Maybe not for me though, as he motions towards a couple of yurts at the end of the paddock, 'We've got a few people to stay — glamping, you heard of it?'

Glamping is the latest venture Eddy has taken on. He's tried his hand at a few unusual things. 'We tried alpacas, and planted a few oaks for truffles — that's a bit long term, eh? The missus is running glamping now, and once she's got her ticket, she's going to run yoga retreats. I just make sure the tents are up and the bogs are clean.'

It's amazing listening to the interviews. Sometimes it's like Pete and Eddy are arguing with each other, like they *are* in the same room. It's almost like a call and reply. I wonder if they've been arguing with each other in their heads for decades.

CTK — 'So you didn't pursue music then? After The 'Tonics split?'

TEE — 'For me, it wasn't really about the music. The other guys thought we'd take over the world and if that happened, I would have been fine with it. But really, all I wanted to do was hang out with my mates, smash the shit out of my drums, have a beer and maybe score a chick. So when we split — I didn't think there was any point to it. I didn't want to play with anyone else.'

CTK — 'Do you still play, Pete?'

PR — 'Yeah, y'know for a musician that's like saying: "Do you still breathe?" Professionally? Nah, not my scene anymore. I have a band here that I jam with, covers y'know. The odd gig now and then.'

CTK — 'Do you cover any of your songs from The 'Tonics?'

PR — 'Nah. They were never really my songs . . . And anyway, that's not really what the punters are into, they want something . . . I don't know. Normal.'

CTK — 'I'm a big fan. I'd kill to hear The 'Tonics live.'

PR — 'A bunch of old has-been punks? Get off the grass. How old are you?'

CTK — 'Thirty-three.'

PR — 'Seriously? So you weren't even born when we broke up? Jesus. I appreciate it, mate, I really do. But you don't have to say it. I never thought we made the kind of music that translated well, y'know, recorded. As a live band — yeah, there was something special between us.'

CTK — 'I've heard about your live gigs, interviewed fans that were there . . .'

PR — 'Yeah, well, I've heard a lot about the Queen's coronation, but it's not the same as being there eh?'

CTK — 'There's a whole lot of younger fans out there. Have you thought about a reunion?'

PR — 'Nah. It wouldn't be the same. I just don't have that rage in me anymore. None of us do. I heard

all I wanted to do was hang out with my mates, smash the shit out of my drums, have a beer and maybe score a chick.

Johnny Rotten's selling real estate these days.'

CTK — **'You said they weren't really your songs . . .'**
PR — 'I thought you'd know that. Tom and Ray wrote all our songs.'

CTK — **'You didn't want to write anything? No ambition to be a songwriter?'**
PR — 'I wouldn't say that. I had some songs, some good ones too — but at the time they didn't really suit the direction of the band. Or rather, they didn't suit Tom and Ray's vision for us. But I did name the band, so that's something.'

CTK — **'The Thequetonics is an unusual . . .'**
PR — 'Unusual? That's almost as bad as saying it's "interesting".'

CTK — **'Yeah, OK. Damning with faint praise — you got me.'**
PR — 'What's really annoying for me is that people didn't get the play on words. They didn't seem to understand that it wasn't so much a name as it was a manifesto. These days they'd call it a mission statement. We grew up drowning in disco, sickly-sweet candy-floss music. Y'know — insubstantial, it just melts away. We wanted to shake things up, destroy the discotheque in a huge earthquake — y'know, tectonics: *thequetonics.*'

it wasn't so much a name as it was a manifesto.

Eddy laughs for an excessively long time after I play him the clip.

TEE — 'Pete's always been a bloody blow-hard. Still is, eh? Even after all this time. Truth is, we had a gig but no name to put on the poster. Tom, Ray and Pete argued about the name for days — and I truly mean *days*. And the thing with Pete is that he's stubborn, he's persistent, man. The other two were coming up with a different name every five minutes and there's Pete just saying "The Thequetonics" over and over again. Until, finally, I think the other two just gave up, let him have that. Threw a dog a bone.'

In Kawerau, Pete's already drained his first pint. I buy him another.

PR — 'I came up with the look too . . .'

CTK — **'The suits? I was going to ask about that, and if you'd been influenced by . . .'**
PR — 'Don't you dare say Split Enz.'

CTK — **'Why? The comparison has been made before.'**
PR — 'By morons. We wore suits, we played music that was a little out there, but we weren't copying Split Enz . . .'

CTK — **'I don't know if I would mind being compared to one of the greatest . . .'**
PR — 'Yeah, yeah, they're a great band. No one's arguing against that. But we weren't copying them. The suits were like, satire. We came out all clean-cut in suits, looking like a Māori showband. And then we'd rip the stage up. We were referencing the big showbands . . .'

CTK — 'Like the Maori Volcanics?'

PR — 'Yeah, all those guys. So, we come out looking like them and people think we're gonna do some old standards, something nice that plays in the background. But we were punk. I know *now* punk is associated with that marketable aesthetic pushed by McLaren — but that wasn't us. Punk was rage, pure rage against injustice, against establishment. It was subverting expectations. That's what punk was all about. Can you get more subversive than four Māori boys in pristine suits?'

Tom would pick up a guitar . . . it was effortless for him.

TEE — 'I think Pete gets stuck on the name and the suits, eh? Because he's always been jealous of Tom and Ray. Pete wrote a few songs, yeah, but they were never as good as what Tom and Ray could come up with. Like, Pete would be slogging over a riff for days, weeks even, and then Tom would pick up a guitar . . . it was effortless for him. Ray too. Pete just can't admit that he wasn't as good as them.'

PR — 'I was a great guitarist. But you can't have three guitars in a four-piece, can you? So I picked up the bass. Because I'm adaptable.'

TEE — 'Me? I always knew my limitations — I mean, there's a reason there was never a drum solo in our set. That's OK. We just needed someone to keep the beat. Steady, I didn't have to be flash.'

PR — 'These days you push a button and there's your drummer. Just loop something and play back. Chris Knox toured like that for years.'

Having met these two, I'm no longer surprised that The 'Tonics split. They're so volatile just *thinking* about each other. I can't imagine what it would be like to have them in the same room. Eventually their rants circle back to the events that led up to the gig at Kings.

PR — 'Well, I guess it's like any other relationship. It may look sudden, it may blindside you — but if you're really honest with yourself the signs were there. You know what I mean don't you? You're old enough to have had a serious relationship, aren't you?'

CTK — 'Of course.'

PR — 'Hey mate, no need for that tone. I mean, I can't presume. Your generation is all over the place. Anyway, it's never just one thing. It's lots of little things; slights, misunderstandings, bad decisions . . .'

CTK — 'Bad decisions?'

PR — 'Here's a classic one. Tom and Ray decide to put Eddy in charge of our finances. The drummer. Eddy. He's a nice guy, but y'know what they say about drummers, eh? They can only count to four.'

TEE — 'Yeah. I took care of the money. I was good at it. I've always been frugal.'

PR — 'He was a tight-ass. We'd play a gig and he'd give us our share of the door or whatever. Some nights it didn't even cover our beer!'

TEE — 'We didn't have anyone on the door, so some-times no one paid the cover. And the rest of the guys would waste the money we did get. One time we did a gig in Taupō, they take all these girls from the gig out to Manuels. We knew a bartender there, a good bloke named Abe. Now, Abe could spot us a beer or two, no problem — but they take a dozen girls there and they all want cocktails . . . that kind of stuff adds up.'

PR — 'I'm not saying that Eddy was light-fingered or what have you, there's no proof of that. But I reckon it's suss. That's all I'm saying.'

I ask about Queenie.

Pete leans back, rolls his eyes and snorts, 'Yeah. And *her*. Another bad decision.'

Eddy is more reserved. 'The Queenie thing was . . . complicated.'

Anyone who's seen that status knows what that means.
I tell Pete that people call Queenie 'Yoko'.

PR — 'Well that's bloody unfair to Yoko Ono. She has talent, she was an artist in her own right before John Lennon. Queenie was more like Nancy bloody Spungen. Just looking to hook whoever could make her famous. She started off with Ray, did you know that?'

TEE — 'Yeah, she was with Ray first. But we all tried it on with Queenie, eh? It was a different time then and she was good looking. She turned me down and I thought that was fair enough, but I think Pete took her rejection hard — probably because she went with Ray. It was another thing for him to be jealous of.'

PR — 'Tom was the singer, Ray played guitar so they got the lion's share of the groupies. Here's a joke for you, make sure you write it down. Do you know the difference between riffs and licks, boy? Groupies don't riff ya balls!'

TEE — 'It wasn't just because Tom and Ray played guitar. I mean, they both had their ways. They were charming. Tom was always super cool — he'd zero in on a girl and make her feel like she was the only one in the room. Ray was funny, he'd make them laugh. Even I had my share of admirers. But Pete, you've met him. He's a bit . . . intense.'

PR — 'Queenie came to our gigs all the time. She'd ended up in the bar with us a few times. Then one night she goes home with Ray and then, all of a sudden, she's with us all the time — before the gig, after the gig, answering Ray's bloody door. Then, somewhere between Taupō and Auckland, she's answering Tom's door. She's sitting up the front with Tom in the van. And Ray doesn't say anything about it. He's just noodling away on his guitar. We play some gigs in Auckland and then we had some time in a studio booked. To cut a demo, y'know? Ray plays us "A Different Door", it was the only song he ever insisted on singing.'

Ray plays us 'A Different Door', it was the only song he ever insisted on singing.

TEE — 'It was awkward, man. Everyone in the room knew what the song was about. Ray didn't even look at Queenie, the whole time he played he just stared straight at Tom.'

PR — 'Tom just picked up his guitar and played some licks. Staring back at Ray. And it was uncomfortable and stomach churning — but it was fucking gold.

We knew it was going to be our first hit single.'

TEE — 'We had a week before we picked up the tour again, so we thrashed that song. You know how when you do something over and over you get used to it?'

PR — 'You've heard that thing, y'know, about how you can boil frogs by gradually raising the water temperature? Because they get acclimatised?'

TEE — 'I never got used to playing that song. It was always awkward.'

PR — 'Every time Tom and Ray would just stare at each other. And that stupid bimbo would fawn and giggle over Tom in front of Ray. Like she was *enjoying* it.'

TEE — 'We get to Ōhākune, and Tom announces that Queenie is going to be our manager — that she'll be taking over the finances.'

PR — 'Y'know, I wasn't hot on Eddy taking care of our money. But it was better him than her.'

TEE — 'Taking care of the money was a hassle, and apparently Queenie had contacts in the industry . . . I didn't mind letting that part go, but it was the way it was handled. It was like they were suggesting I was . . .'

PR — 'Incompetent. I mean the woman could barely balance herself! She was so top heavy, if you understand what I'm saying.'

TEE — 'There was a bit of bad blood before we even took to the stage that night. We ran through our first set, no problem.'

PR — 'Tom and Queenie had been throwing back the gin during the break.'

TEE — 'That would have been all our takings for the night. Gone, just like that.'

PR — 'The crowd was warmed up, had a few drinks in them. We always introduced new material at the top of the second set.'

TEE — 'Tom's a little bit pissed, he slurred a bit when he introduced "A Different Door". I count it off and Ray plays; but Tom hasn't come in. So I looked up . . .'

PR — 'Ray's looking at Queenie, singing right to her. And y'know, if it was awkward before . . .'

TEE — 'It was fucking awkward, man. And then Queenie just looks from Ray to Tom and then back at Ray . . . and Tom just pounced.'

PR — 'I probably should have broken it up, but it felt good to throw a punch y'know.'

TEE — 'It was like the whole place had been holding their breath and then, all of a sudden, they could let go. It was chaos.'

PR — 'The physical stuff, the actual fighting between us fizzled out pretty quickly; but y'know, whatever bond we had was broken. It was like I was standing there with strangers.'

TEE — 'I wasn't hurt physically. But spiritually? I hitched a ride back to Taupō that night.'

I wasn't hurt physically. But spiritually?

PR — 'I grabbed my bass and my clothes and that was it. Got a ride out of town and ended up here. I haven't talked to the others since.'

TEE — 'Ray ended up in New Plymouth and Tom and Queenie are in Tūrangi.'

CTK — 'Have you thought about getting back together?'

PR — 'You're kidding right?'

TEE — 'I've left that life behind me, Clayton.'

The last stop I make is at Kings in Ōhākune. I order a beer at the bar and try to imagine the place thirty-five years ago. It's not hard to do. I'm engulfed by pine panelling — bar, walls, ceiling, all clad in pine — the yellow wood screams 80s. There's black and white chequered tiles on the dance floor: Kings boasts that it's the biggest in town.

I slip in my earbuds and find my 'Tonics playlist — *Live at Kings*. Only a few days ago this would have excited me — I would have felt that I was a pilgrim, completing my hallowed journey. But now it feels hollow.

I close my eyes and let the music take me into the past: imagining the packed room. The 'Tonics decked out in their suits take the stage. Somewhere in the front of the crowd Queenie watches on — their number one fan.

Pete's right, of course, I'd never know what it was truly like to be there. I pause the music and order another beer, opting this time to sit out on the deck overlooking the mountains: I need the air.

Outside, I push play again and I'm surrounded by their music. I know the exact moment that they will break; I can feel the tension of it rising from my stomach. Ray plays the riff and it's as close as I'll ever get; so I raise my glass to them.

Tom and Queenie Southern and Ray Halliday declined to be interviewed for this article.

The Kūmara God Smiles Fatly

BY HONE TUWHARE

Thinner than a silver blade curving
the moon has stopped climbing.
It is turning to me slowly until,
full-faced I see the deep pits and
the nicks it has given itself shaving
without water
without a water mirror.

It seems to hang up there inert;
influential.

I have felt the silver pulse beat
of the moon its sandpaper hands
on my head on my heart my naked body
sanding my eyeballs.
I don't want to look at it anymore.

Face down between long valleys
of meshed kūmara vines the earth smells
of woman flesh just milked.

I am bathing in a river of silver.
I am bathing in a thousand refractions.
The river empties itself into the pits:
my river my tears of silver. The moon

is gone.
And gone forever are things magical
I may never reach out to touch again
as gentle.

At dawn
the kūmara god smiles fatly.
The time of harvest does not eclipse
my regret.

The Potato

BY WITI IHIMAERA

1.

My father, Te Haa, called his grandfather, Manu, Pā.

'Pā had the best horses in Poverty Bay,' Dad told me in an interview in 1997. 'They were chaff fed, grain fed. Manu was a farmer on forty acres of his own land, cropping maize and oats, and he also had some lease-land. He used to grow grass as well to sell as hay and seed.

'In the 1920s, the Okitu dairy factories started up at Mākaraka. One was near the railway station. Manu and my grandmother, Hine Te Ariki, ran a herd of cows and the cream they got was exchanged for flour, sugar and other goods. I recall that no money was exchanged, only goods. Hine Te Ariki was a good milker. She would climb a hill, see where her cows were, sometimes a mile and a half away, put two fingers in her mouth and whistle her dogs to bring the cows in.

'In those days everybody lived close-knit. We stayed in our own homes but we shared everything with each other. Hine Te Ariki used to save milk and take some to my Uncle Tip (Tipene) and others after each milking. If anybody killed a beast they would go around sharing the meat. Any meat left over was preserved in a big drum filled with fat from the pork. The fat preserved the meat and it lasted for months. If somebody didn't have kūmara, resources would be shared so that everybody could get through from one season to the next. It was not unusual for families to feed up to twenty people at dinner, including those who were passing by or staying temporarily.

'Our day normally started at five in the morning. Pā used to start the Ringatū hīmene but sometimes he would call out to me, "Te Haa, māhau rā te hīmene, you start the waiata." When I was very young I used to get frightened of the droning sound and would hide my head under the blankets.

'We had prayers for up to an hour and then we were out of bed by six. Breakfast was cooked in the kāuta on an open fire and normally comprised of a cup of tea and oven bread. We always blessed the food before eating. In fact, there was a prayer for just about everything. Then Pā and Hine Te Ariki would go off to work, "Right-o, haere tātou ki te mahi."

'One of the main occupations was tending the kūmara plantation. Pā would say a karakia before digging the kūmara out of the ground. In those days people were always so careful handling kūmara and other garden crops. I remember helping the old man put the kūmara one by one into a flax basket, carefully, so that they wouldn't get bruised — because if they did, they could go rotten in the kūmara pit. Then I would help him carry the kit to the pākoro, and all the time he'd be saying in Māori, "Careful, careful, grandson!" The kūmara pit was a small raupō house, so low you couldn't stand up in it. It was constructed so that when it rained the water would fall away on the outside of the pit and not come inside. Pā would crawl inside and I would start handing him the kūmara, one by one. Always he would be cautioning me, because I was forever in a hurry, "A! A! Don't tip the kūmara! Be careful! Kei mārū! You might bruise the kūmara!"

'I loved watching the way he put the kūmara into the pākoro: the first row on the solid ground, then the next row on top of it, giving a slight careful twist so that each kūmara fitted in nicely. The big kūmara were always placed at the back of the house and the small kūmara to the front. Always so much care! The reason? Because Māori lived from season to season and those kūmara had to last a year, between one harvest time and the next, so that there was sufficient food to keep everyone alive.

'I remember once I tried to go into the pākoro to help him, but he wouldn't let me, just in case I did a fart, because even that could make the kūmara go off.

'Kūmara was the main diet, supplemented with pūhā, pumpkin, ironbark pumpkin, and Māori bread baked from flour, water and sometimes yeast. Not many potatoes were grown at the time.

'Our main drink was water. Whenever it rained we had to catch water by any means and put it into three twenty-gallon wooden casks. We didn't have a tank. Sometimes, however, we had to get our water supplies from the Waipaoa River.

'I remember one day, Pā said to me, "Haere, tama, ki te tiki wai." We took two of our casks on the sledge down to the river. It was in flood and I wondered why we were getting this silty water.

'"This water is too dirty, Pā," I said. "How can we drink it?"

'"Don't ask too many questions," Pā answered. "Turituri."

'After we had taken the water home, he proceeded to bucket the water into the third cask, which was empty on the kitchen bench. When it was filled he said to me, "Go and get a mug." He turned on the tap at the bottom of the cask and the water came out clear! I was so astonished, until he told me his secret. At the bottom of the third cask was six inches of shingle, which filtered the impurities out of the water. Much later in life, I used this same principle when digging a well. I shovelled some shingle into the well because the water was so yellow. After a while, it came out clear.

'These are some of the ways by which the people showed their simple, natural wisdom. And at the end of every day's work, there was a prayer of thanksgiving before going home.

'Today I have to say that I have never wanted tribal leadership. When my brother Win was alive, I told him to do it. He used to say, "You're the eldest." Today I have realised that I have had to grow into this role of a kaumātua. I have tried to do my best according to Pā's and Hine Te Ariki's teachings.

'It was they who taught me to care, to look after people, to be unselfish, to give more than you take, to look after the kūmara, the royal children who will take the Māori into the future, and to try to stop them from being bruised.

'And always to have aroha.'

2.

I don't know why my father, Te Haa's, two simple tellings of storing the kūmara and of purifying the river water with his pā affected me so much. In the first instance, I think I tried to apply them to my own work, because was writing so different to storing kūmara? I began to think of my work as kūmara, which I could offer to people to enjoy; Māori say that the kūmara does not tell you how sweet it is until you taste it, and I wanted it to be sweet. Second, sometimes I think of the rewriting process as a purifying process, adding a layer of shingle at the bottom, to filter out the impurities. Man oh man, my father's pā would probably reprimand me for the heaps of shingle I have had to sometimes use to ensure that the words come out clear as the water of the Waipaoa River.

And Dad is right: the children are royalty. Every child is a prince or princess, an ariki. They are our future, and I am writing this memoir so that they know.

I didn't realise, however, how much my father's story had affected my own world view until 2009 when I was offered, and accepted, the University of Hawai'i's Citizen's Chair. I followed the Father of Pacific Literature, Albert Wendt.

I found myself living in Honolulu. There, I rented the beautiful apartment of Professor Cristina Bacchilega and her husband, John Rieder. At the time Cristina was chair of the university's English department and when she and John went on sabbatical they left me their car to use, along with 'anything you find in the refrigerator'. Superb wine awaited me as well as fine cheeses and other delicacies.

A month later, at the back of the refrigerator, I found the potato.

Now, I don't want John and Cristina to get upset about this story. Who knows? I probably bought some potatoes when I first arrived and one dropped out of sight where the moist conditions encouraged it to develop a blackish-greenish tinge and stimulated it to sprout knobbly growths, kind of like a miniature triffid. I showed the potato to my friend Glenn Yamashita, who told me I should put it down the waste chute, but I couldn't do that.

'Why not?' he asked, astonished.

I began my explanation. 'In legendary times, a potato could mean all the difference between living or dying. A potato, for instance, figures in our family history because Hine Te Ariki fed my father with one when he was a sickly baby, chewing it in her own mouth and putting it into his so that he would not die of starvation — but its importance is more profound than that.'

Warming to my subject, I related the story of how the kūmara, sweet potato, had been brought from Hawaiki to Aotearoa on the *Horouta* canoe, which had been the first ship of my mother's ancestors. Seedling cargo on the waka was spoiled when *Horouta* foundered at the mouth of the Ōhiwa River.

'A young voyager by the name of Pourangahua offered to return by canoe to Hawaiki to obtain a fresh supply. He came to shore at

Parinuiterā where his uncle, Ruakapanga, had a potato plantation and was only too pleased to offer his nephew a replacement cargo. However, Pourangahua had a problem. When he had left Aotearoa the kōwhai trees were already beginning to bud and the planting season was near. If he didn't make it back by then, and the seeds were not sown in the ground, there would be no crop to feed the people in the spring. They would surely die of starvation.

'As it happened, Ruakapanga had the fastest transport going at that time: two pet giant albatross called Hora-ngā-rangi and Teu-ngā-rangi.

'The birds would carry Pourangahua back to Aotearoa,' I told Glenn, 'but they came with a set of strict instructions. When Pourangahua arrived at Rarotonga he was not to fly them anywhere near Mount 'Ikurangi. An ogre lived there and would engage them in battle. Nor was he to touch or pull out their feathers while flying over the ocean to Aotearoa. And on arrival there, he was to feed them and give them water before he sent them back to Hawaiki. Pourangahua said, "Okay Uncle," and, astride the two birds, off he went! Of course, no sooner had he gained altitude than he disobeyed his uncle's instructions. Maybe he was in a hurry to get back to see his girlfriend.'

'Is that in the story?' Glenn asked, noting the contemporary tone and knowing my penchant for embellishment.

'No,' I answered. 'It's a possibility, though, don't you think?

'Anyway, Pourangahua flew right over 'Ikurangi, the high peak in the Cook Islands, where the ogre attacked him, and the two albatross had to fight back and were grievously wounded. Then, when Pourangahua was approaching Aotearoa, the birds began to circle and circle because they were looking for a place to land. Impatient, Pourangahua plucked a feather from each bird to force their descent.

'Naturally the people rejoiced to see Pourangahua and the new kūmara seeds. But there was no rejoicing for the two giant albatross. Auē, Pourangahua even forgot to feed them and give them water! Knowing that they would not survive the trip home, they began to weep for each other. The tears formed a particular pattern on the sand that Māori call the roimata toroa, the tears of the albatross.'

To get back to the story, Glenn and other Hawaiian friends kept on advising me to get rid of the triffid potato. 'After all,' Glenn said, 'it's not really a kūmara, is it?'

'But it's the same whānau,' I shot back.

My friends even spirited the potato out of the apartment while I wasn't looking, dropping it into the waste chute, but I had nightmares about what they had done so went down and retrieved it. After all, the whole of Ireland had suffered many deaths when the great potato famine began in 1845 (some people say 1846). The statistics are tricky: nearly a million died and the numbers who emigrated depend on what years you include, two million perhaps, mostly to America. But some came to Aotearoa too, including many lads who married into Māori families, so that's another plus we can credit to the potato isn't it?

In the end, after two weeks of eyeballing it, I ate the potato. I made a ritual feast. I roasted the potato, slathered its crevasses with butter, placed it in the middle of a nice lettuce and tomato salad and put every little dried black piece of it in my mouth.

'You owe me, Dad!'

I have never been able to leave any food on my plate or on anyone else's plate. At high-class restaurants I suffer dreadfully if friends don't eat everything. Rather than have me embarrass them in public, they ask for a doggy bag — and even that makes them shudder — so I can take the kai home.

I have a wooden panel in my house in Herne Bay, carved for me by my cousin, Greg Whakataka-Brightwell. When he asked me what story I wanted to have carved on it I immediately thought of Pourangahua on the back of those two pet albatross.

I wonder why Pourangahua wasn't punished? In most mythologies punishment is usually the punchline: 'You fly too close to the sun, you get burnt.'

In Māori myth, however, clearly a Māori Icarus doesn't fall into the sea. Gods and humans with supernatural powers can get away with anything.

It wasn't Pourangahua, however, I wanted to honour. The carving was to remind me of the two birds whose sacrifice saved a nation and enabled it to develop in the new world.

In another way, I wanted to honour my Irish ancestors. Some of my mother's tūpuna are from County Cork; they came here after the potato famine. One of my cuzzies even tells me our Irish kin are still waiting for us to return, 180 years after we left, to fix the gates and fences of our ancestral land.

mythical beings

CHAPTER 11
OGRESSES

———

Kurungaituku

———

Blind

———

Kurungaituku

BY NGĀHUIA TE AWEKOTUKU

She was huge, with long, strong legs and arms that swept across the sky like vast wings, trailing soft, glossy feathers. They sparkled in the sunshine, they glowed in the moonlight. Her name was Kurungaituku. She was half bird and half human. Her face was sometimes beautiful, and sometimes ugly, too. She was especially beautiful when she talked to her pets, and played and sang with them. Ngārara and mokomoko, lizards and skinks; pūngāwerewere and pūrerehua, spiders and butterflies. Kiore and kurī, the gentlest rats and tiniest dogs. And most of all, the birds. So many, it'd take days to name them, for they were all part of her family. One dainty little bird was her favourite — Miromiro — whom she fed special treats on a ledge high above the floor of their home.

They all lived together in a cave overlooking the forest, which rolled out rippling below them, a raw whāriki of dark treetops. It wasn't a very big cave, though, and Kurungaituku didn't enjoy housekeeping very much at all. With the pūngāwerewere and pūrerehua, the kiore and the kurī, the ngārara and the mokomoko, and all the birds busy fluttering in and out, things got very very messy.

Kurungaituku decided to do something about the problem. She decided that she needed a human friend, too, someone who could help keep the place clean, and dust out tired wings, and smooth ruffled feathers, and groom twitchy fur, and peel off wrinkled skins, and talk and play and sing with her family of pets.

She was tramping through the bush thinking about this one day, when she heard a strange, unusual voice that soared high into the trees. Even the birds ceased their own light, lovely melodies to listen.

Kurungaituku looked for the voice, and found its beginning. A young male human, striding along the leafy path, his white teeth flashing, his fine legs bending in time with his chant. He was what humans would call 'handsome'.

With a quick, graceful flexing of her feathered arms, Kurungaituku flew straight up into the air, to rest briefly on a branch. Absolutely silent, and still, she watched him for a while, then she floated quietly down, landing with a soft thud, just in front of him. He jumped back in surprise, and swallowed all his words.

———

The birdwoman didn't know what to do next, as she had never talked to a human before. But she was kind, and curious, and eager to talk to him. So she did.

He said his name was Hatupatu, and he was following the wind for a while, happy to go wherever it took him. Hearing this, Kurungaituku knew he was the one she needed. She invited him home to meet her pets, and maybe even stay for some time.

Hatupatu agreed, his eyes glittering. He had looked at the fabulous, richly feathered cloak she was wearing, so perfectly made it covered her like a shining skin, shimmering in black waves to the mossy ground.

I would like a cloak like that, he thought.

For a while, they were happy in the little cave atop the forest.

Hatupatu tidied up, dusted out tired wings, and smoothed ruffled feathers, and groomed twitchy fur, and peeled off wrinkled skins, and talked and played and sang. All the family loved him, except Miromiro, who shivered high up on her ledge and only came down for Kurungaituku. Instead, little Miromiro watched Hatupatu, and often saw him touching the birdwoman's special taonga that were kept in places hewn out at the very back of the cave, reaching in to the mountain. One treasure was a finely woven mantle of bright fresh blood: a silky soft, sorrowful memory of Kurungaituku's favourite feathered cousins, killed by humans for their beauty, and snatched back one moonless night by a vengeful birdwoman. With the cloak, she had claimed other human treasures — ornaments of pounamu and pāua, fine weapons of stone and wood. These taonga Hatupatu fondled, lovingly, with a faraway look in his eye, and a humming, greedy song upon his breath. Miromiro noticed these things, and drew back onto her ledge, quivering. She despised him.

————

The nights stretched out; the mornings became colder. Far over the forest, closer to the sea where the sun rose, bunches of karaka berries fell upon the ground, bursting and juicy. Hatupatu described them to Kurungaituku, how delicious they were, how plump and tasty. He was sure she'd enjoy them, and the family would, too, though the closest trees were at least a day's journey away, even for someone half bird and half human.

Hearing this pleased Kurungaituku. Her wings felt like a good stretch, and karaka berries sounded new and exciting. So Hatupatu encouraged her to go, promising to take care of everyone, the pūngāwerewere and pūrerehua, the ngārara and mokomoko, the kiore and kurī, and all the fluttering, twittering flock of little birds.

He reassured her, all he had to do was sing to them, and quietly, easily, they'd settle down, not missing her at all.

Smiling, Kurungaituku bade them all farewell, strapping an extra large pīkau across her sturdy back. She sprang from the cave's mouth, catching the wind, enjoying the view, and then, for a change, she paced along in the cool green shade beneath the trees.

————

Hours passed. The sun rose high above the forest, and welcome rays of warmth flooded into the cave.

Hatupatu stood at the entrance, flexing his muscles, admiring his shadow. Slowly, gently, softly, he sang; the family started waking, unfolding, to the new day.

With soundless tread, Hatupatu moved around the cave, his music low and lingering, his touch firm and true.

He dusted out tired wings, and crushed them to a pale ashy powder.

He smoothed ruffled feathers, and snapped thin bones and tufted necks.

He groomed twitchy fur, and hacked through yielding muscle.

He peeled off wrinkled skins, and shredded cool, soft flesh.

He killed. He maimed. He killed. Again, and again. Every one, every one. Except Miromiro, who hid high up on the ledge, drawn back into the weeping dark.

Hatupatu searched about for the largest kete. He found it, stuffed it full with pounamu and pāua, stone and wood. Quickly, he tugged the corded rim together, gathered it tight, slung it across his broad shoulders.

And with the shimmering kākahu draped firmly around him, he strode eagerly through the cave, the soles and sides of his feet reddening, stained with the blood of small broken forms and splintered bone strewn across the floor. Rippling red across his body, leaking red between his toes, Hatupatu smiled at the sky as he left the cave. Again, magical, his voice soared.

———

High up in her hideout, Miromiro waited until the sound faded, seemed to drift further and further away. Little wings buzzing, she flew straight out, not looking down, not weeping either. On and on and on she flew, towards the sea, where the sun climbed strong. Sometimes friendly breezes lifted Miromiro, carrying her along like a tiny floating leaf; other times she had to bend her beak against small fierce gusts, and push and push, thinking of her slaughtered family, thinking of Kurungaituku.

Heavy shadows were deepening the lush meaty leaves of the karaka when the brave one found her mistress, and told her story.

Kurungaituku tenderly placed Miromiro in the scooped fork of the giant karaka tree, lining the nest with soft grasses and sweet moss. She trickled healing teardrops across the tired little face, and settled her down to rest. She kept in all her feelings until she turned away, until she bent her huge feathered knees, and raised her massive arms, and leaped raging over the trees, and into the pale wintering sky.

Her anger was snarling, immense, but she contained it, controlled it, turned it into shafts of speed that glittered through her bloodstream, spiking her feathers, sharpening her talons, stretching her jaw. Her grief was thin and pointed and she directed it, beaming a long fine light from behind her tear-streaked eyeballs. She searched and searched, scanning the forest trails and tracks far below.

———

There it was, a snatch of red, moving swiftly through the trees, a blood drop, a dull spark. Moving swiftly through the trees, pacing himself with song. Hatupatu.

Wordlessly, without a sound, Kurungaituku dropped in front of him. He gasped, pulled the red cloak around himself, and clutched his bag of treasures. Clunk, the taiaha fell to the ground; a cruelly clawed foot spun its length skilfully aside.

Hatupatu began to run. For his life. He dropped the kete, ripped off the plundered mantle of feathers, and sprinted down the trail. Kurungaituku watched him go, as she flicked her kākahu around her hips, a melting band of red. She watched him go, waiting for him to tire, wondering at his feeble human form. On he raced, on, and on.

She lifted herself into the air, following his frantic dash through the trees. She felt grim, and vicious. But not in a hurry, not in a hurry at all.

Every now and then, she'd forcefully land on a weak-looking tree branch, laughing as it crashed madly to the ground, setting Hatupatu off in a spurt of crazy speed.

Every now and then, she'd thump fiercely through the under-growth herself, flattening plants, great feet clawing the soil, and hearing this, Hatupatu would lift his knees in panic, and force his legs harder, longer. On he raced, on, and on.

Soon, Hatupatu tired. And night was falling. He needed shelter.

The rock was there. Simply there, just off the trail. Very large, and warm, with one side hollowed at the base. Scooped out, like a bowl, man-sized, lined with dry leaves.

Squinting, he peered into the rustling darkness. The birdwoman was nowhere to be heard — or seen. Hatupatu listened, concentrating, for what seemed the longest time; he told himself she was off track somewhere, resting too. Feeling safe, he curled into his stony, makeshift nest, and fell asleep in the rock's embrace.

Upon the rock's highest point, her wings like silent, falling shadows, Kurungaituku settled to wait for morning. She dozed, she waited. She was not in a hurry at all.

First light, she awoke in a flurry of sighing feathers, and leaped high into the green branches overhead. Watching and waiting.

Hatupatu unrolled himself, stretched out, rubbed his eyes awake, and looked warily around him. He patted the rock once, hummed a lilting tune behind his teeth, and plucked a small frond from a nearby ponga fern. Giving quick thanks, he dropped it in the hollow, onto the pressed dry leaves. He grinned heartily, feeling rested, and gave the rock his name, too, in gratitude. He lifted his chin at the thought, about to compose a song . . . and saw her. Kurungaituku.

Fright gave his feet wings. He started sprinting again. On Hatupatu raced, on, and on.

Towards the earthy open fragrance of his family home, away from the thickness and tangle of forest trails and bushy tracks he ran.

The greenness stopped, suddenly; the large trees gave way to stunted, brownish scrub whose warped low-lying branches stretched across the earth. Here, he slowed down. He was almost home. For there, the ground breathed in muddy splashes of heat; glopping, stench-wet pools choked and chuckled in bands and blobs of colour; sometimes, higher than the tallest forest tree, a sleek shining panel of hot water shot into the air, caressing the sun.

Kurungaituku delighted in it all; clouds of dense grey vapour enfolded her briefly, gently, and just a few more tears slid down, blending with the geyser's breath. She hovered, and dipped swiftly down, testing the convulsing earth; she could see Hatupatu more clearly at ground level. She realised she had to use her feet, and not her wings; to run, and rush, and risk her life, like a human. He danced among the pools, ducking and diving here and there, pausing dramatically to taunt and sneer at her. He was almost home. On he raced, on, and on.

She chased him; he darted between pits, around clumps of wrinkled plant growth, through spiralling veins of steam. He knew the dangers and the death traps of this place, his family land.

She chased him, though the crust felt perilously thin beneath her claws. The steam billowed. The pool boiled, and hissed. She noticed him leap, skilfully planting his flat human feet; she noticed him leap, far across the pool, in one smooth swift stretch. The steam billowed, dense clouds darkening, concealing; the pool boiled, and hissed. Kurungaituku sensed the earth heave, slightly, the smallest warning; her curved, curling toes gripped the pool's tumbling edge. And then, she knew what he was trying to do.

He paused, again; he looked at her. He smiled.

The rim collapsed beneath her weight. The steam billowed, dense clouds darkening, concealing. The pool boiled, and hissed. She howled, she screamed; the horror of little crushed wings, and thin snapped bones, and frail shredded flesh swelling in her voice, the horror. And the never-ending pain. She howled, she screamed. And then, suddenly, she stopped. Suddenly. Silent, silent as defeat. Silent as death.

Hatupatu stood, utterly still. He listened, concentrating, for what seemed the longest time. The steam billowed, dense clouds darkening, concealing. The pool boiled, and hissed. He listened, then walked away, singing his triumph.

While the pool boiled, and hissed, and another column of bright white water reached breathless heights, thick clouds of spray and dark rich spume rainbowed the air.

Riding the moist winds, streaking swift into the sun, lifted by the geyser's life, Kurungaituku stretched her aching, scalded wings, tasted cool air upon her burning face, and flew, and flew. In retreat, to rest — for a while.

She went home, and she waited, and she watched. She was not in a hurry at all. And Hatupatu, with his thankful, disbelieving family, celebrated his return with feasting and games and festive dance. New songs were sung, and new stories told, and these Hatupatu rolled over his tongue, chanted lustily with his ever glorious, magical voice.

So the legend grew. How bravely he escaped; how cunningly he hid and rested; how viciously she perished. Kurungaituku. Tricked by handsome, wily Hatupatu, she plunged to her death in a boiling pool.

————

Days melted easily into weeks, and Hatupatu's fame spread throughout the land. Kurungaituku listened to these tales, and relaxed in her place high in the mountains. She mourned her little lost loved ones, and set about finding a new family of friends.

Ngārara and mokomoko, lizards and skinks; pūngāwerewere and pūrerehua, spiders and butterflies; kiore and kurī, the gentlest rats and the tiniest dogs. And most of all, the birds. Many visited her, to share her grief, and make her feel better, and many stayed. They knew of her kindness; they learned of her terrible betrayal. They loved her, and they formed another whānau in the cave, and Kurungaituku's heart began to heal, just a little, day by day. Until Miromiro, her faithful messenger, came home with some interesting news.

Hatupatu had been boasting about the kete of precious things left behind in the forest. He said he'd go and get them, bring their great beauty back to the people to admire and enjoy, for Kurungaituku was no more. With lilting words, and shining melody, he had described each taonga, buffing the pounamu, polishing the bone, weaving a spell of expectation that tingled through the village.

Carrying another strong kete he set off, a long, elegant kaitaka cloak draped across one shoulder, the other bared to the warm morning sun. He wandered through the bubbling, mud-pooled landscape, and ventured into the dark, green forest. He searched his memory for the place he'd dropped the big heavy bag on the trail and thrown off the plundered mantle of feathers, as he'd sprinted for his life.

Music, and sun, filled his day. Small birds seemed to guide his way; they fluttered and trilled, and chirped and danced, always, always, just a few feet in front of him, dappled by the spangled sunbeams that spun from dew-moist leaves. They dipped, and twirled, and dived; they stopped, hovering, close to one side of the trail. They circled, once, twice, and two more times, then flashed swiftly into the trees. Hatupatu was puzzled; his song ceased, his stride paused. The kete was there, bunched up, broken, by the path.

He saw her first. Kurungaituku. Horror and disbelief made him noisy; panic and fear made him clumsy.

He was bending down, to grasp the kete, damp and damaged by the rain. Pounamu, bone and pāua gleamed within. He was bending down, and he saw her. Quaking with fear, he dropped the kete, and tripped, muddying his kaitaka.

He scrambled up. He smiled, he flashed his teeth, he plucked and smoothed the mud from his cloak, and with all his dignity and handsomeness, he faced Kurungaituku. Or her ghost, he told himself, hiding his fright behind a wide, charming grin, while sweat oozed and dripped along his collarbone. It had to be her ghost, who would remember his beauty, his specialness, his voice. So he smiled, he flashed his teeth. And again, he began to sing.

Without warning, she struck.

Claws reached down into his mouth, and tore out his tongue. Crushed his back teeth to a pale, ashy powder; snapped the front ones, so thin and white; shredded the cool, soft flesh of his gums, hacked deep into his throat muscles.

Silenced his voice. Forever.

———

Kurungaituku picked up the big heavy bag, bundled it into her pīkau. Leaning over Hatupatu, she wiped her talons on the fine, soft flax of his kaitaka, and she sighed to herself. His voice was gone. His beauty ruined. Kaitoa.

All that would be left of him, from that moment on, was the story. The legend.

That, she grimaced to herself as she left his crumpled breathing body in the fern, should be more than enough.

And so it was.

Blind

BY KELLY ANA MOREY

1964

'Watch out for that one,' the nurse says, leading me through yet another bare room. She points at an elderly Māori woman, sitting in a single square of sunlight, on a straight-backed wooden chair. A blue and green crocheted blanket falls across her legs and tumbles to the floor. 'She's generally got a vicious tongue on her, though she goes quiet in the winter,' continues the nurse. 'We think she hibernates once the colder weather sets in. Barely eats a thing and goes mute, the old crocodile.'

'Are there many like her?'

'Long-term patients, or murderesses?'

'She's a murderess?'

'The Matekai Street Child Killer, would you believe,' the nurse replies, stopping at the door that's on the opposite side of the one we used to enter the room. 'Been here nearly twenty years. But, apart from being mean, she's mostly pretty harmless — and blind as a bat.'

'Oh . . . of course I've heard about her,' I say, hoping I'm disguising how genuinely shaken I am by the information. Though, in many ways, I'm not even surprised she's here, at my final nurse-training placement. It's like I've been waiting my whole life to come face-to-face with her.

'She's like Minnie Dean — kind of infamous,' I continue, consciously keeping my voice soft so the old woman can't hear me. 'I grew up in Grey Lynn, so when we were kids our mum always used to threaten us with the Matekai Street Kid Killer. But I don't even think I was born when they arrested her.'

'It was VJ Day, 1945,' the nurse replies. 'Funny how you remember things like that. It was all over the newspapers. I remember them wanting her to hang for her crimes. But, in the end, they sentenced her here for the rest of her life.'

'But, wasn't she old back then when they arrested her?' I ask.

'They thought so. She couldn't tell anyone when she was born — and still can't. Or won't,' replies the nurse, unlocking the door with one of the multiple keys that jangle on a ring that hangs from her belt. 'But here she is, nearly twenty years later, still going strong. Though it's obvious she's been in the wars. The doctors say her heart is good and she's remarkably active when it's warm. There's nothing wrong with her upstairs either. Still got all her faculties and of course that vicious tongue,' she continues, holding the door open for me before following me out. 'It's incredible really. She'll outlive us all.' There's a click as the door locks behind us. The nurse then opens yet another door, and this one lets us out behind the building and into the grounds.

Outside it's no warmer than it was inside. The sun may be shining and the sky an endless expanse of blue, but the thin wind that's sweeping up from the mountains has the shiver of fresh snow on its breath. I hate winter at the best of times, but out here it's so desolate that I wonder how I'll survive.

'We'll go and get your uniform sorted out and get you settled in at the nurses' home,' the nurse says. 'Then you'll have a quick meeting with matron, then someone will give you the proper guided tour. What did you say your name was again?'

'Jennifer. Jennifer Devich,' I reply.

'Oh, a Dally, eh?' the nurse says, swallowing my name, my fair skin, my Pākehā hair and green eyes without a thought.

'Yes,' I reply, more than happy to be Jennifer Devich the Dally new girl. It just makes things easier. 'If you can pass for a Tararā, you might as well,' Mum's always said. 'My mum and dad are from up north,' I continue, 'but they moved to Auckland a bit before I was born.'

'Rita Stephens,' the nurse says suddenly smiling. 'Welcome to Kingseat, Jennifer Devich. Don't worry, you'll get used to it. It's always a bit of a shock at first. But you'll get the hang of it and it's not that bad really.'

So begins the next year of my life. Long shifts, lousy living conditions and the opening and closing of doors. I have one day's leave a week to go to Pukekohe and one weekend leave a month to go home. Do I make friends? Not really. I'm just one of those girls who is passing through. The lifers, they can smell it on me. I'm soft and they know it.

———

My whole life I've listened to my mother rail against my father. Don't get me wrong, they have it pretty good together — but for one single thing. The house my dad bought dirt cheap in 1946 when he and Mum first came to Auckland as newly-weds.

'Typical Tararā,' Mum says after a few glasses of Dad's home-brew. 'Couldn't resist a good deal could he?' This always makes Lorna and me laugh, because Mum's as much a Tararā as Dad is Māori, even if he doesn't look it. They both have a bit of both, it's just that Mum is as dark as Dad is fair.

But to give Dad due credit, 35 Matekai Street is a beautiful house. It's liberally decorated with wooden gingerbread and made of red brick from the works over the hill, though it dates from many years before Dad got a job there. It's just a little unfortunate that it's also the house where at least five children were killed and thought to have been eaten by a deranged blind old woman.

'And you think, Annie, that we could have afforded this place any other way?' Dad always replies when Mum gets riled up about living in a murder-house. This being the most he will say in his own defence on his one mistake. He's easier with the ghosts than Mum. There's a history of it in his family. Mum and Lorna are more literal. Me? I'm just sitting on the fence. So, my sister Lorna and I grow up overlooking the ground where we believe they exhumed the bones of children. It wouldn't be until much later that I would discover that all the police found when they dug up the backyard were five small skulls that had been thoroughly gnawed 'as if by an animal'.

Throughout my childhood I randomly find children's teeth in the backyard. Pearly milk teeth like chips of ivory. They push up through the soil like crocuses at the first taste of sun. I keep them in a Red Jacket cigarette tin that my uncle from Canada gave to me that one time he came home to New Zealand for a visit. Mum plants dahlias in the backyard every spring. We're the only people on our street who don't have a vegetable garden.

I never wanted to be a nurse. Not one little bit of it. But when I didn't get into teachers' training college, nursing was what was left in the 'good job' basket. So, off I went to start my training, and ended up at Kingseat — with all the loonies.

By the time the spring arrives, I tell myself that I've almost accepted my fate. Though if I'm honest, the place gives me the creeps. Patients and staff, we all know it's haunted. I'm new, so I'm kept away from the patients who are locked up all the time. Almost all the nurses who work in those wards are men. On still nights, lying in our beds in the nurses' home, we can hear the cries of the truly deranged. It seems worse when there's a full moon.

I get to look after the drunk women who are there for the cure. My one and only stroke of luck thus far in my working life. The drunks, everyone tells me, are the easiest. Most of them are regulars, according to the long-time staff of Villas 11 and 4 where the dipsos are kept. Periodically sent here to dry out by their families. At least I'm not serving a life sentence like some of the people here. The moment my time's up, I'm gone. I'll go and work in the sewing factory with my friend Erin if I have to.

I discover that the Matekai Street Child Murderess is called Mereana by the staff, because no one knows what her real name is, and no one ever has. Throughout the winter I periodically come across her, curled up in corners, her hooded eyelids dropped almost completely over her blank reptilian eyes. I see her and I keep walking. If she's dead, someone else can find her.

It stays cold until mid-October when a warm wind finally drifts down from the Pacific and, in a matter of days, brings everything back to life. I'm doing a rare shift in one of the general wards because a couple of the staff have gone to a funeral. Because it's the first truly warm day in a long time, we — me and three other staff — herd everyone out of the common room and into the grounds. Everyone except Mereana, who is sitting in an armchair in her usual semi-comatose state with the ginger tomcat that's a bit of a fixture around the place. He sits on her lap, purring as he kneads away at the wool blanket covering her legs. 'Will she be all right by herself?' I ask the others, who are lighting cigarettes as they watch the patients responding in their various ways to the kiss of warmth on their faces.

'Who?' they ask.

'Mereana.'

'Oh Mary Anne. Yes, she's fine,' the most senior nurse says. 'She's locked in. Nothing much can happen to her other than falling off of her chair.' They all laugh like it's the funniest thing they've ever heard.

Mad old Māori lady falls off her chair onto a concrete floor. Hilarious.

Because I'm young and don't know how to stand my ground, I follow the others out into the garden. We're almost at the collection of broken-down furniture under a magnolia tree when the senior nurse turns to me and says, 'You wouldn't mind going and getting us a cup of tea from the kitchen would you?'

It's not a question, so I turn back, retracing my steps. On the way to the kitchen I pause and look in through the common-room window. From my limited viewpoint I can see that Mereana's chair is empty. As quickly as I can, I let myself back into the building, then into the common room, swearing under my breath as I fumble the keys. Mereana hasn't just fallen off her chair, she's got about three feet away from it. She is painfully inching her way across the floor towards the windows and the patches of sunlight that have just started to paint the linoleum-covered concrete. The woollen blanket has twisted around her legs and trails behind her like a tail. The blanket's scalloped pattern looks like scales in the glittering light that's flooding the room. Mereana's body twists and flexes like an articulated automaton. A grotesque facsimile of the real thing. Though, what that thing is I'm not quite sure.

'Mereana, let me help you,' I say running across to her, slipping as I step through something viscous that's been spilt on the floor. Somehow, I keep my balance, a skill a psychiatric nurse learns to do fast in a place where there's always something — blood, vomit, shit and piss — spilt on the floor. I crouch down and lean over Mereana. Her face is locked in a spasm. Her lips peeled back over her gums as the seizure grabs hold of her. Her teeth are rotted down to blackened points. 'It's all right, Mereana, I'm here,' I say, grabbing her hands and lifting her head off the floor so she can feel me through the fog of electrical disturbance. Her hands are cold and she smells like the muddy creek at the bottom of my grandmother up-north's place. The creek where my cousins and my grandmother's cats hook out eels.

Time passes, I don't know how much. I just suddenly become present and Mereana is calm, as am I. The only sound in the room apart from the ticking of the clock is our long, measured breaths.

'I see you, Girlie,' she says.

'I see you too,' I reply. 'Let me help you,' I continue. 'Can we get you up?' For a frail old lady she's surprisingly heavy and it takes a bit of work to get her upright and back to her chair. I tuck the blanket in around her after I've settled her back in. I'm about to leave to get the tea when she beckons me close. She grabs hold of my arm, running her hands over it hungrily. 'You skinny like a 'Kehā,' she says dismissively. 'No bloody good to Rūruhi-Kerepō. But I have something to tell you, Girlie.'

'What's that, Mereana?'

'Ko Rūruhi-Kerepō ahau,' she says. 'This is the first thing you need to know.'

'I'm sorry,' I say. 'I don't speak Māori.' I wait for her to translate what she said into English but she waves me away.

'No bloody good to anyone,' she says again.

I hear the outside door being opened, then the jangle of keys as the senior nurse lets herself in to the common room followed by an orderly. 'Came to see what had happened to our tea,' she says.

'I found Mereana on the floor,' I explain. 'I think she had a seizure. But other than that she seems to be all right.'

'Oh, Mereana, you're back,' the nurse says, not unkindly.

'Lock up your children,' quips the orderly and they both laugh.

'Nothing to worry about. The old girl comes to life every spring,' continues the senior nurse. 'Come on, Jen, you can find her some clean clothes and since you and her are such great friends you can help with her bath too.' Once again she and the orderly laugh in that unkind way that people do when you're getting the short end of the stick.

As I'm about to leave the room, I look back over my shoulder and Mereana is looking straight at me. She raises a finger and taps the side of her nose, the universal sign of conspiracy. I have no idea what she means.

It's not until a few days later that I realise the ginger tomcat has vanished, and that I have no memory of him being in the room during Mereana's seizure.

I'm home on my monthly weekend leave and Erin's come around. We've gone for a walk, which is our code for sitting in a nearby park smoking cigarettes while we exchange news. From where I'm sitting, Erin's got it made. She has a boyfriend who she's been putting up with for two years — that's Jimmy. She lives at home on Rose Road, a few streets over, with her mum and dad and three younger siblings. Also, she works at a garment factory in Avondale, which sounds like a damn sight more fun than looking after dipsomaniacs in an insane asylum. So much for Mum's, 'You're too good to end up in a factory waiting to get married'.

'How's it going?' asks Erin. 'Still counting the days until your place-ment is over?' She continues taking deep drags on her cigarette.

'Five months to go,' I say, taking a cigarette out of the packet of Pall Mall filterless that lies between us. Her father's brand of choice, so he's today's benefactor of the 'holy nicotine', as Erin likes to say. 'Though, really, apart from being vomited on, it's not that bad. Mainly it's just a little bit boring and a bit lonely. I never thought I'd miss Lorna and her endless prattle.'

Erin gives me a sympathetic look. 'Hang in there, I'm sure you'll get a job somewhere good when you're finished.'

'What if I don't? What if I end up staying there or get Carrington?'

'Better than where I'm going to end up,' says Erin, who's suddenly trying not to cry.

'What do you mean?'

'Well, I've only gone and got myself pregnant, haven't I? Promise you won't tell anyone.'

'Are you sure?' I ask. 'Is it Jimmy's?'

'Well, of course it's Jimmy's!' Erin says. 'Jeez, what kind of question is that?'

'Oh . . . yeah. That was dumb. But won't you just get married?' I ask. 'I kinda thought that was the plan anyway. Work at the factory until you turn twenty, marry Jimmy, get a house and have a million kids.'

'That was the plan, but things haven't been so good between us lately. I'm pretty sure he's seeing some other girl, which is why I . . . you know,' Erin explains. She pauses and drags deeply on her cigarette, sucking the last remnants of life out of it. 'I'm not even sure I want to get married to Jimmy, to be honest.'

'You have to tell him about the baby though.'

'Yeah, I know. I'll do it tonight. After the dance.'

'You've been smoking,' Mum says when we get back from our 'walk'. 'I can smell it on you.'

'See you later,' Erin says, exiting swiftly out the back door.

She'll be back with Jimmy later in his dad's car to pick me up for the dance.

Mum slides a corned-beef sandwich in front of me as I sit down at the kitchen table. 'You should eat before you get dressed,' she says.

My little sister Lorna comes into the kitchen and sits down beside me. 'I wish I could go to the dance,' she says. Lorna is fifteen and already boy-mad. She's allowed to go to dances at the Community

Centre in Freemans Bay with Mum and Dad, but the Orange in Newton is forbidden territory.

'You're too young,' says Mum, who has the final word on all things, as she tumbles store-bought potatoes into the sink to be washed and peeled for dinner. 'Especially for a Valentine's Day dance.'

Sitting there, eating and half-listening to Mum and Lorna bicker, I wonder why I've never told Erin about Mereana, even though I've told her about lots of the other patients. The memory of helping scrub that ancient body of a year's worth of filth a few weeks ago haunts me.

How we peeled the layers of rotten fabric from her body. How she twisted and turned in our hands, slippery and fleshy, until the warmth of the water calmed her and she fell into a half sleep, exhausted by her wakening. The trickle of water running into the drain on the floor and the sound of our breathing. Once she calmed down I could see the scar tissue on scar tissue, thick cords of it slashing her entire body. Bone ends protruded, threatening to push through the thickened skin that contained them. It was as if every bone had been broken and then healed in a fractured state, forming ridges and spines beneath the landscape of her tortured body.

'What happened to her?' I whispered.

'No one knows,' answered the nurse who was helping me.

Once the layers of filth had softened a bit we began to wash Mereana with soapy rags. She started to croon happily, almost purring as we gently soaped her clean. With the worst of the grime dislodged and the water gone tepid and brown, the nurse helping me turned around and started running one of the other baths in the room so we could rinse Mereana off in clean water.

That's when it happened. That first flicker of a vision behind my eyes. Seeing the sharpened bone of an eel gaff coming at me and hearing that thick, gristly crunch as the sharpened bone bit into flesh only to tear through it and vanish upwards towards the watery light. Gone as quickly as it had arrived.

'Are you all right?' the other nurse asked, looking over her shoulder as she turned off the taps.

'Yes,' I said with absolute certainty. 'Yes. Come on, let's get her rinsed off and dressed.'

After that, Mereana becomes something of a fixture in my life. 'She likes you,' the other staff say in amazement. 'It's given her a whole new lease on life.'

I have to take their word for it, but throughout the summer, in the rickety old wheelchair someone's found her, Mereana is everywhere. No matter how much I try to hide, she always finds me. 'Girlie,' she says, and beckons me closer. And I can't say no.

So Erin and I, who tell each other everything, especially those things like Mr Hartley and the things he did when we were in primary school. Things we can't tell anyone else. Erin who held in her news about the baby, so I would be the first to know. Erin and I who swore to be friends forever when we were only eight years old. Erin and I finally have a secret between us. But it won't be just her. I don't even talk about Mereana to my mum. I never speak about the visions that keep coming: the fury of creation, of fire and shaking earth and strange creatures emerging from the fissured ground; the crack of muskets and the sudden terrible bloom of flesh struck by lead; the screams of children and the wailing mothers left behind. I never speak to anyone about how the sights and sounds don't frighten me, not really. It's this place, I think, though really I know it's Mereana and she's telling me a story I don't understand.

A few hours later at the Orange's Valentine's Day dance, Erin and I are dancing up a storm to Ray Paparoa and his band. Ray is known as 'The Māori Elvis from Pukekohe', and Erin and I think he's all that and a bit more. Usually, he plays at the Māori Community Centre in Freemans Bay. It's not often we go to the Orange which has a much more Pākehā — and younger — crowd. Jimmy and the boys prefer it. At the Community Centre the wardens have their eye on them. They know exactly what their game is. Things have got far too 'free and easy' according to some of the older people who have been going to the Centre since it opened after the war. It's still about family, though, but they do let us do the twist. It's been getting quieter at the Centre lately, as families move out to the new suburbs.

Jimmy is hovering around the door, sliding out onto the street every so often to smoke and drink with his friends. He's no dancer. Never has been. 'That's reason enough,' Erin has said on a number of occasions, 'not to marry him.'

Ray Paparoa finishes his set and the dance floor clears as people head downstairs to the basement where the Orange has its refreshment room. Erin and I go outside, hoping to catch a kiss of breeze that will cool us down. Outside is almost as hot as in. We sit on the concrete stairs that are mercifully cool now the sun has gone down. Jimmy breaks away from his mates and comes over.

Erin sighs. 'I need to tell you something,' she says to him.

'All right,' he replies, taking a last drag from the cigarette pinched between his thumb and forefinger.

'Not here,' Erin says, standing up. 'Let's go for a walk. You'll be all right won't you Jen?'

'Sure,' I reply.

'Can I take the smokes?' asks Erin.

'Yeah,' I reply. 'You need them more than me.'

I stay sitting on the stairs as they cross the road and head down St Benedicts Street. The sweat on my skin has cooled and it's nice, so nice, just to be sitting out here by myself.

'Have you been abandoned?' a Pākehā guy says, coming up behind me and sitting down. I don't know him from a bar of soap, but I like his cheek.

'I really think I have,' I reply, 'but for a good cause.'

'Will Murdoch,' he says, extending his hand.

'Jennifer Devich,' I say, taking his hand and shaking it.

'A pleasure,' he says, with a big goofy grin. His teeth are crooked but beautifully white. 'I was watching you and your friend, you know, dancing. You two are pretty good. And now she's disappeared and The Playdates are going to start their set soon. We wouldn't want you to miss that.'

'Are you asking me to dance?'

'Oh good,' Will says, 'thank heavens you understood all that.'

'I'm gasping for a cup of tea. Do you think we have time?'

'Plenty of time,' Will says, standing up and extending his hand once again and helping me to my feet. 'We have all the time in the world.'

Erin and Jimmy return as The Playdates, the last act of the night, are finishing. Erin's make-up has mostly been cried off, but they're both smiling, so obviously things are going to work out for the best. Which I had figured anyway.

'We're getting married,' Erin says excitedly. I hug her and am happy — because what other choice did Erin really have?

'Congratulations,' Will says.

'Who are you?' asks Erin.

'Oh,' I say, and laugh. 'Erin, Jimmy, this is my new friend, Will.'

'We're going to a party in Ponsonby,' says Jimmy. 'You two up for it?'

'Not me,' I reply. 'I need to go home. I have to be back at work by midday, so have to catch an early bus.'

'Ah,' says Erin, without malice, 'you're no fun.'

'You can go if you want to,' I say to Will.

'A gentleman always walks his dance partner home,' he says. 'So where was it you lived again?'

'Helensville,' I say for fun.

'It's going to be a long night then,' he fires back with that goofy smile thing happening again.

Jimmy laughs, 'We'll drop you off up the top of K Road.'

'It's a start I guess,' says Will. 'You don't really live in Helensville, do you?'

'She lives on Matekai Street in Grey Lynn,' says Jimmy. 'That's our Jen. Always the joker.'

The next day I return to Kingseat. It's another four weeks until I get another weekend leave. Will and I have already arranged to go to a dance next time I'm home, but it's far too much in the future for both of us, so he telephones to find out when my next day's leave in Pukekohe is due. We meet on King Street and talk about going to the pictures, but end up in a tearoom talking avidly. I find out that he's from Palmerston North, about to start his final year at law school and works part-time at The White Lady on Shortland Street to make ends meet. He is the first person in his family to go to university, so feels a weight of responsibility.

'I like you, Jen Devich,' he says as we part.

'And I like you too, Will Murdoch,' I reply.

I'm one of Erin's bridesmaids when she and Jimmy marry six weeks later. Her mum does a good job on the dress and she barely shows, not that anyone cares now they've made it down the aisle and back. Will joins the wedding party as my partner. Erin opts for pale blue as her colour and, in years to come, Will and I will derive a great deal of pleasure from the wedding photos. Our first as a couple. 'Baby blue,' I always say. 'What was she thinking?'

Will makes the journey out to Pukekohe at least twice a month for the remainder of my placement and I spend so much of my time with him when I'm home that Mum's already talking white dresses and bridesmaids, even though it's only been a few months.

'Leave them alone, Annie,' chides Dad, who likes Will. 'They're just kids.'

Fortunately for me, Lorna sneaking out to the airport at Whenuapai to see The Beatles takes the heat off me. She would have got away with it too, if her picture hadn't been on the front page of the *Herald*. There's a fair bit of shouting about her 'making a spectacle of herself' with Dad threatening to send her North to stay with our grandmother, Nan. Though, predictably, because it's Lorna, nothing comes of it.

———

I've come off Saturday night duty with less than a week left of my time at Kingseat to go, and it's been a hard night's work with the police bringing three new patients into the drunk-tank villas. I smell like vomit but even that can't get me down as I walk across the grounds to the nurses' home, anticipating a bath. By next Sunday morning I'll be at home in my own bed with nothing much to do for six whole weeks before I start my new job. Mereana is waiting by the front door of the nurses' home in her wheelchair. I'm really surprised to see her as now that the cold weather has set in, she's retreated back into herself. But there she is, remarkably bright and obviously has a bone to pick with me.

'Kia ora, Mereana,' I say, coming to a halt in front of her.

'Oh, kia ora now is it?' she says slyly. 'Maybe you're not so useless after all, Girlie.'

'What are you doing here, Mereana? You know it's out of bounds.'

She gives me a long watery look and then suddenly grins. 'I've come to see you, Girlie.'

'Why?' I say, sitting down on the stairs.

'You're going away.'

'Yes, that's right,' I reply.

'Why?'

'Because I can't stay here. Because I want to see the world,' I reply.

'I'll find you,' she says.

'Maybe,' I reply, thinking she'd have to have an escape plan a bit more dynamic than an old wheelchair. In two months' time, I'll be boarding a boat for England as an elderly woman's nurse and companion. Will is going to follow me at the end of the year, after his last exam — though that bit Mum and Dad don't know about.

'I know you, Girlie,' Mereana says, pausing to cough wetly and hoik up a thick wad of phlegm, spitting it on the concrete. Her chest sounds muddy and heavy like she's swimming underwater and I don't like her chances of surviving another winter. 'And I have something to tell you,' she continues.

'What's that, Mereana?'

'Ko Rūruhi-Kerepō ahau,' Mereana says, growing in stature, her voice suddenly strong.

'I'm sorry, Mereana, I don't speak Māori.'

'Ahhh,' she says, 'bloody useless. I am Rūruhi-Kerepō.'

'Oh,' I say, because to me it's just a name. 'How lovely.'

'Ko Rūruhi-Kerepō ahau,' she says again. When she says it in Māori it has so much more power. In English the statement is somehow diminished.

'Ko Rūruhi-Kerepō ahau,' I say, standing up. 'I'll remember that.'

'You go now, Girlie,' she says, dismissing me.

Erin has her baby a few days before I sail across the ocean — as far away from Auckland as I can get. I wonder, in those days leading up to my departure, if I'll ever come back.

2004

Erin's already waiting at a table when I walk into Alleluya. 'Erin. Hiya. Sorry I'm late,' I say, pleased that she's chosen a table that looks over Myers Park. Beneath the concrete and steel of St Kevins Arcade, I can feel the trickle of the Waihorotiu Stream, the Queen Street river that still percolates deep beneath the ground here.

'No worries,' she replies. 'I've only just arrived. And it's Erina, these days.'

'When did that happen?' I ask, sitting down.

'Back in the 70s.'

'Oh, of course,' I reply. 'I missed all that. We were in London.'

'K Road is so flash these days isn't it?' says Erina, changing the subject. 'I hardly ever get into the city so I really notice the changes.'

'The Las Vegas, a few sex shops and Rendells are hanging in there. George Courts is long gone of course. It's very nice apartments now. Do you remember our mums getting us dressed up and taking us there for special shopping?'

'Ha,' laughs Erina. 'Mum always got people's wedding presents from there, so she could shame the down-country rellies who inevitably turned up with "Māori food" as she called it. Funny really, these days I'd kill for a feed of kina or pāua. Thank goodness for Rendells though,' she continues. 'There doesn't seem to be any parking around here anymore except in their car park. Where did you park?'

'I walked,' I say.

'Why?' asks Erina. 'I'm so lazy Stan says I'd drive to the shops if they were next door.'

'I like it,' I say. 'It clears my head. And it's really not that far from my place. I hardly ever use my car, to be honest. Me, traffic and parking are not such a good mix.'

'I can't believe you still live in your mum and dad's house on

Matekai Street. I'm sorry Jen, that's a bit weird you rattling around that old house by yourself. And these days it must be worth a fortune. You should cash up.'

'I like it,' I reply. 'And remember I spent almost thirty years in the UK, so it doesn't feel like I've been stuck there since time began. Shall we order?' I continue, 'I'm dying for a coffee, and they do a great eggs benedict here.'

'How long has it been?' asks Erina after we've ordered our food and coffees at the counter.

'I was thinking about it last night, and when I left your baby had just been born. I can't even remember her name!'

Erina laughs. 'That baby has just had her fortieth. I called her Nicolette. At the moment we're calling her Nicorette, as she's just given up the smokes and she's as grumpy as a taniwha.'

'Forty years,' I say. 'That's almost forever.'

'Jesus!' Erina says. 'No wonder we look so old. I have grandchildren who are teenagers!'

'Are you and Jimmy still together?'

'Oh, God no, we broke up when the kids were little. He could never keep it in his pants so I thought I was better off if he was someone else's problem. After Jimmy there was Gary, what a no-hoper he was. Still, took me another two kids in three years to work that one out. He went out for a packet of smokes one day and that was the last anyone heard of him. Could be in Oz or could be dead for all I know. We'd been arguing for a while so he probably legged it. So, not a cent of child support. At least Jimmy always provided for his kids. And now I'm with Stan who's Tongan, we met up when we were both protesting the Tour and that was twenty years ago. Stan's been a life saver. He took on all my kids like they were his own.'

'How many kids did you end up having?' I ask as our coffees arrive.

'Six, would you believe. The youngest, who's Stan's, just graduated from university.'

'I thought you worked out what caused them with the first,' I say. 'I clearly remember you saying, never, ever again.'

Erina laughs, 'I kept forgetting — that's the problem.'

'Still, lots of them to look after you in your old age,' I offer in consolation.

'Little buggers ruined my body though. Nobody remembers that I was once skinny. Having babies and giving up the smokes was my downfall. I stacked it on.' There's a long awkward silence as the undeniable fact that Erina has indeed 'stacked it on' hangs between us.

'So anyway,' I say, 'what have you been doing for the last forty years besides having kids?'

'To be honest,' she says, as our food arrives (a virtuous salad for her and eggs benedict gleaming with rich yellow hollandaise for me and my hangover), 'turns out having kids is a full-time job.'

'How are your brother and sister?'

'Well, Jonty and his missus did pretty good for themselves when they sold up a couple of years ago. They moved to the Gold Coast the lucky buggers. They've got a great condo. And Susan's first husband died in a car accident not long after they were married leaving her with two under two, but she remarried and lives in New Plymouth. Nice bloke. Dairy farmer. We don't see her that often. And of course Dad died a few years ago and Mum's just moved to the same retirement village as your mum, thanks to the killing we made selling Rose Road to yuppies. It's pretty funny when you consider how much we all nagged Mum and Dad to move to a nice new house out in Papakura where we all were back in the day. But no, they wouldn't leave their beloved Rose Road. Guess Mum had the last laugh on that one. So all pretty boring really. Unlike you with your exciting life overseas.'

'To be honest, it wasn't that exciting, or as much of a good time as you might think. We lived, we worked, we travelled. But in the end we came home anyway.'

'Yeah,' says Erina. 'Mum told me your husband died. Did you meet him in London?'

'No. Will was the guy I met at the Orange all those years ago.'

'He came to my wedding, didn't he?'

'He sure did.'

'You married that guy?'

'I sure did.'

'It was cancer, wasn't it?'

'Yes,' I reply, 'but it was quite slow, so he got to have time with his family and say his goodbyes properly.' I don't give her anything other than the bare facts. It's not a secret, but even all these years later, the memory of Will dying still knocks the breath out of me.

'How long ago was that? Mum wasn't sure.'

'Eight years ago,' I reply. 'Sometimes it still feels like yesterday, but you box on, you know.'

'No new man in your life?'

'No . . . just Crowley the cat.'

'Are you still working?'

'Yes,' telling her the name of the private clinic I work at.

'Oh,' Erina says. 'Is that the abortion clinic?'

'Yes, I'm a theatre nurse there. Have been for a while now.'

'Wow, that's . . .'

'It's a job. And a worthwhile one at that. When I was in the UK, we had a lot of Irish girls coming through one of the clinics I was working at and they were terrified because what they were doing was criminal.'

'Have you always been an abortionist?'

I laugh. 'I'm not technically an abortionist, but from the 70s onwards, yes. I did a bit of general nursing when I first arrived in the UK, then specialised in theatre. Then I got a job in private practice and found that that was much more my thing. Basically, anything was better than the loonies. After Kingseat, there was nothing that could rattle me.'

'Did you come back when your dad died?' asks Erina.

'No,' I say shaking my head. 'Lorna had to bear that one on her own.'

'How is Lorna?'

'Oh well, you know, Lorna.'

'Mum told me she's been married like a million times. Not that I can talk.'

I laugh. 'It's only five. And, though I admit I've never met any of the others, I really like the current one. He keeps her very well, and Lorna needs that. And he's very good to Ruby her daughter. But, you know, she's still Princess Lorna, even when times are tough. Mum reckons that's what gets her through the day.'

'We all have something,' replies Erina. 'Mine's food and hating exercise.' She holds up a fork-load of organic salad greens and looks at it dispassionately. 'Fuck my life,' she laughs, 'bloody lettuce! So, do you have any hobbies?'

'Hobbies?' I say. 'How old are we?'

'Almost sixty by my count,' she fires back.

'Okay I do.'

'You play bowls, don't you?'

'God no! What a thing to say! No, I have been taking tikanga and te reo workshops for the past four or five years and I've learned to weave. I'm a bit of a master of the ways of the harakeke, I'll have you know.'

'Oh, well done girl. That's very kia ora of you,' jokes Erina. 'All my mokopuna have started out in kōhanga and my kids tell me that half of the kids there are Pākehā so that's a bit of progress for you. So different from in our day when you did all you could to not be like a Māori.'

'You know, because I looked Pākehā people would, and actually still do, say the most awful things in front of me. And every time a new child abuse scandal breaks I pray that it's not a Māori baby in Starship fighting for its life. And if it is, I feel personally responsible.'

'Yeah I know. It's bad isn't it.'

'But what can we do?' I ask rhetorically.

'So that got serious very quickly,' Erina says, finishing up the last of her salad. 'Any other harmless old lady hobbies?'

'I read a lot. Mostly history, especially New Zealand history. I belong to a very nice Grey Lynn book club and I collect Crown Lynn.'

'Oh, that's terribly normal, isn't it?'

'I get out enough,' I say. It's easier than admitting to how much I like being on my own at home, a glass of vodka near at hand, Crowley sitting on the dining-room table eating off my plate.

'Do you want another coffee?' I ask, as our plates are cleared.

'No,' Erina replies. 'I've got to get home. I have the grandkids after school and, as I'm sure you remember, it's a bit of a hike out south. And the traffic these days! It's murder!'

'I'll never be able to forget those bloody bus journeys back out to Kingseat after a weekend at home. The growing sense of dread as we got closer and closer to the turnoff. God I hated that place. I was only there a year and I still sometimes dream that I'm back there.'

I see you, Girlie.

Erina checks her watch. 'Best I get my skates on. Sorry I can't stay longer, Jen, but to be honest I really didn't know if we'd have anything to talk about after all these years — so it was kind of deliberate.'

I laugh. 'I understand. I wondered too — if it would be weird.'

'Was it weird?'

'No,' I say. 'Not at all.'

'We're still pretty funny for two old ladies,' she says, standing up.

'Do you need a lift home?'

'No. I do genuinely enjoy the walk and I might stay for another coffee.'

'It's been great seeing you,' Erina continues. 'Good on our mums for putting us back in touch.'

'Let's not leave it for forty years next time. Though, we'd be chatting to each other underground at Waikumete cemetery by then, I suspect.'

'The women in my family live long lives,' Erina says.

'You keep telling yourself that,' I reply, and we both laugh.

'But honestly,' she says. 'Keep in touch.'

'I visit Mum most Sundays,' I say. 'Maybe we should take her and your mum out.'

'Good idea,' says Erina. 'We should do that. Maybe take them to the museum or MOTAT. Okay, now I've really got to go.'

I watch as Erina walks up to the counter and buys a couple of brownies, slipping the brown paper bag into her handbag. After she's left, I briefly consider getting another coffee and sitting in the sun for a while longer. The world has become brighter and louder than I like though, so I elect to grab a takeaway latte from Brazil on my way home. I stop once more on my wander up K Road.

There's a flicker of recognition on the face of the kid behind the counter of the off-licence as I slide the bottle of Stoli across the counter to him. Fuck you and your judgement, I think, dragging my eftpos card through the machine. I'll be avoiding that particular bottlestore for a few weeks — until he forgets my face or gets sacked. He puts the vodka in a paper bag, twisting it tight around the neck and hands it back to me. 'Thanks,' I say, but he's already back reading a magazine. The weight of the bottle in my handbag feels good — another evening taken care of. I walk out onto the street, dropping my sunglasses down from the top of my head onto my nose.

And there she is, sitting on a bus bench, ancient, timeless and not aged a day since I first saw her forty years ago at Kingseat. She's been turning up everywhere since Kingseat closed in 1999. Her and every other nutter deemed benign enough to be left to their own devices. I walk, so I see them everywhere. Broken husks, blown across the city to gather in doorways and gutters before being slowly washed out to sea along with the stormwater. The gods and monsters of K Road. Kingseat may have been a whole lot of inhumane, but I don't know if this is any better. I stand for a moment and just look at her, Rūruhi-Kerepō, the Matekai Street Child Killer.

'I see you, Girlie,' she cackles.

'I see you too, taniwha,' I say, because at long last I really do.

CHAPTER 12
TANIWHA AND PATUPAIAREHE

———

Te Pura, Warrior Taniwha of Te Wairoa

———

Getting It

———

Hine Tai

———

Īhe & Her

———

Te Pura, Warrior Taniwha of Te Wairoa

BY RENÉE

I ngā wā o mua, Te Pura, the Shining One, was sad, angry and totally cheesed off, all at the same time. Her scales glittered and shook with irritation all over her large shoulders, thighs, arms, legs and hands and her tall towering body.

The last of the day's sunlight danced through the water like stars doing the finale in a kapa haka poi.

She should have taken the eggs with her, but it was quicker to do the trawl up and down the river without them. She often left them and they had always been perfectly safe. Now, someone had stolen the precious eggs and they'd also taken the three pou, Nīkau, Tōtara and Rātā, the kaitiaki who guarded the eggs in the deep hole in the river where Te Pura lived.

Auē . . .

She stared at the empty possie where the eggs had been and the spaces where the three kaitiaki had stood. She had known that one day they would be gone. That was what happened to taniwha eggs. One day, the cracks in the cream and silver-striped shells would appear and the little taniwha would float away to start their own lives in another place.

Te Pura knew everything was for a limited time. She also knew that the eggs had not gone of their own accord. When that happened, shell was left behind. There was no sign of the cream and silver-striped shells. Someone had taken the eggs and the pou that guarded them. They had to be found and returned. Each egg had a destiny — and a destination. Nothing ordinary men did could be allowed to interfere with that.

The drowned tamariki wept with her and held out their hands and one by one she took their hands and smiled. 'All will be well,' she promised.

She felt deep anger about the two thefts. She was sad that the robbers respected her so little, but as she clasped the hands of the drowned tamariki and they mourned together, she began to hear a waiata.

Was it the willows? A younger tree than the tōtara and much younger than the kauri, but planted along the river by people who came as strangers and stayed to build fences. Te Pura did not hold the fences and posts against the wavy trees though. Trees went where they were taken, either by people or sometimes birds.

Some of the fences were pulled out and the posts thrown in the river. Three of them, chosen for the spiritual power they held from the trees they had once been part of, were strengthened by the prayers and waiata of Te Pura. Using her clever hands and a small slender dark stone, she'd carved away gently, gently, to reveal the eyes and the head of each pou. The soul was already there. These pou became kaitiaki and watched over the eggs in her deep, dark, velvet home, in the depths of Te Wairoa.

Although she was angry about the thefts, Te Pura was happy too, because when the wavy trees sang this was a sign she would go on a journey. The wavy trees knew about journeys. The mānuka and harakeke rustled their unease and whispered among themselves, but the older one said, 'Te Pura knows what she's doing, settle down.'

First, though, she must leave her home and go after the young men who took the eggs and the pou.

'I won't be long,' she told the drowned tamariki. She smiled at them and they smiled back, closed their eyes and slept peacefully.

Te Pura swam up out of the deep, secret whare in the river. She surfaced and stood tall as a kauri and took a little sip of air. Not her natural element, but Auntie Air was from the same iwi of Air, Water and Earth. A different hapū, that's all.

Air was not dangerous, she reminded herself, just different.

Everyone had their own element and hers was water, but it was a good thing to be in another element occasionally. A reminder that we were not the only ones, that the universe was large and we were but one stranger among many other strangers. Te Pura had learned early that we were all strangers. Sometimes loving, sometimes angry, sometimes just strange.

Te Pura waited for her scales to adjust. Her scales were slow, like always when she'd just surfaced and the other eyes she didn't need underwater had to open and her water eyes had to give way. Slowly, slowly, the eyes adjusted, took their time to see this different but always vaguely familiar 'other' place.

Down the river she travelled, her beautiful, scaly bulk, shiny as a large blue whale in the air she now breathed in and out, in and out. Then there, across Te Wairoa, was Te Wharenui.

Silently her strong feet padded up the rounded slope of green. She stood for a few moments, thought of the drowned tamariki, sent blessings on the warm air and each of their whānau stirred in their sleep and smiled as they felt the blessing settle over them like a light feather cloak.

Their dreams were now of days when they fished along the river, along the sea, and their lost ones ran along beside them. Days when they were happy and the fishing was good.

Te Pura moved to the door of the wharenui, opened it and stood in the space. She had to bend her great shoulders and head almost halfway to see in.

There they were.

The eggs were in a kete hanging from one of the maihi in the middle of Te Wharenui o Te Wairoa.

The pou? Where were the pou sent by Tāne? They had been delivered silently as all great gifts are. Gifts were like good deeds, you didn't make a song and dance about them.

Where were the pou? Ah. There they were. Nīkau, Tōtara, Rātā.

Their eyes came to life as they saw Te Pura.

She looked at the sleepers. Typical. They'd had their fun. They'd pushed and pummelled each other like young men did, told untrue stories of their talents and skills as fighters and enjoyed play scuffles in the sand. Then, they'd eaten, told more untrue stories to each other about their prowess with patu and taiaha and now, exhausted by the kai and the impact of their own imagination, they slept.

They'd already forgotten that they'd stolen the eggs from Te Pura. They'd forgotten they'd hidden the kaitiaki — and it never entered their silly heads that Te Pura would leave her home and come after them. So, their sleep was unblemished by bad dreams. They were young. They were invincible.

Lowering her shiny head and shoulders Te Pura moved silently through the door and stood and raised her silver head — which was a bare slither from the high middle of the roof. She considered whether to wake the sleepers and dole out some justice, but decided they'd probably end up doing that to themselves with no help from her.

She trod silently across the floor, picked up the pou and put them under one arm, then, she grabbed the eggs and looked at them. Unharmed. Kei te pai. She lifted her head and paced soundlessly back towards the door and — *Oh oh.* Stars did hip-hop flat out.

Auē.

She'd forgotten to lower her head and shoulders before she walked out the door. Her head felt a bit tingly but she'd managed to hold onto the eggs and the pou.

She stood for a moment or two, waited for the stars to settle. Realised two things at once.

The lintel was broken.

There were voices.

She lifted one large arm and rubbed her head. It was swelling already, but the scales had stopped the worst of it. Just go, she told herself, the elders are on their way and you know how men talk, they'll take all night.

So, she moved out into the dark and slowly and carefully walked back the way she had come. Finally, she reached the bank where she had to enter the other element. Her own place. Her own tūrangawaewae. She breathed out and stepped into the water and, 'Ahhh,' she was back, the waters enclosed her like loving arms and she yielded to their embrace. She released the kaitiaki. They needed to cleanse themselves before they returned to the home of Te Pura.

She looked at the eggs. Tahi. Rua. Toru.

There were no cracks in their large beautiful shells but she had a feeling that it wouldn't be long. Destiny — and destination — were waiting.

Her eggs were always in demand.

Everyone wanted another Te Pura.

Still, it was anyone's guess whether the little taniwha inside were male or female. She had a feeling they were all female this time. Female taniwha didn't have more mana than male ones, but as everyone knew, female taniwha were extra good at taking care of places and people. While they could get angry and breathe out fire, just like the males, this was kept for a last-ditch emergency response rather than a common reaction.

More than this, who else but Te Pura would take drowned tamariki into their whare to care for and sing to?

Of course, female taniwha had eggs too. This was another reason for their popularity. Her eggs were greatly prized, although why was a mystery to Te Pura, because wherever the little taniwha inside the eggs went no one would know, until they arrived. The people there would have to wait — and wait. It took a long time for a taniwha to grow big enough to do their job.

But the good news was that once they did, they were unstoppable.

Taking care of places.

Looking after the people.

Seeing off intruders.

Keeping the peace.

She opened her water eyes and yes, there were the drowned tamariki smiling up at her. She floated above them briefly then her powerful arms took her down, down to the deep bluey-green depths. She lowered the eggs one by one to their nest.

Oh, oh. Was that a crack? No. Phew.

Te Pura settled her ample body down beside the eggs and waited.

Back at the wharenui the young men were trying to explain, saying that it was just a joke.

'Oh?' said one of the old men. 'You have a sense of humour? That's good. Then you'll see the funny side of digging over those three big pieces of land down by the river and getting them ready for kūmara planting.'

'Where are the spades?'

'Spades? That's your problem. Funny, ay?'

The elders huffed off, but when they got round the corner they giggled among themselves remembering their own youthful escapades and the punishments that followed.

'Remember when you had to get down on your knees and scrub the wharekai right down to the last big step outside?'

'Sssh,' said one to the others, 'they might hear. The less they know the better.'

So, the young men got up, put the bedding out to air, washed themselves, combed their hair, put sorry on their faces and waited to see if the kitchen kuia would give them kai before they went searching for spades. Shovels would be better. They were out of luck. All they found were some branches. They took off the twigs, walked down to the three large weedy patches and started work.

The sun came up, they sweated, but they couldn't stop because the Nannies had brought chairs and, although they laughed among themselves, their eyes were sharp. They made bets on which of the young men would finish first and they played euchre when it got boring. Their eyes made notes. They had moko. You never know.

One of the young men, Te Teira, decided he was sick of digging in the hard earth with a stupid stick, but he also knew that if he stopped, he'd be for it. He thought of the waka tied up at the beach. He stood up straight then, oh so casually, he moved, still digging, slowly, slowly. He mustn't upset the Nannies. Gradually, he got to the side and slipped around the deep green and yellow leaves of the harakeke, stood still for a moment and listened. No shouts or calls.

He knew what he would do. Follow his dream. He would go on a long journey to the fabled land of Hawaiki. He saw himself returning with great and beautiful gifts and messages from the people of Hawaiki. Te Teira smiled.

He saw his future. He would be one of the great travellers, he would be talked about in kōrero. People would sing waiata created especially to honour him and his prowess. There would be stories and haka. He would be held up as an example of a strong hero.

His chest swelled and his eyes shone as he thought of the fervour and excitement. He smiled. Then he thought, No, no. Heroes don't smile like idiots, they look into the distance, strong and far-seeing. So, he settled his face into a mask of silent heroism, with eyes that looked over the sea to Hawaiki. That's better, he thought.

He moved silently, easily and eventually he reached the waka. His younger brother and sister were playing on the beach and ran up.

'Where you going?'

'Can we come?'

Oh-oh. Problem. If I say no, thought Te Teira, they'll run straight back and tell everyone and if I say yes they'll be a real nuisance. Who ever heard of a brave young warrior setting out for Hawaiki with a small girl and a small boy dragging along behind?

But he couldn't hang about because the Nannies would have noticed there was one short in the digging department and they'd tell the elders and all hell would break loose. They'd come for him and this time the punishment would be even worse. They might make him weed the whole marae with only his fingers. They would definitely make him go down to the bank where Te Pura lived in her deep dark watery whare in Te Wairoa and ask her forgiveness. The thought of going down to that deep dark mysterious place was enough to make his legs tremble. And even if he said 'Aroha mai' to Te Pura, she might not forgive him. She was probably totally hacked off, but . . . the tide was turning. He better make up his mind pretty quick.

'Please, Te Teira,' said Hēmi.

'Please, Te Teira,' said Moana adding, 'I have been given the name. You must take me. It will be an adventure.'

Te Teira knew he was up that old creek with no paddle. If he refused to take his brother and sister, they'd run back and tell the Nannies, and if he took them it'd be a drag and he'd be even worse off. What could he do?

Moana looked at him. 'Have you checked the food? Do you have water?'

'It is not for you to question my actions,' Te Teira grumped. 'You're a little girl. What do girls know?'

'Do you have kai? Do you have wai?' Moana's eyes were steady.

She was seven. She knew a lot for a seven-year-old.

'Can we come? Can we come?' said Hēmi. 'If you don't let me come I'll run back and tell everyone.'

Te Teira looked up at the sun. Going down in the west. No time to muck around. He sighed. 'Get in,' he said.

Moana and Hēmi scrambled into the waka.

'Now sit there and don't move,' said Te Teira.

Te Teira really wasn't a great thinker. What boy of eight and girl of seven are going to sit still for more than two minutes?

Te Teira set off. He was feeling a little bit desperate. He didn't know how far Hawaiki was and, to tell the truth, he didn't actually know *where* it was, but he supposed if he headed in the direction of the sun and kept going he'd end up somewhere. Maybe he'd find a totally new land no one had ever found before. The sea was large and powerful. Tangaroa could take him anywhere. Maybe he'd end up where the ocean joins the sky and go to one of the stars or even the moon. He smiled.

This would show them.

He was not someone to be picking around in a kūmara patch with a stick. He was meant for greater things.

But they were away from shore now and he smiled as his strong arms powered the waka and it swooped through the water.

He had set off just in time. Three small figures appeared on the beach. Their mouths opened and shut and their arms waved and their legs jumped up and down, but Te Teira kept paddling. It was a great feeling. The sun was shining, Moana and Hēmi were sitting quietly, the sea was calm, the waka moved through the waves like his mother's spoon through kānga-pirau.

Moana thought about Te Teira. She didn't know much about setting off in a waka but she did know there should be karakia. Her oldest brother has forgotten the most important part of setting off. Under her breath she whispered words to Tangaroa.

Te Teira was happy. He loved the sea. His arms were his servants, they would row as long as it took.

They were out on the wider sea when Hēmi said, 'I want a drink.'

'Get the bottle,' said Te Teira.

'What bottle?'

So, it was discovered there was no bottle, so no water. Te Teira was feeling thirsty himself, he'd rowed for a long time. His arms were sore and his legs felt like cramp was only a breath away. He started to think. Maybe he'd been a bit quick off the mark. He should have said no to Hēmi and definitely no to Moana.

Then the breeze started up, the waves began to slap froth on the sides of the waka, and Hēmi moaned because he was very very thirsty.

Moana didn't like the waves getting bigger. The way they hit against the side of the waka made it tremble and shake. She sat as still as she could so as not to upset Tāwhirimātea.

It was no good though, the slopping and slapping became harder and louder. Te Teira saw the sky darkening to a bluey purple. The wind was making the waves choppy. He smelled a storm coming.

He thought, *Why is this?* It was a sunny day so why had the sky darkened? Then he remembered. *Oh, oh. Oh.*

He hadn't asked for the blessing of Tangaroa. That was why the storm had come up on a sunny day

Tangaroa was angry.

Te Teira looked at Hēmi and Moana. They were sitting still and he could tell they didn't like what was happening. They were frightened. They were hungry and thirsty, but they sat as though they knew he would get them out of this mess — of course he would — he was their brother.

Oh, oh, oh. Te Teira felt the fear right down to his toes. *Te Pura,* he thought. He sent the message, heart to heart.

Te Pura, Te Pura. Help me.

Deep down in the depths of Te Wairoa, Te Pura felt the vibrations. A faint tremor at first, then becoming faster. She ignored them. She had to settle the pou, sing to them, place them. They didn't want to go back into the holes where they were, they wanted new places. This was the way of pou so it was no good moaning about it. She looked around and thought, Maybe there, there and there? She checked the eggs. Was that a crack on that one?

The vibrations became shudders which got more and more desperate.

And then her ears went on alert. Three voices? A young man, a boy and a girl? One of those young men, she supposed. She had seen it all before. Often it was better to leave them to be terrified enough to get themselves out of trouble, but this time she felt the water calling too.

Te Puraaaaa, Te Puraaaaa, save usssss . . .

Te Pura sighed.

She patted the pou, told them she'd be back. Smiled at the drowned tamariki who smiled back. They knew this was her job. They knew she would come back. What they didn't know was whether she would reach Te Teira, Moana and Hēmi in time. They looked around their home. Was there room for three more? Of course, there would be room. Te Pura would make sure of that.

Te Pura swooshed up out of the river. She stood and sang to the air to help her. She took in a huge breath. This was a tricky business. She needed both air and water to help and they don't always get on. She shook her head. Hapū are like that. Whānau are like that. Iwi are like that. They don't always get on.

However . . .

She sent out her cry, stood tall, sang the karakia across the waters, then, steady and strong, her silver scales glittering against the bluey-green water, she walked purposefully into the waves.

Then she saw the gods ranged across the horizon. Tangaroa, Tāwhirimātea, Rūaumoko. They were not pleased. 'What's got up their noses?' Then, she understood and thought, Oh crikey.

Not only had Te Teira forgotten to sing karakia but when he got into trouble instead of calling on the gods, he called on Te Pura, a mere taniwha, for help. Oh well, she thought. Not the first time a young man has forgotten the kawa. Won't be the last.

Te Pura called to Tangaroa, Tāwhirimātea and Rūaumoko. She sang a waiata asking for their help. She sang for their forgiveness for Te Teira for transgressing against the kawa.

The gods went into a huddle.

Jeepers, thought Te Pura. I'll be here for hours.

She moved further into the water. A tall strong shining blue-green scaly presence. She carried her beautiful head high as her eyes searched across the waters. Her powerful thighs and legs stood strong against the high waves and the winds.

Tāwhirimātea was totally brassed off with Te Teira. This was not the first time the young man had ignored protocol. He wanted Tangaroa to chop up the waves, call down the rain, send the winds, he wanted Rūaumoko to shake the land underneath — maybe even send a tsunami. But there was the girl. There was the boy too.

Tāwhirimātea, Tangaroa and Rūaumoko knew that the girl at least remembered what the older brother had forgotten.

It is always the way.

Wāhine carry the stories, they carry the kawa, they carry the songs.

But, thought Tāwhirimātea, that Te Teira is an idiot. Who but an idiot just jumps into a waka and sets out across the sea? He has to be taught a lesson.

But if he was taught a lesson his brother and sister were goners.

That was the conundrum, it was always the conundrum.

Tangaroa was sick and tired of being faced with these decisions.

It was not easy being a god. There were always idiots and there were always innocents.

'And, somehow,' he said to Tāwhirimātea and Rūaumoko, 'we are expected to choose whether to save the fool because of the innocents, or to make the fool pay which means the innocents pay too.'

Like all the gods, they'd made both decisions in the past and they knew they would do so in the future.

And then there was Te Pura.

Who does she think she is? Granted she's beautiful. Granted she takes care of Te Wairoa. Granted we should keep on her good side, but she doesn't seem to realise she is merely a taniwha and not as important as a god.

Tāwhirimātea sighed and the waves went slopping against the sides of the waka.

It was dark and the waves were high. Te Teira was frightened. He had been a fool. Who had he thought he was, setting himself up against the elders?

Now Tangaroa, Tāwhirimātea and Rūaumoko would take their revenge too.

And what about Moana and Hēmi? he thought. It was all his fault.

He saw clearly that there was no greater task, no greater hero's journey, than to work the land and get it ready for food. He had been a fool. If his brother and sister drowned it would be his fault. He was not a hero. He was a stupid thoughtless idiot.

'Te Pura,' he called, '*Te Puraaaaa . . .*' His voice was frantic with fear.

'Aroha mai,' he called to the gods, 'aroha mai . . .'

There was a huge slap against the waka and it turned over. Three heads vanished under the waves as Rūaumoko got into the act. He made the ground shake. The wind screamed with wrath. The seas shouted their defiance. A tsunami wave rose like a giant silk geyser that wanted to wrap itself around everything in sight.

Te Pura set her shoulders and strode on into the sea. She lifted her large strong shiny legs in and out of the waves, stamped down, stepped forward, stamped down, stepped forward . . . She didn't look like she was moving fast, but she covered a lot of ocean.

Rūaumoko was getting over his hissy. He thought he might have gone too far. He didn't really want to fall out with Te Pura. Taniwha might not be as high up as gods but they're tricky opponents. Anyway, who was going to say to Te Pura that she wasn't as high up the chain as they were? Not me, Rūaumoko decided.

Te Pura faced the gods and kept walking into the fierce wind, the lashing rain and the rods of light that broke the sky into bits. Tāwhirimātea could throw anything he liked in her path but nothing would stop her. An irresistible force had finally met an immovable object.

Rūaumoko had heard of Te Pura's strength and stubborn refusal to admit defeat; now he saw it for himself.

Tangaroa tossed the three heads around in the water. Te Pura, invincible, stomped right into his territory. Her arms pushed against the waves, her thighs and legs forced their way through the mountains of water.

'Sheesh,' said Rūaumoko, 'gave it my best shot and she didn't take any notice.'

The tsunami turned slightly pink with embarrassment.

Te Pura approached. Te Teira didn't see her. All he saw was his brother and sister struggling, their heads just dots against the might of Tangaroa, Tāwhirimātea and Rūaumoko. He made up his mind. He might not be a hero but he knew the right thing to do now.

'Take me,' he cried to the gods. 'Take me. The fault was mine, only mine. Save Moana and Hēmi.'

Te Pura kept on walking.

Tangaroa kept on making up his mind.

Tāwhirimātea decided to have a little lie-down.

Rūaumoko called to him, 'Here mate. Over here.'

The two gods had a brief confabulation.

'One of us has to talk to Tangaroa,' said Rūaumoko.

'Bags not me,' said Tāwhirimātea. 'He's in a real paddy. You know what he's like when he can't make up his mind.'

They watched as Te Teira struggled. Finally, he grabbed hold of Moana and Hēmi. He gathered them to him.

'If you take us,' he cried to Tangaroa, 'you take us. That is your decision. But I am the guilty one. The only guilty one. Take me. Save my little brother and sister.'

At that very moment Te Pura reached out her giant arms, picked them up and gathered them in.

She shook them a little so the water flew off them back to Tangaroa.

She gave Te Teira an extra shake for being such an idiot.

'Settle down,' she said to the gods. 'Settle down. These ones are mine. They are my people. I am taking them home.'

She held Moana, Hēmi and Te Teira high in her beautiful shiny strong arms and the water dripped from their bodies onto her glittering scales, which danced with defiance.

Tangaroa decided he was tired of this fight.

And anyway, he remembered, if you got into a stoush with Te Pura, there would only be one winner. It wouldn't be him. Taniwha had long memories. Best not to get on her bad side.

Te Pura smiled, tucked Te Teira, Hēmi and Moana in her front pocket and held her large strong shimmering arms out to the gods. She raised one arm and drew a tick in the air.

Tahi, e Te Pura.

And her laugh rolled out across the space and all the seabirds chuckled, the kōura grinned, even the pāua managed a smile.

Te Pura turned, checked that Te Teira, Hēmi and Moana were okay then, shoulders straight, walking like the warrior she was, she moved back through the waves to the shore where the people waited. She could hear their cries and waiata.

She sighed.

Auē . . . not another hero's welcome.

All she wanted was to drop off Te Teira, Hēmi and Moana, then go back to her home where the three pou and the drowned tamariki smiled in that deep hole under the waters of Te Wairoa.

There were the eggs to think about too. Would they still be waiting? Or would their shells have cracked and let the baby taniwha set out on their journey to the places that waited for them? She sighed, and looked at the crowd gathered on the beach. Knew all over again. This was part of the deal. Part of being a taniwha.

It was part of looking after the people. People liked to celebrate when things turned out well. The eggs would have to wait. Her head went up.

Then, she felt it. The little nudge at her thigh. She looked down. Three new taniwha were circling around her. Their little bodies with their tiny tiny bright scales flipped and fluttered in the water as they sang their poroporoaki.

'*Haere rā, haere rā . . .*'

So, the eggs had cracked and she hadn't been there.

For a moment there was a sting in her air eyes, then she nodded. This was the way it was.

'Go,' she said. 'Go. My blessings will follow you wherever, wherever.'

And the little taniwha flipped over one more time then, each heading in a different direction, they sped off. Te Pura hoped they would be all right. She hoped they would be happy. She knew there was nothing she could do about it anyway. It was up to them now.

She hauled Te Teira from her pocket, held him up high, then dropped him in the sea.

Splash.

He spluttered and spat water, hung his head.

'Aroha mai, e Te Pura,' he said. 'Aroha mai.'

She nodded at him and shrugged. He would get over being stupid and impulsive or he wouldn't.

She lifted Hēmi and Moana out of her pocket and gently slid them into the water. They stood and laughed up at her.

'Thank you, Te Pura, thank you.'

Then they ran through the little waves, onto the beach, into the waiting arms.

The people shouted their joy and thanks.

'*Te Pura, Te Puraaaa . . .*'

Te Pura squared her glossy incandescent shoulders and walked on into the light.

Getting It

BY KERI HULME

BORING
   BORING
      BORING

So far, we've had the concerned conservationist, a wet-eyed woman of mature years:

'In summation, I *beg* of you to take these cohabitants of our lovely coast, each of them as valuable as you or I.'

— Councillor McMurtry rolls her eyes and snorts —

'in their own way of course, but valuable, please take them into account.'

At least she was concerned about spiders, a pleasant change from the usual birds or trees.

Then, the dour owner of a neighbouring property, sandal-wearing yes, but looking as though he'd sooner eat spiders than save them. *He's* upset at the prospect of lots of trucks and noise and inconvenience to himself and noise and increased rates probably and noise.

'He's had the noise control officer out seven times so far this year. Last time it was about dogs barking. The farm was three k distant.' Sam's whisper is as engaging as everything else about her. 'Ooops, got to brief the next lot.' She tiptoes away.

Now we've got the local iwi rep rabbiting on about spiritual importance and cultural insensitivity and a violation of manawhenua blah blah te mea te mea. When I went to school with him, he was Paddy O'Shea and he used to be rude to my gran behind her back (she'd've cracked him one with her stick if he'd been rude to her face). Now he's Te Paringa Auhei and he had the cheek to ask me just before the meeting began, 'Did your lovely old tāua leave any whakapapa books or things like that e hoa?' He still understands a playground snarl.

Now he's doing a chant and stumbling over some of the words. Giving the hearing his best shot I suppose, but two of the councillors are murmuring together and anyway, everyone knows this hearing is a total waste of time.

Because the council has already decided that a subdivision — 'a boutique tasteful ecofriendly village' is how the developer's pamphlet puts it — a subdivision on the Neck is A Good Idea. More rates for one thing: more work for local builders and roading contractors for another, and more jobs for the large pool of jobless. Win–win for everyone, and besides, the land was going to waste. If Soamy Reischek hadn't been smart enough to realise it was unclaimed Crown land of no interest to Ngāi Tahu or DoC and so up for grabs, it'd just sit there, idle, useless except for breeding sandflies. O, and spiders —

so, boring.

Not that I'm unsympathetic to the concerns being expressed: it's just that, after ten years working round councils and such, I know how the system works. The council's decision is a foregone conclusion and nobody's interested in objectors. One of the councillors has slumped sideways, asleep rather than dead, I think. The Mayor has his forehead resting on steepled hands. Soamy and his sharky-looking lawyer are smirking at each other. The council general manager and his secretary are whispering, totally ignoring Pat. Councillor Mooch is picking his nose in an absent-minded way. Someone really should tell him that's how the rest of his brain went west.

'Tihei mau reee ora!' declaims Pat.

'Ah. Thank you ah, Mr ah,' says the Mayor. 'And next ah?'

'I'm not quite finished, your worship.'

'Ah.'

'You won't believe what's next!' whispers Sam excitedly and her delicious lips tickle my lobe.

I look at the order list and groan. Quietly.

The spider lady; the man with tender ears; Paddy. The elderly hippy clan who were next had been effectively sidelined by the council cruelly holding the hearing on the day before benefit day. So it has to be the nut group next. I had already labelled them The Flax Leaf Scribblers. Imagine making your objection to a proposed subdivision on a flax leaf — way to be taken really seriously eh? Pissed the hell out of the photocopy clerk I can tell you. Still, it made a nice paragraph ('Committed conservationist recyclers should take note' etc.) and I admit the printing was very neat.

We're already an hour over normal sitting time.

And I've got to write up this dreck afterwards.

For crysake put a sock in it Paddy.

But he goes on translating, sort of, what he's already said, 'and if you wound our mother, she will fight back. She will destroy you, yes indeed. Death will take you, yes, that's true. Yes! Yes! Kss kss hei. There isn't really a translation for that.'

'Ah. Thank you. Thank you.'

Paddy doesn't look at me as he pushes out the big double swinging door. Figures I've sold out probably.

There is a short pause. People rustle papers, slump further sideways. Then the doors creak inwards.

Hello, that's interesting: it was cold and raining hard when I entered the meeting. Now it seems to have turned to fog. Little wispy tendrils float into the room.

Sam, standing in front of the council table, announces,

'Speaking to their submission, objecting to the proposed sub-division, ur Te Hā o Neherā.'

Lemme guess, Ancient Nation of Waita freaks. Or maybe SHIT!

He stands about two and a half metres tall and he's covered in long red hair. It drapes down his belly sort of covering his sex. He stinks, rancid meat and freshcut fern and something like ancient sweat.

She is only slightly shorter, and is possibly hairier: she has tied little shells to her belly fur and they hang down right to there and clink and clitter as she lumbers across to stand by the male, facing the Mayor and council —

Whose collective jaw has dropped.

The things stare around with huge black mournful eyes.

I note the male is clutching a long bone, with holes drilled in it. It looks unhealthily like a femur. Fresh primate femur. Which fact goes whizzing round in my brain so hard I don't notice the entrance of the next two —

beings.

One is a little horror, hairless, face pale as foam under moonlight, with eyes that are wholly red. No pupils, no whites. Its nails are red too, bloodred on hands and feet, but any other strangeness is hidden under a wrapping of cloak. A cloak that looks to be made from thick cream twilled silk.

It's best muka, retted and beaten to silken smoothness, such as I have only seen in museums.

And, moving to head the little company is —

o dear, I remember far too many of Gran's stories, and there's only one thing this could be.

Slender and elegant with hair like toetoe in the sun, and large deeply green eyes — imagine almondshaped lenses of clear kawakawa pounamu come very much alive — those kind of eyes.

Dressed in a black kneelength rāpaki, but not like any rāpaki I've ever come across (Gran was the last weaver who made them: they look odd but are surprisingly warm and comfortable. There's a soft loose-weave lining, and many layers of rolled end-knotted strings which sway as you walk. I've never felt so lithe and sexy as when walking in a rāpaki). But *this* rāpaki has little green beetles flying out and around at erratic intervals, tethered on invisible threads. A tiny clematis vine is growing around the waistband. Naturally, it's in full flower. And for a top, the being has a kind of bolero made from kākāpō feathers, soft and gorgeous mottled mossgreen feathers.

Only they move. A subtle lifting, shifting, resettling —

while the tūrehu stands perfectly still on its bare feet, luminous brown skin unmarked by any kind of gooseflesh.

The fog obscures the doorway, and filaments weave around the four.

'I will initially translate for us,' says the tūrehu, and everything Gran said about their music is true. I hear song in these ordinary words.

'We are the five signatories to our objection to the proposed—'

The sharky lawyer is on his feet. 'Mister Mayor Mister Mayor if I may—'

The Mayor's hands are rigidly flat on the table.

'What is it Mr Reiver?' His voice is hoarse.

'If these these — things arnt hoaxes, they arnt human either!'

The tūrehu turns its head towards him and smiles, placidly.

But the lawyer takes a quick step backwards and bangs into his chair.

I can see the smile too. Someone who smiles like that would slice your belly open to check what you had for breakfast, quite playfully and just in the interests of learning. Then they'd tie your intestines in a bow —

'Your objection is rather similar to that which you raised apropos the material our submission was written on. The council has not been specific about what an objection should be written upon, nor has it been specific as to whether objectors speaking to their submissions have to be human. Or not.'

The smile widens a little.

'Happily, we are not.'

'But, but, there's only four of you and—'

'You really wouldn't like the other one of us to come in here with you. Besides he wouldn't ah, fit. See?'

And every eye — except for those of the Others — follows the long slim finger as it swings to the doorway.

There is a wonderful arc, scimitar curve, rearing out of the mist. It is dark, massive, tall as the door, and ends in a point so sharp it can't be clearly seen. It flexes once.

I really really wouldn't like whatever owns that claw to be in here with me.

Nor would anyone else, judging by the absolute silence.

The lawyer slithers bonelessly down on his chair, and the tūrehu turns its head back to the council table.

'We are the five signatories to our objection to the planned roading development and subdivision of the land you know as the Neck. The māeroero and his daughter will speak first.'

'Signatories?' squeaked the lawyer. His sharkliness was gutted, gone, but he was still trying his nastiest. Which I admired, deep down. I wasn't game to do anything except stare, and breathe occasionally. O, and make a note or two.

'The māeroero and his daughter have signed their names in their language, there being no requirement from the council for English or Māori only to be used for such matters. He is

Third-stop and she is Sixth, and you will note the finger directions quite plainly in the two lines of holes at the lefthand bottom end of the flax leaf.'

I see Sam actually check.

'I thought they were nibblings by insects.' No one can hear her, but I know the ways of her lips.

The lawyer slumps a little more. Soamy isn't smirking any more. You can't when your mouth is hanging open.

The tūrehu's smile is beatific.

The two red giants stand a little straighter. One of them farts. We hear the shells tinkle. Then the male lifts the femur-flute and breathes into it. The female opens her mouth and croons.

Is there something narcotic in that damned fog?

It's like quiet tuneful moaning; only it seeps into you and makes you feel vague and sad.

Then you feel — words, words stroking your skin, fingering the inner drums of your ears.

We were here first. We have never left. We own our homelands.
We prefer to be in the shadows. We roam the lands at night.
We were on the Almost-island before you came, it has always been ours.
We will remain there, in company with the first arrivals.
We share with them but not with humans. Go away. Leave us alone.

It seems the flute and crooning have come to an end, although I can still hear the music in my head.

Many of the gobsmacked councillors twitch, shoot terrified — or bovinely puzzled — looks at each other.

'I see I do not have to translate in this instance,' says the tūrehu smoothly. Its English is as inhumanly perfect as everything else about it. 'A ponaturi from the Poutini horde will now speak on behalf of her kind. The signature is that nail scrape to the right of the māeroero signatures.' The tūrehu twinkles in a kindly fashion to Reischek's sunken lawyer who has turned quite yellow. 'It is an old ponaturi clan name meaning "May your throat be quickly slashed", thought appropriate in this instance.'

Ponaturi, ponaturi? Gran had never said much about them, unlike her stories about the bush fairies whom she dearly loved, but I dimly recall it was all terrifying. A clever and vindictive seafolk, who killed humans much more often than humans killed them (although our stories didn't exactly emphasise this).

Note: ponaturi nails are long, strong-looking, and savagely pointed.

The ponaturi's speech goes on for many painful minutes, slashing at all our ears. It crackles and hisses, sounds like highpitched static mixed with strata of loathing and spat hate.

'That was a very brief recital of interactions between ponaturi and humans over the past eight centuries. Most of them concern the previous owners of the land, of whom Mr Auhei was such an eloquent and definitive representative.'

Ouch.

'However, three incidents specifically relate to direct-line ancestors of the Mayor, a councillor, and the applicant land-developer.'

How can you make *applicant land-developer* sound like a tiny perfect lullaby?

The ponaturi grates and sizzles again.

'Mister Mayor, your paternal ancestor of three generations ago fired at a ponaturi of Clan Gut in the dark and loudly claimed he had shot a demmed native. Any similarity between a New Zealander and a ponaturi is, I think you would agree, negligible?'

The Mayor nods, numbly.

More hate speech.

'As well as the insult your ancestor delivered, his bullet severely grazed the ponaturi's back. This means there is a blood issue between Clan Gut and any and all lineal descendants of your ancestors.

'Your life is forfeit and you are unable to make any objective decision on any matter arising from disputes between ponaturi and humans, according to ponaturi law. As the Neck is an ancient place of refuge for ponaturi . . . I do not have to spell it out, do I?'

'That isn't our rules,' says the Mayor, in a very small voice.

'O sometimes, the older laws have their place. The Poutini ponaturi have delivered due warning to you. They do take everything so personally you know. A rather young and hasty folk.' The tūrehu can do confidential smiles too.

'We are also informed that the grandfather of Councillor Mooch'

'Eh? Wot?'

'distaff side, cast urine on the person of a peaceable net-mender working on shore in the late evening. The fact that your ancestor was blind drunk does not exculpate him. Or you. Such insults are a deadly serious matter with the ponaturi clans, and you are in the same unfortunate position as your Mayor.'

'Eh! Wot!'

'Annnd, Mister Reischek? According to the ponaturi — I will testify that they have accurate memories beyond the guess or conception of humans — one of your female ancestors, four generations back on your mother's side, fell upon an innocent young ponaturi, wandering in a carefree fashion down Sevenmile Beach, minding his own business, and slaked her drunken lust upon him. My goodness, you were a jolly lot back then weren't you? My interpolation — the ponaturi do not have this view of you. Regrettably however, your greatgreatgrandmother was a goldfields prostitute and some kind of cross-species infect—'

'That is a bloody lie!' Soamy is a florid flabby man, but he has sprung to his feet quite pale and taut.

Hmm. Note: check out some of the older generations' gossip. Possible goldmine here.

'Bloody bloody lies! Bloody bloody *things*! This a bloody travesty this this this—' spitting sputtering incoherency as he rushes towards the ponaturi knocking chairs aside.

The ponaturi very distinctly sneers. She spreads her longnailed hands —

and that huge claw in the doorway — scraped.

My teeth shuddered. Several people clapped hands over their ears and others were shivering. Reischek has fallen to the floor, whether tripped or crashed is uncertain.

'There is corroboration, or should I say, belief in the facts as stated? This is not regarded a matter of morality by the ponaturi, but as an absolute case for war. Very particular about their gene pool, these folk.' The tūrehu beamed. 'So. The gist of the ponaturi submission is that, should a decision detrimental to their continued occupation of the sanctuary of the Neck be made by this council, war will be declared upon you all and everybody you have any dealing with.'

Everyone round the council table, and longside in the petitioners' chairs, is looking strangely blank.

More crackling and clatter from the ponaturi.

'O, and in the interests of a "fair fight",' musical laughter bubbles under those words 'they wish you to know they are no longer susceptible to sunlight and they have cultivated many new ah, pets. Yes, pets. I particularly like the little leggy ones with pretty blue rings now so well adapted to cold waters, but most of them are *much* smaller.'

It is right then I notice that the tūrehu has no pupils to its eyes either. Just ultimate fathomless green . . . I notice this because it is smiling now at me.

You ever felt your anal sphincter *crunch* shut? And then twist?

'You are still hearing us, aren't you?'

'Uh. Uh. Yes.'

The tūrehu sighs, a sigh with a rirerire trill running under it.

'Well, we tried. We are going now. You probably won't ever see us again.'

'Oh no! I mean, what about—'

'Hmmm?'

'Your submission? And your signature? And and—'

'I am a simple coordinator. My signature? The flax leaf of course. The taniwha has officially breathed on the whole. We sympathise entirely with both given submissions.'

'But going before the summary and the vote and—'

'We came because we thought seeing us clearly might cause wonder, make you realise there is much more than you think you know about our world. We thought our very presence might open minds and change present attitudes. All of us heard most minds snap shut minutes ago.'

'Not mine,' whispers Sam, very pale Sam.

'Nor your friend's,' answers the tūrehu. 'Do give my regards to your grandmother by the way. We spent a happy afternoon together some time ago. She was a charming child.'

'She died twenty years ago.'

'O well. That is the way with you folk isn't it? Something of her thinking must have been given to you because you can still see and think. Look at the others.'

The Mayor is staring at the fog.

Councillor Alley has slumped under the table. No other councillor is moving, all sitting hunched and stone-faced except Councillor Mooch and he's back on automatic again. The general manager is staring at his sheaf of papers and his secretary's eyes are tight shut. There is no sign of Reischek or his lawyer.

'Is — this — real?' I ask the tūrehu.

'As real as your life,' it answers, 'and as real as whatever you call reality. It is just that your kind can't stand very much reality. You much prefer your patterns and your stories and your noisy dirty tramplings over everything. However, you don't last forever and we almost do. We are going now. I would go quite soon too, if I were you,' and it gives a small smile and, horrifyingly, winks. And the mist and Others weren't there any more.

———

Being bored seemed such a desirable state. While Sam and I twitched and quivered, the Mayor and councillors jerked — well 'awake' is as good as any other word here I suppose — and went into recess on the grounds of commercial sensitivity.

I wrote a bland report of the meeting, précising the submissions against the development of the Neck. 'Emphasis was placed by all objectors on the desirability of keeping the Neck in its present state, with some supporting tākata whenua concerns and others wanting protection for endangered invertebrates. However, it is unlikely the Council will give great weight to these matters when' te mea te mea blah blah blah.

A week later, the paper prints a picture of the Mayor and Soamy smiling into the camera, shaking hands across a display, an artist's conception of the tasteful eco-friendly village Reischek planned to build.

Then Sam and I sold what we had and fled to the other side of the hill.

———

We drove past the Neck on our way out. It is a large peninsula, with a high, forested headland. There are seaviews all the way round, seaviews to die for. We know about the deep lake nested in the middle of the thousand-hectare plateau, and had learned that birdlife abounds. All of it unclaimed Crown land and nobody else near it, loving it, except for a few old hippies on a rundown ohu to the north, and a wet-eyed environmentalist and a grumpy lover of silence to the south. You could see immediately why a developer would take one look and see CASH OPPORTUNITY in high golden letters. And that would be all he saw.

———

The news isn't good from what remains of the Coast. Last summer's toxic algae blooms killed off all the salmon farms and ruined the last whitebait season. The goo that developed suddenly in their sewage ponds and sewerage was a huge problem, swelling the contents a thousandfold overnight. I heard Soamy was one of the first fatalities, overwhelmed by a surge from the Hurihuri system as he was out walking his dog one night. Confirmation was pretty hard to come by — and I really wanted to know what happened to the dog — because, by then, the permanent rain had wrecked almost every bridge and length of hill road there was. It had done things you wouldn't believe to electric and 'tronic systems everywhere over there. And finally, the earthquake swarms began —

———

They are creatures of mist and rain and aloneness
 says my gran
 they play water and sadness into our world
 she said.
 They are people of cunning and malice, and sunshine and music and stillness
 says my gran
 they bring together all of the Others, the ancient unborn, the young and the old

she said.

And never forget the dwellers-in-water, shape-shifters, changers
says my gran
and that all of them hate us strangers, who came from the Abyssal Void
yes, I do remember what she said.

And I thought it was just one of Gran's little songs. Now I teach it to our children.

Sam and I live quietly by a far southern lake. I'm a good gardener and she is a good harvester of weka and fish. Life is strenuous and much less certain than it used to be, but we are never bored.

And we hope each evening, while listening to the winds play like flutes in the far mountains and watching the flax bushes sway,

we hope the Coast was enough.

Hine Tai

BY APIRANA TAYLOR

Nan Waikawa Stevens squinted at the text her daughter Jenny sent her. It read . . . *Hukarere on morning bus with Terry*. Late as usual, she grumbled, as she waited outside the Farmers store.

Jumbo the driver always had some excuse. A tree fell across the road. Slips in the pass. Floods. He hit a cow . . .

She heard the bus before she saw it as it grumbled down the hill into Whanga-Tai-Tini. She frowned as she always did when deep in thought. Whanga-Tai-Tini used to be full of people and horses. Now there were only horses. The Farmers store would close after Christmas. The bus service would downsize. The post office had disappeared.

Nan shook her head. As if that wasn't enough, it was harder to see. Her glasses were useless! She needed a telescope!

She had a 1989 Holden. It was over twenty years old and couldn't go beyond third gear. That was fast enough. She only felt confident driving the one kilometre from her house to the Farmers store and wouldn't drive any further because of her eyesight.

Nan heard the bus as it chopped down through the gears, rounded the corner and clunked to a halt across the road opposite her.

Was that them? Was that Terry and her granddaughter? She rubbed her eyes. Yes, that's them, she realised. That's Terry with Hukarere by his side.

'Kia ora Mum,' said Terry. 'How are you? I'll drive.'

Hukarere and Nan sat in the back seat. Terry turned the key in the ignition. The car coughed into action and off they went.

She looked at her granddaughter. 'You're seven and a half now,' said Nan, 'and you look just like your grandpa, Henry. Flat nose and curly hair.' She ran her fingers through Hukarere's bundle of curls.

'Stop that!' snapped Hukarere. 'I'm a big girl. You can't do that now!'

'You're a smarty boots and you're grumpy because you're tired,' said Nan.

'Why did Mum make me come and stay with you?'

'Because she's studying to be a teacher and needs time to study for her exams.'

For a moment Nan wondered about her daughter Jenny. Maybe Jenny needed a break, she decided. Jenny's husband, Tai, worked on the deep-sea trawlers and he was often away at sea for months. Tai is a good man, thought Nan. He's hardworking, he doesn't drink and he's the gentlest man I know. The only thing, smiled Nan to herself, is he sometimes spoils Hukarere a little when he comes back from sea.

Terry headed for the garden shed when they arrived home. He hauled pots of paint, nails, saws and hammers out and spread them out on the porch. 'I'm gonna mend the holes in the roof and paint it, Mum,' he said.

That boy, thought Nan. He's a good boy, but I do worry about him.

He kept himself busy and yet sometimes he daydreamed as if his thoughts were elsewhere.

'Let's eat first,' said Nan.

Later the tides changed and the sun began to set.

'Hukarere, haere mai ki te kai,' called Terry.

'No, I don't want to,' said Hukarere. She clamped her hands on her hips, gritted her teeth and poked her chin out.

Terry frowned. 'I speak Māori to you and you answer in English.'

'Jenny sent Hukarere to kōhanga,' said Nan.

'Yeah. You're lucky, Girl,' said Terry. 'I've had to go to the kuratini to learn Māori and can only say a few simple sentences. You can speak Māori, eh Girl, but you won't. Why don't you?'

'Why should I. You can't talk Māori, Uncle Terry. Nan won't talk Māori and nobody at my school talks Māori, not even the teachers. So, why should I? I don't want to and I won't!'

The sky closed its eye like an eyelid as the sun went down and night fell.

'I'm tired, Nan,' said Hukarere after tea.

'Time for bed then. You're sleeping with me.' She put her in bed and soon she was snoring. 'Are you snoring in Māori,' she laughed.

Talk Māori, thought Nan when she settled in beside Hukarere. She remembered her own grandmother, Nan Tureiti. She grew up in a world where the family spoke only Māori. She told me, when she went to school, the teacher gave her a blackboard and chalk and wrote on the board. CAT, RAT, MAT. She copied this and when she returned home showed her elders how she could write, CAT, RAT, MAT, they were amazed and called Tureiti a good girl because she could write the Pākehā language.

They awoke early the next morning.

'I'm hungry,' said Hukarere.

Nan gave her cornflakes with milk, an apple and a piece of toast with Marmite on it.

Terry was already on the roof. Hammering with his hammer and sawing with his circular saw. 'That noise is driving me mad,' groaned Nan.

'There's nothing to do,' moaned Hukarere.

'C'mon, Girl, we'll go for a walk along the beach.'

'Boring,' chanted Hukarere, copying what she'd heard her older cousins say.

'There's always interesting things to find down by the sea,' said Nan. She took Hukarere by the hand and led her down the path, across the road and down to the beach.

'The sea is very big,' said Hukarere. She stopped and gathered pāua, mussel, and pipi shells and seaweed. Nan also paused and gathered shells which they spread on the table when they returned home.

Nan went to prepare morning tea. Terry had filled the fridge with roast lamb, sausages and smoked bacon. Usually there wasn't much in there apart from bread, butter, milk and sometimes seafood — shellfish, parengo, or whatever could be gathered at the time.

Nan had a garden and an orchard behind the house. They were her husband Henry's creation. 'Here, Girl,' she said when she returned to the table with a Marmite sandwich and a pear.

Hukarere had arranged the shells into a pattern. 'What's that?' asked Nan.

'It's an old lady.'

'So it is. A beautiful old lady, I might add.'

Hukarere had shaped the woman out of seashells and given her pāua-shell eyes. She wove the old lady's hair out of seaweed and sprinkled it with tiny broken bits of pāua shell that glittered like stars.

Early that evening the sea air overpowered Hukarere and she fell asleep beneath the kitchen table. Nan put her to bed.

The weather changed. The glassy flat sea turned rough and hurled mighty waves at the shore. The wind howled around the house.

'I'm scared Nan,' yelled Hukarere as she ran into the kitchen and jumped onto Nan's lap.

'Don't worry, Nan will look after you.' She wrapped her arms around her granddaughter and held her.

'Look,' said Hukarere. She pushed away from Nan and pointed at the photo of Henry on the mantelpiece. 'Grandpa Henry is smiling.'

'What's wrong with you?' said Nan. 'He isn't smiling. He looks sad.' She wrinkled her brow and gazed over the bay as if she was far away. 'Your grandfather was the one person people came to if they wanted to learn anything Māori.'

'What did he know?' Hukarere pricked up her ears, cocked her head and looked at Nan.

'He knew a lot, Girl. They offered the locals money if they could build an airstrip on top of Mount Maungaroa. Grandpa said, they mustn't build there as it was an old pā site.'

'What happened, Nan?'

'The locals wanted the money, pittance though it was. They didn't listen. The money disappeared long ago.'

'Did they buy lollies, Nan?'

'Some did. The airstrip is still there for top-dressing planes that roar around spraying the land with poison and coating us with it. You never know what that dust does,' she continued. 'The creeks around here are growing watercress that's tall as trees.'

Early the very next morning, it seemed as if the world had deliberately set out to rile Nan Waikawa. A top-dressing plane zoomed across the sky.

'C'mon, Girl,' frowned Nan. 'Let's get out of here.'

Hukarere followed Nan down the path, over the road, through the dunes and down to the beach. They walked a little further along the shore than they had the day before. The aeroplane droned on ahead of them.

They reached a rocky outcrop that jutted up above the waves at low tide. The rocks were embedded with pools, one of which was deep and festooned with seashells. It was also full of little fish that darted about and strands of seaweed that swayed to and fro in the eddies, especially when the tide changed and the sea poured in or out of the pool.

Something made Nan pause. She gazed out beyond the waves

to the edge of the horizon and then looked back at the rock pool. Childhood memories filled her and felt so strong it was as if yesterday stood before her.

'Why have we stopped?' asked Hukarere.

'Well, Girl, my grandmother, Nan Tureiti, used to bring me here.'

'What for?'

'Nan Tureiti told me there is a taniwha who lives in this pool.'

The top-dressing plane's noise above them roared even louder as she spoke.

'The name of the taniwha is Hine Tai,' said Nan, raising her voice so she could be heard.

'What?' squealed Hukarere.

'She's a goddess of the sea. She often appears in the ocean as an old lady,' called Nan.

'What's a taniwha?' screeched Hukarere.

'A taniwha is magic,' yelled Nan. 'Hine Tai looks after us, like, a kaitiaki.'

The plane roared directly above them.

'Is a kaitiaki like an angel?'

'What?'

'Is a kaitiaki like an angel?'

'Sort of,' bellowed Nan, yelling her lungs off. 'The old people gathered here to greet Hine Tai and welcome her back from the deep sea. They cared for her. They sang and danced to her.'

'Why?'

'Because Hine Tai would bring them all the riches of the ocean as a gift.'

The plane faded off inland and Nan found herself yelling into a silence broken only by the gentle hush of waves. 'Sometimes she spoke to them and told them things they needed to know!'

Hukarere screwed her face up. Grown-ups said strange things. Grown-ups were funny people. What was Nan talking about?

The sun painted Whanga-Tai-Tini. The ocean was calm until two speedboats rounded the point and whizzed over the water like mosquitos zipping about and making ripples on the surface. The rocks sheltered the pool from the ripples. Hukarere gazed down into the water. She saw the purples, red and greens of the seaweed and the long brown bull kelp swaying around like long hair. Little fish darted to and fro like arrows. Beyond this glittered many seashells that winked at her in the watery light.

The next morning Hukarere went outside and called to Uncle Terry who was on the roof. 'Uncle Terry!'

'Yes.'

'Are taniwha real?'

'What?'

'Are taniwha real?'

'Eh?'

'Taniwha and kaitiaki. Are they real?'

What's that girl thinking of? wondered Terry. 'No, they're not real.'

'Nan says they are.'

'They might've been once, but they've gone now.'

'Why?'

'The questions you ask, Girl!' Terry paused a moment and gazed out over the bay as if listening to something far away and then looked back at Hukarere. 'They've gone because this world has no respect. They have gone because technology has driven them off!' He gazed out over the bay again.

'Uncle Terry?'

'Yes.'

'What's technology?'

'You ask too many questions.'

'What's respect?'

'Ask me later, Girl.' He returned to hammering on the roof.

That afternoon Nan swept the kitchen floor and gazed out the window. She heard them. Those speedboats again. They reminded her of the day when she peered out over the bay and made out a torpedo shape with a little flag on top of it cutting through the waves. When she found out it was a 'kontiki' and realised what they did, she protested.

'That's not real fishing,' she had said when the kontiki man showed up again. 'Don't you come around here to fill up your bloody car boot with fish and wipe the place out. Bugger off! You're not even from here!'

The sea air got the better of Hukarere again that evening and Nan put her to bed early. The room was dimmer and full of shadows. Nan could just see the stove's outline from the bedroom.

When she was a girl the house had no electricity. Her grandmother, Nan Tureiti, had fought the council to get the power connected because she could no longer see by the oil-burning lamps and was tired of cooking on the wood-burning stove. Two years before Nan Tureiti died, she managed to get the power connected, and along with that came an electric stove and electric lights so she could see better.

'Ha,' snorted Nan Waikawa. Nan Tureiti refused to cook on the new stove; she couldn't, because she wasn't used to it. She bought some lightbulbs and soon after that she went blind. Imagine that. For a moment Nan paused in thought. This place is well named. Whanga-Tai-Tini. The harbour of many tides.

When Waikawa started school at age five, she spoke Māori. By the time she was eight, she'd almost stopped and only spoke it at home. You had to speak English at school. Too soon, the few old people who spoke Māori at home died and she gradually stopped speaking it. The language flickered out and died like a light. She had been keen to learn English. Everyone agreed it was for the best. Now, she had to pause and think back before putting just a couple of phrases together in Māori.

She remembered the old people again. They knew all about fishing. When and where to go. They fished from the deep sea, scoured the rock pools and combed the shore looking for food. She remembered how they would catch the tiny delicious piharau that in some places were disappearing from the estuaries and the oceans forever. 'Bah,' she gasped and thought for a moment. 'Rāhui,' she said. That's the word the elders would use, she remembered. If the sea was over-fished, the elders put down a rāhui. A ban forbidding anyone from taking fish or any food from that area until the sea had time to revitalise itself. 'Bah,' she grunted again. That's what the world needs, rāhui all over the show. But who would take any notice of the rāhui? she wondered. Who would listen? She felt sad. The sorrow was sweetened and deepened as she remembered the kindness Nan Tureiti and her old people fed her with when she was a child. For a moment, she felt an urge, a call to talk Māori again as she once had.

After breakfast the next morning Nan looked up from the table, wrinkled her brow and said to her moko. 'Haere koe, kia kite mehemea a Hine Tai kai te koma i ōna makawe.' (Go and see if Hine Tai is combing her hair.)

Hukarere's eyes opened wide like bowls, 'Was Hine Tai real?' She ran out of the house and down to the beach.

When she returned Nan asked, 'I kite koe i a Hine Tai kai te koma i ōna makawe?' (Did you see Hine Tai combing her hair?)

'No, Nan, I didn't see Hine Tai combing her hair.'

Another storm wracked the coast that evening. 'Bah,' grunted Nan. 'Just like that girl to sleep through the rough stuff. I can't sleep a wink.' She felt tossed about like the waves.

Terry wasn't much company that evening. He spent all night on his cell phone. He had bought her a cell phone a few years ago. She had had to go out to Henry's orchard and climb to the top of Henry's apple tree just to get reception on the phone. Once that was sorted out, Terry bought her an updated phone with all the bells and whistles. She seldom used it and hadn't learnt how to ring all the bells and blow all the whistles.

'This young generation,' she said to Terry. 'You spend all your lives talking to people on the other side of the world and never say a word to those sitting next to you. Soon Māori mightn't go to the marae. We'll just text our karanga in and go online with our whaikōrero. We'll text our sad songs in to the funeral and tangi our hearts out into the phone.'

There are so many troubles flowing about like streams. Coming and going like the tides. What can we do, wondered Nan. The storm blew itself out in the early morning and she drifted into sleep.

At breakfast time that morning, Nan wrinkled her brow and repeated to Hukarere, 'Haere koe, kia kite mehemea a Hine Tai kai te koma i ōna makawe.' (Go and see if Hine Tai is combing her hair.)

Hukarere's eyes opened wide. She jumped up and sped off down to the rock pool.

When she returned Nan asked, 'I kite koe i a Hine Tai kai te koma i ōna makawe?'

'No, I didn't see Hine Tai combing her hair.'

'We're off tomorrow afternoon,' said Terry.

Nan felt sad and a little angry. *They will go and leave me with nothing but fading eyesight.*

'We'll be back soon to sort things out, Mum,' he said.

'You'll be back soon, eh?' She stared at Hukarere. 'We will sort things out, eh? Oh yes, we will.'

'What are you talking about, Mum?'

'Never mind.' She felt a tear in her eye and turned away from Terry and Hukarere so they couldn't see her face.

The next day Nan looked up from the kitchen table and peered at Hukarere. 'Haere koe, kia kite mehemea a Hine Tai kai te koma i ōna makawe.'

Why does Nan always frown at me? thought the youngster as she wandered down to the rock pool. Why does Nan keep saying those words? What is there to see? There is nothing! She enjoyed the squelch of water and sand between her toes as she daydreamed and dawdled along. Then she gazed wide-eyed into the rock pool. A breeze sighed and the waves broke into song.

When she returned Nan asked, 'I kite koe i a Hine Tai kai te koma i ōna makawe?'

'Āe, āe, e kui. I kite au i a Hine Tai kai te koma i ōna makawe. I kite au i a Hine Tai!' (Yes, yes, Nan. I did see Hine Tai combing her hair. I did see her!) squealed Hukarere as she jumped up and down and pointed out the window to the sea.

'Ka rawe,' said Nan. Her face wrinkled into a smile. She looked at her moko and paused for a moment. 'We must go and welcome Hine Tai. She is our tipuna and she will bring us pāua, pipi, mussels and all the sea's riches. She will talk to us and tell us what to do. Let's go and get the kina.'

'I don't like kina.'

'What do you like?'

'McDonald's and Kentucky Fried.'

'Forget the greasies. Kina is better for you.'

'Me aha rā tāua ināianei, e kui?'

'Me haere tāua ki te kōrero ki a Hine Tai.'

'Āe, Nan.'

'Me hoki anō tāua ki te moana, e moko.'

Īhe & Her

BY FRAZER RANGIHUNA

Staring at the leafy wallpaper, I'm drawing lines with my mind, going in and out between the leaves, trying to find a way out. Without crossing over the same lines again. Two weeks it's been. Two weeks since I was last inside her. Yet she's still inside of me. This hara, still violating me. And *still* Māmā is trying to soften the blow. She used to rub pages from the *Rotorua Daily Post* between her fists when we ran out of toilet paper so I wouldn't get my arse hurt. And when she couldn't soften the blow, she'd be there to kiss it better. I've told her a million times I don't want to talk about it, but she's still standing there, her mouth is *still* moving! What does *I don't want to talk about it* mean, Māmā? Probably, how I wouldn't want to talk about having cancer of the balls or something. Even if I was worried a ball was going to drop off, I'd still say nothing. Not even point to where it hurts. But my ex-girl, *she's* the disease I don't want to talk about.

'I'm sorry, baby. You two were good together. Hei aha though — you're still *my* chief,' she says, holding up my freshly ironed overalls. With creases that tell everyone I'm only a quarter of the man I used to be.

Out on the road, I don't know how many times I've pulled at my hi-vis vest, listened to it slurp off my bare chest. And how is a man supposed to feel staunch when he looks like a giant fuckin' highlighter, anyway? But I make it work. By pulling my overalls down to my waist and tying the sleeves at the front. This job is *Stop. Go. Stop. Go.* All day. Not me, though. The lollipop sign. In a fit of ingenuity, I found that if I stuck the pole into the hole at the top of a road cone, all I have to do is swat the sign from go to whoa. And now, all the breethas do it. Sometimes when I see a sticky chick pulling up, I take it out of the road cone and swing it around, taiaha styles, to impress her. One time this girl even wound down her car window and panted 'Hot-hot-hot!' at me but before I could reply with, 'Look who's talking!' I realised she had burnt her lip on a Maketū pie. Sticky chicks don't come along often, which is stink, so a man has to find other ways to pass the time. One of the best things is doing the pūkana behind my shades at the honkies pulling up in their audis and beemers. It brings my Nan back to life every time — the *bleh you pigs*! and *garn yas*! she'd grunt at the Pākehā approaching the paepae.

At the sound of crunching gravel, I look up to see a queue of cars, waiting for me to spin the sign to *Go* again. All of their lives play out inside their windscreens in frame-by-frame. And that's my other favourite pastime — a little something I've made up that I like to call The Voice-Over Game with Īhe.

Car one: Girl looks all excited. She holds up her phone to her boyfriend and says, 'Hey babe, look at how many likes I got for this photo!'

Bro grabs her phone from her. He looks all aggro. Flicks through the comments from all of the horny guys who are posting shit like: #girlfriendgoals; and 'Do you have a boyfriend? Lol.' He turns her phone back to her and points. 'Who the fuck are all these clowns? And how come you're friends with them?'

Girl turns away, flicks her hair. 'They're friends. Just friends.' She turns back to him, puts her hand on top of his. 'I'm with you, babe. Do you think I'd show you if I was rooting any of them?'

He flicks her hand off of his, gives her the side look, 'Maybe you're a fucking skank like everyone says you are.'

She tries to touch his hand again. 'Babe, you gotta stop this. I can't handle much more.'

'Well fuck off, then!' he shouts.

I sniff hard up my palm. 'Fuckin' loser.'

'Hey Īhe, smoko time!' the boss shouts.

'I'll E-hey *you*,' I mutter under my breath as I drop my smoke butt onto the gravel and crush it.

'That us?' I reckon to my mate DaShaun who's been snapchatting his missus. He doesn't think I saw him take a selfie with the puppy-dog filter on. Fuckin' puppy-dog ears, puppy-dog tongue, and wagging tail.

When we get into the smoko room — this shed dumped on the side of the road — there's a huddle of psychedelic orange.

'What's up, my breethas?' I ask.

Bronson raises his head. Flicks it at the local rag laying open on the table. 'Fuckin' check this out my bro!' He's pulling that face he pulls when he hugs a sticky chick at the pub — eyes rolled back, snorting the Pantene out of her hair. This must be good! Pushing my way into the huddle I see what all the dirty noises are about. Not even the stank breath and pīhau can put me off.

'Man, I'd dip my wick in that anytime!' DaShaun reckons. And even my uncles, who would usually pounce on the chance to tease him about his pencil dick, aren't taking the bait. My uncles, who pat bloody handprints on the arses of their jeans after butchering a sheep. Chew tero tero like chuddy.

They're all pussy-whipped. First, by our aunties — who they thought of as mythical creatures but found out they weren't mythical at all, just real princesses and now, by *Her and the Patupaiarehe*. Her, eh. This hard-out beauty is doing a show tonight. Only trouble is I'm pōhara as, and yay-day, pay-day, is tomorrow.

'10.30's late for a show, isn't it?' Bronson asks.

DaShaun says, 'Look at that white skin though, bruh. Doesn't look like she's seen much sun.' He giggles, 'Maybe girl likes it in the dark?'

'I'd tan her!' shouts Uncle Dar, his jowls clapping.

Everyone turns to stare at him.

'I'm not joking!'

For ages I stare at Her's face. For so long, it's like staring at one of those pictures of dots, that when you look up, you have a vision.

'Oi, back to work!' the boss shouts at us, but I don't move. Just wait for all of the breethas to leave. Just stand there wiping the cold sweat out of my hard hat.

'Hey, boss. Can I ask you something?'

'Make it quick, Īhe.'

My real name slips off the tip of my tongue, 'Can I have an advance? Please?'

'An advance?' He laughs then lifts a boot up on a chair. 'What for?'

'I just wanna have a drink with the boys after work.'

'Advance means you've actually done some work that I can pay you for. But you've done fuck all. Now, advance out that door and get back to work.'

'C'mon boss! It'll be the last time. Promise, man!'

'Out!'

Stink fulla! I think, ripping out the page with 'Her' on it, careful not to crease over Her's natural ones.

Out on the road again, me and DaShaun are playing kiss, shoot or shag and he's answering 'Yo' mama' to all of them. All I'm thinking is it must be true, how a man can die of thirst. Sculling three cuppa teas does shit to quench my thirst. The slimy backwash from

DaShaun's Coke bottle doesn't either. Man, I need a drink. A real drink. Turning away, I cup my hand and raise it up to a frothy cloud, imagine I'm sucking the head off an icy, cold Steiny when my text tone goes off. It's Māmā.

'Sorry chief . . . A.N.Zilch this week xxx.'

'Fuckin' sun. Just as well you can't get any blacker, eh?' DaShaun says as I'm putting my phone back into my pocket.

'Bei, are you looking for a crack?'

'Bei, what's up your arse?'

'Tūtae.'

'No shit! But what else?'

'Nothing bruh,' I say. 'Just hanging for a drink, eh. Hey, are you gonna come see that chick tonight?'

'Can't, bruh. My missus'd go ape.'

'Can I borrow twenty huck, then?'

'Eh? That's all she gives me for pocket money, bruh. Just enough for a 30 gee. And hey, it's stink about you and that chick, bruh.' Then he goes back to looking at his phone.

'DaShaun? I'm real fucked up, bro,' I say, reaching out my hand to him. But when he turns to look at me I freeze. Then I just pick up the lighter sitting next to him.

'What was that bruh?'

'Nothing. Nothing,' I say.

At home, Mum lifts the lid off a pot of spuds and pours salt in.

'She wasn't good enough for you, Chief. Come to think of it, I never did like her. What kind of weirdo doesn't eat kaimoana?'

'Someone who's allergic to it, maybe?'

'Strange girl, that one.' She shudders. 'Gave me the creeps.'

I pull up my hoodie. Then I feel her tug on the cords. Watch my world close in.

In my bedroom, I move over to the window, push it open and look out at the backyard from two storeys up. Every now and then my bedroom door shudders to a stop with Mum's weight behind it. And every time I make a floorboard creak, she moves away. We — my ex-girl and I — met at kapa haka. It all started off as a flirty and light waiata-ā-ringa. Our tutor, Aunty Tangi, said I had to imagine she was this girl I was trying to woo, which wasn't hard because I was trying for reals. Baby-oiled up, I hoped she'd take a shine to me. The winks, the heel kicks, I even imagined the *rape* spiralling over my arse cheeks hypnotising her. All of the boys wanted her. Each haka was a competition, not only against the other rōpū but with each other, too. We tucked our dicks into the waistbands of our undies in case we got an embarrassing stiffy in front of her, even if it might've proved I was the bigger man. We'd get red tits from scratching at our chests, crossing our hearts, for her. We fell over ourselves to be her partner in the haka so we could play out our fantasies. We all wanted to be the one who got to pump his fist while she held the front of her piupiu open, her face all bloated and amazed.

It was my first relationship and, being in love, I assumed things. No one told me I couldn't carry on being myself. I'd assumed I'd be the one who stayed skinny, while she packed on the pounds. But by that time, I'd be too old to score anyone else so we'd be stuck with each other, forever. At the end though, it was all a mōteatea. And I no longer felt a fake singing one anymore. Before the break-up, I used to just pretend to look sad and bewildered by grief and loss, but suddenly I was living it. The breeze coming through the window crawls up my arms and takes a cold grip. I move forward, until I feel my hip bones press hard up against the windowsill when something in my pocket crinkles. Unwrapping the piece of paper, it's Her again. The window slams shut.

I've put on my best gears. My tan Dickies jeans, a white singlet and my pin-striped vest. In the bathroom, I watch myself doing bicep curls among the white spatter all over the mirror when the thought hits me — what if I actually score this Her chick? Finishing my set, I moisturise with my *Jazz* cologne then I cruise down the hallway to the linen cupboard to look for fresh sheets. I choose the ones with little flowers on them because girls like flowers. After I've made my bed, I rummage through the pockets of my jeans and trackies I've stepped out of and left in piles on my bedroom floor, hoping to find some loose change, but all I find is a Minties wrapper and a strand of hair.

When Māmā hears me coming down the stairs, she shoos Snowy the foxy off her lap. Māmā's got this thick coat of hair stuck to her. She tries to brush off the shitty korowai, but then she realises there's hundreds more where that came from so she just wears it. Then she leans right forward in her chair for a good ol' nohi. Her gold-coloured heart necklace swings out and she says, 'Phuuuu, Chief! You look neat, alright!' Then she sits back and her gold heart beats on her chest, 'Kei te haere koe ki whea?'
    'Out.'
Her eyes light up.
'Nah, not with her.'
'Anei,' she says, handing me a stack of these damp-smelling coins.

The further out of town I get, the fewer lamp posts and cops there are looking for Māori driving on their learner licences and expired regos. Feeling safe enough, I park up on the side of the road and roll a ciggie. Then I check myself out in the rear-vision mirror. My lips blow out smoke that I watch rise then it begins to unfurl over me, but I wave it away, look out the window and up to the maunga thinking it's a strange arse place for a show, that!

The dirt road is so steep and windy that my little Honda's bumhole squeaks as it rounds every bend. And even with the headlights on full, I can only see a few metres in front of me, as if anything beyond that is too dark to imagine. A little darkness never put a Māori off, though. Not Kupe, not me. And we're kind of the same. So, I just grit my teeth and hope no one is coming the other way. Finally, after rounding yet another bend, I come to the summit. A sign on the side of the road says 'No lights beyond this point'. So, I turn off the lights, park up and have a jack nohi around. It's out-of-it how there's no other cars. My watch says 10.25 p.m., just five minutes until the show is supposed to start. In the distance, there's the pub tagging shapes into the moon. Another sign says it's 'The Altar'.

Then I bring my fist down hard on the dashboard. Don't tell me this is one of that fuckin' DaShaun's pranks again! Made a fuckin' fool of me, again! Like that time he poured cordial into my mouth when I was sleeping with my mouth open. Fooled by the ex-girl! How she used to lay her head on my arm and laugh because she wasn't sure whose heartbeat she was hearing. The liar told me our hearts beat as one.

Fumbling with the keys, I'm just about to scarper when I hear this music. The haunting sounds of a kōauau. It makes me think of a ruru calling. How that is scary enough, but you wait for that other sound — the tohu telling you your shit luck is going to get shitter. Then again, how could it? So I get out of my car and follow the music to a figure standing in the doorway.

'Name,' it says.

'Īhenga.'

The figure's head moves slowly from side to side as if it is this speaker picking up some negative feedback. 'Īhenga! Please, come in, come in,' it says, showing the way inside.

It's barely light inside, but what light there is, is so soft, it's as if this lens on my life has been smeared with Vaseline, taking away all of its harsh edges. Across the room the curvy silhouette of a woman sways softly from side to side, her hands following the coasts of her body. On either side of her, there's two smaller versions of the woman, each holding a kōauau up to their lips, playing a tune I don't know.

'All the way from the forests of Ngongotahā maunga,' this Steve Parr, *Sale of the Century* voice says, out of nowhere, 'we bring you, *Her and the Patupaiarehe*!'

The lights don't go up but her face is lit up by something else inside her, something that energises her. She stands still, her eyes closed. Her hair is this mass of glossy red muka billowing around her face, the waves of it a lathe to her sharp features. Then her eyes open and I'm drawn into them, not knowing if the blueness of them is warm or cold but what I do know is that she's showing interest — I think — and anyway, that's enough for me. When she sings, I'm not so much moved by the beauty of her reo, not even by my thoughts of those wet, red lips curling around my dick, the way they're curling around the words, but something that is even more powerful than that. So powerful, I don't realise she has finished singing until she is standing in front of me, in a cat suit of red harakeke in a poutama pattern. It's so tight, it could have been woven hand over hand from the strands of her own skin. My eyes slowly climb up the poutama to her face.

'You look thirsty, Īhe whaiāipo. Can I buy you a drink?' the beauty asks.

After I've sculled it all and wiped the froth off my lips, careful not to swear in front of a lady, I say, 'Jingers, I needed that! Hey, how did you know?'

'Know what?' she asks.

'My name. What I needed.'

'Let's just say you aren't the first Īhe . . .' she shakes her head, 'I mean, *man* to turn up here, wanting a drink, honey. None as handsome as you though!' She winks, then nods at the barwoman — another patupaiarehe — who pours me another Steiny and I lift the glass to my mouth. My shit-eating grin as wide as the lip of the glass. As the beer drains, I see Her's face through the thick glass at the bottom, her eyes look all huge and pleading like that Puss in Boots character in *Shrek*. Man, I'm so in! I've never been with a girl this fine before.

I hope I can satisfy her, I think, squeezing my thighs together. I feel myself coming out of its shell.

'So, tell me about yourself,' says Her.

'Well, I'm 21 and I live with my . . . flatmate and I work in . . . infrastructure.' What else? 'I love kapa haka. Our rōpū won the nationals last year. Second year in a row. I'm a real gym junkie, too. I go three times a week.' Then, of all people, Uncle Dar pops into my brain, telling me I'm talking too much.

'*A ha ka ma na*, boy,' he said to me one day, as he was pulling the bottle-opener out of his toolbelt. We were out in the corrugated-iron lean-to at the back of the wharekai. It smelt of raw meat and smoke. All of us stood in a circle. All pissed. Past the comedy and passing shade. We just stared into our beer bottles, held them up to the light. Thought about how the fuck we got to this point.

'You mean the waiata?' I asked him.

'That's the one, boy. Just remember the woman is singing the *A ha ka ma na pa ra ta wa ngā wha* bits and you're doing the 'echo' *e he ke me ne* bits. Show her you're interested. Come straight back with a reply. The ladies love it when they think you're listening. How'd you think I scored your aunty?'

I turned my face away to screw it up, thinking about Aunty Kino

— gummy, bum front. Then a bottle cap pinged off my head.

'You think she looked like that back in the day, iriot? *A ha ka ma na!* You'll thank me later.'

'So, tell me about yourself,' I ask Her.

'What do you want to know?'

I smile. 'Anything. I want to know about you. How old are you?'

'You're not supposed to ask a lady that.'

'Why not?'

'Because it's bad manners.'

'Bu. . .'

She holds a finger up to my lips but *she* makes the *shhhh* sound then smiles. 'You talk too much,' she says, making her way to the stage again.

She opens her lips over the head of the microphone and says, 'This one's for you, Īhe, whaiāipo.'

A few more steinies later, while Her is singing about needing sexual healing and how she can't help falling in love, with this you-gon'-get-it look on her face, I'm feeling misty blue. I can't help but compare my ex-girl and Her. Her is making this all too easy. It was so different with my ex-girl. Girl made me work. Got my respect for making me chase her. It took so much planning, too. Happening to be in the right place at the right time. At the clubrooms, I'd make sure I was standing across the room when she looked up, so our eyes would meet. Every time one of her friends made her laugh, she'd glance across and I'd join in on the laughter. When she walked around the corner after coming back from the toilet, guess who'd be there for her to bump into?

Then the patupaiarehe start to play some Prince Tui and I really get them feels. 'E Ipo' — was our song. It was playing so loudly in the garage that night. Uncles were outside, pissing in the garden, their slack faces pressed up against the windows, looking on.

Me and my ex-girl just standing there, still, a string of flashing fairy lights above us reflecting in our eyes. She was Missy and I was Prince Tui. Then I closed my eyes. Mouthed Prince Tui's spoken bits to her . . .

'My never-ending love,' I say.

Eyes open again, I realise I've been serenading *Her*! I've unleashed the power of seduction on her. This kōrero tuku iho of my uncles has finally worked. At the wrong time! And now she's blowing me kisses. The smacking sounds of her lips echo loudly from the microphone. While she makes her way back to the bar again — my eyes ride the fleshy wave of her chest that threatens to break over the top — and I wonder if this is fate? Maybe I've got to know what a white girl feels like, just so I won't go through my life wondering? Just so I can rub DaShaun's ugly face in it. All of this wondering is nothing compared to this mate nui I feel for the familiar, though. With someone who knows what to expect. Who some day I might surprise. I've got to get her back.

Sitting down next to me, Her reaches over and takes my hand. 'I feel the same way as you, whaiāipo,' she says.

Slowly I try to pull my hand out of hers but she squeezes my fingertips in her fist.

'Taihoa a minute,' I say. 'There's something I need to tell you.'

'You don't have to say anything, babe. I know.'

'I don't think you do know. Back there . . . Sorry, but I didn't mean you . . . I was talking to my missus. My ex-missus. I fucked things up with her, but if I just tell her I'm sorry I think she'll give me another go, eh.'

Her's ankle circles then cracks. The sound of something breaking makes me jump and I touch the back of my neck.

'Forget about her, babe. You've got me now.'

'I can't forget about her, though. Hey, look. Sorry if I led you on . . . You're really hot and everything . . . it's just . . . no hard feelings? Thanks for everything,' I say, standing up to leave.

Then, I'm swept up in Her's arms. When I open my eyes, Her's lips are wrestling mine. Her eyes are closed. Over her shoulder, I see there's a piupiu spread out and nailed to the far wall. Close by are three decorative baskets hung in a row and I rack my brain, trying to remember what each of them holds. One holds knowledge, another I think, holds memory. When I'm thinking about what the third one holds, kete tuatea — it tilts on its nail and I imagine the contents are pouring out. Then I remember what was in it and I jump back.

'Whoa, fuck this! I'm outta here,' I say, moving in the direction of the door.

'Hang on, I'm not finished with you, yet,' she says, grabbing my wrist.

Shaking off her grip, I'm almost at the door when I feel her grip around my wrist again. This time, it's much tighter. I struggle to get loose but I can't.

'Hey, let go! Before I . . .'

'Before you what, big man? Before you hit a woman?' she laughs, taking hold of my other wrist, too. She pins me to the wall and we struggle. Well, I do. She just stands there looking bored. Forces my hands up and down, like we're playing a game of hei tama tū tama in slow motion. 'You think you can come in here and take advantage of a girl's hospitality like this? The drinks? Massaging your stupid ego? You owe me.' Her grip burns. Almost as much as the shock of being overpowered by a girl — that leaves me wide-eyed and gasping at this new feeling — that there's no use fighting. I just don't believe I can win. Not even if I was to make the most noise. She's not other women.

So, I hum. Fill the air with humming. The tune of *Ka pine koe* I feel thrumming sweetly in my throat and I watch Her's face soften.

Her eyes light up again at the recognition, and the meaning of the song. *Ka pine koe e au*, I hum, *ki te pine o te aroha*. It's what you want, isn't it? I ask Her with my eyes and she nods. Bites her lip.

'Let me make it up to you, eh?' I tell Her, and smile. 'How about I do a little kanikani for starters?' Her's grip weakens, then she lets go of my hands. Another patupaiarehe goes over to the door. Locks it.

In the middle of the dance floor, I slowly unbutton my vest, and ease it off. Cross my arms, pick up the hem of my singlet and peel it off my body. Once I've kicked off my boots, I unbutton my pants, unzip and step out of them. Then I walk over to the wall to take the piupiu down. Tying it around my waist, I move from side to side, watching the strands swing out and in. I'm ready to perform. When I think back about my past performances, it was easy to fool them with our white smiles, framed in black ink. We made the fools smile. Their ties a lump at their throats, they were choked up by the cheery tone, the sleight of hands. They tapped their Hush Puppies while we told them they weren't here for our benefit but for Satan's. But now I'm here for another of his spawn, Her. If I just imagine she's my ex-girl, I reckon I can fool her, too.

'C'mon, babe! Kanikani for me!' shouts Her. Hearing the impatience in her voice, I decide I'm going to tell the story of how my ex-girl and I met. It's time for another episode of The Voice-Over Game with Īhe.

One day, bro was at kapa haka just minding his own business when a new girl captures his attention. He tilts his head, raises his eyebrows and inflates his eyes with a pūkana to get a good nohi at her — to take her all in. He notices her checking him out, too, but he's not sure if she likes him. Only when she doesn't screw up her nose and purse her lips, doesn't squeal, 'Poo! Poo!' does he know he's in with a chance. He moves a cupped hand up to his mouth and shakes his hand, sending out a call to her. Asking her if he can approach, if he can remove his waewae tapu. With her arms out in front of her, and the trembling of her hands she beckons him to haere mai. He treads lightly, though. He bounces, lifts a knee and crosses it over the other leg, his toes pointed, alternating legs as he moves towards her. His fists on his hips to tell her he means no harm. When they are facing each other, at the same time, they bring their arms up to cross over their chests, their fists closed then opening out into fluttering hearts.

And of course, she's in love, I think as I look over at Her. I can feel her moistness from here. With no other option I mumble, 'Ah well, tōia mai te waka,' and I make two fists — one facing up, the other facing down and I pull. Her comes willingly, faster than I'm pulling — she's hooting, her arms in the air, flicking her hair around and I drop the ropes and reel her in the last few metres with the gyrations of my hips.

Then suddenly, some kind of force pushes me down into an open-legged squat. My foot begins to stomp. I get the sensation that I'm pumping my people's blood from out of the land and into my body. As my veins fill, my bloodlines branch out into their intricate networks. Each limb brings another tipuna back to life. Those who never got to tell their stories. All of them fight to break the surface of my skin. They will not be invisible anymore, turning my skin red as they move up my body.

'Īhe? What's happening to you?' Her asks.

I shake my head as they move up my thighs. And I bring my hands down hard to guide them on their way.

Her lunges forward to grab me but the patupaiarehe draw her back to them.

Rising to my chest, I feel them gathering there, so I scratch. My nails digging out flesh while I scream, 'Kss! Kss! Ha!' Making a way out for them through the open wounds. But they just gather inside. Dry the blood into little beady eyes that keep watch, while the others make their way up my neck then I taste blood, pooling in my mouth. It drips out of my nostrils. A rush of blood flows into my eyeballs, it fills them with blood that bursts out in tears, when I'm brought back by Her's screaming.

She screams at me, 'Get out!'

PART FIVE

Rarohenga

CHAPTER 13
JOURNEY TO THE UNDERWORLD

———

Rarohenga and the Reformation

———

Niwareka and Mataora

———

Rarohenga and the Reformation

All intelligence is artificial
— e.ther

I'm sorry that I have to deliver you this in words on paper but that
is what we are reduced to. At the very least I would have liked these
to be black pages — the abyss — a void out of which white words
appeared, but ink is poison. You open a new book and you love the
fresh pressed smell. You breathe it in, but all I smell is poison. Ink
is poison. Bleach to make white pages from tree pulp is poison. A
book is a decadent thing. It kills. A tree died, toxins and poxins are
released from the saws, the trucks, the mills, the printing presses
and the shops. CO_2 footprints stomping on everything, everywhere,
like the Godzillasaurs we are.

But you're not here to hear an old Greenie, well into his anec-
dotage, rant and rave. No. No, you're here to resurrect the dead, am
I right?

. . . Talk to me. This is an interactive experience. Immersive.
We live in a post-narrative world. There's no glory in story. Hell,
you take an augmented reality bath, pick-a-path, use g.iraffe and
p.eriscope to enter any uni.verse you conjure.

D.Avid Gear.y | 349

. . . I know you're shy. If you're somewhere public it will be strange to talk to a book but people have been talking to their phones, their blue-tooths, their google-eyes in the sky, the shroud-cloud, the e.ther for fifty fig.ments now. We're third re-generation homeless-loonietoon-ranters.

And I know in your perfect word.world you have on a SR/VR/AR headset and these words float past you in transambiotic fluid cybeardspace. You are Major Tom floating on 4evah. I.mages, o.bjects, re-memes, instagrammar float by. It'd be a bit like the end of *2001: A Space Odyssey* before you end up stuck in the room with the old furniture forever, like going to visit the great-great-grandma you never met, but she's not there.

We have to get away from these rectangles, these screens, the world is a 4-D, multi-diamondsional and SR sensory experience. Unfortunately, and I don't have to tell you this, despite HU.mans wanting to have our head in the stars, our hearts are in the gutter and all our ambitions for high-techopias are reduced to pornography.

Not that I've got anything against porno4pyrography — after all, it's our bread & butter here at The.Reformation. That's the name of our company. We *re-form* people. Although, I don't like the word *company* in this post-corpor.ant world. Company implies we get together, have a CEO-EO, Executive Washrooms, Lear.y jets, Charitable Foundations, sleepods and spin-cycle meetings. It implies that we're all wearing sync-heart-trackers to reach health goals together, and are constantly aware of each other's BP, Bad Cholesterol, Diabetes, and Biometrindex, but the truth is I've never met anyone who I work with in person. That was my original guiding principle: that if we were to create the next level of SR/VR/AR experience, then we had to model that in our bizniz structure. We couldn't have a skyscraper with corporart in the foyer, a lo.go, and *American Psycho* bizniz cards. Conferences and Italian suits? No. We had to exist solely in the e.ther, surviving without oxygen.

Do you like the name *The.Reformation*? What does it conjure up for you?

I confess that when I came up with it I had no idea what it meant, apart from it having something to do with the church and Elon Musk before they took out all his wisdom blueteeth and he turned into flux. Still, the concept of re-forming people, re-formation, taking dead matter and bringing it back to virtual life seemed like an Act of God/Gods/Atua to me.

That's what you're here for, right? Āe? . . . .

Let me say now that this is an interview/interrogation/inquisition — this is not really a book, this is a wooden horse.

π

pi

in the

sky

When this arrived from Amazon.e on your 1346-storey balcony in our new *Jetsons* retro-drone, we thought you'd be amused to find that the introduction to our select services was via an artefact like a book, but this isn't an ordinary book. It's the latest in sm.art-screen-sensors, so as soon as you held it we were monitoring your pulse, BP, heart-brain-anxietivity waves.

It doesn't matter if you close the book now. You've already been scanned. Like TechCos says: *We're not here to connect you; we're here to collect you.*

If

it's free

you're the product.

☺

:) Smiley Face floats by.

Do you remember E.cstasy? Have you been taking your retro-drugz?

⧗⧗⧗ Is time running out?

Did she have an hourglass figure? What figure does she make now? Congratulations! Balloons fly! You've passed the Psychopath Test. 👍

Humans are simple machines. Like, you can't physically read down the page to see what's coming next faster than we can rewrite the script ahead of you. Yes, you could skim-read, or power.read, or skip to the last page but we're faster, stronger, more intuitive — responsive.

Breathe.
Your breathing has become shorter.
You'll feel dizzy if you keep this up.
Breathe . . . One Mississippi, two Mississippi . . . Breathe . . .

NOW SHOW US THE MONEY.HONEY!

In this post-credit world, where everyone invents their own DNA.crypto-currency, we are reduced to bartering again. So what are you willing to offer for our service? What is it worth to you for us to re-form your dead EX? How much of your DNA have you mort.gauged?

In your encrypted hyper.text you used embedded Emojis to suggest you cut off your ex-partner's head in a crime of passion, and buried it in a box in the park nearby. Since you opened this book we have conducted thermal scans on the common grounds in a 3 kilometre radius of your compl.ex and found no evidence of your DNA.x ∞∞∞✚ being twisted by such trauma. So we are wondering if this is true? ? ?

It doesn't matter. We live in a post-murder-means-blood world since Roe vs Spade was repealed and Adultery-is-a-reform-of-Murder was installed. Has anyone even seen a cop recently? I heard they've gone the way of the White Rhinoplasty, since the digiocrazy-dicktatorship.

Maybe he/she/they just left you and you wanted to behead them? Maybe they e.cheated on you? Ex.sex.texted.u?

e.MO.tive? To make a point. To show them. Maybe you met in a chat-room and nothing was ever made flesh & fluid, so you just decapitated their Ava.Tar?

In a Post-Tinder:Post-Grindr:Mindr world, where you're either a Coder or a Loser — it is the meeting of the minds not behinds that we concentrate on/work with. What matters is that to reach our level, to plumb to our depths, to remove certain e.curtains, you had to expose yourself to us; you had to send us the e.link to your life story, open your digital veins and we have your every-man-data. And thanks to you we've dredged your EX's II.phone2.0, sociaMEdia, photos, we even triggered in your amygdala and hippocampus the sensation associated with their favourite perfume, so they can come back to you better than the real thing.

It's just now a case of haggling at what level, and I'm sorry to be so base, but whether while wearing the headset you want to also hire a real life e.xotic e.scort to ensure you get a h.APP.y ending? . . .

I'm sorry, we have to ask that question to check your pulse and pupil dilation.

Let me say we have accessed all your frequent flyer porn.tortr sites so we can ensure the composite.scort will combine many of the qualities you LIKE/SPIKE/PIN and sub.mit. You will hold her codes.

One final thing.

☐ *Are you a robot?*

Press your right thumb into the square and hold still for 5 seconds. . . . *Buffering* . . .

It seems that indeed you would like to eventually achieve a full SR sensory re-union with your ex-partner, but that it's more important to first just have a chance to be with them, talk with them, say some of those final things you never got a chance to say. How . . . quaint/ noble/old school.

You could of course troll.stalk her while playing some old song about 'Who's loving/driving your car now?' but that's not quite the same thing, and we see that you already did a bit of this, so I guess that's why we're here. So, the price is 33% of your DNAta-soul — most of which you've already given us. Not to mention the access paths to your crypto-currency vault, from which we've already extracted our DNAeposit.

Your palms are getting sweaty. Relax, we are certified by e.Thics.

If you agree to a release we agree not to weaponise your DNAta. That said, how would you know, right? . . .

Think about it. . . .

How much do you want her back? . . .

And if she does come back will you find the right words this time, or will you want to cut off her head again? . . .

In a post-serial killer world, where the Inter-generational-sins&foreskins-of the-fathers are visited on the sons & daughters, we have all been deemed serial killers due to the Privilege of the Whitestream and Trickledown-E.ffect: Generation-Gen-Genocide, so it is irrelevant. *Silence of the Lambs* is a comedy now, as quaint as bad B-grade sci-fi used to be.

NB: You are under no obligation to accept this offer . . . though we have reserved a time share in Puerta Vallarta in your name. Say the words *Puerta Vallarta* and we will flashdrive an SR of being on the beach there into your r.e-tina . . . See?

Are you going to Puerta Vallarta now? No.

If you agree to our terms you will enter *Rarohenga — The Underworld*, the spiritual dimension to our game. We have gone back to the ancients. Back to one of the strongest Indigebrands — The Māori people of New Zealand 2.0. We have drilled down into their stories of the Underworld and mined them. All with deep embedded consultation with their E.lders, some of whom worked on the classic movie *Moana* and gave it the 2 thumbs up. Quality People. We have also secured the E.lders responsible for another classic, *Whalerider 2: Blubber* in which the Māori are less spirit-sentimental about the whales being beached up, butcher them with chainsaws in the spirit of Al Pacino in *Scarface*, and throw a great hākari/feast while the girl from the original (now a Green Party politician) cries the whole time, not because she cares about whales but because she's taken a vow of Vegance.

NB: We have been culturally certified as non-appropriative, and adopted as Wisdom-Holders by a tribe, Kai.e.tāngata. It has been a great honour and responsibility to re-construct these worlds and now offer them to a man such as yourself with a clear pan-tribal bent.

Chillax.e, there will be old skool puzzles and battles just like other retro-games, but you will also be trying to find and re-form your lost, dead, dismembered EX. By so doing, just like Humpty Dumpty, the original good e.gg, you will be attempting to put yourself back together. That's the inner journey. Can you wire your shit tight? Can you get it together, bro?

Are you ready for your Hero's Journey? Your Spiritual Quest, Your Vision Time?

. . . You have resisted the Call-2-Action twice. It is now time to Cross The Threshold.

To SUBMIT, press your right thumbprint into the following Symbol for The.Reformation.

♋

Kia ora! Congratulations! Balloons fly! You have entered Rarohenga and this book is now your game controller.

♠ Black Page ♠※

LEVEL TAHI (1): RĀKAU POSE

In the beginning there was nothing, then the potential, then the night — Te Pō, Rangi, Sky Father, and Papatūānuku, Mother Earth, locked in an endless embrace, and their sons trapped between them in eternal darkness.

You are Tānemahuta — the son who wants to stand up for himself. You must do the original tree pose. Stand up, wherever you are, and do a tree pose . . . NOW!

Know this, in order to achieve your desired goal you must go through several levels of humiliation and degradation, that is the purpose of The Underworld.

. . . You do a tree pose, you wobble, but this is just a tree in the wind. You are crowned Tānemahuta — God of the Forest — Level Tahi is complete. Collect a koha from all the other players . . . Auē! The joke is on you. There are no other players! You are alone here . . . except for your bad bros . . .

LEVEL RUA (2): BAD BROS

Life is short, you stretch it with yoga and continue to push your parents apart to let light into this world. But your bad bros are not happy with your tree pose, they would rather put you in corpse pose, *Savasana* (shah-VAHS-uh-nuh). Prepare yourself for battle with the bad brothers who are angry that their parents are separated: Tū — god of war — and Tāwhirimātea — god of wind.

Tangaroa — god of the sea is more chillaxed about it: *sweet as, bro.*

Rongo — god of kūmara/sweet potato is also fine as there is more sun for his vegeself to grow in: *sweet as, bro.*

The battle is fierce. Tāwhirimātea's wind bends your branches and Tū hacks at your trunk with his mere, but you stand strong.

But then there is torrential rain. These are roimata/tears as their parents sob to see their children fighting, but also because they want to be back together.

Your task, if you choose to accept it, your 'Māori-Missionary-Impossible-Position' is to turn your Mother Earth over, reverse the magnet poles, make her flip, like a pikelet, face down so she can't see her husband.

You do this, but fail to realise your little bro is trapped inside her womb. Trapped — never to be born. He is Rūaumoko — god of earthquakes and volcanoes. In the future, when the e.settlers remark that the quake was 6.2 on the Richter scale, the locals go: 'Yes, because Rūaumoko is angry that he was never born.'

He is a foetus in diapers forever, a big baby, the tiki you see around everyone's neck — symbol of fertility and friendship, but pissed.

Your task is to create a Māori emoji that represents this.

 HINT: Use this 1950s Health Care stamp of a happy Māori baby as the basis for your drawing. Give up? Then Join-The-Dots and Paint-By-Numbers.

Now you must fight the baby. He throws his tūtae at you. It sticks. Hot lava shit burns your skin. You dive into the ocean to cool off. It is Cape Rēinga, the jumping-off place of the spirits. You are swept into a whirlpool, down further into the underworld.

LEVEL TORU (3): MIGRATION AND NAVIGATION

You struggle to make it back to the surface and find yourself emerging out of a puddle in a path somewhere in the Taiwanese highlands. Your task is now to migrate across the Pacific from Asia to Hawai'i (the Stolen Kingdom), to Easter Island for a nose job, and then down to the great Southern Islands we call Te Ika-a-Māui and Te Waka-a-Māui/Te Wai Pounamu. It feels like you're on that old reality TV show, *Amazing Race*. Reality used to be a friend of yours. But you cut her off. She gave you re-reality checks but you didn't like to be called out on any of your shit, so you cut her head off. You did this with all the women in your life you couldn't control.

To gain Kaumātua knowledge of stars, currents and winds and navigate across the Pacific you must give up all the credits you've gained so far. Welcome to Murderer's Bay . . . before it was called Murderer's Bay.

LEVEL WHĀ (4): COLONISATION/COLINISATION — DAWN OF THE COLINS (MEADS & MCCAHON)

You are a Dutch seaman under Abel Tasman. It is 1642. You played the trumpet a bit in the school band, so when Abel sees smoke on the shore of this new island, and the Natives sound a conch, Abel says:

'Hey, able seaman, trumpet boy, play something back! The Natives want to make music with us.'

You must now play either Miles Davis 'Bitches Brew' in its double album entirety, or Chet Baker's cover of Elvis Costello's 'Almost Blue'. You choose the latter. The lyrics are more meaningful.

You are missing a sweet Dutch girl that you rolled around with in a tulip field 'til a Dutch re-formist switch came down on your bare arse, and you were sent off to sea before you could do any more damage. And now, Abel Tasman gives you a nip of Dutch courage and sends you off in a longboat to meet the friendly Natives in their canoe. You take the trumpet, and play a little reprise as you get closer, but these bad bros don't want to trade, and help you replenish the ship. No, their conch shell was asking, *You want to rumble?* And the trumpet you played was, *Yeah, bring it on.*

So, they get close and they club one of your mates (the one who reminded you most of tulip girl and you'd shared a cabin with), and you shoot one, but then they club you and this tragic cultural confusion leads to you being one of the first two white men to land on this new land where you are killed, beheaded, butchered, cooked in an underground oven and eaten. They assimilate you.

The good news now is you *were* the kai, and didn't eat any kai, and that means despite losing your head/life you're still alive in Rarohenga. . . . LIFE/DEATH LESSON no.1: While in the Underground, don't eat the food, it's all forbidden fruit.

Your spirit wanders this new land, a lonely Dutch boy, until Captain Cook arrives. While a rat scuttles down a gangplank, you drift, as smoke, into a porthole and stay on board as he does reconnaissance for the Brits. He records the native pop'n, terrain, vegetation, culture, all the challenges they might face in colonising this green and pleasant land.

You shapeshift and become Captain Cook in 1779, but your goose is cooked when you visit Hawai'i where we update the original argument over a boat to a surf beach. Here, you consider you're like one of the 'Royals' and should get to ride a long board, as opposed to the peasants who just get to body surf with boogie boards. But the surf gang, the Black Shorts, who really ruled the waves, aren't having any of this, or any of your promises of fair deals and treaties and union wages and maternity leave, and coconut-flavoured condoms. And when you jump the queue to ride a wave, they spear a board into the back of your head, and then another, and another.

Then they slice and dice you while singing:

Tell tale tit, your tongue will split
And every little puppy dog will have a little bit.

You get dismembered, and never re-membered, and that should be the end of the story, but your crew have a whip-round to try and get your bits back, most of which is your BBQed butt, and they bury your remains at sea.

LEVEL RIMA (5): THE WHITE TIDE

Tangaroa takes pity on you and washes you up on the shore so, many years later, you're part of the white tide that just keeps rolling in, but you've gone native by then and can't settle . . . settle down.

By now, the Māori gods are all driven underground into Rarohenga by the missionaries who cut their ure/penises off all the carvings, and make everyone 'cover up'.

The Māori gods are unhappy to be locked down with all the other lower-class lost souls, especially as they're now in the kingdom of their baby bro, Rūaumoko, and of Hine-nui-te-pō — goddess of the night.

There's a massive fight sequence. It's *300* meets *Deadlands* meets every samurai movie you've ever seen but with buff Māori dudes. Hine-nui-te-pō, she's just happy to see the place packed and, well, she spies you and sidles on over.

'Hey, honky, what's up? You look like Alice fallen down a rāpeti hole. You're late, for a very important date.' She's all like Beyoncé (girls run the underworld!), puts on her deadly-nightshade lipstick, holds a black cherry between her teeth and coos, 'You want some of this? You want some of this?'

You run for your freakin' life! You use your Get-Out-Of-The-Big-House-of-Death-Free card and Rūaumoko blows you out of a volcano as a piece of pumice . . .

LEVEL ONO (6): TOI MOKO

. . . a piece of pumice used by H. G. Robley to sand the hard skin on the bottom of his feet when he can't convince/buy a dusky maiden to do this for him.

You shapeshift to become Robley and take over his practice of collecting preserved Māori heads. You supply muskets to anyone who will acquire them for you. One musket for one head in Taranaki. It's a win–win–win for the settlers.

You create a fantasy football team *The Once Were Warriors* with the heads, re-form them and whip them up into an unstoppable wairua-militia who try to take over New Zealand, and then the world, in a game of RISK which finally puts us on the board.

You try to take Russia in the winter, fail, and are traded back to New Zealand in a lard-for-Ladas deal where you are put on trial for treason. You are accused by the Crown of being part of the New Zealand Company conspiracy under ex-con, failed-kidnapper/ mystic, Wakefield. You're convicted and sentenced to hang, but the Wairua-Warriors spirit you away to appear on a new hybrid-mash-up game, The Settlers of Catan/Neverland. Here the previously invisible Natives rise up, pull up the survey pegs, and burn the cities. They fly planes into The Two Trump Towers and establish their own Monopolynesian hotel chains.

This is Pearl Harbor. The Americans go all-in: Nuke the Pacific. There's a new bounty for any Māori heads that can be found amongst the survivors.

These heads are used for rugby games. Used in sideshows as rotating clown gobs for ping-pong balls to win a stuffed Kiwi.

GAME OVER!

You play your Post-Narrative Back-Track Card.

RE-SET

Your new mission, should you choose to accept, it is to fly around the world, recover all the toi moko from the museums, private collections, Believe It Or Nots and sideshows. Then you must bring them home on an Air New Zealand Hobbitcraft sponsored by the Govt. as part of ongoing Truth and Re-conciliation.

But the heads have changed since they've had their OEs — overseas experiences. They want the vegan options and are lactose intolerant. They want to fly in first class with Kanye West, who drops his 50-years-on remix of 'Stronger'. . . *what does not kill me, makes me a deadhead.* The toi moko want SR/VR/AR headsets that will take them back to pre-contact, and Wi 3.0 with mere and taiaha. They want to go back to when there were kings and queens, commoners, and slaves, when . . .

WARNING: You've played your Back-Track Card already. You must go forward . . .
WARNING: The.Reformation is deemed an e.nemy of the Digiocrazy. Anyone who uses their services is automatically deemed a Re-former. If you log out now, you can be re-deemed. If you choose to continue, you will be deemed an e.tard.
WARNING: Batteries running low. Please ensure you have e.RAM or The.Reformation will not take responsibility for lowering of anti-virus shields and malware attacks.
WARNING: We offer the truth. But we offer no re-medy.

LEVEL WHITU (7): PONO/TRUTH

The truth is, H. G. Robley/Tama, that, despite your name, you're a very ordinary guy who aspired to be a hipster. You had a girlfriend, but she eventually found you too ordinary, so she left you for a much more hipsterer guy who was the DJ at a boutique microbrewery where she worked as a barmaid. He had some major ink, a design label, and promised to take her away from all this.

You had grown a beard, groomed it, taken the softening lotions, but she said, 'It still feels like a toilet brush.'

'What? How would you know my beard feels like a toilet brush?'

'I'm leaving you.'

'That doesn't make sense.'

'It doesn't have to. I'm leaving you. I don't have to make sense, or anything else, to you any more.'

Dodged a bullet there.

LEVEL WARU (8): OE.STD

You go on a holiday to Thailand, hire an e.scort at the airport, catch an STD that you have to explain first to a nurse then the doctor at a walk-in clinic who can't speak English. You end up having to mime your problem/issue/condition. They don't understand, they bring in the other nurses, and doctors and staff. All of them try to figure out what you're talking about . . . then they all crack up laughing, because of course they all speak perfect English, just like on *Crazy Rich Asians*.
WARNING: There is no game element to this level, just ritual humiliation.
WARNING: If you log out now there will be no more humiliation, but you will not be re-united with your re-former EX.

LEVEL IWA (9): TAMA

You are Tama . . . you . . . you . . . you . . .

You get fired from your job as an IT guy because while you were away in Southeast Asia, and then recovering from your STD, they upgraded the software — the upgrades come every 3 days now —

and you're deemed STR — surplus to requirements.

You can't afford your apartment any more. You move out and live under a bridge, listening to the rumble of army trucks all night long.

This is your Darkest Moment/Rock Bottom/The Death before the Resurrection. You eat at the food bank, dumpster-dive, and use the retro dial-up internet at the library. You help other losers with their emails to family and various government agencies in return for P. You sleep in the Māori section and occasionally read the pukapuka. You are struck by the story of Tama-nui-ā-rangi and Ruku-tia. It is your story.

The original Tama was a man who had wanderlust. He was addicted to searching for female slaves and to stealing. He had cold, wrinkled skin. He had a maro/kilt of dog tails. His wife, Ruku-tia, was taken away by a major magical dude, a total spunkrat hunk, Tū-te-korepango. Tama would have run away with him too, if he'd had the chance, if he'd been so inclined.

You, Tama 3.0, know what to do. You start collecting cans, become a re-cycler, with a bike and shopping cart. You raise enough money to get a Māori tattoo. You want it to make you look a lot more masculine, staunch, cool as bro.

When the tattooist sees you he asks, 'Where do you want it?'

'On my chin.'

'Are you sure about that?'

'Yeah. No one is going to call me a chinless wonder any more.'

'Shit, did they call you that?'

'Can we just do this?!'

'You know, bro, it's um usually only women who traditionally got them on their chin.'

'Yeah, but we're living in a post-gender world.'

'Have you got any Māori blood?'

'Mate, we're all indigenous to somewhere.'

You get the tattoo.

Like the original Tama, you battle thorns, nettles, impenetrable bush, steep ravines, taniwha and whirlpools, determined to find your EX and win her back. You have it all planned. You will appear at the Club that the major dude now runs. Turns out it's actually a strip club, billing Pacific Princesses, and your EX is now having to exotic dance there. You are going to save her from this monster. You're like Mickey Rourke in *The Wrestler*, and she's Marisa Tomei.

You smear your face with mud so they won't recognise you and hang around the back collecting bottles and cans. You sing karakia to yourself, and when your EX is supposed to dance she can't do it, she breaks down and her new boyfriend beats her and throws her out the back door.

You help her up, wash her tears away, wash the mud off your face, and reveal who you are. She is overjoyed that you have come to save her. Together you steal a boat down at the marina. You escape out to sea . . . and then you cut off her head and wrap her body in a cloak and bury her under the bridge where you've now set up a shack.

You are very unhappy. Winter passes, spring comes. One day there's a buzzing, a bluebottle fly singing. It's the song she used to sing, Coldplay, 'Fix You'. You claw the ground with bloody hands, dig up the box, open it up. What do you find?

WARNING: This is a koan (the answer says more about you than about itself).

A. Ruku-tia is alive, and smiling at her husband. #LearntHerLesson

B. The box is empty. #Don'tDoDrugs #TheDrugsDon'tWork

C. Ruku-tia is rotting. #WhenDidWomenStopBeingSacred?

LEVEL TEKAU (10): ENDGAME

Ministry of Social Development / Te Manatū Whakahiato Ora
Opening Hours

Monday–Friday: 8:30am–5:00pm
Wednesday: 9:30am–5:00pm
Wheelchair access
Guide dogs welcome
No smoking
No food or drink
No helmets
No hoods
No sunglasses
No gang patches
The office is protected by security guards
Security cameras may be operating
You may be asked for identification

At the door you're asked, 'Who's your caseworker, bro?'

'Ah, they just shuffle the deck with me. I get a different unlucky one each week.'

You gasp. Her head appears at a counter, behind projectile and chemical-attack perspex. It's your EX, she's been assigned your caseworker. She motions for you to come over — but pretends she doesn't know you. You're dead to her. She's all bizniz.

A. She may not even be real.

B. She may be a holograph that they've created just to torture you.

C. She wants you back and is playing hard to get.

She asks, 'Is that tattoo permanent?'

'Yes. Yes, it is. I got it for you.'

'Tattoos at job interviews can be real deal-breakers. Even Air New Zealand has trouble with the mostess-hostesses having moko as the Asians think they're part of a triad. It's a cultural thing.'

'Yeah, it's a cultural thing. You know there's a story behind mine. I . . .'

'Do you have any specific skills that employers would be interested in?'

'I top-scored on *Detroit: Become Human* for our quadrant.'

'I see, but in a post-gaming world, we . . .'

'I was in IT. I know some coding languages.'

'Which ones?'

'Java, Java Script, Python, C++, C#, PHP, Pal, Swift, R, Rust . . .'

'How about slide rules, the abacus?'

'Um, I don't know those, but I can learn.'

'I'll put you in the re-train/re-frame/re-form pile. We're going back to basics. Re-education. Fundamentalizm is the new orthodox.'

'Tell me, does anyone ever get placed? I mean re-placed?'

'Oh, yes, just last month we re-placed several Māori Santas, and Calvin and Luther set up their own Bros Lawnmowing business — they're our re-placements of the month. You can watch a video on them while you wait. Hold still while I burn a number into your forehead and wait 'til you're called.'

'Will it hurt?'

'Yes.'

'Do you recognise me?'

'No. You're sweating. Are you sick?'

'No, I'm not sick.'

'You can get an exemption from work if you're sick.'

'Okay, I'm very sick.'

'Take this form, fill it out, and line up over there.'

'So, if I say I'm sick, will I see you again?'

'No.'

'Okay, I'm not sick. I'm just . . .'

She cuts you off, 'Security!'

GAME OVER!!
RE-BOOT?

Niwareka and Mataora

BY WITI IHIMAERA

MATAORA, PRINCE OF TE AOTŪROA

The epic story of Mataora, Prince of Te Aotūroa, is the pūrākau which most contributes to my thinking and theorising as a Māori writer.

As a protagonist, Mataora fits the classic male trope. He is nobly born, a chieftain and, from the beginning, destined to become a hero.

Late one night while sleeping he hears sounds outside his sleeping house. They are different from the usual rustle of flax in the midnight wind or cry of an owl navigating the face of the moon.

He reaches for his fighting staff and cries out, 'Who's there?'

His enquiry brings forth a group of shimmering visitors the like of which he has never seen before. They are just as surprised at his powerful, dark appearance. He looks as if he could dominate the universe. 'Are you a man or a god?' they ask.

The question is not surprising as humankind and atua are the main inhabitants of the World Above and Mataora is clearly not a monster.

The travelling party has ascended from Rarohenga — The World Below would be a better description than The Underworld which has unfortunate European connotations. It's the realm of

Hinenuitepō, the Great Mother of the Night, as well as the domain of spirit tribes who serve her.

This begs the question: if Hinenuitepō rules both Rarohenga and Te Pō, are they the same world?

Regarding the latter, Te Pō has always been positioned as a period during the creation of the Māori universe: first there was Te Kore, The Void; after Te Kore came Te Pō, The Night; and following Te Pō arrived Te Ao Mārama, The Dawn of Light. By comparison, Rarohenga has a more specific location.

Bearing in mind Māori physics, perhaps we could posit the Great Mother as the axis around which both realms revolve, double helixes spiralling so fast that the distinctions resolve themselves — time and space — into the one singularity. Is Hinenuitepō therefore the agent by whom the universe is able to expand and contract and connect with fluid time? Through her, do ora (life) and mate (death) find balance and harmony?

Mataora's visitors emerge out of the darkness. Their appearance takes his breath away. They are not quite human. On the other hand, they are not inhuman.

'What are you?' he asks in a hoarse voice.

They are extraordinary beings, and they have crossed the border into Te Aotūroa at a place located solely at Pou-tererangi — a location in time as well as space — where Te Kūwatawata, its guardian, regulates the entrance.

You will recall that the god Tāne sought entrance at this same crossing when pursuing Hinetītama, Girl of the Dawn. And Māui, also, negotiated at the entrance with Te Kūwatawata when seeking to defeat Hinenuitepō and to thereby bring immortality to humankind.

Māui's father, Makeatutara, had earlier made the crossing to become, like Hinenuitepō, a guardian of The World Below. He was fortuitously positioned, wasn't he, to mourn over his son when Māui failed his task. Indeed some people put the blame for the failure entirely on Makeatutara because when Māui was born, Makeatutara had incorrectly recited the prayers at his baptism.

Imagine the gateway as a busy thoroughfare. Human tohunga and priests, wishing to visit the sacred sites of instruction and learning within Rarohenga, gather eagerly on the Te Aotūroa side of the toll-gate. Meanwhile on the Rarohenga side, multi-coloured subjects of that world, curious wide-eyed tourists in rich scintillating gowns, wait on their side to rush into our world to visit its fabled sites.

To Mataora's question his visitors reply, musically, 'We are tūrehu.'

They are a fabulous and stunningly beautiful tour group which has come through the gateway to pass among the tāngata of the human world. Maybe their itinerary includes visiting the Waitomo Caves or the hot pools at Whakarewarewa, for these locations are much talked about in Rarohenga as being among the wonders of The World Above.

Pākehā chroniclers equate tūrehu with 'fairies', ugh. While it might be true that the visitors are ethereal, fair-haired and fair-skinned, they are not elven or gnomic. Imagining them as such — diminutive with red hair — is probably some wish fulfilment by those searching for the Celtic in indigenous histories.

I like to think of them, rather, as ngā tūrehu, an earlier form of humankind, serving the Great Mother. Perhaps they are an inter-species, close enough to the DNA of Māori to be able to couple with humans and to bear children.

Mataora's tūrehu are distinctive in another way.

They are all aristocratic young women and are probably looking for a good night out on the town with some lowly, lucky, likely local lads. The beauty among them is Niwareka, who holds a very high rank in Rarohenga. In fact, although Mataora is human, Niwareka's tūrehu lineage is higher than his. Her father is Uetonga and she is fourth generation direct descendant from Rūaumoko, the youngest of the god brothers. She is also second generation mokopuna of the Great Mother herself.

You can see, can't you, that the Mataora–Niwareka story is rich in detail and meaning. It's a story that has multiple strands and ambiguities. Some have been caused by terrible interpretations of what Rarohenga is, and who tūrehu were — oh, so many acts of wilful interpretation have been perpetrated which rob the story of its original insights. And information freely available on the internet still maintains the totally disgusting, damaging, colonised readings of the contexts as well as the text itself.

Suffice to say that Niwareka and her entourage dance. The dancing is stately and unlike any that Mataora has ever seen. Not like the haka boogie kapa haka of modern dancing which completely robs Māori women of all desirability. Rather, the dancing is slow, sensual and scorching to the senses. During the dance, Mataora falls in love with Niwareka as she shimmers in the moonlight, tantalising him with her beauty. She is a being of glittering light, and moonbeams swirl around her.

And she is drawn closer and closer to the warrior chief. Indeed there is one part of his body that absolutely fascinates her.

The tattoo on Mataora's face.

Entranced, she touches the moko . . . and, impermanent, it smears.

Mataora asks Niwareka to marry him, and she accepts his proposal. They are happy for a time, and Mataora's kinsmen are entranced by Niwareka's strange beauty.

One day, however, Mataora notices that his older brother Tautoru is paying too much attention to his wife. Jealous, you might expect him to fight Tautoru. Instead he beats Niwareka. Savagely. Perhaps because she is too beautiful and he wishes to destroy that element of her that makes her so desirable to other men. Such is the way of the male who, rather than fight his brother, takes it out on the female spouse.

The beating shocks Niwareka.

Is Mataora really the hero that the texts make him?

'Surely, I have not deserved this,' Niwareka says to herself.

She has probably seen enough of humankind to know that an upraised hand is the way all men reprimand their women. And it is not in her nature to wait around for another backhander. Accordingly, she wraps a cloak around her and, fleeing from Mataora, she makes her way to the gateway. Gaining entrance from Te Kūwatawata, she descends swiftly into Rarohenga.

At least Mataora redeems himself by being penitent. Remorseful and distressed, he dresses in his finest cloak, kilt and ornaments. He paints on his tattoo, applying the colours and lines carefully, and tracks Niwareka to Pou-tererangi.

'Has a woman passed this way?' he asks the gatekeeper when he reaches the border crossing.

'What is she like?'

'She is beautiful and pale, with long transparent hair, like īnanga, and fair skin, and a straight nose.'

'A woman of that description passed this way many days ago, weeping as she went.'

'May I follow her?'

'Only if you have the courage.'

'I do.'

Will Te Kūwatawata let Mataora cross the border? Well, this all depends on Mataora abiding by the rules of entry. And the regulations appear to be of a similar kind to those any traveller must declare when going through modern-day customs. No food, no currency that might be used for commercial purposes and, above all, Mataora must, when leaving, acknowledge possession of taxable income or dutifiable goods — and, of course he will not be allowed to take tapu or sacred taonga out of Rarohenga. All countries these days have such rules, to stop the thieving that has occurred in the past of one country's artefacts by another.

Te Kūwatawata steps aside. 'Enquire of Tīwaiwaka for further directions,' he tells the chieftain.

Tīwaiwaka is the very same fantail that accompanied Māui in his own journey through Rarohenga — and which laughed when the demigod tried to conquer Hinenuitepō.

The bird's account of Niwareka's appearance is graphic. 'Her eyes were red with weeping,' he tells Mataora. 'She has passed on with swollen eyes and hanging lips.'

All our assumptions of what the story is going to be about are overturned.

The quest motif widens to become a complex narrative exploring domestic violence, marital love and forgiveness. It makes the story one of the most rewarding and nuanced in our literature.

Hints at Niwareka's constancy.

And Mataora's disturbing psyche.

UETONGA, ARIKI OF THE UNDERWORLD

When Mataora strikes Niwareka she is horrified.

Overturned are conceptions of violence, what is permissible and where it is practised. What is startling, for instance, is that while cruelty, brutality and sadism are a way of life in Te Aotūroa, it is unknown in Rarohenga. Niwareka feels the pain of the blow, the shock of experiencing a barbarous act and the confusion that sometimes inflicts the victim with doubt — perhaps the punishment was deserved? This is what most women have been brainwashed to think when a man hits her. And, like them, Niwareka seeks sanctuary in the house of her parents, there to recuperate from her wounds and try to decide what next to do for herself.

Meanwhile Mataora, in pursuit of her, makes a remarkable discovery.

Rarohenga is clearly not 'Hell' or 'Hades' as conceived within Pākehā thinking. On the contrary, The World Below is a place . . . of *light!* and so another human presumption is overturned. It is Te Aotūroa, which claims to be a world of daytime light, that is in fact dark — with all the connotations of the word.

Not only that, but unlike his own warring world, Rarohenga is a place where the people sing and dance and play, and they live together in harmony! It is as much an escape from the harsh realities of life as listening to a story, or as writing one.

Indeed, no obstacles confront Mataora as he searches for Niwareka, no demons, no dragons, no undead of the sort that The World Below is supposed to be peopled with. Darkness, evil and fear have no place here. Nobody tries to rob or murder him as he makes his way through the various kingdoms. Far from it: the court of the Great Mother is associated with peace and the inspirational arts.

And so Mataora mingles freely among the citizens of Rarohenga until, one day, he comes across a whare where people are watching a tattooist at work. A young man is stretched full length on the ground and the tattooist is cutting lines into his face with a bone chisel and hammer; the blood flows freely. Mataora is dishevelled and exhausted and he can't help but comment on the procedure he sees taking place before him.

'Your way of tattooing is wrong,' he says. 'In Te Aotūroa there is no spilling of blood.'

What an upstart Mataora is to think the human way is the right way! As cocky as a young writer can be. Everyone laughs at him and the tattooist corrects Mataora's thinking.

'Bend down your head,' he says. He looks at Mataora's tattoo — painted red, blue and white. 'Oh, The World Above!' he says. 'Ever is its adornment a farce. Behold how the moko can be effaced as it is merely a marking.'

And he reaches forward and, as Niwareka had done, wipes at the tattoo.

In so doing, not only does Uetonga belittle the human moko. He also discredits Mataora's mana. If Mataora had been wearing a crown, the act of despoiling the tattoo would have been similar to knocking the crown off his head.

The plot pivots in another of those ironies which make the Niwareka–Mataora story so fascinating.

The tattooist is Uetonga, Niwareka's father, a rangatira of Rarohenga. He doesn't know that the stranger is his son-in-law. If he had known that this was the husband who had mistreated his daughter, do you think he would have welcomed Mataora in? No.

And Mataora must be recompensed. 'You have spoilt my tattoo,' he says. 'You must now return it. Or I will seek justice by killing you.'

Remember . . . violence is unknown in Rarohenga. Therefore, Uetonga undercuts Mataora's mounting anger by mediating in a friendly manner. 'Oh,' he smiles, 'let me gift you a better moko.'

He invites Mataora to take the place of the young man whose own moko has just been completed. 'Prepare the visitor,' he tells his assistants, watching as they mark the pattern with charcoal that he proposes to etch on Mataora's face.

Mataora observes with keen and curious interest as Uetonga lays out the uhi matarau, which are the finely crafted instruments used in tā moko: the range of bone chisel blades which will produce the deep grooved lines of the tattoo; the various combs, tapers, handles, mallets and hammers that will assist in the intricate patterning; the pigments that will be tapped into the scarification of the skin.

'I shall begin,' Uetonga says.

To the sound of karakia, and using the method known as hōpara makaurangi, Uetonga follows the marked lines with his chisels and taps the colour into the wounds with his tools. While he does so, an assistant stretches Mataora's skin so that the surface is always taut.

And Mataora is taken to the threshold of human pain. Waves of agony sweep his body. They emanate from the point of the chisel. No matter how fine the instruments are, the gouging and channelling of the grooves and insertion of dark pigment soon makes him feel that his face is on fire.

Mataora must be forcibly restrained as Uetonga continues the work. Spiral elements are applied to his nose, cheek and lower jaws. Curvilinear rays on the forehead and from the nose to the mouth. Using his own artistic eye, Uetonga adds other design elements to accentuate and enhance Mataora's own personal beauty.

Can we think of the process as a symbolic punishment as well as embellishment?

Indeed, as he is being tattooed Mataora tries to mitigate his pain by chanting a song, pleading for Niwareka to come to him.

And when the work is complete, Uetonga is immensely proud.

'You have a living face now,' he says to Mataora.

Ironically, Uetonga inevitably seals the fate of all.

Unwittingly, he endows Mataora with moko that irrevocably joins Mataora to Uetonga's whakapapa. It is a bold visual expression not only of Mataora's authority but also his own.

Unintentionally he also reveals the uhi matarau, the satchel of instruments which will be credited to Mataora when he becomes the 'discoverer' of the art of tā moko. They belong in fact to Niwareka's father.

NIWAREKA, PRINCESS OF TE PŌ

Mataora's song reaches Niwareka where, during her recovery, she has been spending her time weaving cloaks; in creativity she is attempting to find self-respect and worth again.

Can we imagine her receiving care from the women of Rarohenga? In particular from one of her grandmothers, Hinenuitepō, surely the most important kuia rangatira in the entire world? Or Rohe, another goddess of the spirit world? Let us picture Niwareka, therefore, on first reaching sanctuary, seeking an immediate audience with the Great Mother of Te Pō. She runs into her arms just like any child to her kuia.

There, there, Hinenuitepō soothes, *Stop weeping now.*

What kind of emotions must register in the older woman as she reflects on her own abuse? After all, it was her own father, Tāne, who slept with her. Multiple times he committed incest and, from each a child was born.

How else could humankind be propagated?

Or was Hinenuitepō a free agent? The choice was never hers. Her father enslaved her, keeping her a prisoner in a house with talking posts until, at long last, she was able to gain the personal strength and will to escape him. To mitigate her shame as a victim, she took the guilt of bearing the children upon herself.

And then Niwareka hears the waiata of Mataora resounding through the halls of Rarohenga. Regardless of advice from Hinenuitepō to give Mataora the heave ho, her heart opens to him.

Isn't that always the way? Mataora has erred but don't we all make such human mistakes? And Niwareka, isn't she only showing her divinity by forgiving him? Aren't women always doing this, forgiving men?

Niwareka follows the song to the source but, on first meeting Mataora, she does not recognise him. His face is swollen and purple from the tattooing procedure. But he recognises her and, when he begs for forgiveness, she pities his suffering and greets him with tears.

And what are Uetonga's feelings in this matter? After all, by giving Mataora the family moko he has unwittingly acknowledged the man who beat his daughter.

We don't know how the various reconciliations are effected.

But we do know that once the wounds of his carved moko have healed, Mataora wishes to return to his own world. Indeed, he is forceful in making his intention clear. When men command in Te Aotūroa, all must obey.

However, Rarohenga is not his kingdom. He is the foreigner here. Therefore, try as he might to impose his human rangatiratanga, he has to face the humiliation of not having his wishes listened to.

'The matter must be left with me and my kin group to decide,' Niwareka tells him. 'In particular, my elders will make the decision.'

Niwareka invokes the practice of having a third party making the judgement. Uetonga is of the opinion that Mataora should return home alone. 'Leave my daughter here,' he says. 'While the practice of wife beating might be acceptable in Te Aotūroa, it is not condoned in our realm.'

Niwareka's brother, Tauwehe, however, takes a different tack. He endeavours to persuade Mataora to remain in Rarohenga, 'Your world is a place of darkness and warring clans whereas there is no crime and no darkness here. Why not make a clean break from Te Aotūroa?'

Mataora is adamant. He must return to Te Aotūroa — and with Niwareka.

Let's not leave Hinenuitepō out of the debate. She must surely weigh the balance and I like to think that it is she, ultimately, who has the final say.

Let us see if a male child of Tāne is able to learn to alter his ways. Yes, humanity must have one more chance.

And Mataora achieves a personal transcendence. As a tribal chief in Te Aotūroa, he has not been accustomed to any decision-making process of the consensual kind.

He makes a promise before Niwareka's family that he will adopt the customs of Rarohenga.

Indeed, when he begins the return journey with Niwareka to Te Aotūroa he has been transformed and retrained by the Rarohenga paradigm. Physically, he now has a living face, the magnificent legacy of his stay in The World Below. And the citizens of Rarohenga adorn him with a stunning cloak of blinding shimmering colours. Named Te Rangi-haupapa, 'Sky of Peace', the kākahu is a symbol of all the hopes they have that a prince of Te Aotūroa will change not only his own personal savagery, but also the brutality of his world itself.

'My three pet birds will guide you back,' Uetonga tells his daughter and son-in-law. 'They are the ruru, the pekapeka and the moho pererū.'

These gifts are freely given. Not so, however, the other 'gifts' in Mataora's possession — the satchel of instruments known as the uhi matarau and the rangihua Papa which contains the blueprint for tāniko, weaving.

On the arrival of Mataora and Niwareka at the gateway — if I might make a border patrol analogy — Mataora fails to make an appropriate outward customs declaration.

'Are you sure you have nothing to declare?' Te Kūwatawata asks.

'Nothing.'

Whether consciously or unconsciously, Mataora is literally enacting theft — will humanity ever learn? On the other hand, perhaps we should give the prince of Te Aotūroa the benefit of the doubt.

Be that as it may, the instruments must have been of great tapu and mana, priceless and irreplaceable and of great worth and significance to Rarohenga. Their removal, once discovered, leads to pandemonium — and an immediate closing of the border.

From that moment, only the dead can enter.

MATAORA AND NIWAREKA
UNITED IN TE AOTŪROA

Mataora becomes famed throughout Te Aotūroa as the exponent of tattoo by puncture. His first attempt at tā moko is not successful, as must be the case with all artists starting out. However, his story is one of perseverance and he recreates the many designs taught to him in Rarohenga.

Niwareka, also, does not return without a gift for humankind. Hers is the shimmering art of tāniko, Māori embroidery, weaving.

Some people say that you may lose your most valuable physical possession — your home, your personal jewellery and worldly wealth — through theft, robbery or some other calamity, but, through life, your moko will always be your companion. So it has become with my writing.

Your tattoo will also be your passport when you die. It comes from Rarohenga and, therefore, you will be recognised for it.

Ah, this is the moko gifted by whakapapa from Uetonga.

My writing is my moko. The technique of rhythmically tapping a bone chisel lashed to a small wooden haft echoes my tapping the keys of an iPad. But the difference between writing and *Māori* writing is that without the inspiration of tā moko, the inscriptions of our stories would only be superficial and easily wiped away. Unlike other writing, Māori writing is the act of creating incised patterns out of our own flesh. From one line on the page springs the second, third and fourth, as acts of creativity which are also acts against oblivion. The geometric designs of moko, the balance and beauty of them, and the flat incisions into which pigment is inserted take me to kupu — to my genealogy, not any other — which is at the source of my work. And of course it is a methodology that you must have the techniques for, the skill and concentration.

Only with practice and application can you ever hope to tattoo onto the page the same complex interplay that exists in tā moko. The high aesthetic and visual language that underscores artistic excellence and gives expression to our own living face as writers. But there's more. As I tap tap tap away, I get the extraordinary sense of Māori writing as an act of recovery.

The superimpositions of European moko are, thankfully, only superficial after all. And it is possible to retrieve our world, our identity, our politics — our past and present but, most of all, our future — by rewriting back. When we do, the patterns shift and motifs we previously only sensed beneath the surface return to their natural alignment. Just a small correction or additional incision and the pus seeps out. With the careful placing of the chisel and opening up of a new channel the stories are unpoisoned and the red blood rightly flows.

Now, put into place the beautiful pigment. Restore the pūrākau. Redeem ourselves. Return kupu to its origin.

I've said before that sometimes when you shift the universe a little — by a single thought or sentence or understanding — you actually shift it a lot; you open up the future to an alternative that was never there before. But the commitment as a creative writer is something that you have to keep honing and improving and developing even fifty years later. Only now, for instance, am I beginning to understand such things as the spaces between the tattooed designs. They are not empty. Within them are representations of Te Kore which balance the seen with the unseen, time with space, past with present and future — and they are as important as the designs themselves.

There's another matter. The threshold of human pain is involved in the practice of tā moko and so it must also be with writing. Just as the blood flows freely in the tā moko process, so must the toto flow through our words.

The pain authorises us to proceed without fear. To go to those places where evil dwells or explore those depravities that men do. To write about those profound iniquities and atrocities so that those who inflict them are aware they are being watched — that we *know*.

There's more. When the blood flows freely, it allows us to *tell the truth*. In my case I have always felt that I can counter the pain of truth-telling with creativity. Indeed, the moko of writing sometimes takes me to almost unendurable agony — for instance, my conscience often bothers me terribly, saying that when I write I disclose not just myself but others too — and I can only hope for their understanding.

Dad once said to me about a decision I made, 'Look, you made it. Now you *own* it. And *you* take full responsibility for it.' Do you think it is easy to know that what I write is permanent, is there forever?

The kaupapa must remain constant.

I trust to the truth and the pain.

RAROHENGA, LOST FABLED WORLD OF LIGHT

While Mataora's journey was, indeed, heroic, there were two severe outcomes.

One, as you know now, was that the gateway between Te Aotūroa and Rarohenga was immediately closed. No longer would humankind be able to journey to the fabled queendom of Hinenuitepō, The World Below.

That didn't stop some from trying . . . and in some cases succeeding. Among later visitors was Hutu, who sent his soul from Te Aotūroa after his beloved, Pare, to find her wairua and return with it. Others were Rangirua and his brother Kaeo, who sought Rangirua's wife, Hine-Mārama, after she had died — because she had not eaten food, they were able to bring her spirit back and revivify her body. Then there was Ririkoko who, on the death of his daughter, went to Te Rēinga to reclaim her.

While we might therefore praise Mataora for bringing back the gifts that he did, what other undreamed-of taonga could we have possessed?

Undreamed of? Ah! But when we dream, as all artists do, our unconscious can take us back there. As a writer, I therefore owe much of my inspiration to Rarohenga. It comes from the court of Hinenuitepō, the patron goddess of all our creative arts.

The second consequence of the gateway's closure was a more intimate one. Niwareka was forever denied the sanctuary of Rarohenga. From that moment, should she suffer again by the hand of her husband or any human, she would have to turn to the judicial systems that exist in The World Above for redress.

Indeed, it is interesting that the party, guilty of violence towards his wife, goes to Rarohenga, to the spirit world, to obtain his forgiveness. In a sense both husband and wife approach death, but through the intervention of the wife's father and family they achieve resurrection. And by crossing back to Te Aotūroa, they are returned to life.

However, there was a twist. The gatekeeper, Te Kūwatawata, had not seen — or perhaps he did — the 'unseen' gift of Uetonga that both husband and wife carried across the border.

And this unseen benefaction was as powerful a present to us as the arts of tā moko and tāniko, because it offered the wisdom that would forever alter the way that Māori conducted their affairs with one another.

I call it the 'Rarohenga' system of conflict resolution.

Up until Mataora's time, Māoridom was in a state of constant warfare. Any argument over land, food or boundary — or over high-ranking or desirable women — was immediately answered by a declaration of war.

Settlement by sitting down and having peaceful kōrero was un-heard of or, at least, not the first option in conflict resolution. Such an innovative iwi to iwi way of arbitration changed intertribal dealings by offering an example of harmonious existence to strive for.

At the whānau level, both Mataora and Niwareka must also have realised that they needed to establish a method by which men and women could acknowledge the existence of domestic violence and violation; Niwareka's life and the life of all women and children depended on it.

I like to believe that what they put in place led, eventually, to the development of the family court as we know it today.

THE SONG IS AROHA

While I can say that my moko is my writing, and I honour Mataora and Niwareka for bequeathing it to me, it has a greater obligation.

It takes me to a memory of childhood when my grandmother Teria and I are walking in the small plantation of flax bushes at the side of the homestead.

The flax bushes attract the korimako, bellbirds, and Teria takes advantage of the fact that we are there with the bellbirds to remind me of a larger truth.

'Listen,' she says. 'What do you hear, e *Wit*sh?'

There is sunlight all around but, in the breeze, the tall fluted blades are clicking together.

'The flax is asking us, what is the greatest thing in the world?' *The greatest thing, the greatest thing, the greatest . . .*

'E *Wit*sh? What is the answer? He aha?'

Although two important art traditions, tā moko and tāniko, were brought back to Te Aotūroa to fill a savage world with the possibility of redemption through art and beauty, one of the important aspects that we must recognise is that our work is not only creative.

It also has to do with being humanitarian. With having aroha ki te iwi.

Kāterina Te Heikōkō Mataira, in *The Māori People in the 1960s*, referring to the writer's purpose, writes:

'. . . it becomes clear, that if the Māori artist, on the stage, in the graphic and plastic arts, in his music, and in his poetry and writing can imbue society with this quality of *aroha*, then he will have made his greatest contribution to society and mankind.'

Through art, we can and must establish governmental and judicial practices that provide safety for the iwi within a world where the messages are mixed and often extremely violent. Where the powerless require voices. Where those facing death need rescue. Where people need to be fed and have access to clean drinking water. Where the planet needs saving.

Our voices must have moral urgency. In Niwareka's sacrifice of her father's world for her husband's, we are given a duty to repay her through creativity, for forcing her to live forever with human irrationality.

Her return to her own world was certainly closed to her. But for her mokopuna, there is another gateway — to the future — that we must ensure, through every means within our power, will always remain open.

The flax clicks in the wind, the bellbirds await our retreat so that they can return and continue to sip at the honey inside the flax shoot . . .

E Wits*h*, my grandmother whispers in my ear, *he aha te mea nui o te Ao? What is the greatest thing in the world?*

I am able to answer her now. *It is men, women and children, grandmother.*

She nods her head, *Then, e* Wits*h, serve them.*

Āe, e hoa mā, let us do that.

EPILOGUE

THE FUTURE

Waka 99

BY ROBERT SULLIVAN

If waka could be resurrected
they wouldn't just come out
from museum doors smashing
glass cases revolving and sliding
doors on their exit

they wouldn't just come out
of mountains as if liquidified
from a frozen state
the resurrection wouldn't just
come about this way

the South Island turned to wood
waiting for the giant crew
of Māui and his brothers
bailers and anchors turned back
to what they were when they were strewn

about the country by Kupe
and his relations
the resurrection would happen
in the blood of the men and women
the boys and girls

who are blood relations
of the crews whose veins
touch the veins who touched the veins
of those who touched the veins
who touched the veins

who touched the veins
of the men and women from the time
of Kupe and before.
The resurrection will come
out of their blood.

BIOGRAPHICAL NOTES

APIRANA TAYLOR

'Hine Tai' is based on an incident that happened to one of my aunts when she was a little girl and her nan sent her to the rock pool three times to look for the taniwha. Hine Tai is my ancestress from Southern Ngāti Porou.

Apirana, from the Ngāti Porou, Te Whānau-ā-Apanui and Ngāti Ruanui tribes, and also Pākehā heritage, is a poet, playwright, novelist, short-story writer, storyteller, actor, painter, and musician. He has been writer in residence at Massey and Canterbury universities. He has been invited several times to India and Europe and to the Medellen Poetry Festival in Colombia. In 2017, he returned to read at Udine University in Italy and travelled throughout the South of France telling his stories. His poetry and prose have been translated into many languages. He travels to schools, tertiary institutions and prisons throughout New Zealand to read his poetry, tell his stories and take creative writing workshops. He has published five collections of poetry, three of short stories, two novels, and three plays. His poetry and short stories are included in many nationally and internationally published anthologies.

BRIAR GRACE-SMITH

I've always enjoyed the stories about Māui's birth and return and wanted to tell a version from his sister's perspective. While we often hear about Māui's brothers we don't often hear about Hina. I imagine that the pair must've bonded because they were 'different' to the other siblings. Hina later went on to marry Irawaru, and one day while fishing, Māui became annoyed with his brother-in-law's success and, in an act of revenge, jammed him under the canoe and turned him into a dog. On discovering what her brother had done, Hina committed suicide by throwing herself into the sea.

Briar is of Ngā Puhi and Ngāti Hau descent and is a writer of stage plays, short fiction and television scripts. She has also written and directed screenplays. Her awards include an ONZM, the Arts Foundation Laureate Award, Te Tohu Toi Kē a Te Waka Toi Award, the Ramai Hayward Wāhine Māori Directors' Scholarship and the Māori Screen Excellence Award, 2018.

BRIAR WOOD

'Kuramārōtini' was first published in her collection *Rāwāhi*, published by Anahera Press in 2017, which was shortlisted for the Ockham NZ 2018 Book Awards Poetry Prize.

Briar Wood (Ngāpuhi) grew up in South Auckland. She lived and worked as a lecturer in Britain until 2012, where she published poetry, fiction and essays. She is now based in Northland.

CLAYTON TE KOHE

Clayton is of Ngāti Tūwharetoa and Te Arawa descent. He is a blogger based in Wellington. A lifetime ago he studied the law and is a barrister and solicitor of the High Court of New Zealand, but he has never practised. Clayton likes a hoppy pilsner and a peaty whisky. 'Moving Mountains' is his first published story.

To find out more about Clayton, visit https://bit.ly/2NvOZ6g

DAVID GEARY

Both 'Māui Goes to Hollywood' and 'Rarohenga & the Reformation' were written specially for this collection.

David Geary (Ngā Mahanga, Taranaki) grew up in Rangiwāhia, a small village in the Manawatū. He studied law at Victoria University where he discovered Bill Manhire's creative writing course, theatre studies and the University Drama Club. He went on to study acting at Toi Whakaari: NZ Drama School, graduating in 1987. Since then he has written, directed and acted for theatre, television and film. His early works received critical acclaim in New Zealand and Australia and he gained various awards, including the Bruce Mason Award for Most Promising Playwright in 1991 and a NZ Film Accolade. In 2002 David moved to Canada, where his subsequent plays have been performed, as well as in New Zealand. His short-story collection *A Man of the People* was published by Victoria University Press in 2003.

FRAZER RANGIHUNA

'Īhe & Her' is the retelling of the legend of Īhenga, the great explorer and name-giver to Rotorua, and his second encounter with the patupaiarehe — the fairy people — who were the inhabitants of Te Tūāhu a Atua on the summit of Ngongotahā maunga. Īhenga's first encounter with the patupaiarehe didn't go so well. It ended with him fending them off with a burning branch. This time, he was keen to make amends. Surely this wasn't the only reason. No doubt that as an explorer — not to mention a Māori man — he was curious and maybe a bit of a tutu, driven by the prospect of encountering some excitement. So, off he went, up the maunga. But after a while he grew tired and thirsty. When he reached the patupaiarehe's pā, he asked for water and he was obliged by a beautiful patupaiarehe woman who gave him a drink from a calabash (after which the maunga was named). The patupaiarehe were smitten with him and he lapped it up. For a while. Until his amazement wore off and he started to freak out. The mysterious patupaiarehe, their unearthly kāinga — it wasn't his scene. So he took off. As he did, though, someone was close behind him. The beautiful patupaiarehe woman. As flattering as this was, he was afraid that if she caught him, she'd trap him and he'd never see his wife again. Then he remembered that patupaiarehe were put off by kōkōwai (red ochre) and hated the smell of food and oil. In a pocket in his belt he had a small piece of kōkōwai mixed with shark oil, which he smeared all over his body. This stopped the patupaiarehe woman in her tracks, who let out a scream of anger and loss. 'Her' in 'Īhe & Her' is based on the patupaiarehe woman, with some changes. No woman should have to chase a man. Yes, she wants Īhenga, but I wanted to make it clear, she could also crush him. However, there are limits — even to a kick-arse patupaiarehe's power. More powerful than a man. Than both of them.

It was a joy to be asked to create a story for Pūrākau. *Special thanks go to my partner, Tim, who has been so extraordinarily supportive — caring for me so I can care for my characters.*

Frazer, Ngāti Porou, is a self-taught writer of three published short stories. His story 'Piro' won the *Sunday Star-Times* Short Story Competition in 2017. Currently, he is working on 'the novel'.

HĒMI KELLY

'Rata' is Hēmi's first work of fiction to be published, though he wrote a Māori translation of Witi Ihimaera's novella *Sleeps Standing: Moetū*, published in 2017, by Vintage. He followed this publication up with *A Māori Word a Day* in 2018 (Penguin).

Hēmi is of Ngāti Maniapoto descent. He is a full-time lecturer in te reo Māori at the Auckland University of Technology and an assistant researcher at Te Ipukarea, the National Māori Language Institute. Alongside the Māori language, Hēmi has a passion for waiata composition, writing, translation and Māori visual and performing arts. Hēmi is a licensed translator and graduate of Te Panekiretanga o Te Reo, the Institute of Excellence in the Māori Language. He is a highly regarded spokesperson on Māori culture and is often seen on Māori television.

HONE TUWHARE

'We, Who Live in Darkness' and 'The Kūmara God Smiles Fatly' were published in *Mihi: Collected Poems*, Penguin, 1987. Hone also touched on other mythical figures in poems such as 'Papa-tū-ā-nuku', 'Māui makes it with the Death Goddess' and 'To Hine-nui-te-Pō — the fat bitch!', all of which are available in *Small Holes in the Silence: Collected Works*, Vintage, 2016.

Hone (1922–2008) was of Ngāpuhi iwi, hapū Ngāti Korokoro, Ngāti Tautahi, Te Popoto and Te Uri-o-Hau and was crowned the people's poet. He was loved and cherished by New Zealanders from all walks of life. Touring tirelessly, Hone shared his talent and inspired audiences in every corner of the country — from primary and secondary schools to universities, factories to art galleries and prisons. Rights in his work are held by the Estate of Hone Tuwhare: honetuwharepoetry@gmail.com.

JACQUELINE CARTER

As one of my more recent poems says, I am aware that I 'might be Hinetītama, gentle and kind, Mahuika, lighting a few fires, Hinemoana, lapping on your shores, or Hinenuitepō, having to lead you to the underworld . . .'

Jacqueline is of Ngāi Te Rangi, Ngāti Awa and Pākehā descent with links to Ngāti Maru, Ngāi Tai and Ngāpuhi. Her poems have been published in various anthologies including *Whetū Moana* and *Mauri Ola*, edited by Albert Wendt, Reina Whaitiri and Robert Sullivan (Auckland University Press, 2002 and 2010), as well as Anton Blank's literary journal *Ora Nui*. 'Me aro koe ki te hā ō Hineahuone!' was written in 1998 and was previously published in *Puna Wai Kōrero: An anthology of Māori poetry in English*, edited by Reina Whaitiri and Robert Sullivan (AUP, 2014).

KELLY ANA MOREY

Rūruhi-Kerepō was the obvious choice for me really. Evil old child-eater! How could I resist? But there were other reasons why I chose her, the main one being there was pretty much nothing written about her so that gave me the opportunity to take her anywhere I wanted, so I did. I also loved that her name translates as 'Old Woman' and that got me thinking about hierarchies and how to be old, brown and a woman is to have no value. Over the course of writing 'Blind' I became very fond of R-K and she's metaphorically moved in with me. She'll turn up again I suspect, in a novel, one day.

Kelly Ana Morey is of Ngāti Kurī, Te Rarawa and Te Aupōuri descent. She is an award-winning writer of both fiction and non-fiction, and has published novels, poems, numerous short stories, a childhood memoir and a number of social histories. She has been the recipient of the Todd Young Writers' Bursary, has won the Hubert Church (New Zealand) first novel prize, been a finalist for the Kiriyama Award for Fiction (USA), won the inaugural Janet Frame Award for Fiction and was awarded the Māori Writers' Residency at the Michael King Writers Centre. Morey's most recent novel, *Daylight Second*, was a finalist in the New Zealand Heritage and Ngā Kupu Ora Book Awards (2017). She has a BA in English and an MA in contemporary Māori art.

KELLY JOSEPH

Myths help make sense of the world. I've always loved the way many Māori myths explain natural landmarks or phenomena, and the original Hinepūkohurangi and Uenuku story does that in a really beautiful way. Nature-based myths drape another layer of meaning onto the ordinary world we inhabit, allowing us to see the ordinary as extraordinary. I knew I wanted to bring Hinepūkohurangi and Uenuku into a contemporary context, but it was a challenge to figure out exactly how, since rainbows already exist in the here and now. The key was the force of Uenuku's murimuri aroha transcending time and space.

Kelly Joseph, Ngāti Maniapoto, is a writer and artist currently living in the Waikato with her family. She has previously had stories published in *Huia Short Stories 5, 7, 8, 10* and *12* and in *Hue and Cry, Takahē* and *JAAM*, and broadcast on Radio New Zealand. She also has written poetry and articles for the *School Journal*. Recently her work was included in the anthology *Black Marks on the White Page*. In 2009 Kelly spent eight weeks on Kapiti Island as the Tau Mai e Kapiti Māori Writer in Residence. More recently she spent time at the Michael King Writers Centre as one of the recipients of the 2018 Emerging Māori Writers Residency. It was here that she began her short story 'Hinepūkohurangi and Uenuku', while also working on a YA novel. Kelly has an MA in creative writing from Victoria University and a Master of Fine Arts from the Rhode Island School of Design, USA.

KERI HULME

'Headnote to a Māui Tale' was first published in *Te Kaihau: The Windeater*, VUP, 1986. 'Getting It' and 'I Have a Stone' both first appeared in *Stonefish*, Huia, 2004.

Keri Hulme is of Ngāi Tahu, Kāti Māmoe, Orkney Island Scottish and English descent. The author of poetry, fiction and creative non-fiction, she has received numerous accolades, including the Man Booker Prize in 1985 for *The Bone People*, the New Zealand Book Award for Fiction, and the Katherine Mansfield Memorial Award. She has also held several writers' residencies.

NGĀHUIA TE AWEKOTUKU

Kurungaituku was half human and half bird, and lived in a cave with pet birds and animals. She yearned for human friendship, and came upon the handsome young Hatupatu. Some say she abducted him; others say he was invited. He liked the wealth of garments, weapons and finery he saw in her home, but he did not like her companions. Coveting her riches, he persuaded her to go on a long trip to seek special food. While she was away, he killed all her pets — all except a tiny bird, who escaped to warn her. Seizing all her treasures, Hatupatu fled for home. Kurungaituku hunted him, howling with rage and grief. He evaded her, concealing himself in a hollow rock beneath a hill. That rock is revered as a special place, even to this day.

Leaping and prancing about, Hatupatu led Kurungaituku into a valley of dangerous boiling-hot springs. He was safe, home at last. She was not, and she fell. Kurungaituku perished in the scalding water.

Or so the story goes, but I could never accept it. Why didn't she fly away, if she had wings like a bird? And why was she punished, when Hatupatu was the thief and murderer?

'Kurungaituku' was first published in *New Women's Fiction 4*, 1991, and subsequently in *Ruahine: Mythic Women*, Huia, 2003. A precursor to this collection, *Ruahine* was a reworking of various tales of mythic Māori women.

Born and raised in Ōhinemutu, Rotorua, Ngāhuia Te Awekotuku (Te Arawa, Tūhoe) is a veteran cultural activist, scholar and advocate for women and the LGBTQI community. As well as fiction, she has written poetry and non-fiction, including a book on traditional textiles and another on moko: *Mau Moko: The world of Māori tattoo* (2007), which among other awards won the Ngā Kupu Ora — Inaugural Māori Book of the Decade. To add to her other degrees in art history and English, she gained a PhD in psychology in 1981 and is an Emeritus Professor of the University of Waikato. In 2010 Ngāhuia was appointed a Member of the New Zealand Order of Merit for services to Māori culture; and in 2017 she received the Pou Aronui Supreme Award from the Royal Society of New Zealand for outstanding service to the arts and humanities. In 2018, she was made a Fellow of the Auckland War Memorial Museum, which recognised decades of work as a curator, writer, policy-maker and dreamer.

NIC LOW

Nic Low is a Ngāi Tahu writer of wilderness, technology and politics. His polemical story collection *Arms Race* was shortlisted for the Readings Prize and Queensland Literary Awards, and was named a *Listener* and *Australian Book Review* book of the year. He's recently spent several years in and out of the Southern Alps researching his next book, a Ngāi Tahu history and philosophy of mountains, told through walking journeys. He also writes for magazines and journals across Australia and New Zealand, is vice-chair of the Ngāi Tahu ki Victoria taurahere, and loves climbing and mountain biking when not at his desk. Find him at www.dislocated.org.

PATRICIA GRACE

'Te Pō' and 'Hine-ahu-one' were first published in *Wahine Toa: Women of Māori myth*, Penguin, 1991 by Patricia Grace, illustrated by Robyn Kahukiwa. The book depicted eight principal female mythical protagonists.

'Moon Story' was first reproduced in Patricia's collection *Small Holes in the Silence*, Penguin, 2006.

Patricia Grace, Ngāti Toa, Ngāti Raukawa and Te Āti Awa, is one of New Zealand's most celebrated writers; she has received the Distinguished Companion of the New Zealand Order of Merit for Services to Literature, the Prime Minister's Award for Literary Achievement, and the Arts Foundation of New Zealand Icon Award among many other accolades. She has also won numerous fellowships and prizes for her books. She was the first Māori woman to publish a novel and, since her first book in 1978, has published many more novels and short-story collections, as well as books for children and non-fiction. Patricia was born in Wellington and lives in Plimmerton on ancestral land, in close proximity to her home marae at Hongoeka Bay.

PAULA MORRIS

Paula Morris, Ngāti Wai, Ngāti Whātua, is the author of the collections *Forbidden Cities* (2008) and *False River* (2017); the essay 'On Coming Home' (2015); and seven novels, including *Rangatira* (2011), winner of best work of fiction at both the 2012 New Zealand Post Book Awards and Ngā Kupu Ora Māori Book Awards. She teaches creative writing at the University of Auckland and is the founder of the Academy of New Zealand Literature. In 2019 she was appointed an MNZM for Services to Literature, and was awarded the Katherine Mansfield Menton Fellowship.

RENÉE

I was born in Napier and went to Wairoa as a young woman. There I researched my mother's whakapapa and fell in love with the river. I loved Te Wairoa right from the start. The river has its moods but whether it's angry or sad or flowing happily, I love it. I don't see it very often these days but it's always there in my mind. The retelling of the myth of Te Pura appealed to me because of that love for the river. I wanted Wairoa in the title because usually when Wairoa makes the headlines it's because the river is in flood and the bridge is down, or it's silted up, or there's been another rumble between the gangs, but there are many beautiful things about Wairoa and the story of Te Pura is one of them.

Renée is of Ngāti Kahungunu and Gordon Clan descent. She has written many notable plays, novels, short stories and non-fiction works. She has described herself as a 'lesbian feminist with socialist working-class ideals'. As well as being granted various residencies, she has been awarded the ONZM for services to literature and in 2017 was recipient of the Playmarket Award, which recognises a playwright who has made a significant artistic contribution to theatre in New Zealand. In 2018 Renée received the Prime Minister's Award for Fiction.

ROBERT SULLIVAN

'Waka 86' and 'Waka 99' are both from *Star Waka*, AUP, 1999, which was shortlisted for the 2000 Montana New Zealand Book Awards. As noted in the *The Auckland University Press Anthology of New Zealand Literature*, 'In his 1999 poetic sequence *Star Waka*, Robert Sullivan uses the image of the waka as a container for the freight of history — personal, familial, tribal, national. The waka, he says, "is a knife through time", connecting the pre-contact past with the urban present and sailing on towards a possible, if fancifully configured, extraterrestrial future. The waka morphs as it travels, from primeval first fleet to space ship.'

Robert Sullivan, Ngāpuhi, is the author of numerous collections of poetry, a graphic novel, and *Weaving Earth & Sky: Myths and legends of Aotearoa* with illustrations by Gavin Bishop, a prize-winning book of Māori legends for children. He co-edited, with Albert Wendt and Reina Whaitiri, various anthologies of Polynesian and Māori poetry in English. He has held various fellowships and been a Distinguished Visiting Writer at the University of Hawai'i Manoa, where he taught creative writing for some years. Subsequently he has headed up the Creative Writing School at Manukau Institute of Technology and is Deputy Chief Executive Māori there.

TINA MAKERETI

'Skin and Bones' and 'Shapeshifter' are both from Tina's short-story collection, *Once Upon a Time in Aotearoa*, Huia, 2010.

Tina is of Ngāti Tūwharetoa, Te Ātiawa, Ngāti Rangatahi, Pākehā and, according to family stories, Moriori descent. She writes essays, novels and short fiction. Her latest novel is *The Imaginary Lives of James Pōneke* and, alongside Witi Ihimaera, she is co-editor of *Black Marks on the White Page*, an anthology that celebrates Māori and Pasifika writing. In 2016 her story 'Black Milk' won the Commonwealth Writers Short Story Prize, Pacific region. Her first novel, *Where* the *Rēkohu Bone Sings*, won the 2014 Ngā Kupu Ora Aotearoa Māori Book Award for Fiction, also won by *Once Upon a Time in Aotearoa* in 2011. In 2009 she was the recipient of the RSNZ Manhire Prize for Creative Science Writing and the Pikihuia Award for Best Short Story in English. She has presented her work all over New Zealand and in Frankfurt, Taipei, Jamaica and the UK. Tina teaches creative writing and Oceanic literatures at Massey University.

WHITI HEREAKA

The prologue to *Pūrākau* is extracted from the novel *Kurangaituku*, a work in progress. 'Papatūānuku' has been adapted for this collection from the original story of the same name published in *Breakups*, Mongrel Books, 2017.

Whiti is of Ngāti Tūwharetoa and Te Arawa descent. She is a playwright, screenwriter, novelist and a barrister and solicitor of the High Court of New Zealand. She holds a Masters in Creative Writing (Scriptwriting) from the International Institute of Modern Letters, Victoria University. She has had several plays produced and has won Best New Play by a Māori Playwright at the Adam Play Awards in both 2010 and 2011 and won the Bruce Mason Award in 2012. She has published three novels: *Bugs* and *Legacy* for young adults and *The Graphologist's Apprentice*, which was shortlisted for Best First Book in the 2011 Commonwealth Writers' Prize Asia and Pacific. Visit Whiti's Facebook page for more information https://www.facebook.com/whereaka.

WITI IHIMAERA

'Hine-tītama' is an abridged version of 'Ask the Posts of the House' from the collection of the same name, published by Penguin in 2007. 'The Potato' first appeared in *Māori Boy*, Vintage, 2014. 'A Story from the Sea' is drawn from different parts of *The Whale Rider*, Penguin, 1987. 'Niwareka and Mataora' is extracted from the forthcoming memoir *Native Son*, Vintage, 2019.

Witi is of Te Whānau-ā-Kai, Te Aitanga-ā-Māhaki, Rongowhakaata, Tūhoe, Te Whānau-ā-Apanui, Whakatōhea and Ngāti Porou descent. He was the first Māori to publish a novel, *Tangi*, in 1973. He has subsequently gone on to become one of New Zealand's leading writers. He is passionate about writing Māori stories and creating opportunities for the continuing development of Māori and Pacific literature, theatre and film. He recently became the patron of the 100 Books In Te Reo project.

Witi's memoir, *Māori Boy*, won the Ockham Award for the best non-fiction work, 2016. His play, *All Our Sons*, won six Wellington theatre awards in the same year. His opera *Flowing Water*, set in the Waikato during the New Zealand Wars, premiered in Hamilton in 2017. He was the presenter of *In Foreign Fields*, a documentary for Māori Television shown on Anzac Day last year. Witi lives in Auckland.

Of *Pūrākau* Witi writes, 'I've always wanted to work with Whiti Hereaka and thank her for the skill and aroha she brought to co-editing the anthology; after all, she has a legal background. James Ormsby has done another terrific cover to follow up *Black Marks on the White Page* — that tokotoko is full of electricity! And the contributing writers: your amazing work has made *Pūrākau* a privilege to work on.

'There is another person, I can't let her hide from view, and that is Harriet Allan. She instigated *Pūrākau* for Penguin Random House New Zealand, her vision drove it . . . and her love of pūrākau is as strong as ours. Whiti and James join me in thanking you, Harriet, along with editor Carol Buchanan, proofreaders Claire Baker and Gillian Tewsley, and Louisa Kasza and Rachel Clark at Penguin Random House, for helping us to fashion such a strong tokotoko, reflective of the energy and potential of story in Aotearoa New Zealand.'